MM II

THE RETURN OF MARILYN MONROE

MM II

THE RETURN OF MARILYN MONROE

by

SAM STAGGS

DONALD I. FINE, INC.
New York

 Published in the United States of America by Donald I. Fine, Inc. and in Canada by General Publishing Company Limited.

Library of Congress Cataloging-in-Publication Data

Staggs, Sam.
MMII : the return of Marilyn Monroe / by Sam Staggs.
p. cm.
ISBN 1-55611-179-7
1. Monroe, Marilyn, 1926-1962—Fiction. I. Title. II. Title: MM2.
PS3569.T28M57 1990
813'.54—dc20 90-55026
CIP

Designed by Irving Perkins Associates

Manufactured in the United States of America

10 9 8 7 6 5 4 3 2 1

To Roger Farabee,
who taught me how to
look into the heart
of an artichoke.

Grateful acknowledgment is made for permission to reprint copyright material in this book as follows:

Sara Teasdale, "Moon's Ending." Reprinted with permission of Macmillan Publishing Company from *Collected Poems of Sara Teasdale*. Copyright 1933 by Macmillan Publishing Company, renewed 1961 by Guaranty Trust Co. of New York.

E.H. Gombrich, from *The Story of Art,* 15th edition, 1989. © 1972, 1978, 1984, 1989 by Phaidon Press Limited, Oxford. Text © 1972, 1978, 1984, 1989 by E.H. Gombrich.

Anthony Summers, from *Goddess: The Secret Lives of Marilyn Monroe.* Copyright 1985 by Anthony Summers. Published by Macmillan Publishing Company, New York.

"I Won't Dance." Music by Jerome Kern and lyrics by Oscar Hammerstein II, Otto Harbach, Dorothy Fields and Jimmy McHugh. Copyright © 1935 PolyGram International Publishing, Inc. (3500 West Olive Avenue, Suite 200, Burbank, CA 91505). Copyright Renewed. United States rights of Otto Harbach controlled by Bill/Bob Publishing Company and Dorothy Fields controlled by Aldi Music. International Copyright Secured. All Rights Reserved. Used By Permission.

Carl Sandburg, excerpt from "Chicago" in *Chicago Poems,* copyright 1916 by Holt, Rinehart and Winston, Inc. and renewed 1944 by Carl Sandburg, reprinted by permission of Harcourt Brace Jovanovich, Inc.

"Diamonds Are A Girl's Best Friend" by Jule Styne and Leo Robin. Copyright © 1949 (Renewed) by Dorsey Bros. Music, a div. of Music Sales Corporation. International Copyright Secured. Used by Permission.

"A Little Girl From Little Rock" by Jule Styne and Leo Robin. Copyright © 1949 (Renewed) by Dorsey Bros. Music, a div. of Music Sales Corporation. International Copyright Secured. Used by Permission.

"Lost April." Words by Edgar Leslie, music by Emil Newman and Herbert Spencer. Copyright 1948, 1976 George Simon, Inc. (ASCAP). Used by Permission. All Rights Reserved.

"River of No Return." Words by Ken Darby, music by Lionel Newman. Copyright 1953, 1981 Simon House, Inc. (BMI) Used By Permission. All Rights Reserved.

Acknowledgments

Love and thanks to my parents and my aunts and uncles for years of encouragement and for taking me to the movies.

To Vernon Jordan, Leigh W. Rutledge, Patricia B. Soliman, and Raymond Summer for enormous good humor and unending help.

To Donald Fine, my editor and publisher, and to Al Lowman, my agent.

Contents

Moon's Ending

Moon, worn thin to the width of a quill,
In the dawn clouds flying,
How good to go, light into light, and still
Giving light, dying.

—Sara Teasdale

MM II

THE RETURN OF MARILYN MONROE

CHAPTER 1

"Strictly Business"

FRIDAY, JULY 27, 1962

Visiting New Yorkers might have mistaken Los Angeles for their own city that day. Too hot; L.A. was too hot. The air felt like the breath of a stranger on every neck in the city, putting everyone in a bad mood.

A gray chemical haze soiled hills and valleys, canyons and beaches. At the edge of the haze, puny sunlight struggled to shine. The best it could do was reflect pink shadows onto the grayness, which soon absorbed them. Asphalt glittered, tar melted. There was a feeling in the lungs that oxygen had evaporated from the world. Even the palm trees along streets and boulevards looked exhausted.

From Santa Monica, a black Cadillac hurried toward Brentwood. The driver looked as ordinary as a chauffeur always does. He had brown hair, made to stand straight up in a crew cut. Behind green military sunglasses, his brown eyes held the road, never turning to glance at pastel houses, or lawns sparkling under sprinklers in the pale noonday sun. He showed the first signs of sag under his eyes; he was forty years old and gravity had begun to reach up and pull on his face.

As the car sped along San Vicente Boulevard, he nodded

occasionally in answer to a question from the back seat. The passenger in the plush gloom of the soft pigeon-colored upholstery leaned on the armrest. Unlike the driver, he did not look like an ordinary man. He did have an ordinary name—Robert, often shortened to Bobby—but in every other way he was unusual. His hair was unfashionably long for the time, and an unruly lock fell over his forehead. Often, in fact, the hair seemed to dominate the head, lifting it, pulling it, twisting it this way and that without the man's consent or even his awareness.

He smiled a lot. Part of his job was to smile at cameras, and wherever Bobby went photographers were not far away. For these camera smiles, his teeth seemed to jostle each other, shoving and crowding into the front of his mouth. The gleam from their competition was white and burning.

Smiles had etched lines around the eyes, but since he was only thirty-six years old the lines vanished when the smiles did. His knowing eyes concealed more than they revealed. He rarely missed a move, a flicker, a gesture. His intelligence was apparent. Traces of hardness in his expression caused journalists to describe him as "ruthless," "unforgiving," "stubborn." On a day like this, someone looking into those quick-traveling eyes just might have believed those adjectives.

It was a seductive face, too, hinting that this kid of a man could generate secret thrills. His eyes offered the dare: Come on and find out.

The car's windows were smoked, the back ones a darker shade than the front, so no one in the hundreds of cars passing this one could make out the familiar face—a very familiar face indeed, often seen on television. Seen in the newspapers every day, in every town and city in America. Seen around the world. And now bent over papers, reports, and documents taken from an oxblood leather briefcase.

As he worked, Bobby made frequent notations on the papers with his fountain pen. Sometimes he wrote a sentence or a paragraph in the margin of a page. Occasionally he spoke into a Dictaphone, recording thoughts and instructions his secretary would transcribe when he arrived back in Washington.

Bobby—Robert F. Kennedy, Attorney General of the United

States and brother of the President—had come to Los Angeles on business. Although previously he had often come on pleasure, this time was different. Strictly business. Urgent business that couldn't wait. He was headed to Brentwood, to a house where, in the past, he had devoted himself not to business but to pleasure.

His destination was a curious part of Brentwood—curious when examined on a map. It was adjacent to Carmelina Avenue, which was unremarkable. But hooked onto Carmelina were the Helenas—twenty-five of them in all, each one a dead-end street, or in the language of real estate, a cul-de-sac. Beginning with First Helena Drive and running north to Twenty-fifth, these short residential streets looked, on a map, like the vertebrae of a twisted spine, or the legs of a centipede.

As the dark Cadillac traveled further away from the ocean winds of Santa Monica, the hazy inland shadows grew heavier. But, pressing on toward Brentwood, the chauffeur and his passenger paid no attention to the disappearing sun. The driver turned into Cliffwood Avenue so smoothly that the Attorney General didn't look up from the memo he was drafting: ". . . which, in the context of our conversation of 7/26/62, merits immediate intervention. It is, however, essential that all parties to said information act with the utmost speed and accuracy."

When eventually he did look up from the yellow legal pad, his intense blue eyes were wary. Sharpening his wariness was anger, and giving an edge to anger was fear.

As the car reached Sunset Boulevard, the driver half-turned his head as though to speak. The Attorney General, still musing over the memorandum he had just drafted, anticipated the driver's statement.

"Yes, I know. Good," he said, gathering the papers and legal pads and documents, shuffling them into a neat stack, and placing them all in his leather briefcase. Then he spun the combination lock, making sure that what was secret remained secret.

The magical name "Sunset Boulevard" had little effect on either of the men in the car. Both had been there many times before and neither had seen the 1950 movie whose title had transformed Sunset Boulevard from a street name into the name of a mental condition. The Attorney General certainly *could* have seen

Sunset Boulevard. Several members of his family had seen the film, the first and most eager being his father, who was a special friend of Gloria Swanson, the film's star.

But Robert F. Kennedy was in law school at the University of Virginia when the movie came out. Recently married, he was absorbed in plans for fatherhood and a legal career. The driver was already employed by a government agency, which had hired him on the basis of his successful intelligence work behind enemy lines during the last year of World War II. His name then was Daniel Filatoff. Later he changed it to George Bledsoe, more American and so better suited to his work.

On that July day, however, Sunset Boulevard had only one association for both of them: it was leading them to Brentwood. After a few minutes, Bledsoe took the exit from Sunset Boulevard onto Carmelina. On Carmelina, luxuriant with palms, eucalyptus, orange and lemon trees, and dense with grass and flowers, he slowed the car. The normal thing to do on a street like this. He intended every impression of the car to convey ordinariness, to avoid attention.

This, after all, was a business trip. It had nothing to do with Hollywood glamor, or the signing of movie contracts. But if any inquisitive residents looked across their lawns and guessed they saw a slow-moving limousine containing a famous star or a powerful producer, so much the better. Even though the Attorney General was in a great hurry, George Bledsoe knew the right tempo for this part of town. Slow. To keep his passenger's secret, let him blend with the peaceful rhythm of these quiet streets.

This hasty trip to Brentwood in the middle of the day never took place. Officially. In the recorded itinerary of the Attorney General it was unscheduled, unmade, uncontemplated, undreamed-of. On the official agendas and engagement books of the Justice Department, no entry for it existed. The Attorney General's driver was officially not driving the car. The car was officially not on the streets.

Officially, Bobby Kennedy was in Santa Monica with his wife and three of their many children. The Kennedys were spending a long weekend with the Attorney General's sister and brother-in-law, Mr. and Mrs. Peter Lawford, seeking a late-summer respite from the pressures of life in Washington, from the heat of the nation's capital.

The real heat was in Los Angeles.

At Fifth Helena Drive the car turned left and rolled slowly to the end of the street.

At the end of the cul-de-sac named Fifth Helena Drive a high concrete wall surrounded a Mexican-style house nestled under a red tile roof. The only access was through a heavy wooden gate that seemed built to repel hordes. Across the gate five brass numbers had been nailed: 12305. Not a famous address compared to 10 Downing Street or 1600 Pennsylvania Avenue. But a few months earlier a very famous person had moved to 12305 Fifth Helena Drive, a person even more famous than the Attorney General. Was this famous person expecting a visit from the Attorney General of the United States? Since he had come on business—official business—could it be that the famous person behind the concrete wall and the heavy gate had done something wrong? Or was it simply that the Attorney General, as the nation's chief law officer, had come to counsel and advise the celebrity who presumably waited for him in the house behind the wall?

CHAPTER 2

"Her Sweetheart the President"

FRIDAY, JULY 27, 1962

The house was empty. Or at least the walls were empty—no pictures or mirrors, no silver artifacts, no pink and orange masks from Yucatan and Oaxaca. The house behind the concrete wall was Mexican, and it required Mexican things to fill it up. Lacking them it looked blank, indecisive.

Someone was moving out. Or had moved in. Boxed huddled along the bedroom walls. Crates stood upright with cushions on the end, doubling as chairs. One sturdy crate, used as a pedestal, supported a Rodin sculpture of a man and woman in an embrace. Locked together in ambiguous passion, they were either loving or strangling one another.

Exposed wooden beams gave the quiet living room the texture of a small Spanish colonial church. A carved wooden bench from central Mexico resembled a pew, except that a movie script lay on one end of it. Draped across the script, a yellow chiffon scarf turned the flat bench into an austere still life. The cover of the bound script bore the imposing logo of 20th Century–Fox. Below, the words SOMETHING'S GOT TO—but the scarf covered the rest of the title. A white sofa dominated the center of the room like an iceberg in an empty sea.

Somewhere in the back part of the house were three small bedrooms. Little space remained after the living room was completed, so these bedrooms were reduced. One was designated for a maid, one was theoretically for guests but contained such a jumble of furniture and cardboard, umbrellas and pocketbooks and clothes on hangers that a guest would have been instantly swallowed up by the clutter.

And someone was asleep in the third one. Sawdust crumbs speckled the floor. Between this bedroom and a tiny adjacent bathroom was a new door that the carpenters had not painted. They left it because they intended to come back and finish the remodeling of the house, but someone called and told them not to return. Not for a month, maybe longer. The owner was ill and couldn't endure the noise of hammers and saws.

The bed was not really a bed. A mattress lay on top of box springs, without frame, headboard or foot. Makeshift, like a campsite pitched hurriedly inside the bedroom walls. Taped on the wall over the bed was a picture of Abraham Lincoln, brooding and kind.

Under the sheet something twitched, then moved heavily. It rolled to the other side of the bed, twisting the top white sheet into a conical swirl. After a long pause a pale white arm crept out. Eventually a body followed it. Over the three bedroom windows hung dark blackout curtains, but the skin of the woman rising from the bed added light to the room, like the first pale reflections on a gray morning of rain.

She was not expecting guests, not expecting anything. But she licked her lips, a reflex she had learned long ago when posing for cheesecake pictures. Moist lips, loose hips, was the punchline of a joke that aspiring actresses told each other for a time in the late forties. Now she licked her lips because her mouth felt parched.

Before she could stand, she had to sit for a long moment on the edge of the mattress. Her head swayed, heavy as marble. She closed her eyes, craving rest. During the night she had mimicked sleep, but even the pills didn't persuade her mind to switch off and be still. Instead it buzzed and twitched all night, playing feverish scenes over and over. Her brain, like a film editor going over and over the daily rushes on a Movieola, repeated scene after scene, selecting intense close-ups, misty long shots, speeded-up rhythms and bizarre montages. But the result of so much work was not a final cut ready to print. Rather, the film jumped off its reel and piled up crazily. As the last frame went spinning out of control, she woke up.

Her eyes were troubled, as though still focused inward on the turmoil of her dreams. Her beauty was clouded. As she struggled out of bed her foot bumped an empty bourbon bottle. She growled at it, then quickly revised the expression to a smile as she had been taught to do. A beautiful blonde movie star must never look vexed, or angry, or frightened, or dismayed, or confused. Even if her toe is throbbing with pain. Even if she aches all over.

There's a clock in here somewhere. I left it on the night stand. No, that was my wristwatch. The clock must be in the trash basket. So it won't keep me awake ticking.

The water faucets didn't run, the toilet didn't flush in the tiny unfinished bathroom behind the unpainted wooden door, so she trudged off down the hall toward the living room. Like a visitor unfamiliar with the layout of the house, she glanced at various doorways to find the right one. Success on the first try.

She closed the bathroom door and opened the narrow closet beside the shower. *Last night*? When had she uncorked the champagne bottle? It was mixed in with household cleaners and disinfectants. *Gee, it's not so flat after all.* She giggled. She sipped, then swiped a toothbrush across her teeth, gargled with champagne and emptied the glass.

The medicine cabinet over the sink startled her. The long flat surface of the mirror made her look tired. Her face was pinched, needing moisture and blusher and shadow. She dismissed her reflection by opening the cabinet. There she saw what she wanted: makeup jars, shelves of them. Perfume bottles. Pills. She dotted Chanel behind each ear and swallowed two pills with the last of the champagne.

She closed the door of the medicine cabinet and stood on tiptoes trying to look all the way to the bottom of her stomach. "Jet lag, titty sag," a girl at the studio once said after flying nonstop from Europe to Los Angeles. She raised her eyes slowly to her rumpled hair. *I need Alice to make it gorgeous again. Why hasn't she come since Monday? Alice, come fast. Yipes! What if somebody saw me like this?*

Afternoon was advancing. She walked down the hallway and crossed the living room to the kitchen, where Mrs. Bridwell was struggling mightily with a large porcelain platter. To Marilyn's unfocused eyes, she seemed to be trying without success to push the platter down the drain. But it refused to go. She fought with it, and it fought back.

Suddenly aware that someone had joined her, Mrs. Bridwell turned quickly around. "Afternoon, Marilyn", she said in a voice of professional kindness. "How're you feeling, honey?"

Blinking, Marilyn Monroe looked at the sink, then squinted, trying to focus on the blurred outlines of Mrs. Bridwell's peculiar task.

"Don't these eyes tell it all?" she cooed.

Like the nearsighted Pola in "How to Marry a Millionaire," Marilyn opened the refrigerator. Confused even more by Mrs. Bridwell's assortment of eggs, milk, casseroles, puddings, and a baked ham, Marilyn chose a small carton of cottage cheese. She picked up a newly washed spoon from the drainboard and began eating tiny bites of her breakfast.

"How about some coffee, dear?"

"I could stand a cup," Marilyn said, not waiting to be served. Fumbling, she aimed a spoonful of instant coffee at a lipstick-stained mug that Mrs. Bridwell had overlooked. Half of the brown grains scattered across the Formica countertop, but Marilyn ran hot tap water over the remaining ones and drank, occasionally taking a delicate taste of cottage cheese.

Accustomed to these unpredictable snacks and nonsequiturs, Mrs. Bridwell busied herself by picking up one of Marilyn's several white terrycloth robes—this one left on a kitchen stool the previous day—and holding it open for her. In Ohio people wore pajamas with bathrobes and housecoats over them, Mrs. Bridwell often told her son and daughter-in-law when she first started working for Marilyn. The first time Marilyn Monroe drifted across the house stark naked Mrs. Bridwell almost quit. But having found a job that rated companionship above scrubbing, she endured. Soon she learned that the quickest way to end these innnocent displays was to open a robe and hold it up and Marilyn would scamper into it, a young miss ready to accept a grownup woman's authority.

"I tell you, that belt is nowhere to be found," Mrs. Bridwell complained as she covered the famous nakedness.

Smiling, Marilyn slipped one arm, then the other, into the wrapper. But the robe had been bought when she weighed less, and as it now gaped open Marilyn's flesh popped out.

"Overripe," an unkind columnist had written about her when Life ran a series of revealing photographs earlier in the summer. The pictures, taken on the set of "Something's Got to Give" when she played a pool scene in the nude, revealed an expanse of the celebrated curves. The perfect body seemed poised between freshness and fulsomeness.

"Sarah, let's go and sit on the patio," Marilyn urged Mrs. Bridwell, whose role in Marilyn's life was an ambiguous one, even in a city like Los Angeles where servants often blended seamlessly into the social fabric of their employers' lives. She was not really a maid, even though she tidied and picked up. Nor had she come to cook, although no one complained if after chopping and stirring for an hour she bestowed a meal. On the other hand no complaint was heard if mealtime came and went unnoticed, a circumstance that happened infrequently since Mrs. Bridwell knew the value of keeping up her own strength.

Housecleaning was not Sarah Bridwell's forte, and a flaw in her spine prevented heavy lifting. She had learned how to wash walls and windows as a girl in Ohio, but modern California windows defied the straightforward up-and-down motions necessary for genuine cleanliness. She spared herself that vexation.

She couldn't pass for a secretary, being innocent of typing, stenography and filing. But she answered the telephone, kept the house habitable and warded off the spectre of total loneliness. For such assistance Marilyn paid her an excellent salary, which Mrs. Bridwell earned. Phones rang endlessly. Phones in every room rang like electronic birds in an overpopulated aviary. Marilyn had two numbers, both of course unlisted, but both known, in Mrs. Bridwell's opinion, to more people than was necessary. Marilyn's main house number was the one used by the studio, reporters and columnists, the bank, insurance companies, the masseur, the hairdresser, the makeup people and friends near and far.

Her private number, which even Mrs. Bridwell didn't know, was reserved for boyfriends and a few other intimates. That number rang on one extension only, in Marilyn's bedroom, and Marilyn had removed the printed number from under the plastic disk to assure that no one peeked and later surprised her with an unwelcome call. She wanted her private line open unless there was good reason otherwise.

In addition to answering the relentless phones and writing down messages when Marilyn didn't feel like talking, Mrs. Bridwell provided the much younger woman a companion, paid friend, errand runner and, when Marilyn was in a fractious mood, a mother to rebel against.

Central Casting could not have found a more motherly mother. Mrs. Bridwell was a stout sixty-three years old, a lady anchored in the past. She wore dresses, no slacks. Her shoes were oxfords, and a pair lasted five years. She patronized no beauty parlor, contemptuous of such modern innovations as the permanent. Mrs. Bridwell did not make changes on a whim, and for that reason felt misplaced in Los Angeles.

Professionally, her rise had been steady. During the Depression her husband had moved the family from a small Ohio farm to Southern California. When he failed to find work, Sarah looked for a job as a practical nurse, and for the next ten years she performed menial chores for the sick and dying at several hospitals in Los Angeles. One of her patients near the end of the war was a young naval officer who had been wounded in the South Pacific and was invalided out of the service. Recuperating in California before returning home to Massachusetts for more extensive medical care, the young officer charmed Sarah Bridwell as he charmed the nurses who injected him and the doctors who tried in vain to find a soothing therapy for his injured back. Under the spell of his charm Mrs. Bridwell petted and encouraged him, and smuggled a cornucopia of treats into his hospital room.

She followed his career as Congressman, then Senator, and finally President. He didn't forget the comforts she had supplied in that green-and-gray hospital room in 1943, and every Christmas one of his secretaries sent Mrs. Bridwell a bouquet and a greeting, always with the signature "Jack Kennedy."

But that was long ago. Mrs. Bridwell had later become noted as a companion for the distraught, and for fifteen years several excellent Hollywood psychiatrists had recommended her to important clients as a skilled, reassuring, and discreet companion.

Marilyn's suggestion now that the two of them sit on the patio turned out to be another nonsequitur, as Mrs. Bridwell guessed it would. Instead of walking out the back door to the patio beside the swimming pool, Marilyn drifted through the house after her meager breakfast of cottage cheese and instant coffee. She was, of course, on a diet.

Stopping at the bathroom, she visited the medicine chest once more and again poured champagne into the bathroom cup. Removing an amber bottle of prescription pills from another shelf, she shook out two Nembutals and looked at them as though staring at a dark sky full of stars. One, then the other, she dropped the yellow capsules into her drink. They slid down, leaving behind a trail of fizzy wavelets. Marilyn watched them sink to the bottom of the glass, but before they could disappear she lifted her fortified drink and gulped it down.

At the threshold of her bedroom she raised her arms in a ballet motion, elevated her body on tiptoes, lowered it, turned around, and looked, coyly, over her shoulder. Outside, the dying of an expensive motor. A car door closed. Closed with that significant satiny expensive click of a limousine, causing Marilyn to open her eyes wide.

"I thought I heard a limo outside," she whispered. ". . . sounds like a limo. Where is it?" Then, losing interest, she sang a snatch of "Moonlight in Vermont." At the window she pinched the edge of the black curtain, lifting it as though to peer at the audience before stepping out to entertain.

"It's Frank," she squealed. "It's his car." Reminded of lovely Sinatra songs, all her favorites, she went on singing in a little-girl soprano about moonlight and snowlight in Vermont, pausing to breathe after every word. A smile illuminated her exquisite face as she sang the lyric that recalled silvery evenings in mountain chalets, and champagne and kisses.

"Frank's here," Marilyn reminded herself. She dropped "Moonlight in Vermont" and sang a few lines of "One For My Baby," imitating Sinatra's phrasing. Forgetting everything but the song, she twirled around, then flopped onto her bed as the walls and ceiling jumped over each other, playing leapfrog. Her eyes moved slowly to follow the antic games going on in her bedroom. "The ceiling jumped over the wall," she giggled, then dozed for a moment. An instant later, bored, she hoisted herself off the bed.

The doorbell chimed. If Marilyn had been fully awake and lucid she would have noticed that the sound was in the same key as the song she was singing a moment earlier. Eager to greet her friend Frank, she moved out of her bedroom and down the hall, her gait unsteady. The way she walked was profoundly different from her controlled slither in "Niagara," with high heels pointed like daggers. From years of practice she still swayed her hips as she walked, even though she was barefooted. Without shoes the walk was less photogenic. And no wonder—she had achieved the famous wiggle by cutting a quarter inch from the tip of one high heel to make her hips bob up and down. The result was exactly what Jack Lemmon called it in "Some Like It Hot": "Jell-O on springs."

Marilyn, determined to open the door herself before Mrs. Bridwell could deprive her of the pleasure, ran the last ten feet and grasped the knob. Holding onto it, she put a hand over her chest and sighed, catching her breath. She needn't have rushed; Mrs. Bridwell was far away, sweeping twigs and dead insect carcasses off the terra-cotta tiles around the pool.

Opening the varnished front door, Marilyn yawned as though bidding goodnight to departing guests. Robert Kennedy, his boyish smile replaced by a determined frown, walked in, closed the door softly behind him, glanced around to see if anyone else was present, then put his hands firmly on Marilyn's arms as though to correct a naughty child.

"Hello, Marilyn," he said.

Marilyn cocked her head slightly to one side, trying to get a better look at the man. "Not quite Sinatra, but the same shape," she mumbled. Unable to hear exactly what she said, Bobby glared at her as he led her over the beige carpet to the white sofa in the middle of the living room and sat her down on the soft square cushions.

"Marilyn," the Attorney General said, "what the hell do you mean by threatening to ruin my brother?"

Marilyn squinted at the speaker. She had lowered her eyelids to half-mast so often for photographers that the gesture had become not only her trademark but a reflex.

"Do you know what would happen if you really held that press conference?" he was saying.

Marilyn exhaled a little sigh of exasperation. She really had hoped it was Frank, and now she felt disappointed.

Unable to match the name to the face, she tried a game she had often played with her psychiatrists. They called it free association but she called it simply "jigsaw." To figure something out you added all sorts of pieces to a puzzle and finally you got your answer. *Now,* she thought, *I saw somebody like this at Peter Lawford's. When was it? Well, Pat was there, and Jack . . . Jack! Gee, this man looks just like the President!* The awesome similarity made Marilyn jump.

". . . and leave Jack alone," Robert Kennedy was saying as Marilyn's attention focused back on him. "I mean it." Leaning close to her on the cushion, he spoke into her face but in a voice pitched discreetly low. The Attorney General was a gentleman, and a gentleman does not raise his voice—not to another gentleman, and certainly not to a lady. Today he was uncharacteristically formal. His dark maroon-and-blue striped tie was not loose at the neck, and his shirt sleeves were not rolled up as usual. His blue suit coat was buttoned. The content of his message was urgent, his delivery businesslike.

Marilyn's lips quivered. Her nostrils contracted. She broke into sobs, then hid her face in her hands. She gasped as deeply as an asthmatic trying to breathe. Grief seemed ready to asphyxiate her—or rage.

She was furious. Or she tried to be, but for her anger was a thing she stepped over or around. It was also such a big thing that it could threaten to engulf and choke her. The doctors had tried to help her feel angry but she always ended up scared. She had learned as a child to turn the other cheek, and that still seemed safer than fighting. Besides, she hated the way she couldn't take a deep breath when she got mad, as though someone were smothering her with a pillow.

But this man! Who the hell—"Get the hell out of my house!" She tried to yell it at him but it came out more a whimper.

So that's who it is. Her father had come back after all these years to reject her again. No, it was that wrinkled old man with a sagging belly and a studio contract who used to make her kiss him down there.

The violence in her chest and throat subsided. Looking at the man sitting beside her, she smiled, then let out a squeak of surprise and pleasure.

"Bobby!" she called out, as though he were fifty yards in front of her and she wanted to catch up. He seemed at least that far away. Marilyn recalled him walking down the beach early one Sunday morning, engrossed in political cares, while she dawdled to pick up a pretty shell. That was her last time with Bobby. She tried to remember when: was it only a few months ago, or years in the past? A wave had broken on the beach . . . now she remembered why she had liked him so much. He looked like her sweetheart—her sweetheart the President!

The Attorney General dropped his hand from her arm. "Now look," he said, softening a little, "it's okay for you to have a crush on the President." Considering for a moment, he continued, "Marilyn, it was okay but now it's too dangerous. The lid's about to blow off. You understand? Leave Jack alone. Understand? *Leave him alone*. Or else . . ."

Marilyn nodded ambiguously, perhaps agreeing to leave the President alone, or perhaps only signifying that she understood the point Bobby was making. As he explained why the President was vulnerable to such scandal, Marilyn listened carefully to his Boston accent, mimicking in her head the dropped R's and the British-sounding A's. A great mimic, she found his pronunciation more interesting than his message. She imagined that she might be called on someday to talk like this in a movie. *I could play a character from up in Massachusetts. Sure I could. Those girls in "The Crucible" talked this way when Arthur and I went to see it in Connecticut. I'd love to play a witch . . .*

"Now just stop," Marilyn said suddenly. "Jack—oops, I mean the President—promised to make me First Lady. After all, I'm a Democrat, aren't I?" Did she smile now? "It's true that I'm Jewish and he's a Catholic but so what?" Another quick smile? Then she leaned closer and whispered in his ear. "I'm pregnant, Bobby." Standing up, Marilyn looked down at Robert Kennedy still seated on the sofa. "My son will grow up to be President, just like his daddy. And just like President Monroe," she added incongruously. Then she turned to go, giving a haughty farewell shake of her head to her uninvited visitor.

She sauntered toward the hall. Suddenly she felt exhausted and a little sick. *Like I just swam the English Channel*, she thought. The line from "All About Eve" came to her often, that and so much dialogue from her movies. Sometimes the lines of dialogue nearly drove her nuts. Her doctors had explained that it was because she overlearned her lines, fearing she might forget them in front of the camera. Then weeks, months, even years later they popped into her mind again, especially when she was anxious or overtired. The doctors told her to accept them as though they were no more than silly TV jingles running through her head. She had real difficulty with that. She wanted to speak her own dialogue in life, not parrot what some scriptwriter had dreamed up for a girl she played in a movie. But just when she most wanted to be original, to say something she hoped was intelligent or at least witty, one of the damn characters would rush in to speak before she had the chance. Sometimes Marilyn couldn't get a word in edgewise.

Lorelei Lee was the most persistent. Marilyn was convinced that everybody in Hollywood believed there was no real Marilyn Monroe, only Lorelei. But Marilyn loved her, even though she sometimes wished Lorelei would go back to Little Rock and leave her alone. Still, Lorelei had her uses. When Marilyn couldn't think of the right thing to say, when she wanted people to love her, when she craved the limelight, when she wanted to be the most fantastic blonde in the world, all she had to do was summon Lorelei. "Thank you ever so," was all it took, that and a flutter of her lashes, and the world lay down at her feet, rolled over and begged for more.

When Marilyn got mad at Lorelei, envious of her, or bored with her for being so silly, she sent her away and replaced her with Miss Caswell, or Cherie, or Pola Debevoise, or Sugar Kane, or any one of the other dumb blondes who were her close friends but who also always interrupted her just when she was going to say something smart. Marilyn wanted more than anything to be a *smart* blonde. She believed that's what she was, down deep—a smart blonde who could say smart things.

For Marilyn's less sunny moods, these girls were no help at all. So out they went, discarded and quickly replaced by tough Kay Weston, who wouldn't let a raging river of no return, or rampaging Indians with tomahawks frighten her. Sometimes instead of Kay Weston it was "Niagara"'s melodramatic Rose Loomis, who would stop at nothing to get what she wanted. Or Angela Phinlay, the frightened vamp from "Asphalt Jungle." Marilyn knew what the psychiatrists meant when they told her, "You have hidden resources but you must learn to use them." Wow! the doctors seemed to know about all the other girls. But Marilyn had never mentioned them, except to ask her doctors how to stop repeating those hundreds of lines of dialogue that didn't really belong to her.

When she reached the hall she met Mrs. Bridwell, who had finished sweeping around the pool and come inside to check on her employer. Sashaying past her, Marilyn soliloquized, "Bobby Kennedy! Who does he think he is? He can't talk like that to Marilyn Monroe! Jack won't allow it." She walked indignantly into her bedroom and slammed the door. "Imagine saying that . . . to the President's fiancee. I should call Jack." Looking at the other President whose picture she always kept near her, she recited, "With malice toward none, with charity for all, let us strive on to finish the work we are in." *I wish my fans could hear that! Then they'd know I'm no dummy even if I didn't go to college.*

* * *

"Oh, Mr. Kennedy, I didn't know you were here," Mrs. Bridwell said when she saw the Attorney General still sitting on the sofa as through transfixed. Crossing the room toward him, she patted the back of her fine dark hair and smoothed her skirt.

The Attorney General stood up and shook hands with his brother's old friend. "It's good to see you, Mrs. Bridwell," he said quietly. "My brother sends his regards. We're both grateful to you for agreeing to look after . . . You know, I'm rather worried about her. More than ever."

"Yes, sir, she's got a lot of troubles. A lot of stress. She said yesterday that the only thing she has to live for is the President. Imagine that, the President. And I think the poor baby believes he would run out on his wife and family and country for her. I tell you, the drinking never stops. She put away three bottles of champagne last night and I couldn't say how many pills. Dr. Gruber wants me to tell him exactly how many she's taking every day, but Lord, how can I keep track? She's got pill bottles in places I never dreamed of."

"As you know, Mrs. Bridwell, we think you're a very good influence on her. That's why we asked Dr. Gruber to recommend you." The Attorney General looked across the room to be sure they were alone. "Right now, the only thing we have to worry about is her outgoing mail. If she tried to mail a statement to someone, we would have to take steps. But the phones are no longer a problem."

"I don't believe she could write a letter," Mrs. Bridwell said. "At least, not one anybody could read. Her hands shake too much. And she complains about her eyes all the time. Dr. Gruber wants her to have them examined. He said it almost seems like cataracts but she's too young for that. Not too young for bifocals, though. I needed them before I was forty."

"Has she, uh, mentioned a press conference again?" the Attorney General asked.

"Not since Monday."

"Were you in the room when she spoke about that with Miss Hopper?"

"No, but I overheard her when she called Louella Parsons. So when I heard that, I tell you, I ran out and found a pay phone as fast as I could. I had just come in from shopping but I told her I hadn't got that French champagne she likes. Told her the liquor store was out of stock and I jumped back in the car and headed for a phone booth."

"And she didn't suspect anything?"

"Oh no, I wouldn't do anything to upset her. Poor baby, she yells at me sometimes but I pay no attention. I forgive her on the spot and go on with my work." Mrs. Bridwell nodded her head slightly as though to affirm her patience.

"Your call was very helpful. Miss Hopper also telephoned." Pausing, the Attorney General asked, "And you handle all the mail? Incoming and outgoing?"

"Always, Mr. Kennedy. She can't drive, you know. Dr. Gruber's orders. I keep her car keys and when we go someplace I drive. So you don't have to worry about her running out to the post office. The nearest one is two or three miles. And I always sort through the mail as soon as it gets here. It seldom varies—between ten o'clock and ten-thirty every morning. Marilyn's never up that early anyway. The bundle from the studio comes every Wednesday. A messenger brings it, but it's already been sorted. It's memos, fan letters, clippings and the like. So don't you worry. I tell you, we won't let her do anything foolish, or anything to hurt the President. Poor baby wouldn't want to do that anyway. Not if she was . . . well, herself."

Assured that Marilyn was in good hands, the Attorney General shook hands once more with Mrs. Bridwell and walked to the door.

The distance from the cool house to the cool automobile was short, but the gritty heat exacerbated the Attorney General's anxiety. Little drops of perspiration popped out all over his forehead. Moisture seeped from his skin and glued his white shirt to his back.

George, attentive to all details, had kept the air conditioner on high, so that stepping into the car was like finding a shady grotto in the middle of a desert. The Attorney General slid into the back and slammed the door. "It's okay for right now, but she's on the edge, out of control. She could ruin us."

"I heard it all loud and clear," George said. "The equipment's working fine. I heard your conversations with both of them like I was in the room. When she left you, she started talking to herself about you and the President. 'Jack won't allow it', she said. Then she started carrying on about calling him up. The equipment's picking up every sound. After she popped open a bottle I heard her filling up her glass."

One of the lines in the Attorney General's forehead smoothed out. His shoulders dropped slightly; a sigh emptied his chest. "The phones are covered too," he said. "One word out of place and we snap the line. Even the phone company won't know what's up, it'll look like trouble on the line. And Mrs. Bridwell is monitoring the mail. She said—but no need to tell you what she said. You were tuned in, weren't you?"

George looked over his shoulder into the back seat. As worried as he had been this week, Kennedy could have made life impossible, but now it looked like they would fly out late tonight. Security would be a lot easier than usual. Nobody knew they were going back so all he had to do was play bodyguard until they dropped the car at the Air Force base and headed home. They'd hit Washington tomorrow morning and he could drive to his girlfriend Cheryl's apartment in an hour.

The action reversed. Out of Fifth Helena Drive, onto Carmelina, then Sunset, all the way back to Santa Monica. The dark car remained cool and dry, slicing through the haze like a fin.

Again the oxblood briefcase was opened, the papers spread out across the seat. A business trip of great importance. A matter of national security. A friend of the President's, and also of the Attorney General's, risked great trouble. She must be . . . saved. Through her foolishness, Marilyn could bring down tragedy on herself and many others. Her rash actions, brought about by drunkenness and drug addiction, could ruin careers, destroy homes, turn distinguished public servants out of office, give aid and comfort to the enemy.

It sounded melodramatic in newsreels and on television when an unforeseen event or a crafty ideologue brought down the government of a foreign nation. The United States watched these events, knowing such a thing could not happen in a land of elections and representative government. But this impossible woman, her head stuffed full of ridiculous notions, had the power to topple the President.

Marilyn Monroe had become the most dangerous woman in the world.

In Santa Monica the Attorney General's family was swimming in the surf, tossing beach balls, eating hot dogs and drinking sodas. Soon he would join them for a while, then he would be called out on urgent business. He would slip away, the children would be told he had to fly to San Francisco overnight but would return to Los Angeles the following day to continue their vacation. Everyone would remain in high spirits, and eventually the children would be told that daddy was joining them back in Washington, returning on a different flight because his full schedule had kept him longer than expected in San Francisco.

"Mommy, what's he doing in San Francisco?"

CHAPTER

3

"Put a Stop to This Nonsense"

THURSDAY, JULY 26, 1962

Although formed and maintained as a section of the Justice Department, the FBI could not have been accurately described, on Thursday, July 26, 1962, or any other day, as a section of anything else. Unique and fiercely independent, it was the exception to every rule in Washington. If not the heart of the hive, it was certainly the gland whose hormone repelled every threat. No enemy, foreign or domestic, long survived its wrath. Although the Federal Bureau of Investigation had existed since 1908, it was a direct projection of the mind of one man, who took over as Director in 1924 and who ruled thereafter with power and fear: J. Edgar Hoover.

The Director was on the phone with the Attorney General first thing in the morning. Snorting with indignation, Hoover was telling Robert Kennedy what the Los Angeles bureau had just confirmed: "That crazy Hollywood mantrap has just threatened to hold a press conference."

"When?"

"This weekend! She didn't name the day."

"Uh, well, you see, Edgar—"

"And listen, Robert. Do you know what she intends to tell

that gaggle of reporters? After she gets them to her house?"

"What's that?" A patronizing note crept into the Attorney General's voice every time the Director called to report, in a burst of Victorian outrage, that someone in government, or out, was an adulterer or a degenerate.

"Well, *sir*, she plans to tell the nation that the President jilted her. She's going to say he vowed to make her First Lady, then broke his promise. So the communist whore plans to stage a shotgun wedding."

"What else do you know, Edgar?"

A nerve twitched on Hoover's lower lip. A phantom smile passed over his mouth.

"That's it in a nutshell. She asked Hedda Hopper to be her bridesmaid. It sounded like drivel at first but L.A. tapped the Monroe house and phones late Tuesday. She told a caller that she'd either get the President or get even with him. That was as recent as last night."

Knowing fully the extent of the President's and the Attorney General's personal interest in Marilyn Monroe, Hoover delighted in pretending ignorance of it. Otherwise he would have been reluctant to refer to his President's inamorata as a "mantrap" and a "communist whore."

"Robert, I can put a direct stop to all this nonsense. One of her doctors is ready to have her committed. Once she's in, he'll keep her there."

The Attorney General, however, had no intention of letting "the old reptile" (as he called Hoover in the family retreats of Boston and Hyannis Port) handle this one. "No, Edgar, we don't want to cause her any more distress. As you know, there have been rumors that she dated the President. She must have, uh, imagined some kind of affair after she sang at the birthday party last May. But I'm sure you have more pressing matters. I don't think the press will report these fantasies. Thank you for calling, Edgar. We'll keep you informed."

The Director reddened as he carefully replaced the receiver. So the rich boy was whistling in the dark again. Let her pass around that red diary, which the L.A. bureau also learned about, and there wouldn't be a Kennedy left in Washington. Long accustomed to getting revenge for any slight, the Director had a long list of grievances against his boss.

Hoover savored the stink about to break over the White House. It would smell up the Justice Department, too, but without damaging the FBI one iota. Despite his outrage that a Hollywood trollop dared cause trouble for his government, he was more than a little pleased that the Kennedy upstarts had landed in a tough spot, a very tough spot indeed.

He had disliked the Kennedys from the start. They were young and brash, and Bobby walked around the Justice Department in his shirt sleeves with his tie loosened. He brought his dogs to the office, flaunting the regulation forbidding all animals except guide dogs on Federal property. They both carried on with women who were not their wives, and acted as though the approval of the New York *Times* and the Washington *Post* was all it took to run the American government. And Robert let people call him "Bobby," like the kid he was.

Despite his slack habits, his flashy smile and his queer-looking haircut, Robert Kennedy was dangerous. Wanting total control of the Justice Department, he slighted the Director in order to consolidate his own power. It was common knowledge in Washington that the Attorney General would like to replace Hoover. When asked how he might do so, he was known to reply, "Just wait." That impertinent threat got back to the Director immediately. But he lost no sleep over Robert Kennedy's schemes to kick him out. Not all the Kennedys, nor all the Kennedys' men, could move J. Edgar Hoover out until he was ready to go. And that would not be for a very long time.

Picking up one of the dossiers on his great polished desk, Hoover thought, Now let Bobby tidy up his brother's love nest. That smart aleck might decide I know a thing or two he doesn't. Hoover's lips moved faintly as his interior fulminations built. Telling me he'll keep me informed! I was Director before he was born, and I'll still be here when the Kennedys can't get elected dogcatchers.

Rifling through the many items in the dossier, Hoover looked once again at a photograph. In it a blonde woman and a distinguished-looking man in his forties were together in a room with one wall made of glass. Through the glass wall, white-topped ocean waves reared up as though trying to peer inside the house. The man lay on a chaise lounge with his eyes closed. Seated on the floor at his side, the woman was bent over as though hiding her face against him. The photograph was grainy, as though taken from a distance or shot with cheap film. Or perhaps from a clandestine camera. But it was evident that the man's chest was bare. And at the corner of the frame two pieces of fabric—the top and bottom of a bikini—had been flung carelessly. It was the kind of picture that could not legally be sent through the United States mail.

CHAPTER 4

"Girl Talk"

MONDAY, JULY 23, 1962

"Everybody and his brother's calling the house today," Mrs. Bridwell complained. When she walked in the door at eight o'clock, the phone was ringing. She answered, the caller hung up. Before she could take off her hat and put away her purse, two more calls. One from the art gallery owner, wanting to know if Marilyn would like to buy a sculpture similar to the one she bought in April. "R-o-d-i-n," Mrs. Bridwell wrote down the name of the artist. "And how much are you asking for it? She'll want to know." Next, Alice Mulligan, the hairdresser, returned Marilyn's call from Sunday night: "Tell Marilyn I'll be over between two and two-thirty. And tell her not to do a thing herself. I'll wash it, set it, and apply the rinse."

Mrs. Bridwell started the washing machine, brewed coffee for herself, cut a cantaloupe she had bought at the supermarket on Saturday, and ate half of it. During her breakfast she left the receiver off the hook. As soon as she replaced it, another ring. The pharmacy: their delivery man would be there in an hour. The next caller had an intimidating female voice. It crackled on the other end of the line: "Good morning, this is Hedda Hopper. Tell

Marilyn I'm dropping by at four. We'll have tea. I'll have tea, that is. Marilyn might want something else. Now don't forget to tell her."

Marilyn, sealed into her blackened bedroom, could not have been further removed from the enterprise of the rest of her house. Her phones were the busiest ones in Brentwood. A small corporation might have been extrapolated from the volume of calls put through to her numbers. If she had been awake she would have paid as little attention to the calls as she did in the depths of sleep. Having conducted most of her life over the phone, increasingly she talked only to the people that she herself called.

Although Marilyn's life had become frighteningly disorganized that summer, she managed to fool most people most of the time. With the help of her hairdresser, her makeup man, and other key figures of her entourage she could perform her way out of a combined hangover and drug stupor. She could also pull herself out of an abysmal depression and sometimes overcome debilitating anxiety. Marilyn was a chameleon capable of changing colors and moods.

In spite of her emotional distress she still courted the press, manipulating it shrewdly. Although in answer to yet another question about her private life she might feel like saying, "It's none of your damn business," she never said it. When a boorish reporter from a tabloid asked her if she felt old now that she was thirty-six, Marilyn said: "Thirty-six is great when kids twelve to seventeen still whistle." But when another interviewer asked, "Are you happy?" she replied, "Let's put it this way. I'm blonde."

When Marilyn struggled out of bed at eleven she made her usual rounds: the medicine chest for a pick-me-up, the fridge for a bottle of chilled champagne and half a grapefruit, and the kitchen bar, where Mrs. Bridwell's messages filled up two pages in a notebook. Seeing Alice Mulligan's name and an appointment in three hours, she relaxed. The thought of Alice's deft fingers in her hair soothed her, like the first strokes of a massage on a weary back.

Then, blinking, she held the notebook closer and peered at the name of another woman. "Oh, my God, Sarah. Is *she* coming over? I'll just die! Don't let her in, tell her I've split."

"Well, honey, she might break down the door. I tell you, she sounds determined to me."

Marilyn nodded. She had known Hedda Hopper since 1946, and for about eight years Hedda had been fairly pro-Marilyn. In 1952 she wrote, "Blowtorch Blondes are Hollywood's specialty, and Marilyn Monroe, who has zoomed to stardom after a three-year stretch as a cheesecake queen, is easily the most delectable dish of the day." But around the time of "There's No Business Like Show Business," Hedda seemed peeved with Marilyn for some reason and wrote about her more and more ungenerously.

"That mean woman in her silly hat," Marilyn said, swallowing an extra capsule with the cup of coffee Mrs. Bridwell handed her. "But I have to be nice to her, even though I'm feeding the hand that bites me."

The thought of Hedda's visit at least helped to lift Marilyn out of her usual wake-up fog. The bottle of Dom Perignon helped, too, and so did the Dexedrine she took to counteract the two extra Nembutals required to put her to sleep the night before.

For all Marilyn's dislike of Hedda Hopper, she had never been able to resist the lady's blandishments. Hedda was the one gossip columnist Marilyn couldn't manipulate. She was bossy, insinuating, an expert at putting the worst spin on the truth.

A year earlier Marilyn would have resigned herself to an irritating hour with her unwelcome visitor. She would have poured tea and drunk it like a proper English lady, chatting innocuously about clothes, the rewards of acting, and her hopes of settling down with the right man to raise a family. But not this year. Marilyn's life resembled a car skidding on wet pavement, and anything in its path might well get caught up and dragged along.

The hairdresser arrived early. Mrs. Bridwell opened the door, and Alice, a sparrow of a woman, took small hopping steps across the living room to the sofa. Her canvas bag full of implements and potions looked larger than Alice herself.

Marilyn, hearing the doorbell, came slowly down the hall

from her bedroom. Seeing Alice, she tried to move faster, but pain and drugs dragged against her.

"Darling, when are you going to unpack your things and make this look like a real home?" Alice asked. It was the same question she always asked Marilyn, though it never sounded nagging.

"Gee, you're right," Marilyn said, looking around the room as though for the first time. "My stuff doesn't look so great in this hacienda." Scarcely pausing for breath, she went on impulsively, "Let's go to Mexico. Can you leave today? We'll buy pottery, and rugs and gold and silver. And cacti." Before Alice could answer, Marilyn changed the subject. "But at least I have privacy here in my hideaway. You know? They can't gawk at me anymore."

"That's because nobody would recognize you under those tangles. Just wait. We'll have 'em all gawking at you, and whistling, too."

"Alice, I have terrible news. Something dreadful is about to happen to me."

Giving Marilyn a sharp look, Alice said, "What do you mean, pet?"

A frown had settled over Marilyn's face, but hearing the note of concern in Alice's voice she laughed and lowered her eyes. "A witch is coming to get me this afternoon. Hedda, the wicked witch of the west."

"Oh, you. Tell her, 'Oh, yes, I love Hollywood,' and she'll write a column about what a sweet, nice girl you are. Put on your best dress, do your face. I'll make your hair look marvelous, then you'll go out and dazzle the old witch. There's not a thing she can do to hurt you, pet. You're Marilyn Monroe and she's an old biddy. And don't you forget it."

"But Alice, you know how she is. She'll try to make me talk about why the studio fired me. And she's sure to start me saying bad things about the guys in the front office at Fox."

"Well," Alice said, "let's rehearse the interview while I do your hair. Come on, off to the bathroom."

As Alice rubbed Marilyn's scalp, the tension drained away, leaving Marilyn's face relaxed and fresh. "Now, love, tell me how you're going to handle Hedda. Suppose she says, 'Marilyn, why were you fired? Is it true you arrived on the set five hours late, or was it because you skipped town and flew to New York to sing at President Kennedy's birthday party?' How will you answer?"

As soap and water ran down her cheeks, Marilyn said, "Well, it's like this, Hedda. I needed a couple of days off. And it was an honor to sing at Madison Square Garden for the President. It was my way of serving my country. Gosh, I've always been patriotic. You remember—I caught pneumonia in Korea entertaining the soldiers. I wore a low-cut dress in freezing weather."

"Very good. Now suppose she asks whether you intend to get married again. What will you tell her?"

"Well, I'll say it would be an honor to—"

Mrs. Bridwell rapped on the bathroom door. "Louella Parsons on the phone. You want to talk or will you call her back?"

"Don't mention a word about Hedda coming over. Tell Louella I'll phone her before sundown. Tell her I'm taking a bubble bath."

As Mrs. Bridwell went away to deliver this message Marilyn told Alice, "I wish Louella were coming today instead of Hedda. Louella was one of my first friends in Hollywood, and she's always been like a granny to me."

Long before the world discovered Marilyn, Louella Parsons knew; in the early fifties she wrote that Marilyn was "the number-one movie glamor girl." Over the years she defended Marilyn and pardoned all her offenses.

Although Marilyn didn't set out to conquer Louella, she couldn't have done it better by waging a full-scale campaign. The one lesson every starlet learned on her first day in Hollywood was, "Stay friends with both Hedda and Louella, and never help one scoop the other."

In Marilyn's case they had both liked her for the first few years. Then Hedda, aware that Louella intended to "keep" Marilyn, started her detractions. The rules of the game were clear: Marilyn was Louella's fair-haired child. Beyond the politics of the gossip business, however, Louella genuinely liked Marilyn. She liked Marilyn's sunny disposition, her giggle, her good sense (and Louella explained in her column that the real Marilyn was very different from the daffy scatterbrains she played on-screen). Louella also pitied Marilyn's lost quality.

Like everyone in Hollywood, Louella knew about Kennedy. It was old news. Marilyn had carried on with JFK since the early fifties, but no one dared even hint at the affair in print. He was married; he was religious; the influence of the Kennedy family lubricated key parts of the Hollywood machine. And the Kennedys were ferocious when crossed. But the rumors had gone wild this summer. Some said it was Bobby, not the President at all anymore. Still others claimed it was both, and at the same time.

"There, pet, you look like a million dollars," Alice said as she combed the last platinum tress into place. "I've got to skedaddle. You-know-who wants me to make her look like *you* for the premiere tonight."

Marilyn walked Alice to her car and gave her a hug.

"Now remember," Alice said before she drove away, "tell Hedda what she wants to hear. But don't volunteer anything."

Marilyn had almost two hours before her visitor was due. She returned to the bathroom and made up her eyes. "I believe I'll have a little drink," she confided to herself. Reaching into the medicine cabinet, she found a third of a bottle of vodka and emptied it.

Mrs. Bridwell came to tell her that this was the day to shop and to have the car serviced and the oil changed. "The errands never end, I tell you," Mrs. Bridwell sighed. "Honey, would you eat a steak for dinner if I cooked it the way you like? Steaks would be good for both of us."

"You know I have to lose weight," Marilyn said with a frown. "But you go ahead, Sarah. I'll sit with you while you eat yours."

With Mrs. Bridwell out of the house, Marilyn decided to get in shape for Hedda's visit. Reaching once more into the medicine cabinet, she gathered a handful of pills and nibbled them like salted peanuts. Suddenly thirsty again, she went to the kitchen and opened the door under the bar, where a full bottle of mellow brandy had remained unopened over the weekend. She poured half a tumblerful. Marilyn still felt unprepared for the coming ordeal.

"I need a chaser," she said. Finding it in the fridge, she refilled her champagne glass until nothing was left in the bottle with the fancy gold label.

Beginning at last to unwind, Marilyn returned to the bathroom to do her lips. First the three different shades of red, then the thick mixture of Vaseline and beeswax that made her mouth shine like neon. But no more liquids, or the shine would migrate from her lips to the rim of the glass. "I need sequins," she told herself, but settled for a simple black dress with spaghetti straps.

It was 3:45. Marilyn moved books, dark glasses, a terrycloth robe and a bikini from the sofa and sat down. Practicing how she would look at Hedda, she smiled and nodded politely. She pantomimed the answers she had rehearsed with Alice. Now she felt the numbness spreading from deep inside her, reaching her chest, her throat, her shoulders, traveling to her fingers and all the way to her toes. Her breathing was slow, each breath spaced far apart.

And then it was the hour of doom.

The voice from under the wide-brimmed green hat clattered at breakneck speed. A full skirt, lime green, rustled like a roomful of cellophane, and gleaming bracelets on the veiny arms jangled as loud as steel guitars. Marilyn nearly giggled at the circus act coming through the door.

"Well, look at you," Hedda caroled as she brushed a powdery cheek against Marilyn's face in a gesture meant to imitate a kiss, then marched to the sofa, sat down and patted the spot next to her. Marilyn sat obediently.

Hedda started in. "You've had another birthday since I saw you last. How did you celebrate? That was June first, wasn't it? So of course you had already helped Kennedy celebrate his. Well, it's a shame you got fired. Really, too bad. But we've got a new kind of mogul in Hollywood now. Whether you're a bit player or Marilyn Monroe, they expect an honest day's work for an honest day's pay. If Fox takes you back you'll have to be more professional. Or didn't they teach you that at the Actors Studio?"

"I'm looking forward to returning to the picture," Marilyn breathed. She blinked, brushed a strand of hair off her left temple and looked intently at Hedda Hopper. "After all, I love Hollywood. It's my hometown." Marilyn filled the room with light and lipstick.

"I'm afraid it takes more than that, my dear. But I haven't come to lecture you. What I want to know is, exactly what was said when you met with the studio executives on July twelfth?"

Marilyn, with only the dimmest recollection of the abortive meeting at Fox, knew it hadn't resolved her problems. "I'm ever so sure," she beamed, "that I'll be back at work in a couple of weeks." Brushing an imaginary speck from her eyelash, then propping her face against the spread fingers on her left hand, she continued: "A girl shouldn't have too much time on her hands." An exaggerated pout, followed by a polite giggle.

Hedda knew her present line of questioning would lead nowhere, which was where she wanted it to lead. She knew already from insiders at Fox what had been said at the meeting. She had dropped by today to sniff in another direction. She had always been able to squeeze news out of Marilyn, if only a drop or two at a time. This could be the biggest story of the decade, and even though it could not yet be printed because of its explosive nature, she, Hedda Hopper, might start something that wouldn't soon end. Something that would reverberate from Hollywood to Washington, and around the world.

Hedda gave Marilyn a slanting look. Moving closer, she took Marilyn's hands in her own as though for a bizarre game of ring around the roses.

Marilyn raised her shoulders almost imperceptibly; something tickled her somewhere inside. As more drugs kicked in and helped the alcohol do its work, she wanted to take a nap but knew she mustn't close her eyes; that would be rude. She could talk to Hedda in her sleep. That was the easiest way to do it.

Hedda said almost sotto voce, "Marilyn, my dear, everyone in Hollywood is talking about you. They've done it plenty of times before, you have a knack for that. But do you know what I heard not once but three times last week?"

Marilyn licked her lips. "No," she said in her breathiest tones, "please tell me."

"I heard that you're seriously involved with a very highly placed man in Washington. Is that true?"

"Well, you see, I want to stop having so much fun and just find happiness."

"With the man in Washington?"

Marilyn's red mouth opened slightly, then closed as though waiting for a cameraman to find the perfect angle. From far away, behind the bright lights, came the cue: *Quiet on the set. Roll 'em.*

"Yes, it's true." Marilyn demurely pulled up her bodice. "The President has asked me to marry him." She fidgeted with her skirt, tugged at a strand of hair over her ear and looked at the floor for a moment. In a whisper: "But his wife found out, or something, and now the President says he can't do it." She frowned. "But I love Jack. He's the greatest President since Abraham Lincoln. What I have to do is get him away from *her* and I know he'll marry me just like he promised. Oh, Hedda . . . will you be my bridesmaid?"

Hedda rummaged in her handbag for a handkerchief. She dabbed her forehead and stared at Marilyn, who didn't wait for an answer.

"The press can do anything. The made me a star, didn't they? So be a doll, Hedda, and tell *everybody* to come over Saturday afternoon. Here to my house. I'm holding a press conference. Right where we're sitting." Marilyn made a vague gesture, then giggled. "A girl shouldn't announce her own engagement, I guess, but I don't have a soul to do it for me. So what's a girl to *do*?"

Putting her index finger dramatically to her lips, Marilyn said, "Now, don't you dare breathe a word to Louella. Let me call her up; you know she'll be mad at me if I don't tell her first. I want you on one side of me and Louella on the other. The photographers will love us three girls together, won't they? Which dress should I wear?"

Hedda's heart was beating fast. She reached into her handbag again and rummaged for the nitroglycerine tablets she kept there in case of another heart seizure, then slipped the tablet under her tongue like a lozenge.

As Marilyn grew more talkative Hedda seemed turned to stone. The demented plot tumbled out of Marilyn's mouth: an enormous wedding at Hyannis Port, a dozen Kennedy kiddies scattering rose petals in her path, a twenty-one-gun salute. Afterward a honeymoon on the Riviera followed by two weeks in Paris with *no* interruptions. The Vice-President would run the government for a month and Marilyn would pick a favorite charity to occupy her time once they settled into married life at the White House. "I'll sponsor the Freedom Riders," she said with a straight face.

For the first time in her life Hedda Hopper was speechless. She rose to depart. Mopping her forehead, she knocked her hat askew. Unaware that she looked like a damaged figure on a Bavarian clock, she neglected to adjust her cherished trademark. Without turning to look at Marilyn, or to bid her the usual crisp farewell, Hedda rushed out of the house like a character in a farce making a crucial exit from the stage.

"Gee," Marilyn said, all wide-eyed, "that's the first time I ever got the last word with Hedda."

Driving across town, Hedda muttered to herself, "If we had a Republican President this wouldn't have happened." Although her heart beat less wildly, she still felt undone.

At home, she paced for half an hour, then she went to the telephone. "Operator, get me Washington, D.C. JU six, seven-six hundred. Person-to-person to Mr. J. Edgar Hoover. Hedda Hopper calling."

After a prolonged wait, the Director spoke. "Good afternoon, Miss Hopper. What may I do for you?"

"Mr. Hoover, you told me when we met out here ten years ago to call you if I ever got wind of a communist plot in Hollywood. Well, there's one brewing now that could destroy our country. She's really out to steal the President from his wife, then take him to Paris and let Johnson take over. She's so drunk she can't even stand up. Mr. Hoover, you must do something. It's all because of the goddamned Democrats."

Interrupted in the middle of reading his weekly statistics on organized crime, Hoover scowled while listening to this breathless communique. Must be the change, he thought, having no idea what this disjointed narrative was all about. "You mentioned a woman, Miss Hopper. Do you mean someone told you the President is a womanizer? Is that your news?"

"No, no. I'm talking about Marilyn Monroe. She told me not an hour ago that the President has asked her to marry him. She expects to become the First Lady, says he's going to divorce Jackie and marry her. Crazy as it sounds, she's capable of it. You're the first one I've told. It's absolute dynamite, if you want my opinion . . ."

Hoover, displeased that anyone would disturb him in the middle of a crime report, said, "Thank you for letting me know about this. Your patriotism is gratifying, Miss Hopper. The next time you're in Washington I hope you will come by the Bureau for a tour."

When he hung up he buzzed his secretary and asked for the file on Hedda Hopper. Finding nothing damning, he turned to the summary page and read: "A dedicated Republican journalist, sometimes prone to emotional overstatement and jumbled facts. But supports anticommunist activities throughout the film industry." He sat for several minutes reading the specimen snippets from various Hopper columns, then dialed the chief of the Los Angeles bureau of the FBI.

Mrs. Bridwell returned bearing two large bags of groceries and a butcher-bag full of steaks. The anticipation of a juicy filet mignon had sustained her through the long dreary afternoon at the garage, the supermarket, and the liquor store. "I'll have steak, French fries, rolls, sliced tomatoes and iced tea," she had told herself during the tedious hours.

She wrapped thick slices of bacon around two ruddy steaks: one for her, one for Marilyn—if Marilyn would eat. In case her diet forbade it, however, Mrs. Bridwell was prepared to consume the superfluous portion rather than demote it to the status of leftovers.

Marilyn came into the kitchen, her pupils dilated. "Golly, it's been some kind of afternoon. Would you believe Hedda Hopper left here speechless? Couldn't say a word after I told her my news."

"What news is that, Marilyn?"

Noticing the rich round pieces of meat, Marilyn suddenly felt starved. "How about I tell you over dinner? Those hamburgers look yummy."

Resigning herself to make do with one steak, Mrs. Bridwell

turned to inform Marilyn of the meat's true identity. "Why, that's not hamburger, it's—"

"Oh noo!" Marilyn squealed. "I forgot to call Louella." She took hold of the kitchen wall phone and dialed. "Hi, Louella, this is Marilyn. I have something to tell you. I guess it's kind of unexpected. I'm getting married again." A pause. "To President Kennedy." A longer pause. "Louella, are you all right? I wanted you to be the first to know, of course. Will you be a bridesmaid?" Then, "Are you sure you're okay? *Au revoir*, dear. Also, bye-bye." She hung up the phone and poured a glass of champagne, a wide smile on her face.

The steaks sizzled in the pan, but dinner, Mrs. Bridwell realized, would have to wait. She was in this house at the end of a dead-end street to serve her country, and the reward for such service went far beyond the financial expectations for a job well done.

Certainly, she was well paid; not only by Marilyn but by other sources, too. It was all so complicated that Mrs. Bridwell herself couldn't understand it. But a man from the government had approached her about taking this job; he had talked about every citizen's duty to serve his country and fight communism and she had agreed. Her pay—"remuneration," the man from the government called it—would insure security for herself to the end of her days and, after her departure, for her son and for following generations of Bridwells. The sum, deposited in a bank in a distant state, had been available to her since the day she arrived at Fifth Helena Drive. Now, hearing Marilyn's reckless plans, Mrs. Bridwell knew her duty.

"Honey, I couldn't help overhearing. I believe you're not feeling so well. I tell you, you could get in a lot of trouble saying things like . . . like you're going to marry the President."

"But it's true, Sarah, it's true. I am going to be the First Lady. Just like Grace Kelly. Gosh, I meant to tell you"—Marilyn giggled—"but you were out. Guess what? I'm holding a press conference here this weekend. That's when I'll announce it. With Hedda on one side and Louella on the other. And a house full of reporters. Can you make hors d'oeuvres for all of us?"

Mrs. Bridwell looked woefully at the half-cooked steaks and

turned off the flame. "Lord, Marilyn, I forgot your champagne," she said nervously.

But what had happened to Mrs. Bridwell's memory? She had become very forgetful indeed, for in the trunk of the newly polished and serviced automobile was a case of French champagne. Eager to set upon the steaks, Mrs. Bridwell had postponed unloading the bulky carton until after dinner, when she expected to have greater strength.

"I'll go and buy it right now, before the store closes," she said. With that, she rushed out, the second lady that afternoon to flee the house at Marilyn's news. And the second lady to place an urgent call to Washington.

Louella Parsons, at home on North Maple Drive in Beverly Hills, at first worried that a long-dreaded stroke had numbed her. Seated in her reproduction French Provincial armchair, she couldn't hang up the phone for what seemed like several minutes. Her mouth opened and closed, but no words came out. She wanted a drink, needed one desperately, but was afraid that she might not make it to the bar.

"I have to cancel my appointments," she said. "Marilyn has either gone bananas, or this is the exclusive of a lifetime. She's crazy and he's woman-crazy . . . I wish Mr. Hearst was alive to hear *this*."

She called Lana Turner to cancel their luncheon for the following day at the Brown Derby. Next, she left a message with Sandra Dee's secretary: "Tell Sandra I'm so sorry I can't make it to her pool party on Wednesday. Something very big has come up." The last entry on her week's agenda was a nightclub rendezvous with "handsome, broad-shouldered George Peppard," as Louella had described him the previous week in her column. She broke the date, reminding herself as she did so that "Mr. Hearst always said, 'An exclusive before a pretty face.'"

"Collect call for Mr. Robert Kennedy from Mrs. Sarah Bridwell in Los Angeles," droned the operator as though the call had been for John Doe. "Will he accept the charges?"

Standing in the phone booth at an Esso station, Mrs. Bridwell waited anxiously for the operator at the Justice Department to announce the call to the Attorney General's secretary, who announced it to the Attorney General. After hearing Mrs. Bridwell's message, Bobby Kennedy made two calls on his private line: one to the President, another to George Bledsoe.

The three of them, along with one other man, met secretly three hours later in the Oval Office.

CHAPTER 5

"Unnatural Causes"

FRIDAY, JULY 27, 1962

Long before the Attorney General and his chauffeur—his colleague and partner who also played the role of chauffeur—drove through the Los Angeles haze in the middle of the day, long before they were even awake, a spokesman in Washington was preparing the text of a routine statement to be read to reporters at the daily press briefing in the Justice Department. In Washington it was mid-morning, almost ten o'clock. There was no news.

For every man waiting in the Justice Department press room, and for the two women, no news was bad news. In late July, however, this bad news was the norm. Practically nothing ever happened then because August was only a few days away. And nothing, absolutely nothing, happened in August. Newspaper sales slumped, magazines dropped through mail slots and lay unopened because no one was home to read them. At 6:30 in the evening no one, or very few, turned on the national news. Couldn't leave the barbecue; didn't want to stop swimming; weren't able to find a set within miles of the mountain cabin. The United States was on vacation.

The Justice Department was no hotbed of sizzling news even

at times other than the end of July and the month of August. If you were assigned to cover the Justice Department you had to juice things up year round, stretch little items into headlines. True, since the Kennedy brothers had come to town the Justice Department crackled more than it used to. Robert Kennedy had his hand in everything: civil rights, Cuba, organized crime. Investigations popped up all over, confrontations with southern governors, threats, charges, countercharges, everything from Castro to contempt citations. But not in late summer.

So the gathered reporters waited in the Justice Department press room for the worst possible news: none. At 10:05 A.M. the spokesman stepped to the podium and adjusted the microphone. "Ladies and gentlemen," he announced, "the Attorney General and Mrs. Kennedy, along with three of their children, left yesterday for Los Angeles. They will spend the weekend with the Attorney General's sister and brother-in-law, Mr. and Mrs. Peter Lawford. They will all return to Washington on Monday."

The spokesman continued to the next item on his briefing paper: "In the first quarter of 1962 crime rose two percent nationwide over the same period in 1961, with murder leading the total number of reported crimes by . . ." Page six information, but in many of tomorrow's papers it would make page one. August had begun, even though the calendar still called it July.

A few hours after the spokesman's mundane disclosures in the Justice Department press room the Attorney General and his partner, George Bledsoe, made their business trip from Santa Monica to Brentwood. The spokesman far away in Washington, however, had no way of knowing about their activities. He was informed from above that it was vacation, and so vacation it became. The official version. During the reading of the crime figures one of the female reporters made a note to herself to approach her editor about a feature on the Peter Lawfords at home in Santa Monica. With luck her editor would approve the story and rush a photographer to take pictures while the Kennedys were still there. "Kennedy Sister Welcomes Members of the Clan," the reporter planned to call her feature.

At five o'clock after a day of no news Washington shut down.

As the immense gray government buildings emptied, streets of the company town grew still and silent. Washington would reopen, though sluggishly, reluctantly, on Monday.

In Los Angeles it was still afternoon. The Attorney General and his partner, having transacted their business in Brentwood, returned to Santa Monica. Robert Kennedy rejoined his family at the Lawfords' beach house and his partner went back to his hotel.

When the Attorney General walked in no one inquired about his whereabouts for the past couple of hours. Some members of the house party didn't want to know, ever. Others would find out later and would receive instructions on how to handle Marilyn Monroe if she telephoned or tried to visit. They would also receive answers in advance to certain questions that might be asked later.

Shortly before the Attorney General's departure for San Francisco an exchange took place between him and his brother-in-law as they lounged beside the pool, away from the others.

"Did she agree to keep hands off?" Peter Lawford asked.

"Couldn't. Too stoned."

"What's next, then?"

"The problem's under control for a week, two weeks. But it has to be resolved. Permanently."

"How, Bobby? How can you do that?"

"I'll discuss it with Jack tomorrow. The first thing is to cut Hoover out of the deal. Make him think she's, uh, well, quiet. Then use the CIA. Give them exclusive rights, you know?"

"And then?"

And then it was time for the Attorney General to leave for the airport. His flight to San Francisco on sudden business would not take long. An hour or so. But when the dark Cadillac arrived and the Attorney General once again climbed into the back seat, a different scenario began. "San Francisco" was discarded, like a storyline briefly considered for a movie then dropped by the producer because it wouldn't play. "San Francisco" had actually been nixed long before. In fact, it was never more than a fairy tale made up for the children, and they were the only ones in the house who believed it.

The new script was "Washington." It opened with a trip to the airport. Not Los Angeles International or any of the commercial airports nearby. Instead, a trip to Vandenberg Air Force Base a hundred miles away. A military base with no gawking civilians, those television-watching, newspaper-reading civilians who were experts at spotting the famous, especially in Los Angeles. Experts who, after a sighting, loved to tell their friends. For them, a Kennedy was a big prize, almost as big as Elizabeth Taylor or Rock Hudson. The Kennedys had become show biz, big box-office of a kind perhaps never before seen in American politics. Washington stars, closely allied with the jet set. Jacqueline Bouvier Kennedy had pushed Doris Day, Audrey Hepburn and Natalie Wood right off the covers of Photoplay and Modern Screen. The President and his brothers appeared without let-up on the front of Time, Newsweek, Life, Look, Esquire, the Saturday Evening Post. Stories about the vast Kennedy family filled the pages of McCall's, Ladies' Home Journal, Cosmopolitan: "How the Kennedys Spend Christmas," "Jack and Jackie's Favorite Beach Hideaway," "Ten Things You Don't Know About the Brothers Kennedy," "Goodbye Boston, Hello Camelot."

The military flight was scheduled to depart at midnight. Much remained, however, for the Attorney General and his partner to accomplish before then. At the beach house in Santa Monica there was time for only a brief swim in the ocean.

Did the Attorney General think about Marilyn as he looked at the blue Pacific? It was the same ocean they had played in, the same damp blonde sand they had walked on. Today, as then, the Attorney General was preoccupied with government business. If Marilyn had been with him, she might have lagged as before, picking up opalescent shells while he strode on far ahead, a solitary figure on the beach. She might have cavorted again as she did those other times, turning cartwheels on the soft sand and dancing with the tide as it pursued her along the shore. "Bobby! Hey Bobby!" she might have called out, holding up her sea shells in the azure freshness as she did on those Sunday mornings when she had to yell to make him hear her over the waves and the shrieking gulls. If Marilyn had been with him today on the beach he might have turned again to look at her. What is the most beautiful woman in the world doing here with me on this beach? What if the world found out? Then he might have walked on as before, expecting her to catch up to him.

After a swim and a shower they all ate cold shrimp salad with potato chips and beer and a surprise chocolate cake created by the chef of the Chateau Marmont. Pat's surprise. A lot of talk about Peter's new movies. "Advise and Consent" had just been released. "The Longest Day" was in the can and due to open in the fall.

Plenty of Washington gossip. The Attorney General said, "The old reptile and Clyde go away on weekends. Too hot in Washington for those aunties. It's rumored they toddle off to Fire Island in disguise. As Gertrude Stein and Alice B. Toklas."

"Jolly good," Peter laughed, his tanned face glowing in the late afternoon light.

"Where's the Debutante these days?" asked Pat.

"Bonwit Teller, the Hamptons, Bergdorf's, the Hamptons, Cartier, the Hamptons . . ." The Attorney General's jokes about the First Lady were always mild because he liked her.

Then the dark Cadillac was there and it was time to leave. The sun was declining. It pulled the final Friday of July into the ocean with it.

But why had the Attorney General's partner arrived so early if they were catching a midnight flight? The drive to Vandenberg AFB would take a couple of hours, three at most. And it was only 6:30.

The Attorney General had another appointment before departure. Another business engagement, which required careful coordination of his schedule with George Bledsoe's. Because Bledsoe also had additional business to take care of. In order to bury J. Edgar Hoover in the present crisis, the Attorney General had devised a masterstroke. He had summoned a high official of the Los Angeles bureau of the FBI, along with a trusted informant in the Los Angeles Police Department, to meet with him in George Bledsoe's hotel suite at 7:30. With Bledsoe dispatched on his own mission, Kennedy would instruct the two men in what to do, what to see—and what to forget. He would also apprise them of the consequences should they fail to do, or see, or forget as instructed.

The hotel chosen for these deliberations had long been favored by various male Kennedys. Certain hotel staff were trained to escort these V.I.P. guests into and out of the hotel in total secrecy and security. Whether a Kennedy arrived by limousine or sports car, he proceeded to a certain spot in the underground parking lot and was met, taken in a locked elevator to a penthouse suite, then guarded like a Middle Eastern sheik and catered to in absolute privacy. As were his guests.

In keeping with established practice, the dark Cadillac lurched into the underground depository and rolled to a stop near the controlled elevator. The Attorney General emerged, stepped quickly into the elevator in the company of the designated staff and ascended to the top. From there he observed the city spread out in its hazy bed of twilight. Soon the haze would deepen into night. In the darkness the Attorney General's plan advanced another step.

After depositing the Attorney General, the versatile George Bledsoe left the dark underpinnings of the hotel and drove across town to consult a doctor. Bledsoe was visiting the doctor's home, and the visit required neither examination, nor tests, nor medical instruments.

The doctor's house seemed to grow out of a hillside. Long, low and sleek, it incorporated palm trees and stone craters into its design. The house seemed a living organism, with certain rooms flung uphill and others sloping down, while patios, decks, a courtyard and a narrow driveway wrapped these extremities like skin and bones to keep the insides of the house from spilling out and sliding down the cliff.

Bledsoe sat in a brown leather chair with chrome arms. Across from him, on a black horsehair sofa that once had belonged to a cattle baron in Wyoming, sat Dr. Metaxas, a man in his middle fifties with black-and-white hair and heavy dark eyebrows. Between them was a low glass-topped table that supported a garden of cacti in terra-cotta pots. Dozens of Indian arrowheads lay scattered across the tabletop like stone fruits shed by the twisting cacti.

"So this blonde woman is about forty and you don't expect

her to pull through?" George Bledsoe asked the doctor.

"Not a chance. You see, it was apparently a silent brain tumor. It grew until she was almost dead. Two weeks ago they found her in an alley near the bus station downtown. In a coma. The police brought her to the emergency room but she never regained consciousness. She might lie there for weeks, even a month or longer. She won't recover, though. And no one has reported her missing. Obviously a prostitute. A lush, too, I'd say."

Bledsoe said, "The point is, we need her, or somebody like her, in a week. Two weeks at most." He paused briefly, then continued, "You're sure she could pass for Monroe?"

"No doubt whatsoever," the doctor said. "Imagine Marilyn Monroe without makeup. You've seen those pictures somebody took in New York when she tried to sneak out of her apartment. No lipstick, dark glasses, scarf over her head and eyes plain as a farmer's wife. If we lightened this woman's hair a little no one would guess. Of course, we'll need some co-operation inside the coroner's office, but I believe that can be arranged, not, of course, with the coroner's knowledge."

Bledsoe stared at the doctor, waiting for the quid pro quo.

The doctor, having laid out the bait, did not keep him waiting. "How much will you pay for co-operation at the coroner's?" he asked. "I know several good people there. But they need incentive."

"Ten thousand," Bledsoe said without hesitation. "Ten grand to one person only. I don't want more than one involved."

The doctor offered Bledsoe a cigarette. He shook his head, and the doctor lit one for himself. "And to what extent will you compensate for my own risks?"

"Since I know you, and you've helped the agency before, fifty thou. This is a fairly big job."

Dr. Constantine Metaxas blew smoke up toward the ceiling and raised his head to look at it as it evaporated. "So you want to pay me coolie wages, do you, Daniel?" Metaxas smiled for the first time. "Doc Metaxas snatches a body to save the President, but he's paid in nickels and dimes. If he gets caught it's a dollar-day sale—he keeps the initial deposit but the rest of the debt is cancelled." The smile disappeared.

"Take it easy," Bledsoe sighed. "You got it all wrong. Just to show how much we respect you, I'll double my offer. One hundred thousand, in small bills. A third now, a third when the job is done, and a third the day after the funeral."

"So what you want from me is delivery of a body—the body of this comatose blonde woman—to the home of Marilyn Monroe in a week or so. The Justice Department—excuse me, sorry—the CIA, plans to remove Miss Monroe from the scene for a while. If you don't mind my asking, Daniel, just where do you intend to keep the *real* Marilyn Monroe? Will she be alive or . . . ?"

Bledsoe, previously seen as an excellent chauffeur, further displayed his versatility by answering the doctor's question like a diplomat responding to the query of a treacherous journalist. "She has to be removed, that's all. No permanent harm done. As a matter of fact, she's in basic agreement with our plans. She *wants* to co-operate."

The doctor's eyes twinkled as though he had just heard an uncommonly good joke. When Bledsoe finished his speech, the doctor applauded.

"Very damn good, Daniel," he chuckled. "Slick as always, you are. Haven't changed a bit since the war. My brother, God rest his soul, loved to tell about the time the two of you had to assassinate the mayor of that little town in Austria, then slip across the border into Switzerland. He used to mimic the border guards questioning you. Then he'd describe how you looked them in the eye, handed over your beautifully forged papers and advised them that the two of you were on an errand for the Fuhrer. They believed you, of course. Who wouldn't? He always ended the story with the two of you walking safely into Switzerland. By the time the mayor's body was discovered you were soaking your feet in a hot tub and drinking brandy." The doctor's wide smile narrowed slightly. "I still can't make myself call you George. My brother would be surprised by your new name."

"I'm on an errand this time too, Doc. Only this time it's for the President of the United States. As I said a while ago, Marilyn Monroe has made threats against the President, also against his family. Considering the source, we can't take chances that she won't go through with her nutty plans. She's threatening to hold a news conference. She's already told all kinds of things to Hedda

Hopper, all those gossip dames. She's stoned all the time, so we figure she just might do it. *That* could be major trouble. So that's where I come in. That's where you come in too, Doc."

The Attorney General was, of course, eager to cut Hoover out of the deal, as he told his brother-in-law by the pool. But sidestepping the old reptile meant a double problem. First, the actual difficulty of doing anything without Hoover finding out, and second, resolving the Marilyn Monroe affair without using FBI resources.

But Hoover was not the only devious member of the Justice Department. The Attorney General sincerely believed the truth of the saying, "The enemy of my enemy is my friend," and he transacted business with that dictum in mind. Since Hoover loathed the CIA, envied its unlimited budget and enormous power, and denigrated it at every opportunity, the Attorney General was inclined to favor that vast, mysterious organization. The CIA, being the enemy of the Attorney General's enemy, would be his friend.

The President, too, preferred dealing with the CIA, or at least he had before the Bay of Pigs debacle. Holding the CIA responsible for that botched invasion of Cuba, he vowed in his anger to "splinter the CIA in a thousand pieces and scatter it to the winds." His threat, however, was spoken in haste and soon forgotten—at least by the President. The CIA, of course, had a longer memory than any politician. Kennedy was a pragmatic President, as the pundits repeated on editorial pages and on television panels. The answer to every presidential enigma was pragmatism. The clue to future decisions by the Kennedy Administration was pragmatism. And since he could not eviscerate the CIA, even if he wanted to, he gradually came to depend on it more and more as a personal tool.

He liked the CIA's diffuseness, liked the power distributed at key points throughout the organization. How different from the FBI, where one old snake at the top made every decision, then handed it down with no questions asked by subordinates. In the

CIA the right hand seldom saw the weapon that the left hand wielded. It was very convenient for the President to tap a specialized CIA resource for a particular job; much more convenient, and cleaner, than having J. Edgar Hoover privy to every covert move, every overt one and those in between. Sixteen thousand employees, and an annual budget of half a billion dollars, more if needed—the CIA, if played right, was the best friend a President could have.

President Kennedy gladly shared the CIA with the Attorney General. Even if they had not been brothers he would have shared it just to thwart Hoover, to make the old reptile squirm and writhe. For all his venom, the old serpent didn't quite dare to strike. Even he feared the Presidential heel poised over his scaly head. The President sometimes imagined the heel coming down hard, crushing the reptile. For that, the CIA would deserve a special reward. Whoever stepped on Hoover could name his price. The reward would be a new job: Director of the FBI.

In the meantime Los Angeles was a long way from Hoover's lair. Nevertheless, the Attorney General's masterstroke was intended to drain blood from his heart. And potency from his position.

The representative of the Los Angeles bureau of the FBI arrived first at the Attorney General's hotel suite. He did not fit the gray stereotype of an FBI official. He was over six feet four and muscular. His blond hair made him look at least five years younger than his actual age of fifty-six. The son of a jovial Methodist minister, he took a more benign view of humanity than did Hoover, although he could be as hard as his boss and his boss's boss when necessary. An ambitious professional, he sometimes imagined himself as a contender for the top L.A. post and even Hoover's office if that venerable one ever fell. The Attorney General had hinted a year earlier that Los Angeles would be a strong contender for the job if, and when, a vacancy occurred.

The local police official arrived ten minutes later. He, too, was tall, although not as strikingly so as his FBI colleague. He was over sixty. He had gained weight in his long middle age so that he moved slowly and deliberately. But unlike his FBI colleague, he was a Democrat, and so an implicit ally of the Kennedys. He had even worked in their campaigns and had met one or another of them in Los Angeles and in Washington.

After a few minutes of small talk the Attorney General rose and walked to one of the wide glass windows of the penthouse suite. Turning back from the city spread out before him, he addressed the two men he had summoned.

"Gentlemen," he began, "I don't have very much time today. You are both aware of the, uh, situation that necessitated this meeting. First of all, as Attorney General I am directing the Los Angeles bureau of the FBI to follow my orders directly. Translation: mine and not Hoover's. You will, of course, do everything possible to make these orders seem to be the Director's."

Bobby's eyes were steel, set in a granite face. "No one is to be told about our meeting here. Any breach will be a betrayal of national security, and it will be dealt with as such."

Neither of his listeners let their faces show the astonishment that stirred under their starched white shirts and striped ties. Turning to the FBI man the Attorney General said, "I want a teletype transcript of every word spoken in the Monroe house. Send it to me two hours ahead of your reports to Mr. Hoover. I want a report—not a summary but a verbatim report—every six hours."

The end of a long workday. Two tired businessmen on their way to catch a plane were engaged in shop talk. After swapping details of their separate meetings they were going over the fine points of the project that had brought them to California.

"What if the comatose woman doesn't die, uh, at the right time?" the Attorney General asked, disliking the morbid possibilities raised by his question.

"Doc does good work. *Thorough*. And he's got connections you wouldn't believe."

No further questions.

They arrived at Vandenberg shortly after eleven. At the departure gate a military attendant relieved Bledsoe of the automobile. The Attorney General and Bledsoe waited for a quarter of an hour in the officers' lounge, then boarded the plane along with a general and two colonels. As the plane taxied in the darkness the Attorney General opened his oxblood briefcase and began where he had left off earlier in the day. A conscientious administrator, he had many pages to read, and almost as many to write. This potential fiasco in Los Angeles had diverted too much time and energy from the running of the Justice Department. The sooner it ended the sooner the nation's law enforcement would proceed on course.

Shortly after eight A.M. the soldier-steward served breakfast. An hour later, the plane landed at Andrews Air Force Base, where another dark Cadillac collected the Attorney General. A separate car waited for Bledsoe, and in an hour he was in Cheryl's apartment. How Cheryl would enjoy knowing that he had driven a car into Marilyn Monroe's driveway just a few hours earlier, but she would never find out. Cheryl didn't even know that Bledsoe belonged to the CIA. This steady girlfriend believed he worked for the FBI. Beyond that, she knew nothing about his travels and his overtime. She once thought it odd that he didn't keep regular office hours; she remembered reading that everyone in Hoover's organization had to punch a time clock. After a while, though, she accepted it, like most everything else in his life.

CHAPTER

6

"Breakfast at the White House"

SATURDAY, JULY 28, 1962

The White House looked serene but empty in the grainy heat of Washington on Saturday morning. A few cars passed on Pennsylvania Avenue, a few early-rising tourists straggled across the Ellipse and drifted down the green corridors of the Mall. Surely the First Family had gone away for the weekend. They had probably left yesterday at five o'clock when Washington shut down. Passersby glanced at the majestic front entrance as though expecting to see a rolled-up newspaper and milk bottles left for the absent Kennedys.

The First Lady was indeed away for the weekend, riding horses in Virginia, in the company of friends. She was relieved to be out of the fishbowl for a few days, happy to be uninvolved in this latest intrigue that had so occupied her husband all week. If it was a political crisis she wasn't interested. If it was a personal matter she was curious. She knew, however, that unless it concerned their children, the health or reputation of someone in the Kennedy family, or an event at which the President required her presence, he would not discuss the problem with her. But somehow what he had on his mind seemed more than a casual matter.

Galloping across the hills, the First Lady did her best to dismiss it all.

The Attorney General now walked briskly down the hall to the President's bedroom. John F. Kennedy, wearing a blue bathrobe that concealed all but the most prominent part of his back brace, hobbled out of the bathroom as his brother came in. His valet had just brought in breakfast on a tray.

"Top o' the mornin', Jack," the Attorney General said, speaking in the exaggerated brogue the two of them used as their private joke. The Attorney General, always solicitous of his older brother, put his arm around the President's shoulder and helped him settle into a rocking chair. The valet moved a table to the side of the rocker, set the breakfast tray on it and left.

The President looked older than on television. His stiffness came from his aching back. His sour expression was from more than the affairs of state.

"A tad under the weather, are ye, laddie?" the Attorney General continued as the valet went out.

"I feel like hell, Bobby." The President had lost his banter and his brogue. "I woke up a hundred times. I can't stop thinking about this California mess."

The President tucked into the eggs and bacon on his tray. He handed a biscuit to the Attorney General, who pinched a big chunk from one side of it, ate, and put the damaged bread back on his brother's plate. "After you called," the President said through a mouthful of mangled food, "I, ah, outlined our options. Drew up several courses we could follow." Coffee with sugar and cream, and the presence of his kid brother drove the sour expression off the President's face. "But what about this doctor? You trust him?"

"He's done good work for the CIA," Bobby said. "Besides that, he knows what Bledsoe will do to him if he even thinks about a double-cross. Plus, he's getting a hundred grand." The younger brother eyed the older one for approval. The President's face was almost relaxed. Bobby continued, "That'll guarantee job satisfaction. He'll be on call later if we need him. In Colorado, for instance." Bobby grew more enthusiastic. "He's the best one Bledsoe has found. The blond prostitute in a coma could be Marilyn's double, Metaxas says."

The President considered for a moment, scooping the last chunks of bacon and egg onto his fork and taking a final mouthful. "Would she have talked to the press if you hadn't gone out there to see her?"

"It's hard to say. I can't tell whether she really knows what's happening. Drugs and booze in megadoses. She recognized me but it took a while. At least I believe she did. Of course Mrs. Bridwell will alert us to any immediate problem. And we've got the house and phones bugged." He paused a moment, then said less confidently, "Loose lips sink ships."

"Bledsoe thinks abduction is feasible?"

"He does. He'll guard her as long as necessary. Body snatching, plastic surgery, relocating Marilyn to another country, it's all risky, no two ways about it. But as long as she's on the loose, let's face it, Jack—she could destroy us, compromise the country."

The sour look returned to the President's face.

"Even if she keeps quiet we've got 1964 coming up in two years. God, what a mess. Marilyn has made herself a *serious* liability."

"What about destabilization?" the President asked glumly. "Suppose we got the CIA to start a press campaign: Marilyn's a drug addict, she's become paranoid, she's been found roaming the streets of Brentwood with no clothes on. Then anything she said, the press would dismiss as ravings, the public would see her as a madwoman—"

"Takes too long," the Attorney General said, shaking his head and chopping the air with his right arm. "This thing has to end *now*. If we'd never been seen with her, your idea might work, but as it is . . ."

He stood, walked about the room picking up papers, scanned them, put them carefully back in place. The President remained in his rocking chair, moving slightly forward and back. A moment later Bobby continued, "Once the lid pops off, we're likely done for. Too many know too much already to wait any longer. If Pandora's box flies open nothing can help—not money, not the

CIA, not the Party—*nothing* will put Humpty Dumpty together after that."

The President stopped looking for alternatives. He knew they had to go ahead regardless of the gamble.

"The way I see it, Jack," his brother continued, "we let Bledsoe handle it the way he sees fit. However he must. Which means that later he'll do what's necessary to keep Marilyn quiet." He thought but did not say, "Whether temporarily or permanently—that remains to be seen."

CHAPTER

7

"Wear Red for Good Luck"

SATURDAY, AUGUST 4, 1962

Marilyn was trapped in August. Nothing had happened so far, the first four days of the month had melted together in uneventful monotony. And yet, the concrete walls around her had thickened. When she peered through her windows or sat by the pool in the sunlight, the wall enclosing her property seemed not only heavy and inescapable but also higher, as though it grew a few inches every night like a relentless vine.

Peering at this ineffable growth, Marilyn recalled her terror in grammar school when teachers told stories of kings who locked up their queens in castles. To this day she identified with those poor princesses enchanted by witches who put the girls to sleep for years until the love of a noble prince revived them from the evil spell. "The President could save me from Hedda," she daydreamed. After all, didn't everyone say he was the most powerful man in the free world?

Those stories made her cry and run out of the room, her breath caught in her chest because she feared she might unintentionally offend a powerful ruler and he would imprison her for her crime. In those dark fantasies no fairy godmother arrived to rescue the child Norma Jean. But Jack could rescue her.

More than a week had passed since Bobby came to frighten her. She hadn't recognized him at first, he looked so different in that suit and tie. He didn't smile and flirt as usual, and in his anger he sounded like Bugs Bunny. Even now she couldn't suppress a giggle over that. "I shouldn't make fun," she told herself, "but all those teeth, and he sputtered some, too." She tried to say, "Eh, what's up, Doc?" in Bobby's Boston accent, but before she could get it right she collapsed with a fit of the giggles.

After he left that day she had no doubt he was angry with her. But she hadn't done anything to him; she used to like him when they dated, all those times when the President couldn't come and instead sent Bobby so she wouldn't get lonely. She was flattered that the President was so thoughtful, even though his brother was not such an exciting man—he was too close to her own age, for one thing. She was glad for his company, and she often made jokes to lighten his preoccupation with work. When he seemed distant, as though his mind had stayed behind in Washington, she called him "Your Regency," which she used on Laurence Olivier in "The Prince and the Showgirl." "Hey, snap out of it, Your Regency. What's the big idea, working overtime when you've got a date with Marilyn Monroe?"

She also worked hard to please him. On their first date they talked about art. Marilyn told him she loved Renaissance painters. She had learned a lot about them when she took an art course at UCLA years before. "I'd sure like to do my face in those Renaissance colors. You can't buy makeup like that today." She smiled when she said it. She also told him about her frequent museum visits when she lived in New York. "I'd love to paint," she said, "but I'd have to start from scratch. I'd have to start below scratch. The only thing I can paint are my nails." She looked down at them for a moment. "But, you know, art takes so darn much time and I'm always exhausted from making movies."

"Oliver Wendell Holmes said, 'Life is painting a picture, not doing a sum,'" Bobby remarked. A speechwriter had included the quotation in a commencement address the Attorney General delivered the year before.

The next day Marilyn had her secretary go looking for a book by Mr. Holmes. None of the bookstores in Hollywood had one, so the secretary went to the Public Library and checked out *The Dissenting Opinions of Mr. Justice Holmes.* The long sentences were full of words Marilyn had to look up but the next time she saw the Attorney General she said, "Hey, you know that Mr. Holmes you told me about? I read one of his books. I looked him up in my *Bartlett's Quotations,* too. Some kind of funny old guy!" She snuggled closer to Bobby. "You know what? When he was ninety years old he saw this real pretty girl go by and said, 'Oh, to be seventy again.'" She giggled. "I wish I could have met him." She resolved to read some more books by this new Mr. Holmes who, she said with a twinkle, sure sounded different from the private eye, Sherlock. Bobby seemed impressed.

But now something had gone wrong. The President *had* made that promise to her one night when they were at the Carlyle Hotel in New York and she had made his back stop aching. She knew how to massage his pain away by sitting on him. He didn't have to move around and exert himself at all. Movement caused awful pain. He had to take Darvon or Percodan to kill it, but that would put him in a bad mood. That night in New York had been the best time of all. When she finished he said, "Marilyn, I wish you could move into the White House and do that every night. Think you could arrange it?"

Marilyn, pouring champagne, couldn't believe her ears. "Oh, Prez, I'd love to be your First Lady. I could stop making movies, I'd be in politics! That's what I call *real* drama . . ." The President, relaxed, went to sleep without mentioning it again.

Some time later she asked him if he was truly serious about having her come to the White House. When she told him she wanted to make sure he really meant what he had said he looked at her and flashed a big television smile. "Marilyn, no question. I need somebody to make me feel the way you do. Every night, Miss Monroe." Suddenly he looked serious. "You don't like to ride horses, do you?" She smiled. She knew his wife was always riding horses somewhere.

The two of them had often joked with each other. Before he was elected President they had loads of fun when they dated. For sure, he wasn't a Gloomy Gus like Bobby. He could even outdrink her, at least champagne.

Their only problem in the early years was that Jack was a married man. Which meant they could never go to nightclubs and premieres. Marilyn would have loved dating a Senator in public. She had studied politics, memorizing the states that voted Democratic not only in the election but in the primaries. She was sure she could answer any question those columnists asked about elections and the Cold War. Budget deficits were harder but she got a handle on that too: "It's like the country has a big hole in its pocket forever," she said.

"Doug Dillon couldn't have said it better," he told her, and half meant it. She was flattered; she knew Douglas Dillon was Secretary of the Treasury.

Over the years he had repeated that line about making her the First Lady, always after she had made his back feel good. Marilyn enjoyed the idea, turning it over and liking it more and more. By the time he was elected President in 1960 she let herself start to think more seriously about her prospects. Her marriage to Arthur Miller had ended by then, so she was free, and from what she heard, Jack slept with his wife only when he wanted another child.

Of course she would have to cut down on her drinking and get off drugs but she wanted to do that anyway. If only she could sleep, she wouldn't need pills. A glass of champagne now and then wouldn't hurt, but she was serious about breaking her addiction to tranquilizers and barbiturates and speed. When she raised the subject to her psychiatrist she received little encouragement. "This new prescription will help calm your nerves," was his answer.

But something had gone wrong with all her plans. Until last week when Bobby actually threatened her, she had had it all figured out. This small house in Brentwood, she'd bought it because she felt she didn't really need a large place. Not if she was going to move to Washington. She and Jack could use it for weekends. They could add a room for the Secret Service. She'd be on the road a lot, entertaining the troops and things.

She couldn't recall Bobby's threats exactly, but his tone said it all. He scared her real bad, so she decided to clam up. Not another word to any reporter. Especially not to Hedda and Louella. She had told them too much already about her marrying Jack. She had Mrs. Bridwell call both of them and say she was in bed with a virus but that she'd phone the minute she felt better.

Marilyn was afraid she had screwed things up real bad this time. She had a feeling something was going to happen to her. She was uneasy; paralyzed, almost.

On that momentous Saturday in early August Marilyn woke up earlier than usual, thanks to Mrs. Bridwell. "Marilyn, honey, the doctor's coming at one," she called, rapping her knuckles on the bedroom door. Hearing no movement inside, Mrs. Bridwell repeated, "Doctor's coming at one, honey. Get up."

From the darkened chamber came a muffled groan. A few seconds later an unconvincing assertion from Marilyn, drowned in the fuzzy accents of sleep: "I'm up."

Although she wasn't really awake her conscious mind had switched on and accelerated. It was processing the dream that had scrolled across the landscape of her sleep like a caravan on the dark desert. In the dream, which had lasted longer than "Gone With the Wind," familiar forms had materialized. They were shrouded in masks and veils that covered their features, yet all the while they passed before her Marilyn knew who they were. They didn't reply when she called to them but their silent movements and gestures identified them beyond a doubt. Now her mind was trying to sort out and interpret the figures in the dream.

While asleep she watched a line of Kennedys that stretched across a misty horizon like figures in a Chinese painting. The women—discernibly Pat, Eunice, Rose, Jacqueline, Ethel, Joan—wore veils and bowed their heads, looking at the ground as they moved silently on. A great space separated the women from each other, as though their procession had been carefully choreographed and each one told to stay precisely ten paces behind the one in front of her. Beside the women, and with heads also bent toward the ground, were black dogs with elongated figures. As the line of women vanished in the distance the Kennedy men appeared.

They, too, were disguised, their blurred faces looking like out-of-focus photographs. Or did they wear distorting masks over their features? Joseph Kennedy, Sr., led the file. Behind him, with heads turned away from Marilyn, came the President, Bobby, Teddy, and the brothers-in-law. Each wore a long black stovepipe hat that was taller and blacker than Abraham Lincoln's.

The Kennedy men disappeared, like the women, into mist. In their wake came a long, dark rectangular box. Peering at it, Marilyn made out that it was closed. But zigzagging out of control, it tilted on one side. The lid popped off. Garish lights zoomed onto the body of a woman strapped in the box. She might have been waiting for a magician to saw her in half. Or maybe he had already done so. Her eyes were closed. She was wrapped in black curtains, and black velvet rope gagged her mouth.

Marilyn tried to scream, because the woman in the box was—herself! Before she could utter a word, though, rough hands grabbed her from behind. No words left her lips, as Mrs. Bridwell's familiar voice rang out across the darkness . . .

"Doctor's coming at one, honey." Mrs. Bridwell's voice, usually plain and dry, for once sounded reassuring. It heartened, like a physician telling a patient, "Wake up, the operation's finished and you're fine."

Marilyn lay in bed with eyes wide open. Her mind flipped the dream over and over, scrutinizing it. It didn't seem like a dream to take seriously—it was as stagy and amateurish as any dream she could remember. But it wouldn't go away, wouldn't stop reverberating.

Marilyn turned on the lamp beside her. The echo of the dream receded only as far as the shadowy corners of her bedroom. She sat up, energized by an instinct that overrode the lingering effects of drugs and liquor. This dream was like a message, only it wasn't easy to read. No, it was more like those puzzles that began, "First go to the corner and look under the loose brick in the wall." But there wasn't time to search for clues. The message seemed urgent; it had to be deciphered.

This morning she swallowed one pill—a tranquilizer—and made do with a single glass of champagne. When she went to the kitchen for half a grapefruit and a cup of coffee she moved like the Marilyn of earlier years. Preoccupied, she greeted Mrs. Bridwell with a hasty "good morning" and returned to her bedroom, closed the door and phoned Terry Pavka.

"Terry? Excuse me for calling you on Saturday, sweetheart, but I'm real worried."

"What's wrong, Marilyn? What's upset you?" Terry tried to sound matter-of-fact. He was concerned, however, by the anxiety tossing about under her voice. He had known her for six years and had learned to trust her instincts. As a trained psychic he had sensed from the first time they met Marilyn's ability to feel impulses from outside of consciousness. He knew she was sensitive when she walked through the door for her first reading. Since then he had told her many times that if she would stop numbing her powers with liquor and drugs she could be a major psychic herself.

"I'm scared," Marilyn was saying breathily now. "You see, I think I'm in trouble, I had this dream last night . . . talk about a nightmare! This one you could ride on a merry-go-round."

As Marilyn described her dream Terry gazed out the window at the courtyard below his second-story apartment in this pastel building in West Hollywood. In a corner behind a banana palm strong dark green ivy reached for the delicate roses in a neglected parterre. Soon these ropy vines would grab the pink buds and blossoms, the tiny rose thorns powerless against the inexorable grip of the thick vine.

"Marilyn, is something growing on your body?" he asked suddenly. "I mean, something new, like a mole? Or an abscessed tooth that needs to come out? Anything like that? An infection, a rash?"

"Not that I know of. I'm fine, I think. I just feel terrible. And nothing helps. You know what I mean? I can't stop thinking about that box with me in it. Or somebody who looks a hell of a lot like me." Marilyn exhaled, relieved that someone was willing to listen while she spilled out her anxiety that sounded crazy, she knew, but was also so real.

"Well, you know I can't give you a good reading on the phone. You say you have a doctor's appointment today?" He looked at his calendar. "So you can't come over. What about tomorrow? I could come to your house. In the afternoon. And I'll bring the cards."

Marilyn took a deep breath. "Okay, I'll wait." She sounded depressed. "I'll be here if I wake up." She started to ask a question, then changed it. "What I mean is, okay, I'll be here tomorrow. Just one thing, Terry."

"Yes, Marilyn?"

"I want you to know something. There have been . . . well, presences, I guess you could say, around my house this week." Marilyn's voice rose, becoming high-pitched the way it used to be when she was Norma Jean but as it seldom was in the movies. "I can't tell anybody else about them because they'd say I'm cuckoo." She talked faster, her voice rising. "But you know, sometimes when somebody is around you don't have to see them, you just feel them? Well, I've felt them all week. Several different ones around my house." This was the excitable, nervous, high-strung Marilyn who took pills to forestall hysteria. Terry had met her before.

"Inside or outside?" he asked patiently.

"Gee, I don't know, really." Marilyn slowed down, thinking. "Well, you know I take pills to make me sleep, so I'm a little out of it sometimes. But I always know who's near me, and where. And there have been others besides Sarah. All week long." She giggled, though nothing funny had been said.

"Marilyn, wait a minute, I see colors. What are you wearing right now?"

"Nothing, really. But I'm looking at my robe. It's white. It's draped across the foot of my bed."

"I see colors but it's hard to tell which one is important." Terry closed his eyes to block out the green ivy and the pink roses. "The colors run together. That could mean stripes. It could also mean confusion. Stripes, prison. You haven't done anything illegal, have you? God, don't tell me you're in trouble with the cops."

"Of course not, Terry. I haven't driven my car lately, so the cops couldn't even give me a ticket."

"Confusion. Let's see, are you trying to make a difficult decision? A new man in your life?"

"No, kiddo, just the same old guys."

Terry considered, his eyes still closed. "Now I don't want to sound like a carnival gypsy," he said slowly, "but there's something about a trip. Colors, and a trip." Then he laughed. "Next thing, I'll be telling you there's a tall dark man."

"Oh, I don't mind that," Marilyn laughed. "Send him over. Toot sweet."

"I'll meditate about this overnight. Tomorrow we can puzzle it out. By the way, there was no red in the colors I saw. No bright red, that is. I saw pink and orange and lavender, but nothing really red. Try to avoid all these colors as much as you can. Except red. Put on your lipstick, and wear a red dress." He laughed again. "Now I sound like Edith Head."

"Okay, Terry, I'll do it. Hey, I feel better already. I'll wear red for good luck. I'll call you first thing when I wake up. Bye now, sweetheart."

At one o'clock Dr. Gruber arrived. A regular visitor to Marilyn's home, he made house calls more suited to a country doctor than to an L.A. psychiatrist. This odd practice had aroused comment not only among his colleagues but among Marilyn's friends as well. Marilyn herself was deeply grateful to the doctor, whom she had first consulted two years earlier.

The first year she went to his home three times a week. When she moved to Brentwood the doctor started coming to her; he lived less than a mile away and Marilyn was often not in shape to drive. His visits at first followed a regular schedule of three times a week, then he suggested to Marilyn that she might profit from a fourth weekly consultation and she eagerly agreed. By the spring of 1962 Dr. Gruber was ringing the bell at 12305 Fifth Helena Drive five times a week, and after the studio fired her in June Marilyn was convinced she needed to see him every day. Often once a day was not enough and her dependence required that the doctor make two trips.

Rumors had it that he and Marilyn were having an affair, at least that the doctor was running her life. One of Dr. Gruber's skeptical colleagues told another, "He's taking orders from somewhere else. This is very unorthodox. A hundred years ago we would have said she was in his power. Now she's just his *patient*."

Mrs. Bridwell discreetly left the house during Dr. Gruber's

visits, did household errands or used the time to relax from her duties. She had known the doctor for years. Together they made a considerable team.

When Mrs. Bridwell admitted him now to the house she wore the expression of a devoted nurse who understands the style and purpose of the doctor she assists and knows she's as vital to the team as he. But never had Mrs. Bridwell felt such pride in their joint efforts as today. Now they were not just treating an addicted star; they were actually controlling a threat to the President, soldiers on a patriotic mission.

"Marilyn's expecting you, Doctor," Mrs. Bridwell announced.

He went to the bedroom, where Marilyn always received him. Wrapped in one of her white robes, she reclined, propped on pillows.

"Yesterday," he began, "we talked about your fixation on famous men. Famous older men." Marilyn looked intently at him, nodded slightly. "Of course, you understand that this continuing quest is a search for your father, whoever he may be." Dr. Gruber went on, sure that psychoanalysis was the true faith. Every day he invoked Freud like a priest intoning *Introibo ad altare Deo*. "And you said the prestige of going out with well-known figures makes you feel less exposed, more protected from the public, in other words."

"Yes," Marilyn agreed. "As a child, you know, I used to dream about dating Clark Gable. Oh, yes—I wanted him, and the others, too, for my lovers. Let's see—Gary Cooper, Errol Flynn, Walter Pidgeon—"

"What attracted you to these men?"

"You see, I thought movie stars were exciting and talented." She picked a piece of lint from her robe. Looking sideways at the doctor, she added, "And I wanted to be kissed, of course." She giggled, looked down at the bedclothes and busied her hands by smoothing the sheets.

He had heard it all before. He waited for her to go on, and looked forward to lunch as soon as he could get away.

"You know what? It wasn't just movie stars. I used to wish Lindbergh would call up and ask me for a date. And President

Roosevelt." Lowering her voice to a whisper, she said, "And get this. I even had a fantasy once about going out with Amelia Earhart."

The doctor didn't remember hearing *this* one before. "Oh?"

"Flying in her plane, I guess. Then when we landed, all those photographers would want to take my picture, too, as I squeezed out of the rumble seat."

"You've told me you don't like it when people imply or hint you've had experiences with women."

"Well, it's true that I used to resent those rumors. They were unfair. They made me sound like a diesel dyke. Now, really! I'm the nelliest girl in Hollywood."

Dr. Gruber, unsure what she meant, fell back on proven technique. "What do you mean by that?"

"People never said, 'Marilyn has had fantasies about women like most other women.' Okay, maybe even a few encounters. Instead they would say snide things like, 'Marilyn and Natasha Lytess? Sure, they were doing it every day.' *And* they said, 'Marilyn prefers her girlfriends to men.' That's what they'd say if I so much as had dinner with another female. I mean, really! That's so stupid. Of course I enjoy going out with my girlfriends. But it's because I get so tired of men talking about themselves. With other girls I can talk about myself at least half the time."

The doctor nodded, kept silent. Sometimes she wondered whether his nods meant *Continue* or *I'm so sleepy I can't hold my head up*. She pressed on. "I don't know what Natasha might have had in mind. To me, she was like an older sister. A sister who knew *everything*. She was the best teacher I ever had, until I met Lee Strasberg at the Actors Studio in New York."

The doctor looked up, making a connection best known to himself and Dr. Freud. "Why do you need to destroy people? Remove them from your life?"

She was hurt by his seeming accusation. "I'd rather say I'm sometimes so afraid someone will reject me I drop them like a hot potato. Sure it hurts, but not as bad as *being* the potato."

Earning his salary now, the doctor pressed on. "What if you hurt one of your famous men? For instance, John F. Kennedy?"

Marilyn kept few secrets from Dr. Gruber. "Gee, I don't

want to do that. I never wanted to hurt Joe, or Arthur either." She looked at the doctor, then down at the sheets. "I mean, if the President didn't mean what he said he shouldn't have said it. He promised. Said he wasn't happy with his wife. I asked him, 'Do you really mean what you've told me? It's not baloney? Because if it is, that's okay, but I want to know the difference.' And he just smiled and said he wanted to marry me. Sometime."

"But the President now seems of a different mind, from what you've told me recently."

"I'm not so sure of that. He's the best President since Abraham Lincoln. But now he won't talk to me. Maybe somebody told him not to. I want to know why not. You know what they say about a woman scorned." She pouted, an exaggerated pout, then laughed and shrugged to show she wasn't too serious.

He made a note in his small vest-pocket pad.

"I don't think the President intended to do me wrong. Bobby's behind it all, if you ask me." She pulled her robe tight over her chest, as though a chilly breeze had suddenly blown across her from the mouth of a dark cave.

At the end of the session he asked, "Have you had any more symptoms of pregnancy?" She'd mentioned them before.

"No, I'm sure I'm not." She smiled. "After all, how would it look if I had the President's child before we were married? But I *do* want children. You know, the best scene in 'Something's Got to Give' is the one with the children. I loved playing a mommy. I've got to finish that picture."

She said nothing about her troubling dream. Long ago she had learned to compartmentalize her terrors. Doctors heard the common fears; the scariest ones she kept hidden from them and told only to her psychic, who responded, she felt, more sympathetically.

When the doctor left in mid-afternoon Marilyn felt depressed—more so than usual, as though she had consumed a pound of sugar and couldn't stand up. The doctor had also presented her with drug samples given him by pharmaceutical salesmen.

In her languid depression, Marilyn wondered if this cycle

would continue forever. *My life isn't tragic, it's boring*, she thought. *They all say, Poor Marilyn, lost her husbands, got fired, never had the children she wanted, turned into a lush. But if I could just get away from Hollywood and the boredom . . .* She poured glass after glass of champagne. Looking out the window at the pool, she found little help in the bright afternoon sun infused with a premonition of autumn. The day was changing color. The dazzling summer light, now slanted, was turning from gold to sallow brown.

She went to the bathroom, picked up a pill bottle, shook out two capsules, then frowned at them. *Not now. I'll try to wait. 'Til bedtime. Gotta stop this. I'm no junkie . . .*

She shivered. *I am a junkie. I'm a drug addict and a drunk. And I've been used by men all my life. I'm tired of being passed around like a piece of meat. The President sends his brother to scare me, the studio fires me, everybody uses me. And I pick up the tab! I spend the day talking to doctors because I've been chewed up and spit out by jerks . . .*

When Mrs. Bridwell came into the house with her parcels, Marilyn called out. "Sarah," she said, weaving a bit from the mix of champagne and adrenaline, "you know what? I've made a big decision. I'm going away. I'm going to leave Hollywood. Going back to New York. So, I have to give you a month's notice." She embraced Mrs. Bridwell, kissed her on the cheek. "I'll pay your salary for the next six months."

Mrs. Bridwell said nothing. Grateful for Marilyn's generosity, she nevertheless remained loyal to her true benefactors. And they were far from Brentwood.

"Will you be a doll and tell Dr. Gruber I won't need to see him again before I leave," she went on, "and Monday morning . . . Monday morning, can you help with my . . . arrangements?"

Accustomed to Marilyn's mood swings, Mrs. Bridwell kept silent.

"Sarah," Marilyn said, following her to the kitchen, "everything is going to be so different." She leaned close to Mrs. Bridwell. "I've decided to stop taking drugs. That's my New Year's resolution—it's either real early or real late. Pull my life together. You know that little engine that could? Well, I think I can, I think I can, I think I can . . ." She poured another glass of champagne. "I can't stand being blue all the time. And that's that. And taking crap. Bobby Kennedy, that squirt, came to my house last week. Can you believe it? He tried to scare me. The hell with him. I'll marry the President if I want to. But maybe I *don't*. Anyway, who's going to stop me? Soon as I get straight, anybody tries to stop me had better watch out." She tossed back another glass.

Unleashed anger, along with the notion of deliverance, was too much. As before, she sought help from the other girls. And this time it was Roslyn Tabor who rushed in. "*Killers! Murderers!*" she said, exactly as she screamed at Clark Gable, Montgomery Clift and Eli Wallach when they overpowered the mustang in "The Misfits." The scene in the kitchen was every bit as scary and despairing as the one in the movie.

CHAPTER 8

"Sooner or Later Delicate Death"

SATURDAY, AUGUST 4, 1962

Mrs. Bridwell was not a cynical woman. In the Ohio of her youth, cynicism was unheard of. A true daughter of the Midwest, she had learned early on to accept things at face value. If a transgressor professed a change of heart, Sarah Bridwell was not the one to gainsay it. As a young woman in the early decades of the century she had listened to the sermons of Billy Sunday and his imitators. Their message was: "Change your ways, Brother! It's not too late to get right with God." And Sarah Bridwell saw no reason why anyone couldn't do exactly that, straightening out material tangles as readily as spiritual ones.

Until she moved to California.

That sunny land of cults and sects, of prophets, astrologers and priestesses had clouded the mirror of her faith. Though she rubbed it and polished it, Truth never shone as unambiguously as it previously had in Ohio. Her psychiatric charges had further clouded that mirror. Their wrenching ups and downs (the doctors called these bouts "manic depression"), their vain attempts at reformation and recovery, their staggering setbacks had made her wonder and question. What, after all, could you believe? Nothing was the way it used to seem. People denied they were sick; then lo and behold, they vowed to recover. Good intentions, however, seldom led them back to health. Money and possessions, which should have made them happy, only seemed to vex them more. If they had to work like I do, Sarah Bridwell often said, they wouldn't have time for malarkey.

Hearing Marilyn's vow to leave off drugs and abandon her disorganized life, Mrs. Bridwell thought of how many times Marilyn's mood had shifted before, like a sunny day invaded by clouds. Occasionally her mood changed for the better: the clouds were chased away by a piercing yellow sun. Still, today's declaration did sound different. Never had Marilyn sworn to change her life so drastically. In the past her threats were specific, directed against a person or situation—an unsympathetic director, for example, that she wanted the studio to fire, or a particular scene she was determined not to play. A few months earlier she had even threatened to sue her dentist, imagining he withheld Novocaine while drilling her molars.

Long before Mrs. Bridwell's arrival there had been the profound depressions. They continued, along with suicide threats and, increasingly, actual attempts. More than once, on the other hand, Mrs. Bridwell had seen depression vanish and tears melt into beatific smiles when, say, a current boyfriend telephoned.

Not knowing what to do now, Mrs. Bridwell opted for a square meal. Fortified, she would invent an excuse to leave the house, then use the phone booth at the Esso station. Shaking her head, she reached into the cabinet for pasta and a can of tomato sauce. How times had changed. Years ago a respectable woman wouldn't even buy gas at a filling station. She left that for her husband. Now she was on the pay phone every night like a woman up to mischief.

Unaware that the walls were listening, Mrs. Bridwell waited a couple of hours to do her duty as a good citizen. Spaghetti noodles boiled furiously in the big pot while tomato sauce with chunks of beef sizzled beside it. Marilyn, at the other end of the house, was apparently packing clothes and sorting through belongings.

Meanwhile, other good citizens had delayed dinner. Already a coded transcript of Marilyn's stunning declaration to Mrs. Bridwell and her earlier conversation with Dr. Gruber was humming over the wires to Washington. Like bullets hitting a target, these words came pop-pop-popping onto the teletype at the Justice Department. The code was immediately deciphered, then relayed to the Attorney General, who took the call in the study of his sprawling home in McLean, Virginia.

The word-bullets that pinged into Washington set off a complex chain reaction. The Attorney General, learning that Marilyn intended to leave Hollywood, banged down the receiver. This was the last straw. If she had obeyed him surveillance might have lasted indefinitely, postponing the action that he now had to take. Before she could escape he had to catch her. Tonight she must be removed from the scene.

His fuse was short this August evening. In fact, he had retired to his quiet study because he had no fuse left. The scampering children, barking dogs, twittering birds circling his house before roosting for the night—everything irritated him. Here in his study, where heavy draperies and thick carpets filtered out every sound, he hoped to calm down.

He was tired from his eighty-hour work week, coping with his own troubles and the President's, too. Bobby Kennedy was, in effect, moonlighting as co-President. His brother consulted him on all major questions—the ones he barely mentioned to the Vice-President. Blood, after all, ran thicker than politics. Since the President planned to dump Lyndon Johnson in 1964 anyway, he wouldn't include him now. The idea of Bobby as Vice-President had become fixed. The President knew he would face strong opposition to such a tactic, but he might as well coach Bobby in the event they pulled it off.

And so enormous pressures and possibilities, all demanding the Attorney General's attention and his wisdom, overwhelmed the patience he might otherwise have reserved for Marilyn Monroe. She wanted to escape? He'd put the bloodhounds on her. Despite his sang-froid, Bobby Kennedy believed Marilyn Monroe, in a matter of minutes, could reduce his eighty-hour work week to zero. And she was a loose cannon.

He waited a moment after slamming the receiver, took a deep breath, reclined in his soft brown leather desk chair and kicked off his loafers. He buzzed for the maid to bring him a sandwich and a cup of coffee. With a long strategy session to be conducted by phone, he must remain alert.

First he spoke with Bledsoe, who had returned to Los Angeles earlier in the week. The Attorney General instructed him to phone Dr. Metaxas with orders to get moving. A call to the President to inform him that it had to be done now, tonight. That done, the Attorney General spoke with the Los Angeles bureau of the FBI. With Bledsoe. With the Los Angeles bureau again. With the President a second, a third, a fourth time. With the FBI in Los Angeles once more: ". . . and delete the entire section about her plans to leave Hollywood and move to New York. None of that goes to Hoover." He asked Bledsoe, "Just the two of you? Metaxas himself will put the body in her bedroom? Okay, where is Cathcart meeting you?" A pause. Then, "Go ahead—move!" Finally, a call to Mrs. Bridwell, who was surprised to hear from the brother of her old friend. And far more surprised when she heard what he had to say.

By ten o'clock Saturday night the arrangements looked final. The Attorney General in Washington was waiting to hear from Bledsoe on a couple of points. In Los Angeles, where it was only seven, two men were preparing to meet again for the first time in a week. George Bledsoe would collect Dr. Metaxas in a cream-colored van. Together they would drive to Brentwood shortly after midnight.

By then the big iron skillet would be cleansed of its red tomato stains, the pasta pot hung on a hook in the pantry and the smell of braised beef would linger but faintly if at all in the still, silent corners of the shiny modern kitchen. The dishes would be washed and dried and stacked away, the house tidied up, the occupants asleep. Not a soul stirring in the household. All normal. Or so it might have been if Mrs. Bridwell had not received a telephone call at nine o'clock.

She and Marilyn had eaten early, just after six. Marilyn, preoccupied with the imminent changes in her life, was at first subdued. She looked at her plate of spaghetti, took a few bites, drifted into daydreaming, winding the long thin strands of spaghetti around the tines of her fork, trying, it seemed to Mrs. Bridwell, to take up the slack in the soft pasta. When she managed, finally, to wind a strand so neatly around her fork that none of it was left dangling, she looked up and smiled.

"Sarah, you're not mad at me, are you, dear?"

Mrs. Bridwell, all contentment as she finished her second generous portion of spaghetti, said, "Why, honey, what makes you ask a thing like that?"

"Well, I've got the jitters, I guess. That's all. But I wouldn't want you to think I'm dissatisfied with you. Why, I'm satisfied to death."

"I hope you'll make the right decision, honey. I tell you, it won't be easy for you. You know, to pull up and leave here and resettle in New York City. Your health's not good. Not good at all."

"Jeepers, it's always tough to move," Marilyn said, disregarding Mrs. Bridwell's tone. "I've lived fifty different places since I was a kid. No joke. Can you believe it? But you know, my life is spinning, round and round. Like that Perry Como song. So I want to change. Before I'm too old."

When Marilyn finished dinner—or the charade of dinner, since she took barely a dozen bites—she resumed sorting the items scattered over her bedroom floor: white gloves, a pair of red hoop earrings, a single stocking with a run halfway up the back. She rummaged through her closet until she found a red sheath dress with a raised pattern of darker red ovals and circles that she smoothed by hand and hung on the wall beside her bed, ready for tomorrow. "My Sunday best," she whispered as she cleared a corner of her bedside table and put the earrings on it. Under the bed she located a pair of white high heels. She tucked the pair of white gloves into one shoe, then stood the shoes in the middle of the room.

"Terry said wear a red dress. He didn't say a word about accessories. I guess white ones are okay." She searched for an unopened cellophane envelope containing an undamaged pair of stockings. Her phone rang. She answered, but heard only a click.

She picked up two books that had slid off the bed and landed in the garment piles on the floor of the small room. Unable to touch any book without opening it, Marilyn flipped the pages of *The Story of Art* until she reached the Renaissance chapters. There she paused, as always, to gaze at the color reproductions of Botticelli's Venus, Raphael's Madonnas, and Titian's portrait of the gorgeous young man with a beard. Enraptured, she imagined her own face painted by one of these artists. Looking in the long mirror attached to the inside of her bedroom door, she struck the pose of Venus emerging from the great scalloped seashell. She took off the jeans and cotton blouse she had worn all afternoon. She bent her right leg at the knee, draped her left hand demurely over her thigh and fluttered her right arm over her breasts, with hand relaxed and fingers open into a fan. Like Venus, Marilyn revealed more than she covered with her modest hands. "My hair's too short," she said to her reflection as she tilted her head gracefully to the side. "It's too blonde, too. Hers is almost red. Well, Alice can match it, I'll bet."

Venus eventually grew tired and dropped her hands. Her eyelids fluttered from their wide, innocent Renaissance openness to the languid repose of Technicolor seduction. After holding that pose for a moment, Venus metamorphosed into Marilyn . . .

. . . Who sat down on her bed and turned the pages slowly, as she had done so many times before. From Renaissance to Baroque, on to Neo-Classicism, finally to Realism, Impressionism, Expressionism. She paused at a disturbing picture by Edvard Munch: "The Scream." A woman on a bridge held her hands up to her face. Her mouth was open, her eyes blank with terror. Two dark figures hurried away from her at the other end of the bridge. Marilyn had always puzzled over the connection of these two male figures to the woman. What had they done to terrify her like that?

She read again the author's comments on the picture: "'The Scream', a lithograph made in 1893, aims at expressing how a sudden excitement transforms our sense impressions. All the lines seem to lead toward the one focus of the print—the shouting head. The staring eyes and hollow cheeks recall a death's head. Something terrible must have happened, and the print is all the more disquieting because we shall never know what the cry meant."

Marilyn shuddered, closed the book and tried to forget the gruesome picture. Yet she was fascinated by it, she doted on it, and in truth she had bought the book years earlier because of that one picture and not for the ideal beauty of Botticelli's Venus or the exquisite Raphael Madonnas. "The Scream" was like a hole in a tooth, growing larger and more ominous each time the tongue visits it. Or in this case, each time Marilyn's eyes visited the shrieking head the more obsessively personal it seemed. She heard the scream as clearly as she heard the ringing of her telephones. But what did it mean? And how could the woman be helped?

Somewhere, deep down, Marilyn did make the connection. The woman and her never-ending scream on the bridge was herself. That realization was too dreadful for her conscious mind. She repressed it, and the more it pounded on the walls of her unconscious, the tighter she barred the door. The picture was an omen sent to warn her. Terry Pavka would have told her that if she had shown him the picture. But she didn't show it to him. She didn't want to appear melodramatic, even to a sympathetic friend like Terry. And so she missed the warning.

Putting aside the art book, she picked up *Leaves of Grass*, a worn and crumbling paperback that she loved. Walt Whitman was her favorite poet, even more than Carl Sandburg. She loved him from the moment a New York friend gave her the book years earlier.

She turned to page 265, "When Lilacs Last in the Dooryard Bloom'd." She didn't read the long poem straight through; she seldom read anything from beginning to end. She skipped around, reading favorite lines over and over. "O powerful western fallen star! O shades of light—O moody, tearful night!" The words thrilled her. "Coffin that passes through lanes and streets, Through day and night with the great cloud darkening the land . . ." She often read Whitman for relaxation. The rhythm of his long lines of free verse lulled and stimulated her at the same time. Tonight, though—night had dropped quietly over her house as she laid out tomorrow's clothes and perused her books—these poems that she loved upset her; each image seemed to warn her of something about to happen, yet she had felt better as the day wore on, knowing that she would soon leave Hollywood and go back where she had once been happy. "Come lovely and soothing death, Undulate round the world, serenely arriving, arriving, In the day, in the night, to all, to each, Sooner or later delicate death." She closed the book. Far away she heard a telephone ring. Mrs. Bridwell must have answered it.

Marilyn waited to see if Sarah would shout from the kitchen, "It's for you, honey." But no voice came. Come to think of it, no one had called her all day. Odd, she thought. I wonder if the telephone's out of order. No, at least the main number isn't because Sarah just took a call.

Glancing at her plastic ivory-colored electric clock nestled beside a scrapbook full of last year's press clippings, Marilyn noticed that it was already nine o'clock. *When I'm back in New York, I'll read a lot and go to the Cloisters and the Museum of Modern Art. The days will fly by so fast I won't even miss my pills.*

Exhilarated but jumpy, Marilyn dug into one of her pocketbooks and brought out an amber drugstore bottle. She shook out two Nembutal capsules, then slowly put one of them back. Swallowing the other one, she scowled. She resolved to taper off but she was impatient to reach her goal! She knew as much as a pharmacist about the dosages and side effects of all major sedatives. She consulted the *Physicians Desk Reference* regularly. She knew that to suddenly stop taking her various drugs could bring on serious withdrawal effects, possibly even a coma or death. Marilyn also knew the truth: she was an addict, had been one for years. But she had learned from Natasha Lytess, Lee Strasberg, Terry Pavka, and other teachers and friends that if you plunged far enough inside yourself the prize you brought up could be something stupendous.

Although it was still early, she went to bed. *I'll see if I can sleep a couple of hours on just one pill. If I wake up I'll drink a glass of champagne.*

Opening another of her favorite books, Marilyn remembered cold winter nights in Connecticut when she was married to Arthur Miller and they lived in the country. She loved the idea of being a brisk, sharp-minded, sharp-tongued New Englander like Katharine Hepburn, Bette Davis or the terse spinster who lived down the road from the Miller farmhouse. Nothing tentative about those girls. She'd love to be like that: gritty, no-nonsense, formidable, and vulnerable only when she chose to be. Of if not that, then a real tough New York broad, like, say, Paula Strasberg or Elaine Stritch. *Well, that'll take longer. But if I read Thoreau I'll at least maybe learn to be independent.* Was it Arthur who told her that?

She opened *Walden* to one of the dozens of dog-eared pages and started reading. "I find it wholesome to be alone the greater part of the time. To be in company, even with the best, is soon wearisome and dissipating. I love to be alone. I never found the companion that was so companionable as solitude." Yawning, Marilyn sank further down into bed, hoping to find happy dreams. The book slid quietly out of her hands, hitting the floor with a little thud.

Of all the strange telephone calls that had come to this house recently, Mrs. Bridwell found this one the strangest. It was Mr. Kennedy—the younger one, who had paid a visit just the other day. Now he was calling to tell Mrs. Bridwell that she was fired. He didn't put it like that, of course. He said, "We are grateful for your services. You're a loyal American we can count on. But for now we want you to rest awhile. This job has been strenuous. That's why we're asking you to return home tonight. Miss Monroe's plans have changed, too. She is entering a hospital where she'll get the help she needs."

He was as nice as you please, Mrs. Bridwell told her son and daughter-in-law when she got home at ten o'clock. And he said what a good job she had done. But Lord! he sounded worried, sounded like there was a lot more going on than he wanted to talk about. And how in the world did he know about Marilyn's plan to go traipsing off to New York? "I guess the poor baby called him up. She must have changed her mind. She told me at the supper table how scared she was. Course, it's silly for her to be afraid of Mr. Kennedy. But she said she wanted me to help her get ready to move, and so on and so forth. And she wanted to make sure I wasn't mad at her."

Mrs. Bridwell talked on and on, trying to sort out the rapid changes in her situation. "Well, that's the end of that job, I tell you. And Mr. Kennedy made me swear I wouldn't say a word to a living soul. He said I don't know anything about anything. As if I'd start talking now. I tell you, I know what I know, but the things that go on in that house . . . Well, I'd hate to try to make any sense of 'em."

Her son and daughter-in-law, tired of movie-star gossip and the same old stories about nursing the President when he was a young man, finally asked the important question that had been on their minds for weeks. "Say, Mama. We were wondering. You know, our car's been giving a lotta trouble lately. Could you help us get it fixed? Or it might be cheaper in the long run just to buy a new one."

CHAPTER

9

"Habeas Corpus"

THE NIGHT OF SATURDAY, AUGUST 4–SUNDAY, AUGUST 5, 1962

George Bledsoe was behind the wheel of a plain, ivory-colored service van with no name on the side to identify it. Beside him sat Dr. Metaxas. On this summer Saturday night in Los Angeles it seemed everyone was out for a good time. The week had been stifling, seven scorching days of late July and early August. By Friday everyone in the city was groggy. On Saturday they fled to the beach, came home in late afternoon and went out again that night—dancing, to a movie, or just driving. By midnight most were on their way home. The streets and freeways were crowded with a midnight rush hour.

Bledsoe and Metaxas had not been to the beach, or dancing, or to a movie. But they had done a lot of driving. Bledsoe had obtained the van a few hours earlier. He had the knack of producing whatever was needed—quickly, quietly, without fuss or apparent inconvenience. Word had come from Washington that there was a job to do. Something unexpected, though not a total surprise. Anyway, Bledsoe had expected to do this job in a week or two at the latest. Besides, it wasn't as if he had made other plans for Saturday night. Not when he was on standby twenty-four hours a day, every day. He knew where to get a van on short notice.

Finding Dr. Metaxas was less easy. The doctor had patients to care for, even on weekends. When Bledsoe's orders arrived from Washington he phoned Dr. Metaxas at home. No answer. He tried the hospital, the doctor was paged, not located. Finally just before ten o'clock Bledsoe reached him. Although the doctor wanted to have a drink, smoke a cigarette and go to bed, the extraordinary events that Bledsoe detailed made a change of plans imperative. It took an hour for George Bledsoe to reach the doctor's hillside home. Almost as long for them to get to Brentwood, what with the midnight traffic rush. But finally they were there, turning off Sunset Boulevard onto Carmelina Drive. At this time of night in this quiet neighborhood no one was about. They and their unremarkable conveyance went unnoticed.

Thinking how truly unremarkable they were, George grinned and said something to that effect to the doctor as they came to a stop on Fifth Helena Drive. The doctor finished blowing smoke from his mouth, and agreed.

The third passenger in the van remained silent, as she had throughout the long drive to Brentwood.

12305 Fifth Helena Drive was asleep. Mrs. Bridwell had departed at 9:30, shortly after the Attorney General's phone call. She had packed into a shopping bag the few possessions she kept at Marilyn's: a tattered copy of the *Ohio Home Demonstration Club Cookbook*; fuzzy pink house slippers, slightly soiled; a fresh pair of nylons; two packs of Gayla bobby pins; and an African violet nurtured on the kitchen windowsill.

She had left one lamp burning in the living room and a small night light in the hall. A sudden impulse to say goodbye to the poor girl and to wish her well had led Mrs. Bridwell up the hall to Marilyn's door. But she mustn't wake her up, oh no. And better not leave a note, either. Something fishy was going on, so least said soonest mended, Mrs. Bridwell decided. She had trudged back down the hall and left the house. Forever.

Marilyn's bedroom harbored the darkness, unwilling to relinquish the black night that kept her packed in sleep. She didn't dream; the time of dreams had passed.

A car door closed. Through the heavy blackout curtains and the thick darkness of the room came a muffled sound. It might have been only a dilapidated shingle dropping off the roof, or a tree branch touching an outside wall. Marilyn did not open her eyes. Except for that small pressure on the texture of the night, the house remained asleep in the shadows.

Two men got out of the van. The driver first, then his passenger, who slid across and maneuvered himself under the steering wheel to economize on the closing of doors. Using a key obtained earlier, they passed quickly, easily through the heavy wooden gate. Another key opened the front door.

In the living room that imitated a small Spanish church, George Bledsoe extinguished the lamp that Mrs. Bridwell had left burning. Dr. Metaxas turned out the night light in the hall. A powerful flashlight, its beam aimed at the floor, guided the men. Bledsoe, who had memorized the layout of the house from a floor plan, had visited once before. Earlier in the week he had delivered a prescription order from the Brentwood Rexall Pharmacy. At least, that was what he had told Mrs. Bridwell when he rang the bell that day, and when she left the room for money to pay him Bledsoe took a quick look at Marilyn's house.

Outside the bedroom room, the two men paused. Dr. Metaxas opened a small leather satchel the size of a ditty bag. He removed a glass vial and a hypodermic needle, then handed the satchel to Bledsoe. The doctor bent forward. Bledsoe raised the flashlight. Dr. Metaxas drew chloral hydrate into the hypodermic syringe until the vial was empty, then carefully replaced the vial in the satchel Bledsoe was holding. Neither spoke.

When she woke up and saw the man standing over her, Marilyn for a moment thought it was Don Murray trying to abduct her the way he had in "Bus Stop" a few years earlier. And the other one must be Arthur O'Connell, who played Murray's sidekick in the movie. Suddenly Cherie was right there in bed with Marilyn, bawling in her Ozark accent, "I'm bein' abducted!" Cherie thought fast: *I better keep 'em tawking. Somebody's gonna come and hep me in a minnit.* Aloud, Cherie said tearfully, "Aw, naw, Bo, you cain't do this. It ain't right, you hear?" Marilyn had withdrawn, but she watched from far away, terrified. They had come like this to take away her mother. They had come like this to get Norma Jean and put her in the orphanage.

Cherie was docile. When Bledsoe held her wrists tightly and turned her over on her stomach, she only whimpered. And Marilyn only whimpered when the needle descended into her flesh and stayed there, pumping fluid into her until she was sure that this was what dying felt like.

The third passenger in the van lay in the back, eyes closed, pale yellow hair disheveled. Her skin was waxy, like artificial fruit. The departure of her life a few hours earlier had removed the curving posture of sleep and replaced it with gradually hardening geometric lines.

"Imagine Marilyn Monroe without makeup," Dr. Metaxas had told George Bledsoe a week earlier. And here indeed was something that bore a plausible resemblance to Marilyn—the essential, unvarnished Marilyn. Dr. Metaxas had bought the woman a few days earlier, bought her from the hospital where he was licensed to practice medicine. Working with a vast freemasonry that included necrophiliacs, body-brokers, medical suppliers, emergency room attendants, nurses, and hospital employees at all levels, he had had the woman declared dead, even though technically she was not. Soon after the death certificate was written a member of the cadaver network delivered the woman late one night to the doctor's home. The deliverer was a nurse who attended the comatose woman until it was time to terminate the coma. When Bledsoe called with the dispatch from Washington, Dr. Metaxas ordered the attending nurse to downgrade the patient's condition. Minutes after the nurse's injection, life flickered out and the body was ready.

And now it reposed in Marilyn Monroe's bed. If the woman had come to Hollywood to be a star, she had finally made it. She lay in a famous bed in a famous house, and for the next few days she would play the part of the most famous blonde in the world.

High irony. Marilyn had never trusted stand-ins. Not for a minute. As she became a bigger star, and more difficult on the set, lookalikes spent more and more time standing in her place, representing Marilyn Monroe while the real star tried—often unsuccessfully—to compose herself off the set. Marilyn was sure they were up to something. She saw them trying to impress directors and producers, watched as they ingratiated themselves with the other actors, flirting, laughing, telling jokes. She knew how fast these girls could steal everything: a role, a boyfriend, a whole career. She had watched Eve Harrington do it to Margo Channing in "All About Eve." That's why Marilyn so often threw tantrums at the studio, yelled and swore.

Now, however, she made no noise at all. Stretched in the back of the van where they put her, *she* had become the stand-in for a corpse, even as the corpse had taken over the role of Marilyn Monroe.

With their two blonde actresses in place, Bledsoe and Metaxas busied themselves like executive producers; they must make sure everything on this set was convincing—this set where Marilyn Monroe's suicide had just been enacted. Their job as producers was first of all to produce. That they had done; Marilyn's double now occupied the star's bed. But that deft feat was not enough. It had remained for these producers, in the absence of a set designer, to decorate the set themselves. And everyone admitted to the set must be convinced she really had killed herself.

The most important part of dressing the set was—to strip it bare. Bare, above all, of any Kennedy connection. Bledsoe began by pulling out the small drawer of Marilyn's night stand. In addition to pill bottles he found her address book. Flipping to the K's, he read one of the President's private phone numbers, as well as the main number of the White House. These two entries were near the top of the K's. Near the end of that section Marilyn had entered in red ink: "Bobby RE 7–8200." Although most entries in the book were in pencil, the Kennedy numbers were all in ink—red for the Attorney General, Presidential blue for John F. Kennedy. Like an efficient secretary Marilyn had also noted under K: "Pat K. Lawford, look under L." The President's number—

US3–1600—and the White House switchboard—NA 8–1414—were adorned with little red hearts.

For less skilled perpetrators, dressing the set in silence—and undressing it—would have been problematic. But Bledsoe and Metaxas had rehearsed. Knowing any word they spoke would be overheard by listeners in Los Angeles and Washington, they performed a pantomime that insured not only secrecy but protection. If this operation failed, their voices on tape would be a one-way ticket to jail, maybe worse. Their gestures, therefore, were elaborate; they became Harlequin and Pierrot, articulating with arms, hands and faces.

Bledsoe offered the address book to Dr. Metaxas, shining the strong beam of light onto the entries. Reading them, the doctor pretended astonishment. He pointed to the satchel. Nodding, Bledsoe dropped Marilyn's address book into the black bag.

Meanwhile Dr. Metaxas had searched drawers and closets. It was Bledsoe's turn for surprise when he looked through the assortment of Kennedy memorabilia. "Dynamite," he mouthed soundlessly to the doctor, who read his lips, then moved his head up and down in agreement.

Before Dr. Metaxas put his discoveries into the satchel, Bledsoe gazed at a black-and-white snapshot of Marilyn and Robert Kennedy holding hands on a deserted beach. A smaller photograph, apparently taken in May when she sang "Happy Birthday" to the President in New York, showed Marilyn with her head thrown back in laughter. Beside her, the President smiled broadly, looking as amused as she did. Crouching in front of them was the Attorney General.

There was also a letter, unfinished and unsigned but dated July 20, 1962, in Marilyn's handwriting. "Dear Prez," it began, "Just before going to sleep I'm writing to say I love you. I think you do a terrific job as chief exec., especially on Civil Rights. When I called you tonight I couldn't reach you via extension 1600 so then I called the switchboard. They said you were delivering a speech about equality. It's amazing what you've accomplished in a very short while, if you ask me. When you're re-elected in 1964, *and* I'm by your side, there's no telling what the two of us . . ." The letter stopped. At the top of the page, held by a paper clip, was a long strand of platinum hair.

Into the satchel went the letter, the blonde hair, and more. Someone had transformed a "Kennedy in 1960" campaign button by replacing the face of the candidate with a minute reproduction of Marilyn's famous nude calendar pose. Bledsoe found it under a utility bill on the night stand.

The satchel was too small to contain several telltale books located throughout the house: *Profiles in Courage* and *Why England Slept*, both by John F. Kennedy and both with date-due cards stamped "MAR 3, 1959" from the Los Angeles County Library; *The Enemy Within*, by Robert F. Kennedy; *Jacqueline Kennedy: The Warmly Human Story of the Woman All Americans Have Taken to Their Heart*, by Deane and David Heller; *PT 109*, by Robert Donovan; and *First Lady*, by Charlotte Curtis.

These books Bledsoe stuffed into a pillow case, along with a red diary fastened by a small, dainty lock. The men found no diary key anywhere in the bedroom. Bledsoe tossed the white pillow case into the back of the van.

Years later Sergeant Jack Clemmons of the Los Angeles Police Department, commenting on what he saw at Marilyn Monroe's home the night of the suicide, would say: "It looked like the whole thing had been staged. She couldn't have died in that position. To me it was an out-and-out case of murder." He was, of course, referring to the body found in Marilyn Monroe's bed. Inadvertently he paid Bledsoe and Metaxas a compliment: although he guessed their "staging," he was taken in by their shrewd casting.

Sergeant Clemmons was the first law officer to arrive at Marilyn's house after a caller informed the police that she was dead. The call came from a man identifying himself as Henry McDavid, who claimed to be a friend of Marilyn Monroe. He said: "I'm in Marilyn Monroe's house. She's dead. Come and get her." He was never heard from again, and no one ever learned that the caller actually was Dr. Metaxas.

Metaxas, a.k.a. Henry McDavid, also telephoned Dr. Gruber. "Your patient, Marilyn Monroe, has taken an O.D. She's dying." Then he hung up.

When Sergeant Clemmons arrived, Dr. Gruber was already

there. He explained to the officer that a friend of Marilyn's called him to say she had threatened suicide. Dr. Gruber used his key to get into her house. But it was too late; she was dead. Unaware that the police were already en route to 12305 Fifth Helena Drive, Dr. Gruber telephoned police headquarters to report her death. Dr. Metaxas and Bledsoe, of course, wanted the body discovered. They wanted it quickly identified as Marilyn's, and buried as such. With the arrival of Sergeant Clemmons and Dr. Gruber, neither of whom guessed that the dead woman was not really Marilyn Monroe, the scenario had begun to unfold as Bledsoe and Metaxas hoped. If Marilyn's own psychiatrist and an officer of the law accepted the suicide, then why wouldn't the whole world?

Sergeant Clemmons scrutinized the embellishments left behind on the set by Bledsoe and Metaxas. He did not suspect that this was a stand-in, but he was unsettled by the neatness of the death bedroom. He had investigated many suicides; they usually didn't take time to clean house before they went. But here was a stack of folded underclothes on a chair; a pair of white high heels placed primly in a corner; stockings, earrings and white gloves packed tidily into a reed basket at the foot of the bed. On the bedside table, pill bottles—some empty, others full—all aligned as though on a drugstore shelf. One large open amber bottle lay dramatically turned over, empty except for a single yellow capsule inside.

The sergeant looked everywhere for a drinking glass but saw not a one in the room. How could she have swallowed that many pills without water to wash them down?

The body, too, made him suspicious. Not because it didn't look like Marilyn Monroe, but because of its graceful position. It lay prone, with the right cheek up and a telephone receiver held tightly in its right hand. But, the officer reasoned, wouldn't the receiver have slipped out of her hand as the barbiturates took effect and killed her?

The dead woman lay with limbs artistically arranged, but stiff, like an Egyptian priestess. And like a woman who had been dead a long time, more like seven or eight hours than one or two. The sergeant knew that when suicide resulted from an overdose of barbiturates the body was usually contorted—the force of the overdose poisoning the victim, causing convulsions and choking. But this woman was draped across the bed as though for a nude photo shoot. The sheets were spotless.

Later, when he made these points at police headquarters, he was told to keep quiet. When he insisted that things in the room looked like they had been arranged, and that the body was *not* in a suicide position, he was asked whether he wanted to remain in the LAPD.

While Sergeant Clemmons, Dr. Gruber and soon a host of police officers, reporters, photographers, forensic experts, detectives, studio personnel, publicists, neighbors and curious onlookers gathered at 12305 Fifth Helena Drive in the dawn hours of Sunday, August 5, a plain ivory-colored van was headed away from Los Angeles. George Bledsoe was no longer the driver, nor was the passenger beside him Dr. Constantine Metaxas.

Tired after a long night of demanding work, both were resting. Dr. Metaxas was asleep in his bedroom on a picturesque hillside, and George Bledsoe slept in the back of the van beside Marilyn Monroe. The new driver was Grady Cathcart, who had never seen Marilyn Monroe and felt slightly apprehensive about the project. But Cathcart, well trained by the CIA in the techniques of abduction and detainment, was indispensable to this operation. When he had received orders a week earlier to report to Los Angeles, he left his home near Washington and boarded the first available flight, taking with him the things he would need for a prolonged stay in the West.

As crowds increased outside the heavy gate of Marilyn Monroe's house, a man arrived who urged police to let him through. "It's urgent," Terry Pavka told the officers standing guard to deny entry to the morbid and the curious. "I believe I can help with the case if you'll just let me in the house. She was my client. And my friend." The police dismissed him as a curiosity seeker. The house was sealed to all but those who could prove business. Official business.

CHAPTER

10

"The Late Miss Monroe"

SUNDAY, AUGUST 5, 1962

"Niagara, Mr. President."

From Los Angeles at dawn came the message the thirty-fifth President was waiting for. He had arrived in the Oval Office very early—seven o'clock, which meant it was still the dead of night in California. Since he couldn't sleep anyway, he informed the Secret Service that he would spend most of the day at his desk. He told the First Lady nothing. When she awoke hours later her maid informed her at brunch that the President was working in the Oval Office.

The budget, congressional relations, Martin Luther King and the Southern Christian Leadership Conference, Governor George Wallace of Alabama, the Berlin Wall, military advisors in Laos, the Alliance for Progress and the test-ban treaty—all these and more occupied John F. Kennedy until nine o'clock. The In basket on his ornate polished desk still looked as full as when he started; to the Out basket he had added four sheets of handwriting and two initialed documents.

And then the call came. The call he would have preferred not to take. The call that could only mean trouble for him whether the operation had gone badly or well. CIA men weren't a chatty bunch, so it wasn't necessary to remind them to send terse messages. One word was agreed upon, the one word that meant "mission accomplished."

"Niagara, Mr. President."

The voice of George Bledsoe, unmistakable, velvety soft; you had to strain to hear what he said.

The President hung up fast, as though someone might overhear his conversation; but there had been no conversation to overhear. He swiveled from his desk to face the morning light falling through the Oval Office's long, spacious windows. Another crisis added to the throng he had to deal with. While this one was now "solved," it remained a crisis, although different from all the others. For this one touched his conscience. Often he had to overrule conscience in favor of pragmatic solutions. But in the matter of Marilyn Monroe did the interests of the American people play a part? Perhaps. An election could ride on it, Bobby had said. But in his fashion he loved her too . . . her pale skin and dazzling blonde hair that changed from platinum to gold to silver depending on the quality of light touching her head. Her whispery voice—and the incandescent red of her lips. And her giggle, sometimes boisterous, often timid. He loved making love to the world's most famous blonde, the woman every man wanted. He loved the image of Marilyn Monroe, but beyond that he didn't really know her. Long ago he had realized that no one knew her, especially not Marilyn herself.

"Miss Monroe," he always called her. Even when they were alone it was "Miss Monroe." He had trained himself to call her that; anything more familiar might arouse suspicion. When she sang so provocatively at his birthday party in May, he thanked "Miss Monroe" and joked, "I can now retire from politics after having had, ah, 'Happy Birthday' sung to me in such a sweet, wholesome way."

But now Miss Monroe was dead. Dead to everyone but him, Bobby, and a few men in the CIA. And he could never bring her back.

He picked up the telephone again. "Bobby," he said when his brother answered, "the, ah, project has been completed. Now . . . what should I say to King about the situation in Mississippi?"

When their conversation ended a quarter hour later and the President again faced his incessant crises, he felt alone and dejected. Where was Miss Monroe, who was so beautiful and so much fun? If only she had kept quiet he wouldn't have dreamed of letting this happen. Imagining Miss Monroe's fright and bewilderment as her abductors drove her from Los Angeles, the President frowned. If he were anyone but the President he could abort this unsavory scheme. But the Presidency, the good of the country, left him no sensible alternative. Gone she was, gone she must remain.

Answering the phone a few minutes later, he expected to hear Bobby's staccato. It was the First Lady. "John," she said in her tiny voice, usually slow and measured but now agitated, "Have you heard? Marilyn Monroe is dead."

"Dead?" For a moment it sounded real. He forgot that Miss Monroe was alive, traveling on a highway somewhere thousands of miles from Washington. His reaction convinced his wife that he had not heard the news.

"Yes, dead. Lee came home very late from a party. She wanted something before going to sleep. She woke up her maid to cook breakfast at six o'clock. The maid switched on the radio and heard the news."

"What did your sister tell you?"

"Suicide. Dead from an overdose of barbiturates." With increased agitation she asked, "What shall I say when reporters ask me to comment?"

Though nonplussed, the President quickly regained his poise. When answering his wife's occasional questions, he tended to be formal. He was, in fact, more casual with the White House staff than with Jacqueline Bouvier Kennedy. With them he often joked.

"Ah, the truth is that Miss Monroe has been deeply troubled lately. Or so Bobby told me. She was raving and ranting and he informed me, ah, that she had threatened to call a press conference. Say as little as possible, of course. Say, ah, 'Miss Monroe will live on in the hearts of her many fans.'"

The President heard the message behind her silence. He resolved to be more discreet and never again to become involved in such a mess. He had taken the heat after the Bay of Pigs fiasco;

worse than that humiliation, however, would be his wife's public fury. If she ever found out that he and Bobby had spirited Miss Monroe out of Hollywood and sent her for safekeeping to . . . No, contemplating the row if the First Lady should learn this secret, the President felt tremors in his stomach.

He pictured Miss Monroe in the custody of CIA agents with orders to hide her without harm. Part of the plan was to alter her appearance slightly in case she ever escaped. A few months from now a plastic surgeon would make a house call at the hideout. His mission: to transform Marilyn Monroe's face into a mere likeness of itself. The new woman who would emerge would be Marilyn's fraternal twin, so to speak—not her identical one—

No, it wouldn't work, the President decided. Too crazy. He dialed Bobby again at home in Virginia. One, two, three rings—four, five—"Yeah," Bobby answered, out of breath.

"Bobby," the President said, "call it off. Have Bledsoe and Cathcart terminate the operation. Tell them to release her on the roadside. That way it'll look like any other of her bizarre escapades. Remember the Marie MacDonald kidnapping? She claimed she was taken to the desert, then she turned up in Las Vegas or someplace . . ."

"Wait, Jack. Hold it. Calm down." Bobby, who had been playing football with a yard full of kids, still panted a little. "It's too late, for one thing. Even if we could, you don't want her to blab. I don't either. So forget it, okay?"

CHAPTER 11

"Stripped and Abandoned"

MONDAY, AUGUST 6, 1962

The headline in the Washington *Post* proclaimed the news that everyone had already heard:

MARILYN MONROE IS FOUND DEAD
Sleeping Drug Overdose Is Tentatively Blamed

A photograph of Marilyn, radiant, singing for American soldiers in Korea on a freezing day in February 1954 accompanied the grim words. Or contradicted them, so beautiful was she in life and so terrible, so unbelievable was the news of her death. To the left of the photograph and the headline, smaller letters announced on page one:

STRICT DRUG
LAW ASKED
BY KENNEDY

President Kennedy read the headline about himself first. An instant later he read about Miss Monroe, and on through the rest of the *Post*. The New York *Times* was full of the same news. Even the *Wall Street Journal* carried front-page coverage of Miss Monroe's suicide, though only a four-line item among the tidbits of "What's News, World Wide." Finishing these papers at breakfast, the President moved on to the news summary prepared by his staff.

But this Monday morning the White House newsgatherers had added too much color. Or too much black, for mourning. Their clippings indicated that the world had stopped to grieve for Miss Monroe. Headlines and analyses of the tragedy dominated the thick news folder that lay on the table beside the President's cereal, eggs, toast and coffee. Jack Kennedy scrawled a message across the front of the folder: "Is Khrushchev still alive?"

In Los Angeles Mrs. Bridwell was also reading the newspaper. *The Herald-Examiner* told the same story, using many of the same words: *barbiturate, overdose, tragedy, coroner, autopsy*. Shaking her head, Sarah Bridwell said to her son and daughter-in-law, "I tell you, it's a shame, that's what it is."

They had heard the news on Sunday. A special bulletin preceded Mrs. Bridwell's televised church service, and all day she talked of nothing else, saying "I tell you" this, and "I tell you" that, until her son and his wife looked at each other and rolled their eyes toward the ceiling.

But at least their chances for a new automobile were excellent, especially if they clucked sympathetically while Mrs. Bridwell talked on and on about "the poor girl." Several times she repeated the events and chronology of recent days, recent weeks. "And then I said, 'Why, honey, what makes you ask a thing like that?' and she said, 'Well, Sarah, it's the jitters, I guess.' So I told her, 'Well, honey, you better talk it over with some of your friends.' She said she was afraid of Robert Kennedy—he's the one who used to visit her, you know. Why, she even thought he might do her harm. And all the time he was only trying to help." Mrs. Bridwell looked at her listeners. Her son, taking his cue from her long pause, asked, "Did you believe her, Mama?"

"Humph! I tell you, *he* wasn't the one to be afraid of. Those others coming around—well, it wasn't none of my business, but some of her friends who drove up in their fancy cars, they're who she should've worried about."

"Do you mean—" Mrs. Bridwell's daughter-in-law prompted. Her husband shot her a look that made her halt in mid-sentence. His expression meant, Don't get her started on *him*.

"Oh, the poor baby. That's just what she was, in a lot of ways. A baby. Acted like one, even sounded like one a lot of the time. Lord, sometimes she would cry like she didn't have a friend in the world. And couldn't take care of herself any better than a baby. Why, it's a wonder something terrible didn't happen to her before now. Well, I tell you, I could just cry about all this. To think she killed herself before those nice Kennedy boys—well, I mean President Kennedy and his brother, they both seem like boys to me." Mrs. Bridwell carried on, remembering long-ago days when she was the doting nurse of the helpless, handsome boy Jack Kennedy. "Before they could get her to that hospital. It seemed a little strange to me Saturday night. I mean, Mr. Kennedy calling from Washington to tell me they wouldn't need me any longer. He knew how sick she was. They hoped to get her into a hospital. If only they could have got her there in time."

Her son, perusing automotive ads in the paper, changed the subject. "Mama, here's just what we need, a 1962 Valiant. We can get it from that dealer in Downey for . . ."

A good automobile being more important than a dead movie star, the younger Bridwells turned to practical matters. But Sarah Bridwell continued to shake her head. As she cooked Monday's meals and washed the clothes that had accumulated during the past week while she spent long hours in Brentwood, she thought continuously of that poor girl. If only, if only the Kennedys could have saved her life . . .

But Sarah Bridwell held one thing in reserve. She told no one about Marilyn's outcry that Saturday night in the kitchen. *Killers! Murderers!* And Marilyn had dropped to the floor like a deflated white balloon. Why, thought Mrs. Bridwell, it won't do to tell that. She didn't even sound like herself when she said it. And the poor baby wouldn't have wanted the police to start accusing innocent people. Still, Mrs. Bridwell couldn't forget the implications of that scene, even though Marilyn was awful good at imagining things. In the end Mrs. Bridwell could only conclude that it was God's will.

After a grueling summer Mrs. Kennedy was going on vacation. Her plane was to leave Washington late in the afternoon. She would spend Monday night with friends in New York, then on Tuesday fly to Italy for two weeks.

She instructed her maid to pack all her Chanels. She really did not want to go but her husband had insisted.

Merely a coincidence that the President wanted his wife far away. Or was it? Concerned for her peace of mind, he wished her removed from persistent, prying reporters who would no doubt bother her for comments on the sad fate of Marilyn Monroe. Because in the press, Jacqueline Bouvier Kennedy was as big a star as any woman in Hollywood. When fan magazines began putting her on their covers, she joined the dazzling elite—those sumptuous goddesses whose faces and bodies sold movies and magazines. Now reporters considered her their property; they could ask her almost anything, just as they asked Marilyn and Jayne and Sophia questions like "Do you sleep in the nude?" and "What kind of man does it take to please you?"

Though their questions to the First Lady were less blatant, still they wanted her opinion on every topic. So when her plane landed in New York and she and her maid and the rest of her entourage entered the terminal, the Secret Service did not shield her from the press.

No pushing and shoving took place, however, as it always did when Marilyn arrived at an airport. After eight years of Mamie Eisenhower, reporters were overjoyed to have a glamorous, photogenic First Lady. In spite of their excitement, however, they respected Jacqueline Kennedy; they also understood the message on those stern Secret Service faces. But the press formed a gaggle nonetheless. "Whaddaya gonna do in It'ly, Jackie?" yelled a reporter from a large New York daily. "How many dresses did you pack?" asked a young female from a garment trade paper.

The First Lady's serene expression never wavered. She gazed

over them. Was that really a smile on her lovely face, or merely the shape of her mouth? The dark hair, lustrous and elegant, swayed as she walked through the terminal, surrounded by her votaries.

"Mrs. Kennedy, do you have any comment to make about the death of Marilyn Monroe?" The question came from a dignified man with a pencil poised above his reporter's notebook. More polished than his colleagues, he was, perhaps, from Time or Newsweek.

The First Lady paused. A troubled look passed over her serene features. For a long moment she gazed at the reporter. "She will go on eternally," said the First Lady, although some said it was hard to make out her words.

The *Times* reporter rather liked it. It had class. Marilyn's long obituary, however, had appeared in that day's editions, so there was nowhere to include the statement. Too bad, he thought as he wrote his lead a short while later: "Mrs. John F. Kennedy arrived in New York yesterday for a one-day visit before starting a two-week vacation in Italy." The story appeared on page eight the next day under the smallish headline, "Mrs. Kennedy Here; Off to Rome Today."

In West Hollywood Terry Pavka stared once more into the courtyard. Overnight, a thin green shoot of ivy had embraced the youngest, most delicate of the pink roses, which now looked exhausted and doomed. Two friends sat with him in his apartment trying to cheer him up.

Three psychics in the same room tended to generate a powerful triangle of energy-perception, as they called it. Behari, an Albanian refugee who had come to Southern California in the late forties, moved nervously in his seat, shaking his foot as though tapping rhythm for a jazz band. Gladys Turvey, a lapsed Mormon, was the only one of the three who might have been picked out as a fortune teller by the panelists on "What's My Line?" To be sure, she didn't wear a turban, nor was she dressed in flowing robes. But her jewelry hinted at exotic connections, perhaps Rosicrucianism, or at least the Order of the

Eastern Star. Her lavender blouse was fastened at the neck with a small sword pin encrusted with sparkling rhinestones and rubies. Pendant earrings with tiny silver stars on chains drew attention to her wide face, which resembled a friendly jack-o'lantern. Bracelets—gold, silver, copper, and Bakelite—migrated up and down her plump arms.

"I sure as hell don't think so," Gladys said to Terry. Behari nodded, perhaps agreeing with Gladys, or possibly extending his rhythmic preoccupation from his feet to his head. "Don't you think somebody would get wise if it was a hoax? You're too close to her. That's why you think she's not really dead."

"Gladys, listen to me. When I went to her house yesterday I *knew*. Marilyn's aura wasn't there. Somebody else's was." Terry sounded exasperated. "Besides, the cards back up my vibrations." He knew Gladys's perceptions were seldom off, which was why he sought confirmation of his theory. "Behari, what do you get when you concentrate on Marilyn?"

"Not much I get, but a leetle," he said. When he spoke, his body became still and he seemed completely alert. But when he stopped talking his feet, hands and head returned to their beat, apparently tuned in once more to his internal music.

Terry addressed Behari again. "Is she dead?"

The beat stopped. Behari's beatific look recomposed itself.

"Well," Terry repeated, "do you think she is? After all, you're the expert in reaching spirits. Is she there, or here?"

Gladys leaned forward to absorb Behari's conclusion. Terry crossed from the open window to the floral sofa and sat beside Behari.

"What I tell you is a riddle," he said quietly, cryptically, in his peculiar accent. "She is not dead but she is asleeping."

Monday was the second day of confusion in the Los Angeles Police Department. Since the death of Marilyn Monroe the place was haywire. Reporters wanted a scoop, or at least morbid details; photographers begged permission to photograph the corpse; crazies phoned to say her death was a sign the world would soon end;

other lunatics confessed they had murdered her.

Despite the madhouse atmosphere, the officers of the LAPD managed to do their job. The carnival aura was inevitable, but much of it was fostered by certain infiltrators. Like the one who had come from CIA headquarters to make sure that the dead woman's dental records matched those of Marilyn Monroe. He also arranged a fingerprint match and, posing as a medical expert, ridiculed anyone who questioned the conclusion of death by suicide.

The Agency did not overlook the Los Angeles Coroner's Office. Creating confusion in that branch of city government, CIA disinformation specialists obscured certain facts, doctored and destroyed certain evidence so that even the highly competent staff was powerless to reach a conclusion other than suicide.

A quarter of a century later Dr. Thomas Noguchi, who at the time was a young deputy medical examiner, would say to Anthony Summers, the British journalist who wrote *Goddess: The Secret Lives of Marilyn Monroe*: "For some reason I felt uncomfortable, and shortly after the case was formally closed I called Toxicology and requested test results." Dr. Noguchi was told that the organ specimens had been destroyed.

That was later in the month of August 1962. By then, however, the CIA's job was neatly done. The few shreds of evidence that surfaced in later years, being almost entirely circumstantial, implicated no one. Indeed, each piece only deepened the mystery. Some investigators wrongly attributed blame to the LAPD and to the Coroner's Office, unaware of the CIA's involvement and success. Nor did these investigators guess what really happened at 12305 Fifth Helena Drive in Brentwood between midnight and dawn on the night of August 4–5.

And it was forever impossible for Marilyn herself to tell them, because she really was "asleeping," just as Behari said. Her sleep was, at first, almost indistinguishable from death. But while in the van, moving away from Los Angeles in the company of George Bledsoe and Grady Cathcart, she woke up. She stayed awake, so to speak, and yet her life was delicately suspended, like a seed dropped into a deep furrow with the possibility that someday it might once again, in a very different form, appear in the familiar world.

"There was a Coroner's investigation, and it was flawed. There was a police investigation, and there was a cover-up." So wrote Anthony Summers in *Goddess* twenty-five years after Marilyn's "death." But during the week following her supposed suicide none of her fans, none of the millions of newspaper readers and television viewers, guessed that something very suspicious had gone on behind the scenes in Los Angeles and in Washington. The world had no inkling that the body in the morgue was not the one it was thought to be.

Headlines in every country, television newscasts and special programs, even a rash of sympathy suicides, all proclaimed the death of the blonde goddess. *L'Osservatore Romano*, the Vatican daily newspaper, reported the death, adding piously, "We hope that, in the desperate solitude of this poor woman, and at the last moment, there was Someone who during life was kept away, and we wish that hope and peace has made the dying actress smile." *Pravda*, the Communist party daily, propagandized that "capitalism, and the decadent values inherent in it, made this unhappy woman its victim. Not Marilyn Monroe, but the society that exploited her, must be blamed. She herself rose from the working class, but soon became trapped in the vortex of capitalism and imperialistic destruction. In Hollywood, U.S.A., as throughout the crumbling capitalist world, the few control the many."

On August 10, 1962, CBS aired a special report about Marilyn's death on its "Eyewitness" program. The report was initially called "Who Killed Marilyn Monroe?" After a call from Washington, it was said, the network broadcast the program as "Marilyn Monroe, Why?"

In movie theaters throughout the world newsreels showed footage of the 1950s Marilyn—stepping off a TWA flight from New York to Los Angeles; pressing her hands into wet cement at Grauman's Chinese Theatre; attending the premiere of "There's No Business Like Show Business"; leaning out the second-floor window of an East Side brownstone during the filming of "The

Seven-Year Itch" in New York; and wiggling out to the microphone to joke with Jack Benny after making her television debut on his show.

A number of newspapers carried an Associated Press report quoting the Reverend Billy Graham as having been worried about Marilyn for a week preceding her death. He had even tried, he said, to reach her by phone. At the time no one, or very few, made any connection: that the Reverend Mr. Graham was a friend of the thirty-fifth President, as he had been a friend of the thirty-fourth, and was in the future to befriend the thirty-sixth, thirty-seventh, thirty-eighth, thirty-ninth and so on. No one asked, then or later, if his unease over Marilyn might somehow have been extrapolated from recent visits to the White House, or through telephone conversations with Washington.

In the tons of newsprint devoted to the death of Marilyn Monroe, the millions of words written about the shocking event, one headline never appeared:

MARILYN MONROE DIES

Norma Jean, Raw Material of Marilyn, Lives On

The plain, unmarked, ivory-colored van rolled unobtrusively out of Brentwood, onto San Vicente Boulevard, onto the San Diego Freeway, then the Santa Monica Freeway, eventually heading east, always east on the San Bernardino Freeway until the far-flung collection of towns called Los Angeles was far behind. Beyond the San Bernardino Mountains the desert began.

In a drugged sleep in the back of the van was not Marilyn Monroe but Norma Jean Baker, the neglected, wistful orphan. Marilyn Monroe was, indeed, dead, although not the way everyone thought. Her identity had been killed; Marilyn Monroe would never again light up the films of Hollywood. She would never again squeal, wiggle, or make those coy, suggestive movements with eyes, lips, shoulders, hips and fingertips. Marilyn's identity lay stretched in the chilly morgue, embedded in an unclaimed corpse that was buried a few days later.

Marilyn was stripped of her fame, her home, her reputation, her clothes, her books and records, her makeup, her friends, her lovers, everything that formed the context of her life. The only things left her by her abductors were her body and her talent. And the old, out-of-date identity she had cast off years before. Norma Jean was the only straw left for the drowning woman to clutch.

CHAPTER 12

"Deep River"

SUNDAY, AUGUST 5, 1962

"Jane! Jane! Help me get out of here! They've buried me and I'm not even dead!" Lorelei screamed. Or was it Marilyn from inside her nondescript ivory-colored coffin? Jane Russell, a friend of Marilyn and of Lorelei and a sensible take-charge girl would know what to do, if only Marilyn could make her hear.

But Marilyn was dead.

The coffin was enormous. And not completely dark, the way you'd expect those long eerie boxes to be if you ever got shut up inside one of them. Where was the soft satin that cushioned the corpse? It was put inside a coffin to look pretty, and to keep the body from rolling around. But these walls were bare—they were metal, covered in ivory paint and streaked with dirt and grease.

"Oh God, it's moving, they're taking me to the graveyard. Jane!" She fought the rope that bound her hands and feet. She couldn't breathe, it was as though a cliff at Malibu had slid down the mountainside and swept her under the sand. She heard the humming motor in the hearse that was taking her to the graveyard. "Please, dear God . . ." She tried to remember the prayers that Aunt Ana Lower and Aunt Ida Bolender had taught her. "Evil is unreal," the Christian Scientist Aunt Ana had often told young

Norma Jean. Now, many years later, Norma Jean in the coffin tried to make sense of it. This is evil, but it *is* real, she thought. Then she screamed again.

"Jesus loves me," she sang again as she had sung in Sunday school thirty years before. "For the Bible tells me so." Still the motor hummed underneath the casket. Norma Jean remembered the beginning of a psalm she had read when Marilyn was studying Judaism with a rabbi: "God is our refuge and strength, a very present help in trouble." How did it go in Hebrew? *Maybe they're taking me to the funeral. Maybe they'll hear me if I yell loud enough.*

A telephone, if only she had a telephone she'd call Jane, or Joe or even the operator. "Hey, operator, you gotta help me get out of this coffin. I don't belong in here, I'm the wrong girl." Oh no, it's not funny, she thought, and wept again, wept until her tears were used up and only dry air poured through her mouth and nostrils while drops of moisture on her eyelids hardened to crusts.

She heard another motor, then it was gone. A truck had whizzed past the hearse. If only she could make somebody hear. If she could scream or wave something or write a note and drop it out the door. But the coffin was probably locked. Even if she were able to bang her fists on the lid they might not hear her. But she couldn't even do that, her wrists were tied. Her throat felt raw, as if it had been scraped with sandpaper. And dry, dry. She tried to coax moisture into her mouth by licking her lips but her tongue was dry too and no moisture came.

Fever seared her skin, gnawed her joints. She was thirsty yet the water her body needed was leaking out: her panties were wet. The dampness set up a vibrating chill that quenched her fever heat.

Somebody called her across the darkness. "Can you sit up?"

Several times the man repeated the question as Norma Jean listened from far away, unable to respond because her mouth was too parched.

"Can you sit up?"

"I'm up," she murmured, thinking for a moment it was Mrs. Bridwell calling outside the bedroom door. Norma Jean *thought* she uttered those words; she intended to speak them but the man heard nothing at all. He saw her bottom lip move slightly. Then it stopped.

Chloral hydrate, administered regularly since the trio left Los Angeles hours earlier, was beginning to wear off. She couldn't have any more, not for the rest of the day at least.

Grady Cathcart held her wrist, feeling her pulse. Far from the trans-desert highway the van was parked on the narrow shoulder of a remote dirt road deep in the Mojave Desert.

Bledsoe opened the back of the van and climbed up beside Cathcart and the woman. "How's her pulse?" he mumbled.

"Normal," Cathcart answered. "She's still too groggy to eat. Here, help me get some of this water in her mouth." Bledsoe supported her head while Cathcart poured from a plastic bottle. "Like giving medicine to a cat," Cathcart grumbled as water dribbled out the corners of her mouth and ran down her chin onto her neck. He persisted until she sputtered, gagged, then swallowed some water. Afterward he dried her mouth with his handkerchief. Her head rolled to one side.

The preacher was baptizing her and some of the water dribbled into her mouth. Norma Jean remembered it now. Her grandmother Della had often told her about it, or was it her mother who told her that? Anyway, when Della Monroe had her little granddaughter baptized at Sister Aimee Semple McPherson's Four Square Gospel Church this is what it must have been like, with water dribbling into her mouth.

"Maybe I'm in heaven," Norma Jean sighed as water cooled her burning tongue. Just a minute earlier she was afraid to open her eyes because she knew she was burning in hell, she even felt the devil's pitchfork in her fevered flesh. But what about the funeral? How had she gotten into heaven if they hadn't given her a funeral yet? Then she remembered she was still in the coffin. Her head rolled to one side, she fainted in the arms of the strong preacher, who seemed to be baptizing her at the Four Square Gospel Church . . .

She had no way in the world of knowing that she was in the desert, far from Los Angeles and traveling away from everything familiar in her past. And that this was no preacher. It was Grady Cathcart, pouring water into her mouth like he might with a sick kitten.

The fever-dream continued. The huge ebony woman who looked like Marilyn's old friend Ella Fitzgerald, only without Ella's open smile, rose from her seat in the choir and floated to the pulpit. She looked ready to preach a long and mighty sermon. Instead she clasped hands together, threw back her head, opened her wide mouth and emitted a heavy, rumbling sound like the rushing, tumbling river that had carried Marilyn and Robert Mitchum and Tommy Rettig to safety when they escaped from Indians in "River of No Return."

"DEEE-EEEP RIIVEER," rang out to the back of the chapel and beyond, penetrating the heavy oak doors that had been locked against the crowds.

The melancholy notes splashed through the crowd of mourners in the chapel. The women wore heavy veils, yet they were recognizable to Norma Jean, who hovered cloudlike over a long, silver rectangular box decked in flowers. From high in the top of the chapel a soft light filtered through the wooden beams, bathing the face of the woman laid out in the silver coffin. Norma Jean looked down at her. The woman was asleep. No, she must be dead since she was in a coffin. Her hair was arranged in a pageboy. She wore a green Pucci dress and a green chiffon scarf around her neck. Whose funeral was this, anyway? Marilyn owned a green Pucci just like that one. On a back pew sat a beautiful lady all alone. Wearing a wide-brimmed hat and a thick veil, she occasionally lifted a white handkerchief to her eyes. Her face, lightened with powder, did not move even when her eyes filled with tears. Greta Garbo had come to Marilyn's funeral.

Nearby sat Maureen Stapleton, who had played scenes with Marilyn at the Actors Studio. Beside her, Marlon Brando. Flowers from everywhere were stacked in rows of purple, white, red, yellow, and pink around the bier. Fans in every country had sent them to Marilyn's funeral. At the head of the casket was a wreath of orchids, wildflowers, and calla lilies twisted to form Marilyn's motto: "Hold a good thought for me." An embossed card floated across Norma Jean's vision, informing her that the Strasbergs—Lee, Paula and Susan—picked the flowers in Central Park and wove this wreath for Marilyn's funeral.

At the foot of the coffin lay a bower of sweet-smelling carnations interwoven with giant daffodils, a farewell gift from 20th Century–Fox. Planted deep in the flowers, a leather-bound script bearing the studio's impressive logo. The words "SOMETHING'S GOT TO" could be made out, but the rest of the title was obscured by drooping yellow daffodil heads.

Outside the chapel were rolling hills of grass, trees and tombstones. It looked like Forest Lawn. If so where were Clark Gable and Jean Harlow? They were both buried there and they should have come to welcome Marilyn.

Fans who had come for Marilyn's funeral whispered to each other and ate popcorn, hypnotized by the minty fragrance of eucalyptus trees. The crowds swayed in waves, eulogizing the blonde they loved. "Remember the scenes where she played the ukelele? She was great." Another said, "I got her autograph on Wilshire Boulevard one day. She smiled and said 'Thank you' as though *I* had done *her* a big favor." Someone else sighed, "I'll miss her so much."

Newsreel cameras panned across the faces gathered for Marilyn's funeral: Jane Russell, Sidney Skolsky, Montgomery Clift, Dean and Jeanne Martin. On the pew behind them, Alice Mulligan, Wally Cox, Frank Sinatra, Carl Sandburg, Hedda, Louella, Darryl Zanuck. The president of the International Marilyn Monroe Fan Club. And Mrs. Bridwell, carrying a picnic hamper filled with an assortment of deviled eggs, milk, casseroles, puddings and a baked ham.

Scattered through the crowd of producers, directors, agents and fan-magazine writers were Marilyn's friends and favorites: Judy Garland, Charlie Chaplin, Betty Grable, even Abraham Lincoln was there, wearing a black stovepipe hat, looking sadder than usual.

But where, she wondered, was the President? And Bobby?

Norma Jean peered into each face, trying to find her Washington friends. She couldn't find a one.

As the van hit a rut and bounced, Norma Jean screamed and woke up. "It's not a coffin, thank God, and I'm not at my funeral, either." The nightmare was over. She wanted to shout that she was awake and alive. But the pain hit her again. Every cell in her body needed pills, and a drink to wash them down.

Dr. Metaxas had given George Bledsoe detailed instructions on the medical care. He had supplied enough chloral hydrate to last the first day, after which a tranquilizer was to be administered in large doses. "Don't forget the Valium," Metaxas had warned, "or she might have a convulsion. You know, her drug withdrawal is going to be rough, even with the Valium."

Remembered as a frightening, though pleasurable, fever dream, the funeral seemed to Norma Jean to have dragged on for days. And yet Cathcart and Bledsoe had driven only two hours. They were on schedule: medicine and water for their patient at two-hour intervals until midnight. After that they would stop every three hours until dawn.

Now it was sundown, the time when light suddenly left the desert like liquid spilling from a bottle. Bledsoe and Cathcart were tired and edgy from no sleep and the strain of their responsibility, which was only beginning on this first long day of driving through the desert. And as far as they knew their assignment might last a year, two years, even longer.

"It's five past six," Bledsoe reminded Cathcart. "Better pull over."

No one was around; they hadn't met a car in half an hour. So Cathcart didn't look for a side road, instead pulled onto the shoulder, hitting a hard, dry rut that made the van bounce rudely.

That was when Norma Jean thought the coffin had tipped over and, waking up, realized she wasn't dead.

When Cathcart and Bledsoe knelt beside her pallet she opened her eyes. At first they didn't focus. Leftover pieces of the dream still clouded her mind and she wondered if this was the President and Bobby viewing the woman in the casket.

"I din' tell reporters," she moaned.

Cathcart laid his hand on her forehead. He raised her head with his other hand while Bledsoe popped a Valium into her mouth. Hoping it was aspirin for her splitting head, Norma Jean washed down the pill with a long draught of water. And more water, until the plastic bottle was empty.

"Are you hungry, Norma Jean?" Cathcart asked. "Could you drink a little ginger ale?"

"Ummm."

He filled a paper cup and held it to her lips. The sweet drink cleansed her mouth, even seemed to wash some of the haze from her mind.

"Did Dr. Gruber send you?" she asked. "I didn't mean to take an overdose." Moving heavily against the restraining ropes, she flopped a few inches closer to Cathcart. "Which hospital am I in?" she asked, then closed her eyes. "Please, please, I need a painkiller. And how about a little drink?"

"I just gave you a Valium," Bledsoe said in his muffled monotone. He might indeed have been a doctor, one so immersed in routine that he had little interest in the patients.

Cathcart said, "Drink some more ginger ale."

"Please," Norma Jean said, "who are you? Why am I here? I want to go home . . ."

Cathcart looked at Bledsoe, who shook his head. Their instructions were specific on this point: she was to be told nothing, especially not her whereabouts. Word had come from the Agency: she was to be neither harmed nor cosseted. During the captivity, or at least during the initial phase, she would live an existence of emotional and physical neutrality. A blank life, with few impressions of any kind. She must not be overstimulated; she must not be stimulated at all.

Her incarceration was modeled on the Soviet system, except that she was to live quietly on a farm rather than in a psychiatric ward. She might even thrive in such an atmosphere. To be sure, she would no longer bother members of the press. Nor would she harass the Chief Executive and his Cabinet. The Agency had adapted this Soviet method of handling troublesome citizens. The advent of powerful new drugs facilitated the removal of perceived misfits and hoodlums from society. And the new pharmacology proved more efficient than a former technique: lobotomy. Norma Jean was one of the first subjects for this new and improved therapy for major troublemakers.

"Let's just say you're okay, you don't have to worry," Cathcart said. "Nobody's gonna hurt you. We'll see to that." His matter-of-fact tone carried a note of reassurance, and Norma Jean, lacking strength to ask another question, dozed off again.

She had no idea whether she was traveling north, south, east or west. As disoriented as a pet locked into an airline crate, she might almost have been hurtling through outer space. Her new life, which had already begun, was as strange to her as if she had landed on a distant planet. Wherever she was, it was obvious that she had shed Marilyn, left her far behind. Even these men called her Norma Jean. And Marilyn's glamor had vanished, too, along with her lipstick.

Had she somehow gone back in time? Was it possible? Disoriented, she wondered, in her pain and confusion, if things might really be the way they were in those movies like "The Time Machine" and "Forbidden Planet" and "Queen of Outer Space." It wasn't all that different from drugs, once you got high enough. The right combination could make you forget where you were, even who you were. But then, at least, you had a high, relief. Or at least she—Marilyn?—used to, especially with champagne added.

What was it Scarlett O'Hara said to Mr. Gable? "I'll cry tomorrow." Something like that. *I probably will, too,* Norma Jean thought as she relaxed and the pain flowed out of her body with the water and ginger ale. *Oh, that lovely doctor. He slipped me a Mickey and I don't care in the least.*

And then a moment later she was singing "Lazy," squirming on that red sofa while Donald O'Connor and Mitzi Gaynor did their *shtick,* smiling from ear to ear and tap dancing up a storm. What fun it was being back on the set of "There's No Business Like Show Business." Marilyn, playing Vicky Parker, had a big number coming up. She took up the verse of "Lazy", swinging a leg across the sofa, turning to give the audience a look over her shoulder. And, of course, a wink as the number ended.

But she didn't have a minute to waste. "Heat Wave" was coming up, she had to slip into her halter and that wild skirt, fast. But first the director wanted to film the opening of Vicky's night-club debut: "Ladies and gentlemen," the emcee said, "Gallagher's has a little surprise for you tonight. A new young talent, Miss Victoria Parker. Let's give the little girl a great big welcome."

And there she was in front of the cameras again, swinging her arms, wiggling, blowing kisses to chorus boys who lifted her high over their heads, and carried her about. She sang through a dazzling smile from six feet up in the air. The boys set her down on the floor and she continued her song about the tropical heat wave without missing a beat.

"Print it!" yelled the director, Mr. Lang. Then for some reason he wanted them to rush ahead to the finale. "Places every-one, lights, camera, action. Roll 'em!" They began their long strut down the staircase, singing and flashing million-dollar smiles. Donald, Mitzi, Ethel Merman, Dan Dailey, Johnnie Ray and Marilyn, with showgirls behind them.

They were halfway down the long staircase when somebody called her from out of camera range. "Hey, Marilyn"—she mustn't turn to look, it would ruin the take—"hey, Marilyn," and this time it was louder. No one else had heard. At least no one turned to see who was calling her. It wasn't Mr. Lang, he was a hundred feet in front of his cast, motioning them slowly forward.

"Marilyn," the voice called again. She couldn't tell whether it was a man or a woman.

"HEY, MARILYN!" She couldn't ignore it any longer. She looked to the left. But everything was dark; every light on the set beamed on the actors. There it was; that strange reedy voice. "We heard you were dying and we came to say goodbye."

Who had heard *that* horrible thing? "MARILYN, WE HEARD YOU WERE DYING AND WE CAME TO SAY GOODBYE." This time she cried out, but no one paid attention.

The stars and the showgirls belted out the last line of "There's No Business Like Show Business," holding onto the word "showww."

Marilyn screamed again, and fell. Down the long staircase, down and down, tangled in her dress, high heels flying off her feet, she could not stop falling. Rolling out of control, she heard Mr. Lang call out, "Perfect. Print it." No one had noticed she was in trouble.

The cast and crew burst into applause for each other and for themselves. Marilyn, rushing down and down the stairs, tried to stand up and smile for the cameras. She made another vain attempt, but it was no use. She slid to the ground in a slow-motion collapse. The frame faded, her co-stars vanished, and she went to sleep for the first time in years and years.

CHAPTER 13

"Up Ahead, in Shadow, the Past Waits"

MONDAY, AUGUST 6, 1962 AND THEREAFTER

Strong fresh air made her feel better. They had stopped at the end of a gravel road—a trail, really—high on a windy plateau in Arizona. She was eating breakfast: ginger ale, Valium, saltine crackers and Campbell's chicken noodle soup from a can. For Norma Jean, who disliked mornings, this was no picnic. Yet the wind, pushing big hunks of gray and white cloud across the endless sky not far above their heads, seemed friendly. She could use a friend.

"Hey, fellas," she said weakly to the two men: "C'mon, you can tell me. Are we on location?"

Bledsoe said nothing. Cathcart looked at her and said, "No, I wouldn't say that."

"Well, where are we?"

No answer.

"We're on the way to Nevada, I'll bet. To film 'The Misfits.' I mean, we've already filmed it once. Are we doing retakes?"

Chapter title is taken from the poem "Still-Life with Stranger" by John Ashbery which originally appeared in *The New Yorker* (September 18, 1989).

Cathcart shook his head.

"Where's Arthur?" she asked, worried. "And where's Clark—is he out of the hospital yet?" Remembering, Norma Jean blinked to clear away tears. Her chin trembled. Clark Gable was dead; it happened right after they finished the movie. How could they do retakes without him?

"Hey guys, I'm a mess. I'm not trying to be *au contraire*, but I can't go on the set. Not 'til Alice does my hair." Lowering her voice to a whisper: "I'm a bottle blonde, you know." Resuming her normal tone, she said, "For crying out loud, I can't even find my lipstick."

"We're all tired," Cathcart said. "Don't worry about it. More ginger ale? How about some more soup?"

Norma Jean's hair looked like a yellow cactus. Her dry face was sallow with purple half-moons under the eyes. Pale lips, stripped of Marilyn's luscious red that magnified them, were plain and narrow. Her body, refusing to follow directions, wobbled.

She wore slacks, a yellow cotton blouse and a tweed jacket—the clothes Bledsoe had put on her at the removal from her bedroom. This was her only outfit, although others waited at their destination.

At the end of their rest stop Cathcart and Bledsoe supported her back to the van, one holding each arm. They hefted her in and laid her on the pallet of blankets and pillows on the van floor. Cathcart, who had become Norma Jean's de facto nurse, helped make her comfortable, then stretched out beside her to rest until it was his turn to drive.

Norma Jean's sense of geography was never acute. Even if her captors had explained their location to her, she might have still been confused. After leaving the Mojave Desert they had climbed into the Hualapai Mountains in Arizona before reaching the Coconino Plateau. To the right and left of their route were mesas, gorges, canyons, valleys. And Indians. The Hopi reservation, as well as the Navajo, Apache, San Carlos and Papago. All around were places with peculiar names: Wupatki, Kaibab, Kenab, Havasupai. Nothing like the familiar-sounding places in Western movies: Carson City, Durango, Death Valley.

Late Monday afternoon they reached Colorado. Norma Jean, who had dozed intermittently since their last stop, felt nausea pushing into her throat. Her unending headache was bad enough, along with chills, fever, and bad dreams. Now, added to everything else, she had motion sickness from the curves. Bledsoe drove the van up and down the curling roads of the San Juan Mountains, making Norma Jean and Cathcart feel like riders on a crooked Ferris wheel. His goal was to get down these mountains by nightfall. Then they would stop and sleep in a motel, shower and eat a decent meal for a change. Tomorrow they would begin the last leg of the trip, crossing the Sangre de Cristo Mountains early and reaching their destination not long after sundown.

Though Valium smoothed the rough edges of her pain, Norma Jean was still trapped in an agitated fever-dream. Her mind roamed a make-believe landscape, dragging her body along, or so it seemed. Fatigue overwhelmed her when she awoke for short periods, as though she had been making a movie for weeks, months, without a single day off. She felt as though she had memorized long, difficult scripts and performed intricate scenes while the relentless cameras turned and the director demanded take after take. But during her brief trips to the surface of the dream, when the men woke her up for a pill or ginger ale, she couldn't recall the film. The few lingering details made her feel more lost than ever.

The long movie that was shooting in Norma Jean's head might have been called "The Life of a Blonde," with the subtitle: "The Story of Marilyn Monroe."

The lights went down. A piano tinkled a tinny rendition of "A Bird in a Gilded Cage." A woman's face in close-up. Her mouth moved, soundless words tumbled out. She turned to a man walking quickly, stiffly, out the door. The domestic scene was replaced by a screen with writing. The title told what she said to him: "Please don't leave. Norma Jean needs a father."

Again the music changed to "O Mio Babbino Caro." The woman ran across the room. She flailed her arms. The man slammed the door in her face. An iris shot of the little girl. Light streamed down on the head of the Orphan. Her lips moved, then her face dissolved in tears. The title told her words: "Mother dear, we'll get along. Be brave."

A white Ford ambulance sped up to the neat bungalow. Two men and a nurse jumped out. The three walked jerkily into the house. They brought the woman out in a straitjacket. They drove away. The title read: "Insane."

Again the music changed; the tinny piano played "Going Home." At the foundling home a matron welcomed the Orphan with a stern smile. Title: "We are one big family."

Light again streamed down on the head of the Orphan. She turned her head upward. Her lips moved. Tears rolled down her face. Title: "But I'm not an orphan. My mother is alive."

A car drove through the wide palm-studded streets of Los Angeles. It pulled up in front of the foundling home. The woman had come to take the Orphan shopping for a new dress. The title: "The Long-Lost Aunt."

In the department store. The aunt and the Orphan admired the frocks, the coats, the hats and shoes. The Aunt chose a school dress for the girl. They went to powder their noses. Looking in the mirror of the ladies' room the Orphan patted her dark blonde hair. The aunt looked down at her. The title spoke the Aunt's words: "You are growing up. We'll have your hair marcelled."

"I won't dance, don't ask me. I won't dance, *merci beaucoup*," Fred sang to Ginger. When the movie ended two girls mimicked the romantic dance number on the sidewalk in front of the theater. How lovely Ginger was, and Fred *soo* debonair. "I'll get finger waves just like hers," said Norma Jean. "Me too," said her friend. They paused in their re-creation of the movie long enough to sip sodas at the drugstore. Then they played Fred and Ginger, swapping roles, for the rest of the afternoon and the rest of the thirties.

Or at least until Norma Jean saw "Jezebel." She saw it again. And one more time, playing hookey to watch Bette Davis the mantrap, the southern vamp. At Aunt Grace's—Norma Jean's home for the past year and a half—the girl whose body was sprouting into womanhood closed the door to her bedroom. In front of the mirror she unbuttoned her blouse and lowered it until her neck and shoulders were bare. She was Jezebel! "This is eighteen fifty-two, dumplin'," she drawled in the thickest southern accent ever heard outside of Warner Brothers. "Eighteen fifty-two, not the Dark Ages. Girls don't have to simper around in white just because they're not married." She blinked her Bette Davis eyes, opened them wider than she ever would again in her life.

After "Jezebel" came a string of thirties movies, all starring young Norma Jean Baker. In her bedroom she played Scarlett O'Hara, Marie Antoinette, even Ma Joad. She replaced Jean Harlow in "Dinner at Eight." A big studio gave her a contract. Norma Jean's face flashed from the cover of Photoplay, Motion Picture and every other movie magazine. She out-tapped Ruby Keeler. She bought a pair of dark glasses at Woolworth's and told everyone at University High School that she "vanted to be alone."

But the boys wouldn't let her. Suddenly Norma Jean was popular. She was "stacked." Her lipstick was "Jungle Red." The boys buzzed around her in jalopies. "Get a load of that dish!" "Hey, c'mon, sister, let me take you for a spin."

But she wouldn't. She was getting married.

Cut to the establishing shot showing a trim bungalow in Westwood with roadsters and coupes parked in the driveway. Young people, and a few older ones, laughed and talked as they sauntered to the front door. Everyone seemed happy that Norma Jean was marrying Jim Dougherty.

Inside, a long shot of young men in uniform; it was a few months after Pearl Harbor. The camera moved closer. It held the bridegroom's dimpled Irish face in close-up.

A medium shot of the bride and her attendants. On the sound track "The Wedding March" played as Norma Jean entered the parlor from the hall. Cut to Aunt Ana Lower at the piano. The bride was sweet sixteen. In her hands she carried a bouquet of carnations and daffodils. Pan to the minister: "Do you, Norma Jean, take this man . . ." A medium shot of the happy couple: Norma Jean looked lovingly at Jim and whispered, "I do."

A jump-cut to Norma Jean and Jim doing the jitterbug on

their wedding night. On the sound track, "In the Mood."

The screen went black, then a small suburban California house faded in. The camera tracked up to the kitchen window, tracked right into the kitchen and watched the child bride Norma Jean, her hair in a snood, cooking for her husband. She set the table, checked a steaming pot on the stove and walked into the tiny living room. She turned on the radio. Electronic organ music flooded the room: "One Man's Family" was on the air.

She sat on the edge of the bed in long shot. The camera moved closer, slowly closer until it was watching her hands at work. She cut a quarter inch off the heel of one of her mules—the left one. Then she put them on and walked across the bedroom. The camera filmed the mirror that caught Norma Jean's reflection. She walked like a movie star! Forever after that, she trimmed the heel of the left shoe on every pair of shoes she bought.

"Norma Jean. Norma Jean, wake up." It was that man again, feeding her a pill with ginger ale. She couldn't remember what her dream was, but she knew she wanted to go back to it, and she did.

"We're ready for the horseback scene," the assistant director called. Everybody on the set—no, it wasn't a set, they were on location, high up on a plateau, close to the clouds—but everyone scrambled to get in position. "Take one. Norma Jean and Jim on horseback." Clomping music on the soundtrack. The young couple looked at each other, very much in love. His horse was in front so he turned his head often to look back at his young wife.

"Hey, we'd better go back," Norma Jean called to her husband. "It's getting dark." He didn't hear, so she spurred her horse and rode up beside him. "I said it's getting dark. What'll we do? I mean, how can the horses see when it's dark?"

"Oh well, babe," Jim said playfully, "you just turn on their headlights."

Norma Jean looked at him for a moment, then said, "Well,

hon, where are they? The headlights, I mean."

Jim guffawed. Was she serious? He didn't know, he couldn't tell. Not then or ever.

The forties black-and-white movie ended, but the American Couple did not live happily ever after.

Previews of Coming Attractions: The Navy sent Jim around the world, and while he was gone Norma Jean turned into Marilyn Monroe. She modeled for layouts in pocket magazines with names like Laff and Peek; she made a screen test; got walk-ons that led to bit parts, then larger bit parts in which she spoke a few lines of dialogue. Finally she landed supporting roles. By the end of the forties no one remembered Norma Jean, who had disappeared without a trace. Even Marilyn forgot her. Marilyn was going to be the Technicolor goddess of the fifties. But the fifties ended, and Marilyn died. And then Norma Jean, the inventor of Marilyn Monroe, came back.

When the man woke her for Valium and ginger ale and more food, Norma Jean suddenly knew where she was. In Colorado. She recognized it from "A Ticket to Tomahawk," in which she played a chorus girl. Although Marilyn's scenes were shot on a sound stage at 20th Century–Fox, much of the movie was filmed on location. Now Norma Jean recognized the scenery from the film: enormous blue mountains wrapped in white snow; plunging valleys and rushing streams full of big gray rocks; and evergreen trees taller than skyscrapers.

She raised her head. The men had opened the back of the van and were unloading their things. "Hey, why didn't you tell me we were going to Colorado?" she mumbled, still sleepy. "I made a movie here once. Well, at least part of it was filmed here." Frowning, she said, "Oh no, it can't be. Don't tell me we have to do retakes for 'A Ticket to Tomahawk.' I don't remember my lines." She raised up on her pallet, putting her hands to her face. "Hey, that's because I don't have any lines. I had a bit part." A wan smile crossed her face for the first time since she left home.

"Well, uhm, you see, Norma Jean," Cathcart said, "it's not Colorado. No, this is not Colorado, not on your life." He chuckled uneasily as he looked at her. "It's Montana, that's where it is. Yep, Big Sky Country. Montana . . ."

She had been so engrossed with "The Life of a Blonde" that she had entirely missed the last day of the journey. Monday had ended, they had stopped for the night at a remote motel and Norma Jean had not fully awakened when her companions guided her into this room and tucked her into bed. Except for Valium and ginger ale and unremembered food, she had filled the long hours filming the story of Marilyn Monroe.

And now they had reached their destination. Although the man insisted it was Montana, it sure looked like Colorado to Norma Jean. Well, it didn't matter too much. If you're a prisoner, you might as well be in one prison as another, she decided. *But if I'm ever going to be a smart blonde this is the time to do it*, she thought, sinking into a soft feathery mattress in a cold bedroom painted beige.

She woke up with light creeping under the muslin curtains. Mornings had always been difficult for Norma Jean, and for Marilyn. Her first impulse was to seek refuge again in sleep, in the Technicolor dreams of Hollywood that had enchanted her, making her forget pain and trouble. But anxiety was running round inside her, up and down her soul. *Montana*, she thought. *That's somewhere in the mountains*.

She pulled herself stiffly out of bed in slow motion. When her feet touched the cold wood floor, she flinched. Quickly she tiptoed over the brown painted planks. At the window, she noticed for the first time that she was wearing a flannel nightgown. *Like the one Aunt Ana wore*, she remembered.

Behind the curtain was a backdrop more dazzling than anything in "A Ticket to Tomahawk." In the foreground a well-kept white barn two stories tall. Far away, but towering over the barn like King Kong, enormous blue mountains, more than she could count as she shivered, dancing up and down on the floor to push the cold away from her feet. The mountaintops were as white as cream. From the angle of her bedroom window she saw a large plowed field behind the barn, and rising up beyond the field a dark forest that was almost black in the shadow of the mountains. The sunlight made her squint; there was no smog to dull its brilliance.

On a wooden chair near her bed was a green robe—a man's robe, long and heavy. She climbed into it and hurried to bury her feet in the brown corduroy slippers beside the chair. There was no mirror in the room but Norma Jean looked down at herself in the new clothes. The shoes made her feet look awful.

A line of dialogue popped into her head: "Give him a rocking chair and a corny old tune like 'In the Gloaming.'" Who said that? Then it came to her—it was what Rose Loomis said about her husband, Joseph Cotten, in "Niagara." Norma Jean thought, *Now they'll say awful things like that about me in these shoes. I look like somebody's granddad.*

And the room, oddly enough, did resemble the motel room in Niagara Falls where Rose and George Loomis stayed. Not that it was modern; just plain, and it looked even plainer in contrast to the gorgeous scenery outside the window.

She slowly opened the bedroom door and peeked out. A couple of other doors were closed along the sides of the hall. At the end of this corridor she saw a big black stove with a silver pipe running out the ceiling. In a semicircle around the stove were chairs, some upholstered and others of varnished wood.

Peering cautiously out the door to see if anyone was there, Norma Jean felt like Debbie Reynolds in "Susan Slept Here" or Doris Day in "Pillow Talk." But this was no bedroom comedy; these men had *kidnapped* her—maybe they intended to kill her.

She pulled the robe tighter. Bright sunlight streamed into the house from all directions. Norma Jean tipped down the hall, half-expecting to discover her own bathroom with a waiting bottle of champagne and Sarah Bridwell in the kitchen cooking a meal.

As she reached the black stove and stuck out her hands to warm them a door opened from outside. Two men walked in, one carrying an armload of wood and the other an ax. An *ax*? She screamed and ran back toward her bedroom. But she ran the wrong way and collided with the man holding the ax. She shrieked again, emitting breathy, chopped-up phrases that sounded like, "I won't say anything . . . I promise . . . don't *touch* me."

Bledsoe drew back the ax, but only to keep the woman from hitting it and cutting herself. During the histrionics he stood still and muttered a soft curse. Cathcart dropped a neat stack of logs on the floor and grasped Norma Jean's shoulders.

"Okay, that's enough," he said firmly. "You're okay. What the hell's wrong?"

"*Murderers, killers!* Get away and leave me alone—"

Cathcart nabbed her again. Instead of shaking her, he patted her back as though she were a frightened animal needing reassurance. "It's okay," he said. "Settle down."

Bledsoe approached with a glass of water and a pill. "Take this," he ordered.

Cathcart guided her to a comfortable armchair beside the warm stove. Through her sobs she said, "Please, please let me . . ." but she didn't know how to finish. She was at the end of her rope, her only recourse was to call for help. And it dawned on her what she must do—"I'll be *her*."

Lowering her head like a comedian arranging his face for the next impersonation, she followed Lee Strasberg's advice to "get in touch with your emotional memory and experience." Where *was* she? Where was *Marilyn*? How would *she* handle this predicament?

"She'd play it for laughs," Norma Jean decided. "After all, these two guys are men. And Marilyn knows how to handle men." She raised her head. A knowing smile was on her lips. She lowered her eyelids. Norma Jean was a portrait of worldly innocence. Because of her recent trials, she certainly didn't look her best. Still, she was close enough to Marilyn's persona to play the role.

"I'd adore a cup of coffee," she said, blinking her lashes, which were no longer dark with makeup. "If it's not too much trouble," she added with a winsome smile.

Cathcart looked as startled as Cosmo Topper when the mischievous ghosts, played by Constance Bennett and Cary Grant, appeared in his drawing room and suavely took over. "Sure," he said to Norma Jean. "We were about to put a pot on the stove." Then, abruptly awkward, he busied himself in the large open space where kitchen, dining room and sitting room joined.

"Thank you, Mr. . . ." she said when he handed her the mug of coffee. Well, who was he? She almost said, "Thank you, Mr.

Fabian," the way Marilyn said it in "All About Eve"—so suggestively that it deserved a wolf whistle. Instead Norma Jean said in a stage whisper, "I'm afraid we haven't been introduced."

Cathcart said, "It's . . . my name is Tom."

"Pleased, I'm certain," she replied.

"Yoohoo," she called to Bledsoe, who was moving about the kitchen with his back turned. "May I ask how you'd like to be addressed?"

It sounded like a foreign language to Bledsoe's ears. The sweet childish voice, the theatrical dialogue.

"What's your moniker?" she inquired again, smiling sweetly.

Bledsoe, lacking any sense of humor, turned and just looked.

Cathcart said, "And he's, he's Frank, over there."

"Charmed," to Bledsoe, who had paused with an egg in his hand. "Sorry to interrupt," she added. "Please scramble my omelette over easy." She caressed the green bathrobe.

"Tom," she said earnestly to Cathcart, "if we're staying a while in . . . Montana, did you call it?" She waited for his nod. "Well, I'd adore some books to read." She quickly added, "As a matter of fact, I'd adore them the sooner the better. Could you drive into Boise and borrow some from the library?" As an afterthought she inquired, all seriously, "Isn't Boise the capital of Montana?"

The round country table was set with unmatched plates, cups, and stainless steel cutlery. Bledsoe motioned them to come and sit. He brought eggs, biscuits from a package, a coffee pot and hash browns. The three sat down tentatively, like travelers forced together in a crowded diner.

Norma Jean, aware of their discomfort with a vivacious girl like Marilyn, proceeded to surprise them again.

"Fellas, you can't eat yet." Bledsoe and Cathcart suspended their forks in mid-air. "Well, we haven't said grace," she explained. Sitting straight in her ladder-back chair, she folded hands over her lap, bowed her head and waited for her companions to do likewise. Now, how did it go in Hebrew? She was groping for the words Arthur's mother had taught her for the Passover seder. "*Baruch atah Adonai, eloheynu melech há-olam ha-motzi lehem min há-aretz.*" *Well, I muddled through that*, she thought, seeing her companions as nonplussed as she had hoped. Chanting, she went on and on, making up words when she couldn't recall the actual prayers.

"Delicious, Frank," she said after her first mouthful of scrambled eggs. "I haven't breakfasted in ages, you know." Bledsoe mumbled like Marlon Brando but unlike Brando did not follow with something intelligible.

Norma Jean guessed that he was asking how she took her coffee. "Blonde and sweet," she said.

"Huh?"

"Oh, don't they say that in Montana? You see, in Hollywood that means with cream and sugar."

Changing the subject, Cathcart said, "About those books. I saw a few in my bedroom. *Reader's Digest* condensed. You can take a look at 'em."

"Gee, that's not exactly what I had in mind. Couldn't I get some real books? And when you go to Boise, please buy a deck of cards." Looking around, she added, "How about a radio? Or a television?"

Cathcart shook his head. "Nope, sorry. Nothing like that."

"Oh, I see." She paused dramatically, then said, "You wanna know something? I think you're in cahoots with Bobby Kennedy." She tossed her head and added, "Did he tell you to dump me out in the desert somewhere?"

"You just shut up," Bledsoe snapped from across the table. "There's nobody involved in this that you know. Don't go trying to figure anything out. You'll get in a lot of trouble if you do. Understand?"

Cathcart looked at him, hard, then said to Norma Jean: "Let's just say we're gonna stay here awhile. So you might as well get used to it."

In the case of Norma Jean Baker the all-powerful CIA provided not only a 3,000-acre ranch in a setting of natural beauty, but a comfortable house, fully furnished, and a closet full of clothes. Not to mention electricity and running water, heat in winter and air conditioning in summer, paid companionship, and free medical service.

The Agency, however, did not buy this ranch especially for the sequestration of Norma Jean. Rather, the CIA had taken possession of it years earlier—about the time Marilyn Monroe was starring in "How to Marry a Millionaire"—as a potential site for the internment of communists. At that time it looked as though Senator Joseph McCarthy might overcome his adversaries and rise to the position of President—in which case the government would need plenty of camps for its enemies.

This particular one, a hundred miles southwest of Denver, was designated a sort of glamor ranch. Here certain show business figures and intellectuals would be transported; their talents would be used in propaganda production for the McCarthy regime. Although Bobby Kennedy had worked for six months as assistant counsel to Senator McCarthy, he was unaware at that time of his boss' suggestion to the CIA that internment sites be readied around the country.

After McCarthy's downfall the ranch lay fallow until the early sixties. Then the Agency decided to spruce it up and sell it. The house was painted, the barn repaired and the fields leased short-term for tillage. But no buyer was found. Consequently, neighboring farmers still leased the fields; they plowed their crops and paid little attention to the occasional comings and goings at the ranch house. The government was said to own the farm, but no one seemed to know any more than that.

From her bedroom window, Norma Jean looked west toward mountains, barn and forest. In the other directions, rolling land in shades of brown, tan, green and yellow surrounded the house like geometric patches on a great quilt. The nearest neighbors lived two miles away but their houses were not visible from the ranch. The landscape seemed sculpted in such a way that the Agency's ranch, while open on three sides, was shielded against any attempt at *lèse majesté* by wolds, ridges and crests. The topography of the ranch functioned like louvers, permitting those inside to see out while obstructing the view of anyone looking in. Somehow a chilling, unfriendly atmosphere radiated from somewhere inside the tract, making any passerby reluctant to venture onto the property. Children were not drawn to these parts as they searched for Indian arrowheads or stalked imaginary foes. "Posted" signs alerted their parents to keep them away from this vacant-looking spread whose owners insisted on strictest privacy. No salesmen called, nor was mail delivered.

To reinforce the privacy of the present guest, Cathcart and Bledsoe used some of the most sophisticated technology owned by the CIA. Invisible alarms protected doors and windows; anyone seeking egress or ingress without the proper code would set off a shrill howl. Cameras mounted in the barn monitored the property, while smaller, more secret ones in the house scrutinized the captive's every move. The absence of radio and television made Norma Jean's confinement quieter than that of hardened criminals, who were seldom without the companionship of voices and images from their sets. And no phone rang. Cathcart and Bledsoe communicated with the outside world by a short-wave set located in the ivory-colored van.

Although someone at the Agency had provided a closet full of clothes, they were not the kind a former movie star would have picked for herself. Four pairs of slacks, of a mannish cut, in charcoal, gray, mustard and beige. Blouses that a spinster schoolteacher might have chosen, along with army-issue bras and panties. Since the closet contained no dresses, there was no need for a slip. Nor was there a girdle, Norma Jean noticed as she perused her closet for the first time soon after her arrival. Folded on a shelf were several pairs of jeans and two matching denim jackets; plaid flannel shirts, warm socks, woollen kerchiefs, a Western hat and earmuffs. Hanging at the back were two coats, one dark and heavy for winter, the other a windbreaker.

Norma Jean sighed. Who had assembled this stark wardrobe? *I saw better-looking things on the soldiers in Korea,* she thought. *And why no lipstick or eyeshadow?*

She marched back to the common room and told Cathcart, "Tom, I sure hope you'll go to Boise soon. I'm writing a list of things I need. Gee, whoever picked out those outfits must hate women. You know what I mean?" Then, leaning down to whisper in his ear, she explained the items of feminine hygiene that he should fetch from Boise.

"What if the drugstore doesn't have the large economy size?" he asked.

"Well, *silly*, then get two of the smaller ones." Sitting at the table, she completed her list:

lipstick—"Fire" by Max Factor
eyeshadow, liner and mascara
blusher
Chanel No. 5

She looked up and asked, "Is there a Saks in Boise?"

Told there probably was none, she said, "Well, at least try to find Macy's. And please, please get a library card. These are the books I'd adore to read in my spare time." She worked on the list for a long time; when she finished it read:

Remembrance of Things Past, by Marcel Proust
Catcher in the Rye, by Salinger
The Brothers Karamazov, by Dostoyevsky
Growing Up in Samoa, by Margaret Mead
World Atlas
Agatha Christies
something on Renaissance art—with pictures
poems by these poets: Carl Sandburg, Walt Whitman, Edgar Allan Poe, Lord Alfred Tennyson
plays by William Shakespeare

CHAPTER

14

"Scenes of Everyday Life"

They had been at the ranch for weeks. When they arrived it was summer; now, just past mid-August, the landscape anticipated autumn. Leaves looked less green. Wisps of haze crept in, even at midday, diffusing the bright sunlight so that its golden fire softened to the color of honey. The mountains were a darker blue, as though overnight they had added a layer of warmth for the coming winter.

Cathcart had made his trip into "Boise" several days earlier. Actually, he drove into Pueblo, a small, orderly market town for farmers, ranchers and mountain folk. Dressed in jeans, plaid shirt and cowboy hat, Cathcart could have been one of the locals shopping for his wife or daughter. Except that the women of southern Colorado didn't draw up such specialized shopping lists.

He couldn't find "Fire" by Max Factor—not in the drugstore, not even at Sears. Finally he settled for "Strawberry" by Caro Nome, which the salesgirl pronounced "Caranoam." Maybelline eye shadow was a disappointment; Norma Jean was crestfallen when he presented it. Trying to cheer her up, Cathcart said, "You know, Norma Jean, women in that town don't use as much war paint as you do. And when I asked for Channel Number Five at Sears they sent me to the hardware department."

Norma Jean had to giggle. She was still taking Valium regularly, so her laughter was lower pitched and less shrill than in Hollywood days.

"Where are my books, Tom?"

"In one of these grocery bags. I found one or two you wanted. The librarian never heard of most of 'em, though."

Digging through celery and toilet tissue and canned tuna, Norma Jean touched the slick laminated cover of a book. Pulling it out of the bag, she had another disappointment: the author was not Proust, but Prouty—Olive Higgins Prouty. The novel was *Stella Dallas*. "Oh Tom, that's not it at all."

"Well, I told the librarian what I wanted. That first one—" he pulled Norma Jean's shopping list out of his shirt pocket—"she said the library didn't carry books like that. Written by a degenerate, she said. She said Prouty was more uplifting than Proust any day."

"But *Stella Dallas* was a movie. I saw it when I was a kid. Barbara Stanwyck and Alan Hale." In Hollywood Norma Jean had seldom dared talk about books; someone always made fun when she did. Now she took a chance. "I don't want to read it, though. That's what Arthur Miller calls schlock. Rots your mind."

"Well, take a look at the others then," Cathcart said.

Retrieving more books from another bag, he held them out. *Tales of Horror*, by Poe; *The Complete Plays of Shakespeare*; and *The Mirror Crack'd*, by Agatha Christie.

"Super," she said, delighted to find three books from her list. She thumbed through the collection of Poe stories. "Wow, here's 'The Masque of the Red Death.' We read that in high school. I shivered every time. Just thinking about it still gives me the willies." Her eyes widening, she told Cathcart the plot. "You see, this Duke throws a big party and at the end Death appears and starts whacking them all down. Talk about a party pooper!"

Unnoticed by Norma Jean, Bledsoe came in carrying a case of beer that Cathcart had left in the van. He dropped it on the table with a bang, startling Norma Jean. She yelled.

"What the hell's wrong with you?" he snapped.

"Haven't you bothered me enough, you big banana head?"

She said it before she could stop herself; or was it Angela Phinlay, repeating to Bledsoe what she had yelled at the cop in "Asphalt Jungle"?

"Shut up," he said. "Don't gimme any lip. You're not in Hollywood now, and we don't play your game. You play ours. Understand?"

"That's enough," Cathcart said. Whether he meant it for Norma Jean or Bledsoe, or both, was unclear.

Bledsoe had spent an irritating morning. Checking equipment in the barn, he had accidentally damaged a sensor on the most important camera. He glowered at Cathcart and Norma Jean, then sulked out of the house and back to his technological challenges in the electronic barn.

When he had gone, Cathcart told Norma Jean, "I've got a surprise. In the van. Sit down here." He pulled a chair from under the table. "Close your eyes and count to a hundred."

Cathcart removed from the van a small cardboard box with air holes cut in the sides. Norma Jean was dutifully counting aloud when he set the box in front of her.

"One hundred forty-nine, one hundred fifty . . ."

"Okay, open them."

"*Meow.*" The cat was out of the bag but not out of its box.

"Tom! Oh, thanks. Thank you ever so," she said, picking up the fragile-looking ball of fur that squirmed with surprising strength in her hands.

By the end of the afternoon, the bond was established. The strong-willed yellow kitten had found a new mommy. And Norma Jean had found a friend.

There were no mirrors in the house. Bledsoe had decided the first day, while Norma Jean was still asleep, to remove the wall mirror in her bedroom and the medicine cabinet in the bathroom as well. He took both to his own room, which, like Cathcart's, was always locked. It was better if she didn't see how she looked. Not that she was frightful; she just didn't look like Marilyn Monroe. Her hair was straight and unruly. The roots had also darkened. Her face, usually full, was now lean, almost gaunt. It seemed lengthened by her recent ordeal, angular to the point of boniness. She resembled a hospital patient whose struggle to survive precluded daily grooming.

Bledsoe, however, was not pleased that the woman *was* beginning to revive. The better she felt, the more chance she'd talk. And the healthier she became, the longer they might be stuck here guarding her. The next time he spoke with the Agency liaison he voiced his concerns. Not only about Norma Jean, but about Cathcart as well.

She named the kitten Grushenka, even though she wasn't sure it was a female. Animal anatomy, especially on a tiny creature, was much more confusing than on men and women. Grushenka was a name she adored—she fell in love with the sound of it when she first read *The Brothers Karamazov*. She had yearned to play the earthy Grushenka, but when Hollywood filmed the story Maria Schell got the role. She was considered a brilliant actress just because she came from Europe.

And they made fun of Marilyn for daring to dream of such an ambitious part. Producers and directors who could barely read the newspaper, let alone Dostoyevsky, had chortled. Hedda Hopper made catty remarks in her column. When a reporter asked Marilyn, "Is it true you want to play *The Brothers Karamazov*?" she replied, "I don't want to play the brothers. I want to play Grushenka. She's a *girl*, you know."

Now Grushenka was at her feet. Or at her hands, actually, since Norma Jean was sitting on the floor stroking the kitten in its box, which she had lined with a warm plaid shirt and one of the unfashionable pairs of slacks from the closet.

"My angel," Norma Jean whispered. "Who sent you to me?" The kitten slept on, probably unaware that Terry Pavka, convinced Marilyn was still alive, was holding a good thought for his vanished friend at the very moment Cathcart passed the Pueblo Animal Shelter. He had stopped, on an impulse, to pick out a pet for Norma Jean.

His kindness won her heart. But it also left her confused. After all, he had helped kidnap her, and she remained his prisoner.

His and Frank's. So why was Tom good to her, while Frank seemed ready to bump her off? She was fascinated by Tom's craggy face. It reminded her of Clark Gable, and the eyes, too, were kind; sexy Gable eyes. He didn't have a mustache, but if you looked closely at his ears, they were almost as big and floppy as Clark's. All the same, he was a kidnapper. He had removed the date-due cards from the books so that she wouldn't know the library's name.

The other man, ugh. Norma Jean shivered just thinking about him. Yesterday, reading "The Masque of the Red Death," she grew very frightened at Frank's resemblance to Poe's description: "The figure was tall and gaunt, and shrouded from head to foot in the habiliments of the grave. The mask which concealed the visage was made so nearly to resemble the countenance of a stiffened corpse that the closest scrutiny must have had difficulty in detecting the cheat." Well, Frank, didn't look literally like that, she told herself, but those dark green military glasses he put on before going outside gave her the creeps. He was tall and thin, too. Not gaunt, really, because his clothes fit rather well, she reasoned. And I wouldn't say he's shrouded in the habiliments of the grave, whatever wardrobe that is. He's dressed just like Tom and me—Western style.

She decided, however, to win him over. Realizing the folly of antagonizing him further, she made up her mind to talk with him, include him in the card games, let him know she didn't hate him even though he had kidnapped her. Norma Jean was never one to hold a grudge. More to the point, if she intended to escape she had to win his trust as well as Tom's.

Like shipwreck survivors washed ashore on a desert island, the three inhabitants of the ranch house had soon established a daily routine. As far as Norma Jean could tell, it was something like this: The men ate breakfast early, several hours before she was up, then washed dishes. One of them adjourned to the barn while the other one took up guard duty in the common room. She couldn't imagine why they spent so much time in the barn. She wanted to ask if they kept cows and horses out there, but decided against seeming curious. Instead, she decided she'd look and listen.

How astonished she would have been to discover, in a certain section of the tall barn, enough equipment to blow up the Russians—or at least that's how it would look to an outsider.

At first Cathcart and Bledsoe had devoted alternate days to barn duty; now, however, the pattern had evolved so that Bledsoe spent far more time there, while Cathcart stayed in the house. On duty. Norma Jean observed that neither man's clothes got soiled, so they were obviously not ranchers. Then what were they doing in the barn?

Norma Jean got up late, chatted with Cathcart during breakfast if he was the one in the house that morning, then showered, dressed and applied makeup. Since the arrival of lipstick and mascara her spirits had improved as well as her looks. She spent close to an hour on her face: tweezing her brows, adding fullness to her mouth with lipstick, darkening her lashes. When she finished she went to her room to read and play with Grushenka.

Cathcart and Bledsoe ate lunch around one o'clock, sometimes followed by naps. Later in the afternoon they used the weights and the stationary bicycle the Agency had set up in another section of the barn. Then all three sat down to dinner at seven, after which they tidied up before going to their separate rooms for the night.

One evening Cathcart and Norma Jean were playing poker near the warm stove. The night air, crisp and dry, announced an early fall and foreshadowed a frigid winter. Seeing Bledsoe's attention on them, Norma Jean said, "Frank, come on, play a hand. I'll deal you in." He grunted. Norma Jean half-expected him to walk out of the sitting room but instead he approached the table where their cards were spread, looked down at their game for a moment, then pulled up a chair. Norma Jean smiled as she dealt his cards.

"This reminds me of a movie set," she said. "You know, playing cards is a good way to pass the time between takes. It took me forever to learn poker. Once I caught on, though, I never wanted to stop." Turning from Cathcart to Bledsoe to include both in her conversation, she went on, "Bridge is another matter. When we made 'Gentlemen Prefer Blondes' Jane Russell wanted to teach me how to play. But it was like a whole new job. I mean, who wants two hard jobs at the same time? What's that called?"

"Moonlighting," Bledsoe said.

"You certainly have a good vocabulary. Did you go to college?" Play it dumb, she told herself.

Caught off guard, Bledsoe frowned. Why was this dame so nosy? Norma Jean kept her friendly gaze on him; Cathcart looked too, although more indirectly than Norma Jean. Finally Bledsoe answered, stiffly but with an unaccustomed shade of sociability, "I studied physics. And math."

"You know what?" Norma Jean said, "In high school I took algebra but I flunked it. All those positives and negatives—no matter what I did it always turned out wrong. Two negatives make a positive, two positives make a negative—or was it the other way around? Anyway, as Mae West said, 'Five'll get ya ten if ya work it right.'" Her eyes widened. "Say, maybe you could teach it to me. I mean, a girl never knows when she might need some algebra. In this day and age," she added. "Does it help you balance a checkbook?"

Bledsoe didn't know how to respond. Was this dame putting him on? She sounded like Gracie Allen. Or was she a flirt—even away from Hollywood, out here in the sticks? Could she really be that dumb and dizzy?

"Yeah, could be," he mumbled.

The card game continued past midnight. The glimmer of detente made relations less strained, even though Norma Jean did not feel she had charmed Frank, the quiet, smoldering one.

When Cathcart gave Norma Jean her Valium—which she still took four times a day—she put it into her mouth as usual, sipped water, and wished the men goodnight. The tablet, fortunately, didn't disintegrate as she held it between cheek and gum. It sustained water damage, but in her bedroom she quickly dried it as best she could and added it to the others she had been hoarding. There might be a time when she would need them more than now.

* * *

Long after the abduction, Norma Jean's body wouldn't accept the loss of its drug supply. Valium was not enough. Her opiate craving exceeded a starving belly's desire for food; even when she slept, partially relaxed by the tranquilizer, her brain broadcast its red alert: Mayday! Mayday! like an aircraft losing fuel and plunging to destruction.

Though her body ached, throbbed, quivered, threatened to shatter, her guardians did not relent. They administered Valium on schedule, and noted that her addiction seemed to be lessening despite her craving.

But her greatest dependency was not drugs. Nor booze. No, the addiction embedded at her core was more tenacious—how would she ever break free of *Marilyn*?

Now Marilyn was wrecked; even her beautiful name was gone, replaced by an unflattering old handle that recalled mousy hair, one-piece bathing suits, shyness and shoulder pads. This body that Marilyn inhabited so long was different, too. Norma Jean—if that's who she really was, as the two men seemed to think—lacked strength to reconstruct that shimmering personality.

Underneath, however, new growth stirred. Unknown to the woman called Norma Jean, and certainly unknown to her captors, small branches of a new personality were sprouting in darkness. The sun would soon disappear for its winter rest, taking with it warmth and moisture. Nevertheless, certain of its rays had caressed these new young roots. The first sprouts, hidden in shadow, were, to be sure, tentative and fragile. But behind them a force pushed, pushed, urging them up. During the cool nights her new identity pressed upward like green leaves from a dry, brown earth-patch.

September was a month of gold in Colorado in 1962. The soil gleamed, golden brown. Amber leaves decorated trees across the ranch and far beyond. Pollen spread over mountains like powdered topaz. Norma Jean, strolling one day near the ranch house, wondered if the sun's midday warmth might tan her pale skin.

She was not alone as she walked, even though no one else

was visible. A pair of eyes followed her from inside the house. Other pairs, electronic ones, watched her from the barn. Because of her good behavior she had the day to herself, let out like a semi-trusted child to play until the afternoon ended.

The soft dirt felt strong and springy underfoot. The autumn air, at once warm and cool, buoyed her. Full of energy, she yearned to stride across the fields and even climb the mountains. Dressed in beige slacks, a tan blouse with a windbreaker over it and a wide-brimmed cowgirl hat, she resembled a composite of Marlene Dietrich and Doris Day in costume for "Calamity Jane."

She chewed her thumbnail, not from nerves as Marilyn used to do, but in concentration. She might have been searching for a solution to one of the algebra problems she had insisted that Bledsoe give her, or even memorizing lines from a new script. But now she did it alone, without Natasha Lytess or Paula Strasberg just beyond camera range to reassure her with their approval. Now she had only herself.

Since the first day the men let her out to walk on the property she had studied fields, mountains, forest, wondering if someday she might go for a walk and never return. Norma Jean knew the time was near. She must not stay here long . . . otherwise she would risk growing secure. She might even come to like the role of prisoner. Then that false, perverted security would never let her leave. She would always be the victim. It had happened in Hollywood. The role of helpless victim had lured her back there after she had escaped to New York, in a try for maturity. She loathed, and was afraid of, the pleasure of suffering.

The sky was expressionless. The endless blue told her nothing, gave her no clue. Far away toward the mountains the forest seemed alternately beckoning and forbidding. She considered how she might survive there; eating berries? Trapping small animals? She recoiled at the thought of killing anything. She had seen it done often enough in movies, but even to save her own life she couldn't imagine *doing* it.

Straying further and further from the ranch house, she even thought that perhaps this was the day. The day of escape, with only the clothes on her back. Until Cathcart walked briskly toward her across the flat field, motioning her to return. A moment later he reached her and escorted her once more within camera range. "Now remember what I told you," he said sternly. "Otherwise I'll have to put a stop to your exercise."

She noticed that her captors wanted her always near the barn. That mysterious, busy barn. She couldn't figure out why it was such a rallying point. She never imagined, of course, that the President sometimes saw her televised image as she strolled out-of-doors, or that he regularly received information about her. On that golden day in late September of 1962, Bledsoe was sending a coded message to Washington.

Decoded and delivered to the Oval Office a few hours later, it informed Lancer that "her behavior is no longer erratic. Her last apparent anxiety attack was on 16 September 1962, at which time she wept, saying she wanted to go home. She was asked why she wasn't happy and answered that she missed her friends. She asked to write one letter. Permission was denied. Later she was heard telling her pet kitten that 'Bobby Kennedy did this.'"

After her walk Norma Jean told Cathcart she was tired of playing poker in the evenings. "And goodness gracious, Tom," she added, "can't we have something besides hamburgers and tuna sandwiches for a change?"

"I'm not a chef," he told her. "It's about time for you to cook again."

"Swell," she said. "I'd adore it. Besides, I'm old-fashioned. I think men should never have to fix their own meals." She opened a cabinet door, then looked in the fridge. "Let's see, what'll I need from the supermarket? Beets, garlic, cucumbers, sour cream—that's for the borscht." Closing her eyes to think for a moment, she said, "Oh yes, and a chicken. Better yet, buy chicken soup in a can. And matzo balls—have you seen any in that supermarket in Boise?" Suddenly she burst into giggles.

Cathcart said, "Is this some kind of joke? I mean, what are matzo balls? Some kind of fancy cheese? And beets, no thanks. I got my fill in the army."

"No, no, I'm not joking," she laughed. "I just remembered a funny story. You want to hear it? The new girl at the studio was having lunch in the commissary with a producer. He ordered Louis B. Mayer Chicken Soup With Matzo Balls. So she was real puzzled. She asked her date, 'What do they do with the rest of the matzo?'"

Cathcart wondered what was so funny about that. He laughed just enough to let her know he got it, even though he didn't.

CHAPTER 15

"The Weird Sisters"

The weather had turned cool. A touch of winter in the air made Norma Jean shiver; she decided not to take her daily stroll. In the kitchen she was concocting a meatloaf, her first in years. Determined to make it tasty, she chopped, minced, diced and measured her ingredients.

She would have preferred making one of the Jewish dishes her former mother-in-law had taught her to make. But it was almost impossible to cook Jewish food with the ingredients Tom brought from Boise. He and Frank had disliked her borscht, anyway. "Tastes like red dye," Frank grumbled. Her attempt at matzo ball soup had also been less than successful.

So she had changed cuisines, reverting to dishes which, as a teenage housewife, she had cooked for Jim Dougherty: meat and potatoes, in as many forms as possible. The first time she successfully baked a ham and managed to mash all the lumps out of the accompanying potatoes she received compliments. "Dee-licious," said Cathcart. Even Bledsoe agreed.

Bustling about in an apron, Norma Jean looked like a character actress, although a young, attractive one. She had regained the weight she lost during the ordeal of Marilyn's last days and the reappearance of Norma Jean. Moving about the kitchen, she combined the vestige of a wiggle with the poise of an experienced stage actress. (When Marilyn tried this sort of stagecraft after studying at the Actors Studio the Hollywood big shots hated it. "Be a *dame*," they ordered.)

In her new role of cook-captive she wore no makeup other than a light coat of lipstick. Her brownish blonde hair, undecorated eyes, and full cheeks would have seemed right in a Flemish genre painting. But something extraordinary transcended her homespun appearance—Norma Jean still shimmered. It was Marilyn's afterglow.

"More?" she asked Cathcart halfway through dinner.

"Don't mind if I do." He grinned, taking a generous slice of meatloaf and half a plate of potatoes, which he doused with gravy.

"Frank, please have seconds," she urged.

"I'm not crazy about meatloaf," Bledsoe said.

"I'm sorry you don't like it," she said. "Tell me your favorite dish and next time I'll try to make it." She turned to him and confided, "After you mentioned a soufflé last week I tried to make one. The only problem was, I needed wire to pull it up."

Even Bledsoe smiled faintly at the image.

After dinner, at Norma Jean's instigation, they put on a show. This had begun a week earlier when she persuaded the boys, as she now called them, to read a play with her. She chose *The Taming of the Shrew*. The men were at first bored and confused. But what else did they have to do in the evenings? They had no radio, television or record player, and card-playing eventually became a bore. They had tried Chinese checkers for two nights but soon agreed with Norma Jean that the game could make them lose more than their marbles.

"Imagine me directing a play!" she said as they took their places around the stove. "Why, I couldn't direct traffic. At least, that's what I always thought."

Tonight they tackled *Macbeth*. The boys read the various male parts while Norma Jean played Lady Macbeth, Lady Macduff and the three witches.

Shakespeare wasn't new to her. Marilyn had played scenes from *King Lear* while studying with Michael Chekhov. She also memorized scenes from the tragedies when Lee Strasberg gave her private acting lessons in New York.

To play the witches she used an aluminum skillet, wore it as an outlandish piece of millinery. She wrapped black masking tape around her front teeth. For each of the Weird Sisters she assumed a different grotesque pose. The First Witch spoke; Norma Jean stood up. When the Second Witch answered, she sat down. She moved three paces and crouched, then spoke the Third Witch's line: "A drum, a drum! Macbeth doth come." Clanging a spoon on her aluminum hat, she gave herself a headache. The witch had a whisky voice.

Suddenly Norma Jean's inflection changed. The First Witch said, "All hail, Macbeth! Hail to thee, thane of Glamis!"

Grushenka uttered a fortuitous, though tardy, "Meeoow!"

"I come, Graymalkin!" Norma Jean ad libbed, wishing Grushenka wouldn't miss cues. Why didn't she "speak" at the beginning of the scene? That's when the witch addressed her evil tabby. Norma Jean remembered the Hollywood saying about working with animals and children.

For Lady Macbeth's mad scene Norma Jean swaddled herself in sheets. Entering from her bedroom, she hoisted a flickering candle. "Out, damned, spot!" she moaned. "Out I say." "One: two: why, then 'tis time to do it." She blew the candle out, plunging the room into darkness.

"Hey, wait a minute," Bledsoe said. "What the hell—"

"Hell is murky! Fie my lord, fie! A soldier, and afeard? What need we fear who knows it, when none can call our power to account?"

Lady Macbeth continued her soliloquy. Even Bledsoe didn't interrupt.

Cathcart and Bledsoe applauded, impressed by—what? Something strange had happened in the room: Norma Jean had departed, briefly replaced by a strange, unknown actress.

The next morning she studied a very different kind of book. Sitting by the warm stove, she occasionally added another log as she pondered a page of the World Atlas. Grushenka, curled in her lap, purred and kneaded Norma Jean's woollen slacks.

Although the doors and windows of the house had no bars,

still she had to plan as though she were escaping from prison. She remembered Paul Muni in "I Am a Fugitive From a Chain Gang." Surprise was the key to success. She needed to catch the boys off guard, then vanish without a trace.

She gazed at the detailed map of Montana, a yellow state surrounded by Wyoming in pink, Idaho in green, the Dakotas in orange and purple. She searched everywhere for Boise. "I wish I'd paid attention in geography class. Maybe I played hookey to go to the movies the day they studied Montana." She had to smile at herself.

She did locate Billings, Butte . . . "And all those mountains," she said to Grushenka, who didn't open her eyes. "I'd sure like to know which ones these are." She gestured toward the mountains outside the kitchen window. The nearest one, with its summit now covered in snow, resembled an inverted ice-cream cone sticking into the sky. Still, as always, perplexed by geography, Norma Jean mused, "How can you read a map if you don't know where you are to begin with?" Squinting at the green state wedged beside Montana, she spotted Boise. "But Tom can't go there," she said, "that has to be a zillion miles from Montana." Then where did he get the books and makeup, if not Boise?

She looked at the top of the page. "Canada? Yes. That's where I'll go. Hey, I've been there already. 'River of No Return.' I just hope I can find it again." She had to smile. "This time without Indians." Caressing Grushenka she promised, "In a few days, kiddo, we'll hit the road. I hope you know how to catch mice. 'Cause where we're going, there's no supermarket."

The sun's pink evening rays were stretching behind the white mountain as the van pulled up. Cathcart had been gone all day. Supposedly he was on another expedition to Boise, although Norma Jean now realized that Boise was nowhere near. Not if they were really in Montana, which she also doubted. He came inside with both arms full of supplies: food, beer, several new pots and pans that Norma Jean had requested. As a surprise he had brought her a box of chocolates. A Whitman's Sampler.

Grushenka scampered to the kitchen. Noticing the door that he hadn't closed, the cat peered outside, then slid through the narrow crack. Norma Jean, helping Cathcart put away groceries, didn't notice that Grushenka was gone. A short while later she called her, looked through the house, and realized what had happened. Norma Jean, continuing her search outside, called and cajoled, but Grushenka didn't appear.

Looking toward the barn, Norma Jean saw the end of a yellow tail disappear through a second-story window with a missing pane. Grushenka had climbed a tree beside the barn, then jumped from a branch onto the roof. Now she was intruding in a place where neither she nor Norma Jean was welcome.

Norma Jean, warned to stay clear of the barn, rapped now on the door. Cathcart, seeing her through the kitchen window, called out: "Get away from there, don't you remember what I told you?"

Just then Bledsoe opened the barn door. He was livid. "Can't you keep that goddamn cat in the house? And you, get back in there now. Get *away* from here."

"Gee, it's only an old barn," she said innocently. "Just give me my cat and I'll be most happy to leave." Then, pushing past him, she ran in and called, "Grushenka, Grushenka?"

She was barely inside when Bledsoe grabbed her. "Get out of here, you bitch—"

The raised voices excited Grushenka, who skittered into view, then leaped onto a metal table covered with wires and switches.

Even in the midst of her scuffle with Bledsoe, Norma Jean realized this was no ordinary barn. It looked like the inside of an airplane, the cockpit where the pilot operated the controls. Buttons, knobs, screens—a whole roomful of machinery. No wonder they wanted to keep it secret.

"Let *go* of me."

Bledsoe pushed, she retaliated with her elbows, tried to kick him in the groin. He shoved her again. She lost her balance and ended up on the floor. Her leg hurt, it might be sprained but things were happening so fast the pain barely registered.

Bledsoe reached into an inside jacket pocket and pulled out a silver pistol and pointed it at Grushenka. "Curiosity killed the cat," he muttered. A moment later, Grushenka was gone.

Everything inside Norma Jean froze—tears, anger, terror.

Her mind retreated. She looked on from far away, like a departing spirit gazing back at the body it has left. She stood up, walked past Bledsoe out of the barn and returned silently to the house. Cathcart, who had seen the violent end of the squabble, came into the barn and closed the door behind him. Walking away, Norma Jean heard loud voices. "Let them kill each other, I don't care," she raged to herself. She went to her room, lay on the bed and looked at the ceiling.

An hour later she got up and went to the kitchen. As she stirred the pot of vegetable soup, she added all the Valium she had saved for weeks.

One of the phones on the President's desk buzzed discreetly. His chief of staff reminded him that Ambassador Dobrynin had arrived from the Soviet Embassy. The advisors slipped out through a side door without encountering Dobrynin.

"Mr. Ambassador," the President said, standing to shake hands. "My wife and I look forward to seeing you again soon at the White House. You and the lovely Svetlana Alexandrovna." The President had summoned him to explain the troubling intelligence reports of Soviet intermediate-range ballistic missiles in Cuba.

"We enjoyed Madame Dobrynin's piano-playing. Please give her our warmest regards. In the meantime," President Kennedy added as though it was an afterthought, "I should like to point out that I've heard certain rumors. You will understand my concern—my deep concern—that your government might have misunderstood our resolve on Cuba."

"*Nyekogda*," said the Russian emissary. The buttons of his gray suit strained to retain his corpulence. "Naver, Gospodin Presideent. We know all about Monroe Doctrine." His narrow eyes behind thick spectacles revealed nothing.

For a moment the smile froze on the President's face, then, recovering his poise, the President said, "Yes, of course, Mr. Ambassador, the Monroe Doctrine."

He felt foolish—a rarity for JFK. The ambassador hadn't, of

course, been referring to Marilyn. But the President couldn't stop thinking about her . . .

"It is imperative, of course, that Mr. Khrushchev realize the full implications of any Soviet nuclear presence in Cuba."

"*Da, da,*" intoned Dobrynin.

CHAPTER

16

"The Lady Vanishes"

Playing Lady Macbeth the night before was a cinch compared to the new role she had undertaken. Unfortunately for Norma Jean, tonight's performance had no script. It was strictly ad lib, and her life depended on it.

It looked easy enough on the surface. All she had to do was serve dinner, as she had done often before, and pretend that tonight was like any other night. A smile, a bit of repartee, the usual game to make her captors believe she didn't mind being there all that much. It was practically routine by now, like playing a character in a soap opera. She had been biding her time, but now, suddenly and dramatically, time had run out. What had happened to her cat Grushenka could also happen to her.

Lying on her bed, staring at the stark ceiling, Norma Jean had been tempted to swallow all the Valium. There weren't enough to kill her but at least they would offset her pain. The pitiful final image of Grushenka hovered in her vision. The cat's horrible death, now etched on her brain, would never leave.

She decided to escape. Maybe she wouldn't make it, maybe Frank would kill her too, but if she stayed he would certainly kill her sooner or later. She now realized that Frank was a killer. A man who would kill with slight provocation. Tom wasn't like that, but suppose Frank turned on him, killing Tom and then her? After all, the two men had quarreled violently after the incident.

Still frozen inside, she presided over dinner as though she had forgotten the afternoon's nightmare. "Tom," she said gaily, "do you think it might snow? I didn't go for a walk today, it was so darn cold outside. I didn't dare go out without mink." She batted her eyes and giggled as though she were being interviewed. She was Marilyn again.

Cathcart barely responded. He, too, was troubled, and he didn't try to hide it.

Bledsoe was late coming to the table. He looked sly and defiant at the same time. Norma Jean couldn't bear to look in his eyes. Instead she looked just past them, at one of his ears. "I'm so sorry I was bad," she said. "I've made a dinner you're sure to enjoy." The words choked her.

The table was spread with an array of wholesome food. A green salad; garlic bread; candied yams; roast chicken. "This vegetable soup is special. It was invented by a chef in Beverly Hills. It's named for Will Rogers."

The first spoonful burned Cathcart's tongue. But the soup was uncommonly good; even Bledsoe refilled his bowl. "Save some room, fellas," she said. "For dessert I've made something yummy. Lorelei Lee's Diamond Rice Pudding." Her laugh ended in a near-squeak. She fought to suppress tears.

Passing the chicken, she observed with satisfaction that the boys were chewing more slowly than usual. "Is everything delicious?" she asked with a lilt. "Frank, how about another beer?"

She thought of the marvelous irony of this situation. She, who had recently left off drugs and booze, was now plying her companions with both. From long experience, she knew that alcohol and Valium packed a double whammy.

"You want to hear something funny?" she chattered. "I always had the reputation of being too dumb to cook. Well, I never told anyone in Hollywood, but I learned to cook in the orphanage. That was my job. When I was twelve I became the cook's number-one assistant. And I never spoiled the broth. At least, not too often."

Bledsoe had stopped eating and gazed into space. Cathcart yawned so deeply he couldn't chew. Pushing the food around her plate, too agitated to swallow it, Norma Jean told anecdotes at breakneck speed. "So that summer Joe DiMaggio proposed. And you know what I told him? I said, 'Joe, honey, you'll have to teach me all about baseball before I marry you. Why, I don't know a strikeout from a Lucky Strike.'" A quick smile.

Bledsoe left the table without a word. They heard him flop across his bed. For the first time ever, he had neglected to close the bedroom door behind him.

"Are you ready for dessert, Tom?" she asked brightly. Cathcart made a vague gesture with his hand and smiled at her. He tried to say something but his words became entangled in another gigantic yawn. Pushing his plate aside, he rested his head on the table. His heavy eyes drooped, his tongue lolled out. A moment later he was asleep.

"The sleep of the unjust," she muttered as she tipped up the hall and peered into Bledsoe's room. "Macbeth hath murdered sleep." She worked quickly in the dark. His rattling snores guiding her, she stood beside the bed, where he lay sprawled. She removed the silver pistol from his pocket and aimed it at his head.

No, I don't want his filthy blood on my hands, she said to herself. She put down the pistol, picked his trouser pockets and found money. He lay still as a corpse. She hurried down the hall to her bedroom and put on a warm coat. Into an old handbag that someone had left in the closet she stuffed gloves, scarves, socks and every warm item she could grab.

She ran down the hall, afraid that Tom might have awakened from his deep sleep at the kitchen table. He hadn't moved. She picked his pockets and found more money. She considered using his keys to drive away in the ivory-colored van, then remembered that their electronic gadgetry might easily pinpoint her when they woke up in a few hours. "Just what I don't want to be, a marked woman," she said as she pulled her coat tightly around her and opened the door.

She slipped out the door and ran across the big back yard, avoiding the barn except to blow a kiss to the memory of Grushenka, whose death had liberated Norma Jean.

* * *

The President had once thought of visiting her in Colorado, but the Cuban missile crisis had interfered. Bobby opposed the visit from the beginning. It was too risky. The President, however, seemed unmoved by his brother's arguments, so in a way Bobby was relieved that the Cuban crisis happened when it did. At least it kept the President away from the most dangerous woman in the world.

One day as Bobby tried to dissuade his brother from the mad adventure of visiting MM in the wilderness, he said in frustration, "Jack, tell me one thing. Just one. Are you still interested in her? I mean, the way you used to be. Or is this your misplaced sense of duty? The fact that you, uh, that is, we, put her there, you know, doesn't mean you have to pay a charity visit."

"Sure an' ye're a cheeky lad, ye little squirt." It was their grandmother Fitzgerald's retort to impertinence.

Taking it up like a football, Bobby replied. "Mind ye don't get me riled, ye bloody imp." Another family phrase. An eavesdropper would soon have lost the conversation entirely as they spoke in dialect for a quarter of an hour, laughing and slapping.

The comic relief of their blarney at an end, they went back to the realities of Washington.

"Well, *are* you?" Bobby persisted.

"I don't think I'll ever lose interest," the President answered. "We had to remove Miss Monroe, yes, of course. She was a danger, a threat, I agree. But I *have* thought of seeing her again." His voice dropped. His pale eyes were pensive.

The phone rang. "No, I haven't forgotten. Bobby and I will finish by half past seven."

"She's reminding me not to be late," he reported to Bobby. "Truman Capote is the court jester tonight. I've tried to tell her not to trust him. Someday he'll turn on her." Finishing a glass of white wine, the President shrugged. "But she doesn't believe Tru, as I think she refers to him, would ever snitch. That's his word, I believe."

The President sighed. "If only the world didn't think Miss Monroe dead it might be different. As long as I could watch her—on screen and off—it was tremendous. She made every red-blooded man hot. The biggest turn-on since . . . well, I don't know who.

But now," he added, slumping in his soft, leather chair, "it verges on necrophilia. She's a dead woman for all practical purposes. In the papers, on TV, everywhere. People speak in hushed tones when they say her name."

"All the more reason to forget her," Bobby urged.

"I still think she's the sexiest woman—alive," the President said. "Yes, Bobby, I think I have to see her again. If only to explain why I can't keep my promise to make her First Lady. I think she actually believed it."

When Bledsoe and Cathcart awoke from their Valium sleep, they informed CIA headquarters that their captive had escaped. It was immediately decided within the Agency that she had died of appendicitis. This was to be the official version, the version eventually reported to the White House. The Agency amplified its version with the rationale that Bledsoe and Cathcart had not dared take her to a hospital for fear she might talk. And anyway, the official version continued, it would have been too late, since her appendix ruptured and killed her an hour after the first severe pain hit her in the stomach.

Bledsoe and Cathcart were given details of the official version of their captive's death. They were informed that they had buried her body deep in a forest. Then they were ordered to join the search for her. The CIA later informed the President of her death, choosing as the perfect time to break the news the very day that a U-2 spy plane verified the presence of Russian missiles in Cuba.

Even the CIA slips up occasionally. Marilyn Monroe's appendix had been removed in 1952.

CHAPTER 17

"A Long Voyage Home"

Norma Jean pushed further into the silent forest. She had always been afraid of the dark, but now she plunged into it. Here was safety.

Nothing moved. The stately trees were like skyscrapers in a blackout. She looked over her shoulder, suddenly afraid the men might have followed despite her advantage. The only sound was her rapid shallow breathing. Nothing moved but her chest, driven by her pounding heart.

The forest floor was soft with pine needles. Sitting on it reminded her of straw mattresses at the orphanage. For a long time she couldn't draw a deep breath; tension had padlocked her lungs, denying her access to the enormous gulps of air she needed.

Slowly fear subsided into grief and hurt. "Grushenka, poor baby . . . we shouldn't have done Macbeth. Actors say it brings back luck." She yearned to share her grief, yearned for someone, any stranger, to speak a word of consolation. Only the forest heard, and absorbed her weeping.

She dozed, a shallow sleep punctuated by discomfort. Propped against a tree trunk, she shivered. The coat left her uncovered from knee to ankle; try as she might to curl into a ball and draw her legs under her for warmth, some part of her body still stuck out. Her toes were stiff, as though she had dipped them in ice water. Her nose felt blue.

The night seemed endless. The sharp assault of cold was made more painful by images: Grushenka sprawled in the corner, her own escape from the house of death. The evening recurred in bits and pieces, a jumble that left her exhausted.

Streams of light trickled down the huge trunks and soaked into the soft brown crust beneath. The tree tops were moving. She tried to bring them into her vision but her eyes wouldn't cooperate. The forest was upside down. Untangling the stiff knot of her body, she grasped a nearby sapling and pulled herself up. In daylight, the forest assumed its correct proportions.

Something struck her in the stomach. It was the first dreadful thought of the new day: "He killed Grushenka." Another assault followed instantly: "Run or they'll kill you." She turned to escape. Trees and underbrush blocked her. The forest seemed alive, waving its arms. It seemed ready to deliver a forlorn message. She looked up, turned her head and saw a pathway. Or what might once have been a passage through the maze.

She entered it, bending, straightening, stooping, shielding her face from the lash of twigs. Two hours later the timberland thinned. Scrub brush impeded her but she saw the sky. Picking her way through the tangles, she emerged abruptly from the forest. A field of black dead weeds stretched before her. Beyond the field was a lofty mountain, and to one side of the mountain was—"Oh *no*." Turning, she loped back into the brush, cursing her bad luck. Like anyone lost in the woods, she had gone in circles. And one of the circles had brought her in sight of the ranch.

Sometime late in the afternoon, when the sunlight had deepened and the trees had begun to turn dark, she emerged again. This time there was no mountain; instead, she saw rolling hills, and between them, far in the distance, a road.

She was paralyzed. What if they were patrolling the roads in the ivory-colored van? If they put her in that coffin again she would never escape. Still, she did not dare spend another night in the forest. The cold would kill her. Or worse. There might be wild animals; or wild humans.

The road seemed to recede. The faster she walked over the

empty countryside, the more distant the road. She rested often and thought about food. Was this the desert? Walking uphill and down, she saw other woodlands dotting the landscape. Sagebrush and short brown grass covered the world. No water, and she was very thirsty. "If it's not the desert, it's the next thing to it," she said.

Eventually, to her amazement, she reached the road. It was a narrow blacktop without a line in the center. She heard no motors, not even in the far distance. Night was falling—again. She worried about coyotes; bears; starvation. What if *they* came? There was no place to hide.

Was it a sound-mirage? She thought she heard a motor. A miracle? It buzzed like a faraway lawn mower. She listened again; it was a vehicle.

And then it rolled into view, occupying most of the meager road. A faded blue pickup truck with hay stacked high in back. Two people rode up front. Why hadn't they turned on the headlights? Dusk was rapidly changing into night.

While the truck was still half a mile away Norma Jean jumped into the road and began waving both arms across each other like a signalman flagging a train.

"*Buenas tardes, señorita,*" said the woman, leaning her head out. She might have been young, she might have been old—her face had set long ago, like a terra-cotta mask. Her straight black hair was plaited in pigtails that gleamed even in diminished light. Norma Jean approached.

"*Bonus noches,*" she said, attempting Spanish. She wondered what she'd do if they didn't speak a word of English.

The driver looked at Norma Jean as though accustomed to being stopped this way. "Does your car break down, *señorita*?"

"Oh no, it's much worse than that." How to sound believable? "You see, I was kidnapped. Then they killed Grushenka and I spent the night in the woods." The couple listened attentively to the deluge of words.

"You need help?" the woman asked.

"I'm not a very good Girl Scout," Norma Jean said, trying to smile.

"Where do you want to go, *señorita*?" asked the man.

"Well," Norma Jean said tentatively, "how far is Canada?"

The man glanced at his wife. She did not turn to look at him. He thought for a moment before answering, then said solemnly, "A long way, *señorita*." At Norma Jean's look of dismay he asked his wife, "*Quantos kilómetros*?" She thought about it, then shrugged. Finally he said tentatively, "I would say one thousand miles from here."

"But I looked on the map, and Canada was the next state. I mean, it was on top of Montana—"

"*Si*," said the woman sympathetically. The man nodded.

"How far is Boise?"

No answer. "*Como*?" the woman asked her husband.

"Boise," Norma Jean repeated. "I know it's a long way from Montana but I thought maybe I could get a plane to Canada. You see, I don't dare go back to Hollywood."

"*Señorita*, you say you feeling okay?" the man inquired.

"That's a laugh. I haven't felt *okay* in years. I'm starving, and I'm thirsty and I don't know where in the hell I am." She smiled, then started to cry.

The woman opened the door. "You come with us. We take you into town. You eat something, you drink, you feel better." She moved over and Norma Jean squeezed in.

As they drove down the road Norma Jean asked, "What's the name of that town you're taking me to?"

"Pueblo," the man said.

"Excuse me for being dim, but I've never heard of it. What'd you say it is?"

"Pueblo," he repeated. The woman added, "A town with many stores. We take you to buy food."

A few farmhouses, then an occasional service station, finally clusters of small stucco houses and a string of street lights. "At least I'm out of the desert," Norma Jean said. "Now, promise you won't let anyone see me. I mean, if they get me again my goose is really cooked."

They ate at Rosie's Cantina. Norma Jean insisted that her rescuers join her for a feast of tamales, tortillas, fajitas, guacamole and pitchers of cerveza. "I used to eat Mexican food in Hollywood," she said. "But my husbands didn't like it. So I only went to Mexican restaurants when I wasn't married."

At the end of the meal Norma Jean excused herself. In the ladies' room she removed a $20 bill from the roll of money stuffed in her bra. She had forgotten to count it last night but now she realized she wasn't exactly poor. Looks like a couple of grand at least, she thought as she glanced in the mirror. Like insurance money, if you could buy kidnapping insurance.

But who's that woman looking at me? The black felt hat covered the top of her head, but the hair that tumbled below the hat onto her shoulders was no longer blonde; it was the color of wet sand on the beach at Malibu. Her brows were light brown, her eyelashes neutral. The black mole on her left cheek was the only reminder of Marilyn. Except the eyes—they were only one touch away from Marilyn's. If she made them up ever so slightly, lowered them and tilted her head back . . . but that wouldn't do. Not yet, at least. Not until she found out where she was and what had happened.

At the bus station she thanked José Juan and Natividad, whose names she had learned during dinner. "*Vaya con dios*," they said as Norma Jean climbed out.

"God bless you, too," she waved as they drove slowly away. "I wish the world was full of people like you," she added, but the old blue truck had already pulled away.

Greyhound and Trailways shared the same small terminal in Pueblo. Norma Jean hoped the change from the twenty would be enough to buy her ticket; otherwise she would have to delve into her underclothes again. Now that she was accustomed to the stack of bills next to her skin, she didn't mind. After all, this was her nest egg; why shouldn't she warm it with her body? More to the point, it was also the only indemnity she'd ever get from Marilyn's killers.

"I'd like to know what time the bus leaves for Ottawa," she told the young man selling tickets. Who said that? Norma Jean suddenly felt as though she had stepped into the past. It was more than déjà vu; everyone had those. This one was more like walking into a cyclone that picked you up, whirled you around, then set you down in a different dimension. The way Dorothy got scooped up in Kansas and dropped in Oz.

The young man pushed his glasses further up on his nose. "Did you say Ordway? That's the next bus, and it takes half an hour."

"*No. Ottawa.* I've got to leave immediately. Do you *hear*?" Rose Loomis had suddenly appeared. She was in a hurry to get out of this tank town, as big a hurry as when she was leaving Niagara Falls.

"Excuse me," he said. "You mean Ottawa, *Canada*?"

"And make it snappy," Norma Jean commanded in the surly voice of Rose Loomis.

"It'll take a while. We don't get many passengers going there."

Norma Jean wasn't paying attention. In her head "Kiss," Rose Loomis's favorite song in "Niagara," had started up. In the movie Rose sang along with the record, getting a dreamy look on her face every time she heard it—except at the end when it chimed from the belltower, telling her that the murder hadn't succeeded. A guy said to her in one scene, "You kinda like that song, don't you, Mrs. Loomis?" and she answered, "There isn't any other song."

Norma Jean started to hum it. The empty little bus station faded away, replaced by the busy one in Niagara Falls. Norma Jean, still humming "Kiss," turned around, put her hand over her chest exactly the way Marilyn used to do, and saw him. Joseph Cotten—no, George Loomis, Rose's husband—was spying on her as she bought her ticket. So he knew—but how did he get wise? Or was it somebody else, somebody looking for Norma Jean?

"Quick, gimme that ticket, you potato head," she hissed at the astonished ticket seller. "Give it to me, do you hear? I've not got all night."

"Sorry, miss. I had to look up the fare as well as the schedule." He adjusted his glasses again. "Now, from Pueblo, Colorado, to Ottawa, Ontario, you have to change in Denver, then again in—"

"*What*? Who said anything about Colorado? Is this *Montana* or isn't it?"

"Why no, you're in Pueblo, Colorado. The friendliest little town in the lower Forty-eight."

She reached to brush a strand of hair from her eyes. But it wasn't there; instead she brushed the black hat. The awkward gesture brushed away Rose Loomis as well.

"I'm so sorry," Norma Jean whispered. "You see, I thought someone was following me and I was scared." She smiled at the man, whose glasses had slid further down his perspiring nose.

"Well, we've got a bus leaving in fifteen minutes for Denver. Like I said, you have to change there for Ottawa."

"Yes. I'll take it."

She paid for the ticket, then asked again, "Is this really Colorado? You know, I thought so from the start. But Tom told me it was Montana. You can never trust a man, I should know."

Lowering his voice, the young man said, "Just between you and me, some of these bus drivers forget where they are. I'm sorry if one of them told you the wrong state. But you've got a good one tonight. Makes the Denver run every day. Don't you worry about him getting lost."

A few other travelers had drifted in. Norma Jean still felt uneasy; suppose they were on her tail—they'd be sure to look in places like this. She returned to the ticket counter. "Say, I wonder if you'd do me a favor. You see, they—well, two men—might be after me. Do you think I could wait back there in your office? Just 'til the bus leaves, of course."

"Uh, that's for employees only," he said. "But the station manager's away tonight. If you won't tell a soul I'll let you sit back there. Your bus leaves in fifteen minutes."

She dozed in his wooden chair until he came in to check on her during a lull at the counter. "Everything okay?" he asked.

Her lids were heavy, and when she looked up at him with a wan smile he stared at her. He couldn't take his eyes off her.

She smiled sweetly. "You're a real pal." Why was he looking at her that way?

"Oh, uh, well, sure," he said. "You know, I could swear I've seen you somewhere before. But you're not from around here, are you?"

"No. That is, I wasn't 'til they brought me to the ranch. And I asked them if it was Colorado—you see, I recognized it from the movies but they said it was Montana. To make a long story short, I hightailed out across the forest to reach the border . . ." Pausing, she added, "If that makes any sense?"

"You look a lot like that singer, Rosemary Clooney. You know, she has that TV show. When I heard you humming a little while ago, I thought, my goodness . . ."

"Oh no, not a chance. I mean, I could never sing like her. My voice is small."

"I can't figure out who you remind me of but I know I've seen you somewhere."

"Is that my bus?"

"That's it. You can board in five minutes." Looking around, he said, "By the way, where's your luggage?"

"Oh, I'm traveling light. Just this tote bag. You see, I didn't have time to pack." Giving him a peck on the cheek, she said, "Thank you ever so. Toodle-oo."

In the dark quiet bus she dreamed about Grushenka. And also about Terry Pavka. She wished she dared call him. At least he could advise her what to do next.

At the Denver Airport departing passengers were scrutinized. Word had come from two local CIA men that a woman fitting a certain description was armed and dangerous and on a suicide mission for a foreign power. The men had alerted airport officials to the threat. This woman might try anything. She was insane and likely to tell wild stories about government officials attempting to silence her. She was also thought to be carrying explosives.

If spotted the woman was to be quietly arrested. The CIA officials were on hand to take over after the arrest. At the departure gate passengers boarded planes headed for many destinations, unaware that they were being carefully evaluated. Throughout the night and during the following day hundreds departed, thousands. But not the dangerous Norma Jean.

Eating breakfast in the Denver bus station, she realized that she had to sleep. She must sleep in a real bed; otherwise she couldn't face the long trip ahead. As she finished her coffee she noticed a woman across the counter reading a newspaper. The headline proclaimed: QUARANTINE ON CUBA. Under it, in smaller letters, Norma Jean read: "*Kennedy Acts to Avert Nuclear War.*"

She bought copies of the Denver *Post*, Time, Newsweek and Glamour. In her hotel room she intended to learn the details of the scary headlines. She had seen these big black words on every paper at the newsstand. What was happening? She thought of "On the Beach." Charlton Heston, Ava Gardner and Fred Astaire had ended up in Australia trying to escape nuclear fallout, but at the end of the movie they were waiting to die. Was that going to happen here?

The warm hotel bed enveloped her. If the United States was at war with Russia no one would survive anyway. Jack himself had told her that. She had discussed hydrogen bombs once with Bobby, too, and he didn't think anybody would come out alive. Maybe I'll die in Denver, she thought. She read the first three lines of the *Post* story. She wanted to race on down the page, but suddenly her body twitched, it felt like an electric shock. The newspaper slid out of her hand. Exhaustion having caught up with her, she succumbed.

She slept for twenty-four hours, dreaming once more of Grushenka, who was riding through the air on a B-52, meowing in terror as bombs rained down on Los Angeles. And then Mrs. Bridwell knocked on the door, calling out across the darkness, "Marilyn, honey, time to get up. The bus is leaving without you. Bus stop, bus stop, bus stop . . ."

Enormously relieved on awakening to realize that she was not back in Hollywood, not in a coffin and not in the woods, Norma Jean stretched. Her joints were stiff, as though they had been glued while she slept. Light seeped into the room from behind the closed draperies, making her curious about the city outside and at the same time anxious. She wondered why she always felt like this when she woke up: eager to discover the next chapter of her life, but also frightened that the new day would crush her.

She picked up the newspaper spread over the floor beside the bed. The memory of the scary black headlines made her stomach quiver; maybe bombs had exploded during the night.

She read several paragraphs about the missile crisis in Cuba. Jack and Bobby, of course, were deeply involved. So where Khrushchev, Castro and others whose names she remembered from conversations with the Kennedys: Robert MacNamara, Gromyko, Dean Rusk, Dobrynin.

She turned the page. More on the Cuban crisis. Violence in Mississippi and Alabama over school integration. Paging through advertisements and comics, she came to the entertainment section. As she scanned the first lines of "Voice of Broadway," Dorothy Kilgallen's column, she rubbed her left eye. Something was causing pain, like a loose eyelash irritating the cornea. But rubbing didn't help. Of course not, she realized, as her heart jumped, stopped for a second, then raced up into her throat.

A small line of print had hit her eye with the force of a bullet, penetrating until it smashed into her brain. The message was so sharp that it caused physical pain. She stared at the words, reading them over and over, not able or willing to comprehend the ghastly implications.

At first it had barely registered: "*Miss Monroe's Will Is Contested.*" Then her eye picked up the following lines, whose impact would have knocked her down if she hadn't been lying flat. "The will of Marilyn Monroe has been contested in a Los Angeles court by Inez Melson, former business manager of the late actress. Claiming that undue influence was exerted by the two principal beneficiaries, Miss Melson's attorney, Allen Stein, petitioned the court to block the will from being admitted to probate."

Her *will*! The principal beneficiaries were Lee Strasberg and Dr. Marianne Kris, the psychiatrist who treated her in New York. She had named others as well, but this was horrible; no one should know about her will yet—not 'til she died!

Yet there it was in the newspaper: "Miss Monroe died of an overdose of barbiturates on August 5." So it was a coffin she woke up in; they really had killed her! But how did she get here? It was too much, and she was too lonely. She tossed the newspaper on the floor, buried her head in the pillow and cried herself to sleep again.

This time she had lots of company. They kept coming until

the room was full. Lorelei sat on the bed. So did Miss Caswell and Pola Debevoise, still taking her glasses on and off the way she did in "How To Marry a Millionaire." There on the floor sat Roslyn Tabor, and Sugar Kane beside her. Kay Weston stood by the window. Angela Phinlay paced nervously up and down, while Rose Loomis, in a red blouse and black shirt, stared coldly across the room at Vicky Parker, still wearing plumes on her head and diamond spangle earrings from the finale of "There's No Business Like Show Business." Norma Jean felt like a little girl at a birthday party, only this time the party was hers. And it wasn't even June 1.

"You know what I think?" Rose asked everyone and no one. The girls turned toward her. "You gotta learn how to handle men. There's always a way." Lighting a cigarette, she continued, "Only you've let 'em get away with too much, honey." Tough, scheming Rose softened a bit. She sashayed over to the bed and put her arm on Norma Jean's shoulder. "Go to Washington. Find your lover and knock off anyone who tries to stop you. Buy a pistol."

"If you've nothing more to say, pray scat," Lorelei chimed in. Nudging Rose aside, she said, "Take it from a girl like I, someone's trying to bump you off. You know what? You'd better lay low for a while." Bouncing gleefully up and down on the bed, she seemed to have lost her marbles. But Norma Jean didn't mind it; Lorelei always made sense, even when you couldn't understand a word she said. The other girls looked at each other with "get her" expressions on their faces.

"You can't get away with murder," Lorelei went on. "I mean, they can't get away with murder." Wide-eyed, she paused. "You know where the bodies are buried, right? Not your body, silly. 'Cause you're not really dead. But mum's the word right now. Just wait. You'll get your turn. When you do, tell those Kennedy louses to go back to their spouses. But not 'til you get diamonds. And plenty of 'em. Otherwise you'll sing like a bird. Call a press conference—you know what I mean?"

Sugar Kane spoke up. She was standing in front of the mirror, looking over her shoulder. "Are my seams straight?" she asked Roslyn, who nodded. "Don't be blue, honey," she said, winking at Norma Jean. "You're not dead. It's *her*. They killed poor Marilyn, but you're ginger-peachy." She picked up her ukelele and sang a few bars of "Runnin' Wild." Then she said, "But guess what—you've got your whole life ahead of you." Leaning down, she said in a stage whisper, "You didn't like being a bottle blonde anyway, did you?" Norma Jean, hesitant, nodded. "Okay, what's your beef? Here's your chance. Go back to New York and—"

"Stop having fun and find happiness," Lorelei interrupted.

"Bingo," Pola Debevoise interjected. "And when you get there, find a rich man and marry him so you can retire from the stage."

"Who said anything about the stage?" Miss Caswell asked, puzzled.

"She wants to act, of course," Vicky Parker put in. "Finally she'll have a chance. As long as Marilyn stays out of sight."

Kay Weston, in jeans and a white scoop-neck blouse, snapped her fingers. "Honey, you gotta remember one thing. We'll help you. Natch. We're all pulling for you." She motioned toward the others. "You remember what a jam I was in? I mean, I was a has-been saloon singer, with Indians on my tail and a big angry river trying to swallow me. But I came out okay. And you will too. Yes, indeedy."

"Yeah," Vicky said, putting her arm around Kay's shoulder. "I don't have to remind you how I went from hat-check to headliner in "There's No Business Like Show Business." You know what I said to Donald O'Connor. 'I have a new manager, and he's doing me over completely. New name, new clothes, new . . . I guess everything else is pretty much the same.'" She shook her head and the plumes brushed across Kay's face. Kay frowned. "Hey, Norma Jean," Vicky giggled, "that's the line I flubbed for a week. They almost fired me, it took twenty takes before I got it right." Norma Jean giggled too. "But with you it's different. *Nothing* else is the same. Marilyn can't help you now, kiddo. You gotta find a new name, new clothes, new way of talking, new everything." They all looked at Norma Jean. "I mean, this is when you seek your fortune. And your destiny—"

"And stay off the sauce," Angela Phinlay reminded her. "If you want them to think you're a smart blonde."

"Maybe you're right," Norma Jean said to the roomful of girls. "I'd love to start over. Even though I'm thirty-six years old, I'm really not." Even Lorelei looked puzzled. "Because," explained Norma Jean, "I spent sixteen years as Marilyn. Okay, subtract sixteen from thirty-six and what do you get?"

Pola Debevoise put on her glasses and started counting her fingers. But Lorelei beat her to it: "Twenty!" she said incredulously. "You're twenty years old!" The others gasped at Norma Jean's cleverness. Pola looked at Kay; Kay turned toward Sugar Kane; Angela gave Rose an anxious look, but even hard-boiled Rose was smiling.

Cherie, who had slipped in quietly during the party, burst out laughing. It was a signal to them all. Laughter and giggling, once started, wouldn't stop. Norma Jean buried her face again in her pillow, only this time she shed tears of laughter. Pola's glasses were damp; Sugar Kane and Roslyn collapsed on the floor, unable to stop their hysterical squeals. Much later, when all the girls had stopped laughing only to start again, they pulled themselves together and quietly left the room. Norma Jean had fallen asleep.

In the department store she bought a suitcase and carried it from the luggage department to Women's Casual Wear, where she picked out two pairs of jeans and a matching denim jacket.

"Would you like these wrapped?" the salesgirl asked, wondering about the suitcase.

"No, thanks," Norma Jean said. "I'll wear them. I mean, I'll wear one pair." In Hollywood she had learned the trick of moistening jeans before putting them on so that they would accentuate her curves. Now she was so delighted to escape from the slacks she had worn since her escape, and which she had disliked the first time she saw them, that she hurried into the new jeans without so much as a critical inspection in the mirror. A white cotton blouse and the denim jacket completed her basic traveling outfit.

"If you don't mind, dear," she said to the salesgirl, "I'd like to leave my old clothes. They're nothing but awful reach-me-downs. May I toss them in this wastebasket, please?"

"Oh, uh, yes, that's fine. And the other pair of jeans . . . ?"

"Right here in the suitcase," Norma Jean said. "You see, I

left home in a big hurry. No time to pack my duds."

When she left the store her suitcase was full. Three white blouses; a white terrycloth robe; a black dress; a couple of slips and panties; nylons; two pairs of shorts; and a new winter coat.

"Taking a trip, are you?" the taxi driver asked as he drove her to the Greyhound station.

"You bet. I'm going to New York. To be an actress."

"You don't say. How long does it take?"

"Well, several days, I guess."

"No, no—I mean, how long does it take to be an actress?"

"Well, it's like this. I've already done some acting. And I've taken lessons, too." She hesitated. Would he catch on?

"You know, you kinda look like an actress. I mean, you would if you wore a lotta lipstick, maybe a mink coat."

"Some people have told me I look like a famous movie star. Do you think I do?"

Before he could answer, she yelled, "Hey, stop!"

Tires screeched. The back of the taxi seemed to jump up, dumping Norma Jean on the floor. "I'm awfully sorry," she gasped, scrambling back onto the seat. "I just want to go into this bookstore for a sec. You see, I don't have a thing to read."

If the driver commented on her impulsiveness, Norma Jean didn't hear. She was already running through the door of the Denver Book-a-Rama. "Hi," she greeted the proprietor. "I want a book by Carl Sandburg and one by Walt Whitman."

The tall gentleman smiled, directing Norma Jean toward the shelf containing *Leaves of Grass* and Sandburg's *Selected Poems*. "I can tell you like poetry, young lady."

"Oh, yes. And I'd also adore an art book. If it's not too heavy." On a shelf labeled "ART" she picked up *Picasso's Picassos*, full of gorgeous reproductions.

"That's a lovely book," the proprietor said. "New, too. We just got it in a few months back."

"I really shouldn't," she said. "It's terribly expensive." Unable to put it back, she repeated, "Oh, I really can't, I mustn't." Glancing at it again, "I'll take it. Like they say, you only live twice."

The man said, "Yes, uh, quite so."

When she left she also had a biography of Abraham Lincoln and a new play called *Who's Afraid of Virginia Woolf?*

"I've seen 'em in that kind of a hurry to get to a liquor store, but never to a book shop," the driver commented.

"Yes, that's true," she said. "But I don't drink."

They had reached the station. He pulled over to the curb—this time without spilling her on the floor—and turned to give her a look. "You know, you do remind me of an actress. Right off, though, nobody comes to mind. Unless it's that girl on television. Foxy McNamara's her name on the show." He scratched his head. "Ann Sothern, yeah, maybe you look a little bit like her. She plays this crazy dame—"

"I beg your pardon," Norma Jean said.

"Oh, no offense, miss. I mean, crazy dames are a lot of fun—at least on television."

She waved goodbye to the driver. Inside the station she checked her face again in the ladies-room mirror before boarding the bus. It didn't look at all like Ann Sothern's. In fact, it didn't look all that different from Mar—except that *she* wasn't there any more. "That's why they don't recognize me. No Marilyn," Norma Jean said to herself. "But at least she didn't take her beauty mole when she left."

There were those, however, who might recognize her—even without lipstick, eyelashes and glamorous gowns. Which was why she bought a pair of dark glasses in the station and put them on immediately. It didn't pay to take chances.

Lugging her suitcase, she stepped into the bus. It was full. Immediately, however, a young cowboy halfway back stood up. "Howdy, miss. You need a hand with that bag you're totin'?"

"Why, thank you . . ." She was surprised to see real cowboys, but of course she was no longer in Hollywood; this was the true West.

Another cowboy, older and weathered, also stood up. "Won't you take my seat, ma'am? This bus is mighty full."

"Now jist a cotton-pickin' minute," the first one said. "I'm aimin' to give the little lady my own seat once I git her luggage put away."

While they argued over who could take better care of her,

Norma Jean squeezed down the aisle. "Please, fellas," she said, "take it easy. Haven't you ever seen a girl before?"

"Yep," said the young cowboy, "but you're kinda different. I mean, you ain't too much like the girls around here."

Both men were still standing as they awaited her decision.

"Thank you ever so," she said, not meaning to sound flirtatious, and melting both cowboys as she said it. "You're so kind. I'll sit with you part of the way," she addressed the younger one, "and then I'll change seats." She turned, smiling, to the older man.

Although she, too, was wearing denim, the man didn't mistake her for a cowgirl. Nor for a local. Norma Jean was relieved to find friends. After all, somebody might be tailing her, and a girl never knew when she'd need the kindness—and protection—of strangers.

"My name's Curly McCord," said the young cowboy as soon as she was seated. "And he's Andy Wheeler. But everybody calls him Tunafish. You can too."

"Charmed, I'm sure," she said to Curly. Stretching across the aisle and back a row to shake hands with Tunafish, she said, "Delighted." With a big smile, "I've always been fond of tunafish—especially with lettuce and tomatoes," she stalled, searching desperately for a name. "I've got it," she said. "I mean, I'm Zelda. Zelda Zonk." One of the aliases Marilyn sometimes used. Whew, she thought, even a girl in my shoes should know her own name.

"Howdy-do, Zelda," Tunafish said. Curly pumped her hand vigorously, holding it a few seconds beyond the handshake.

"How far you travelin', Zelda?" Curly asked.

"To New York. The isle of Manhattan."

"Wow! I ain't never been there myself. Matter of fact, I ain't never even met anyone from there."

The bus was now out of Denver, headed toward Kansas.

"I'm from Nebraska," he told her. "Me and Tunafish been ridin' in a rodeo in Denver. We work on a cattle ranch 'bout fifty miles from Lincoln."

"Lincoln is also my favorite President," she said. "There's never been a better one."

"Are you married?" Curly asked suddenly.

"Am I what?" she said, as though he had asked her if she was Marilyn Monroe.

"Married. I don't aim to be nosy, but . . . are you?"

"Why, no. That is, you see, I was married but it didn't work out. So now I'm an old maid."

"The reason I asked, Zelda, I was wonderin', well, if"—he couldn't say it, and then he rushed on—"if you'd marry me. I fell in love with you back in Denver, the minute I saw you, and we could settle down in a real house somewhere . . ."

"Why, that's the sweetest thing anybody ever said to me," Norma Jean said softly. "But I can't do it. Marriage takes so much time, and I have to start all over as an actress—"

"You're an actress?" He fell deeper in love.

"Yes. That's why I'm going to New York."

"I'll come with you. Do they have rodeos in New York?"

"I don't know. But, Curly, it's like this. I can't marry anyone. Not for a long time. Maybe never." She looked down, remembering how excited Marilyn was a few months earlier when she thought she was going to marry and settle down in the White House. "You wouldn't even like my cooking. How would you like to come home after a hard day at the rodeo and sit down to a bowl of borscht and a plate of gefilte fish on rye bread?"

These exotic words further incited him. If she had told him to fall on his knees, raise his arms and bow down he would have scrambled into the aisle to do it. "I could learn to like any kind of fish," he said. "And I'd never complain."

"You're a dear to say that. But you see, I have unfinished business. That's why I'm going to New York. To start all over. And this time I have to get it right." He had no idea what in the world she was talking about, but every word she said struck him as an answered prayer. "Because I won't get another chance. I mean, how many people even get a second chance? But I did, and I have to use it. It's sort of like a comeback, I guess."

As the bus crossed Kansas that night, Norma Jean thought about herself while Curly and Tunafish snoozed. Or tried to think about herself; first she had to determine exactly who she was. It wasn't easy; the cowboys snored and she poked them from time to time.

Although she didn't altogether understand her situation, she did realize that Marilyn was dead. But in a sense Marilyn was only a role she had played for sixteen years. A long time to play any part, she thought. I played it so long I almost forgot about Norma Jean. I never thought she'd come back, or I'd come back, or whatever . . .

It was so complicated. And yet everyone close to Marilyn, all her real friends, had known all along that Marilyn wasn't real. The voice, the mannerisms, the dazzling blonde hair and the blonde girl underneath it—all invented by Norma Jean, with help from studio publicists and makeup men.

But these cowboys, especially Curly, responded to her as though Marilyn were still there.

She dozed but woke up early still thinking of her long run as Marilyn. Looking at the flat fields of Kansas framed by the shallow horizon, Norma Jean thought of the many times in New York when she and Susan Strasberg, Lee and Paula's daughter, would walk down a street unnoticed. No one guessed that Marilyn Monroe was nearby until she—Norma Jean—would say to Susan, "You want to see me be *her*?" Susan would say "Go ahead," then suddenly Marilyn would materialize. And stop traffic; cars would honk, taxi drivers would lean out and yell, "Hey, Marilyn," and autograph seekers would converge on her from every direction.

She wondered if she could make it alone, without the familiar presence of MM. (Like the columnists, she often thought of Marilyn as a pair of . . .initials.) A twenty-year-old girl in a thirty-six-year-old body, with a world of experience, most of it sad and useless; and unable to tell anyone about her past. No one, ever, must know; they'd laugh and call the men in white jackets, for one thing. And even if they didn't, word would get around and then *they* would get wise and find her again. This was the worst possibility of all. That she must avoid at all costs. "But I'd sure like to know more details about *her*," Norma Jean thought. "They really bumped Marilyn off, I guess."

It was tempting to say yes to Curly. He would protect her; adore her; they could have children and a home and dogs and cats and horses. Maybe she could forget the past, or at least the worst parts. It would be so easy: all she had to do was say yes and they'd get off in the next town and wake up a preacher. They even had their best man—Tunafish. And the preacher's wife could be matron of honor—how many times had the very same thing happened to Susan Hayward? Plenty—Norma Jean had seen every one of those movies—

"Hey, Zelda," Tunafish said. "Mind if I cut in? You promised to sit with me, too."

She moved back to his seat without waking Curly. Tunafish must be as tall as Gary Cooper, although it was hard to tell unless he stood up.

Just then the driver announced, "Manhattan, next stop. We'll have a twenty-five-minute rest stop in Manhattan. Change buses for Lincoln, Omaha, Council Bluffs, Wichita, Tulsa, Oklahoma City and Springfield. Passengers for Topeka, Kansas City and points east please reboard this bus in twenty-five minutes." In case someone missed it, he repeated, "Please reboard in twenty-five minutes. Right after breakfast."

"But this is where I get off," she said, gathering her things. "How'd we get here so fast? I thought we were still in Kansas."

"Yep, we're still in Kansas, Zelda," Tunafish reassured her. "Manhattan, Kansas. You got a few more miles 'fore you get to Manhattan, New York City."

"Someday I've got to learn geography," she sighed. "I can't tell you how many times I've ended up in the wrong place."

When Tunafish smiled, the crow's feet around his eyes reminded Norma Jean of Arthur Miller. Tunafish liked listening to her talk; he wanted her to go on and on. Her distinct enunciation, with every syllable in place, made him wonder if she was a foreigner, although the foreigners he had met all had black hair and dark oily skin. But maybe she was; after all, he had overheard her talking some kind of lingo to Curly.

"Once," she continued, "I wanted to take a plane to Atlantic City but you know where I went instead? Kansas City!" Tunafish laughed. "Actually," Norma Jean confessed, "that happened to a close friend of mine, Pola Debevoise. And she couldn't help it; she lost her glasses, so of course she didn't know which plane to take. But you know something? It also seems as if it happened to me."

Tunafish laughed. "You're a pretty girl. Yep, pretty as a picture. I believe Curly's wild about you already. Could you stop off at the ranch for a few days? I live with my sister and she'd be glad to have you stay as long as you want."

"Thanks loads but I'm in a hurry. When a girl's in show biz she never gets a rest."

"What kind of performin' do you do?"

"What I've done in the past doesn't count. But I want more than anything to act on the stage. I know I can do it, too. My teachers told me I could." Norma Jean looked at Tunafish as though seeking his approval as well.

"One day I betcha I'll turn on the TV and there you'll be. 'Starring Miss Zelda'—how'd you pronounce your last name?"

"Zonk," she said.

"And I'll run out my back door and call across to Curly in his bunk. 'Hey, Curly, Miss Zelda Zonk that we met on the bus has turned into a real star.'"

"Oh, Tunafish, I hope it happens just like that. Except I don't care about being a star. No more—I mean; I just want to show them I can act."

He was as warm and comforting as one of her aunts, except that he didn't smell of kitchens and cologne; instead he gave off the odor of hay in a warm barn in midsummer. If she could marry either of the cowboys she thought she would prefer Tunafish.

"What's it like on the ranch?" she asked.

"Lots of horses. Other animals, too, of course, but me and Curly deal with horses. Did you ever ride one?"

"Yes. Quite a few, actually. Once I was riding with my husband—Jim was his name—and it was almost dark. He told me to turn on the horse's headlights, and I asked him where they were." She giggled, and Tunafish laughed with her for a long time in his resonant bass. "After all, how was I to know? I was just a kid who had never been out of L.A."

After their laughter died she said, "I really love all animals. I had a collie when I was little, but this mean guy next door killed him. Then I had a cat. Her name was Grushenka." She slipped her small white hand into Tunafish's big hairy one. "Another mean man killed her."

And then they had reached Manhattan. "Looks like a one-horse town," she told Tunafish. Curly woke up and said sleepily, "Whose horse you talkin' about, Zelda?" He was enchanted, and every word his enchantress uttered seemed to hold private meaning for him alone.

When they boarded the bus again after breakfast, Curly whispered something in her ear. She smiled and shook her head. In a couple of hours they reached Topeka, where the cowboys had to change buses and go north to Lincoln, while Norma Jean headed east.

"Promise you'll write me a letter," Curly begged. "Since you don't have any address yet, you gotta promise. I couldn't stand it, Zelda, if I thought I'd never see you again."

She promised. When they parted she kissed Curly, then Tunafish. They waved, and she waved as the heavy silver bus lumbered out into the street. She kept waving until the bus turned a corner and they vanished. Half an hour later she looked back. Topeka had also disappeared into the shallow horizon.

CHAPTER 18

"Poison Ivy"

The world might explode any minute. The United States and the Soviet Union were in a confrontation, the worst one ever. Khrushchev versus Kennedy. The big dispute was over little Cuba.

In the middle of all this word came to the CIA that a prisoner had escaped, contrary to first reports of her death. A dangerous prisoner. This one carried no guns, no ammunition, but she had the ability to bring down the house. FBI, CIA, NSC, a rainbow of acronyms—buzzed on a twenty-four-hour schedule.

Deep inside the Agency, in a bureau not preoccupied with the missile crisis in Cuba, the uproar was quiet. Quiet but deadly. Those responsible for losing her must suffer the consequences, although not yet. First she had to be found.

The escape of Poison Ivy—the code name for Norma Jean—was so far still a well-kept secret. How long it would remain so, however, was debatable. At least the President didn't know. Nor the Attorney General. This was not the time to bother them. Let them save the world first, then hear bad news on the domestic front if they must.

In the small office deep within the Agency, voices were hushed. Those who labored there seemed never to leave; no one saw them come to work, no one saw them go. Operating as though behind a thick veil, separated from other branches of the CIA like a distant colony, they were nevertheless within shouting distance, so to speak, of the awesome machine that tidied up the government's dirty work. Much of the operation was done by telephone.

"Poison Ivy has been traced to Denver."

"The airport?"

"No. A bus driver remembered her. Boarded late at night in Pueblo, got off in Denver."

"Does he remember her clothes?"

"Said she was wearing slacks. And a coat, but he couldn't describe it."

"Any leads after that?"

"Nothing yet. Nothing substantial from ticket sellers in the Denver station."

"Los Angeles is covered. Poison Ivy's house and the whole shebang. If she shows up there we've got her. At her house or any of her friends'."

"What about newspapers?"

"Who'd print such a story? Even without the Cuban headlines."

"Yeah, you're right. They'd look like asses."

"When you find Poison Ivy—"

"No sweat. We got that taken care of. Planned out in advance. No escape permitted this time. We nab her, it's goodbye, Poison Ivy—the calamine lotion's all ready. And waiting. No more Poison, no more Ivy."

"And you got a good story for the W.H.?"

"Sure, the W.H. gets spared all details. Too unpleasant for Lancer."

"The story we worked on, right?"

"Yes. Poor Poison Ivy. She got very sick. Chills and fever. The fever kept on going up, and the chills shook her 'til her teeth were about to fall out. Worried to death. Who to call? Local doctor? What to say: 'Hey, Doc, we got a real sickie on our hands. How about making a house call? But promise you won't tell a thing you see over here. Even if you recognize Poison Ivy, Doc, promise you won't breathe a word.' "

"No. Even the W.H. wouldn't want that."

"So we tell the W.H., our only alternative was to let Poison

Ivy terminate. Rest in peace. And that's that." The voice paused. Becoming thicker and softer, it added, "Just as soon as we find her."

"What is in a name?" she wrote in the Blue Horse spiral notebook. Now, how did the rest of it go—"Would not a rose by any other name smell just as sweet?" Well, pretty close.

The notebook was filling up fast. To pass the time she jotted down thoughts and impressions about the passing landscape. She wrote poems, chewing the end of her ballpoint pen while searching for the exact word to convey her meaning. After an hour of writing poetry she had to stop; her brain was fried.

The first half of the notebook was poetry; past the heavy divider were whole sentences, pieces of sentences, lists of words she liked, and favorite quotations that came to mind. The last page was filled with names. On that page she wrote first names in one column, last names in another, as though devising a "Match the word in column A with the correct word in column B" game. Perhaps it was indeed a game, although a serious one. Thinking up names, while fun, was more important than mere amusement. For the name she eventually chose would last the rest of her life.

"Zelda" was at the top of the first column; "Zonk" began the column of family names beside it. Of course, that name was impractical; too many people knew that MM had used it as her moniker for traveling incognito. "Harriet Brown" was a name that Greta Garbo supposedly used. "What if I borrowed it?" thought Norma Jean. "No, Miss Garbo might not like it if I did that."

"Lincoln," she wrote in the second column. "Well, Shakespeare was right," she thought. "What *is* in a name? What if I called myself—" and she scrawled "M-a-r-t-h-a" in the first column.

"In about an hour, ladies and gentlemen, we'll be arriving in Chicago. All passengers change in Chicago."

"How appropriate," she wrote. "I'm in Lincoln's home state, and I'm thinking about him. Staying in Chicago for a couple of days to rest and see the sights." Chicago interested her especially because of Carl Sandburg's description of it: "Hog butcher for the world, tool maker, stacker of wheat . . ." She put aside her notebook long enough to reread his poem, "Chicago."

Returning to her own writing, she flipped pages until she found a poem that had occupied her all morning as the bus crossed the flat countryside:

America—
I was born on the wrong side of you
Too much light and sky made me blind
A little fog and snow might have helped me
Instead I looked at so much dazzling blue
That I turned blue myself

What did it need? All her life she had wanted someone near who could tell her what was missing—from a poem, from her *life*. Norman Rosten was like that. He was a writer she met in New York who had befriended her and taught her about writing and a lot about life. She had written several poems after that, which she sent to him.

Arthur, too, had helped her. The only trouble with him, he soon began telling her all the things that were missing—particularly from her life. And, of course, their marriage had ended.

This fantasy-someone who could tell her what was wrong and right in her life had always hovered in her mind, like a cobweb hanging in the corner of a room. It was stronger than a fantasy; it nudged her inside, like hunger. It had inhabited her since childhood, and still nudged her.

The poem she had just written, for example; should she add, "I was born on the wrong side of you, in Los Angeles," or would anyone who read it know that without being told? And had she made it clear that she wished she had grown up in New York or a city like it where everyone you talked to seemed to know so much, seemed to have read half the books in the world?

She felt somehow deprived. The cobweb blew back and forth, never revealing the enormous secret: where do you start to make sense of life, who do you ask for pointers? She had no time, she was in a hurry.

She looked out the bus window at the suburban houses and, far in the distance, the skyscrapers of Chicago. How did you learn about all these people, where they worked, how they spent their money, what they did for pleasure? She was so hungry to *know*. You couldn't just walk into a university and say, "I want to learn about the lives of people in Chicago. Please tell me which course to take."

At the Actors Studio she had glimpsed ways of finding out—not about skyscrapers and people you passed in a bus—but finding out who you were and why you were that person and no other. Lee Strasberg had compared the process to excavating the ruins of an ancient civilization, then assembling them so that they made sense once again. The only problem—there always was one—happened to be she *wasn't* one person and no other. She was MM, but also Lorelei, Kay Weston, Rose Loomis and the others. Even back then when she studied at the Actors Studio, Norma Jean also dropped by from time to time. Suppose she went digging inside herself as Lee suggested; the pain was tremendous, and so was the confusion. Picking the real girl out of that crowd was like trying to regain your normal shape in a hall of mirrors.

"Yeah, we got lucky in Denver. This dame at the Greyhound station sold a ticket to Poison Ivy. Seems they had quite a little chat. Poison was real friendly, told her where she had come from. And where she was headed."

"What else did she tell?"

"Not much. She's buying a ticket, and while she's rummaging around for money in her handbag she asks the dame if she's heard any late news about Cuba, for crying out loud. So the dame tells her about Lancer's speech on TV, and next thing you know they're exchanging life histories. Only Poison made herself sound like Mrs. Jones from Fresno."

"No details from—"

"Not a one. As the dame remembered it, Poison said, 'I'm worried about international problems. This Cuban thing is a big one, isn't it? My friend is involved in it.' So the dame says, 'The President's speech made me a little less worried. He seemed so confident, you know.' Poison didn't say anything else about that. Told her about growing up in an orphanage in California, a couple of happy marriages, reading some book of poems. It was a kinda slack time at the ticket counter, apparently, so Poison goes on and on. Tells her she's crossing the country by bus from California. She asked the dame if Washington, D.C., was on the way to New York."

"Sightseeing, huh?"

"Yeah. So we've increased the stakeout. We figure, look for her in New York in a few days. Maybe D.C. She's also screwy enough to stop off at Podunk on the way, so we've got a few eyes watching points east. East of Denver, that is."

"The thing is, if she was all there we'd already have her, more than likely. But she's just loopy enough to head in the wrong direction. Or at least the unexpected one. Talk about a loose cannon, she's more like a ricochet bullet."

"That's all for now. Talk to you later."

Every time she turned a corner she looked quickly back over her shoulder. Just to make sure. But she couldn't spot what she was looking out for. It was early afternoon, a bright Indian summer day that had brought crowds into the streets of Chicago. Office workers devoted lunch hours to shopping; suburban matrons swarmed, buzzing from store to store on the Magnificent Mile, then off to the Loop to meet friends at the Art Institute. Businessmen from all over the Midwest whizzed by in taxis, on their way to butcher more hogs, make more tools, stack more wheat. Despite the liveliness and the blue Chicago skies, however, Norma Jean was not having a good time.

Since her arrival the day before, she had been hounded by anxiety. Every time she tried to fall into the rhythm of Chicago's streets, anxiety nagged her again. It bothered her like a crooked eyelash dangling across her vision, creating a thin shadow she couldn't brush away.

Norma Jean had seen the girl in the bus station looking at her. At first Norma Jean paid no attention. A few minutes later, however, inquiring about departures for New York, she noticed the girl again. The girl had blonde hair teased into a beehive. She wore a navy blue wool suit and a white silk blouse. Although she pretended to be looking at something slightly to the left of Norma Jean, she was a bad actress; it was obvious that she really had her eye on Norma Jean and nothing else.

In order to save money Norma Jean found a hotel within walking distance of the station. On the sidewalk, as she shifted her suitcase from right hand to left, she caught a quick glimpse of the same girl. Except that it wasn't a girl. A coarse, hard quality in the face made her look more like a woman well along in middle age. Or even—no, Norma Jean felt silly. She knew all about that, and this wasn't one.

This morning in the hotel coffee shop she almost saw the woman again. Turning to look through the large plate-glass window as she finished her coffee, Norma Jean saw a bit of navy blue. It was no more than a reflection that disappeared around the corner. Yet catching the outline of a vanishing figure, her eye held it, pressed it into her brain. All morning she had been unable to concentrate on anything else.

Standing on a street corner, Norma Jean tried to read her map. It was no bigger than a baseball card, or so it seemed as she squinted at the small print and the grid of black lines. She consulted it again, then looked up and down the street. She was in front of Marshall Field's. "On State Street," she hummed to herself, trying to get her bearings from the song lyrics. "I'm on State Street." She looked at a yellow sign: N. State Street. She closed her eyes the better to concentrate and raced on to the end of the song.

"I beg your pardon, Miss, can you please help us find the Art Institute?" The speaker had on a hat with a veil that drooped to the eyebrows; Norma Jean saw that first when she opened her eyes. Caught in the veil were little furry black dots that resembled tadpoles in a fishnet. The hat above the veil was small and demure and matched the lady's floral print dress. That is, it matched the olive green stems attached to the dress flowers.

"We're not from Chicago but we read about the Institute in our newspaper at home. Mr. Shelfmore and I come from Missouri."

"Yep, sure do," affirmed Mr. Shelfmore. "The Show-Me State."

"In that case, maybe you can show *me*," said Norma Jean, shaking hands with both Shelfmores. "I'm as lost as you are. You see, I'm trying to get there myself. I have this map but I really can't tell which way anything is on it. North, south, east or west—it's all the same to me, I'm afraid."

"Well, now, I was a Boy Scout," said the rotund Mr. Shelfmore. "And Boy Scouts learn their directions by the sun in the daytime and the moon at night."

"Yes, dear," said his wife. Turning to Norma Jean, she said, "We'd be glad to have you join us, once we find the way. If you'd care to, that is."

"Why, thanks, I'd love to." She couldn't help thinking of Sir Francis Beekman and Lady Beekman as played by Charles Coburn and Norma Varden in "Gentlemen Prefer Blondes." Except that the Shelfmores probably weren't addicted to diamonds. "You know, I've had the worst luck in Chicago. And I wanted more than anything to have a good time." She smiled wanly. They wouldn't understand if she told them about that odd—woman?—who was tailing her.

"That's too bad, my dear," said Mrs. Shelfmore as the three of them turned off State Street onto—Norma Jean gasped. "Oh no, it can't be," she said nervously.

"Whatever is the matter, Miss . . . ?" Mr. Shelfmore realized that he hadn't caught her name.

"It's Monroe," Norma Jean quivered, wringing her hands and staring up. "Monroe Street."

". . . Miss Monroe Street?" said the bemused Mr. Shelfmore. "But you can tell us your trouble, Miss Street. We have a daughter . . ."

"I'm so sorry," Norma Jean said quickly. "My name isn't Monroe Street. Nor Monroe . . . what I mean is, look up there." She pointed to the street sign above them.

"Oh yes," Mrs. Shelfmore said, patting Norma Jean's arm. "It's probably named for President Monroe." A second later she added, "We're Democrats. We both grew up not too far from Harry Truman's hometown."

By this time Norma Jean had calmed down and introduced herself as "Martha Lincoln." Perhaps it was only the bright sunshine in her eyes; but the moment she had seen that street sign with the name "Monroe" on it she could have sworn the strange woman peered around the corner at them. Or at her. Still wearing that navy blue suit and white blouse and carrying a black handbag on her arm.

"We want to see this picture called 'American Gothic,'" Mrs. Shelfmore announced once inside the museum. "Connie—that's our daughter—told us not to miss it." And so the trio went searching for the farmer and his wife and the prominent pitchfork. The museum was uncrowded; in fact, parts of it were nearly deserted. Walking in the direction indicated by a guard, they passed through enormous galleries where the life of the past was frozen in tableaux along the walls.

They passed Rembrandt's "Young Girl at an Open Half-Door." A few minutes later, still in search of the biggest crowd-pleaser in American art, they walked in front of Renoir's "On the Terrace." Down a long corridor Norma Jean saw a familiar painting, one she had often gazed at in her art book. Ladies wearing bustles and long skirts and holding parasols; gentlemen in black top hats; children, dogs, a monkey—all in relaxed formality beside a lake—Seurat's "Sunday Afternoon on the Island of La Grande Jatte." She was astonished that it was so large; the reproduction in her book had given no indication that the painting was so big you could take a stroll through it.

"Oh, Mrs. Shelfmore, and Mr. Shelfmore, will you excuse me, please? Down there," she said, pointing, "is a painting I'm crazy about. It's scrumptious!" She arranged to follow on a bit later and catch up with the Shelfmores as they stood in front of "American Gothic."

As usual a small crowd surrounded Seurat's sixty-seven-square-foot canvas filled with millions of colored dots. Norma Jean joined the circle of admirers. The soft colors, the peaceful scene, the tranquil gathering of Parisians beside the water kept her transfixed. Remembering her promise to join the Shelfmores, she backed away reluctantly, paused to look a while longer, then turned again down the long corridor through which she had come. Halfway down the corridor she turned to look at the painting once more. It now seemed even brighter in contrast with the dull gray light in the long hallway.

A door marked "Private" opened a crack while Norma Jean's head was turned for a final look at the picture. Someone flipped a switch that made the corridor even darker, and suddenly the door opened wider.

A silhouette wearing a navy blue skirt walked briskly out the door. Norma Jean, hearing the click of heels, turned in time to see a small silver pistol held in the woman's large hand. A low voice: "Say one word and you're dead. Get in here."

The large hand was on her, pulling her coat, which she had removed and draped over her shoulders. The pull became stronger and stronger as she tried to move. The woman's other hand grasped her arm just above the elbow. For a moment she was frozen in place, unable to move or speak. She could only shuffle her feet on the polished floor in a vain attempt to escape.

The woman dragged her closer and closer to the door marked "Private," released the coat and clapped a hand over Norma Jean's mouth. Silence returned to the obscure passageway. The scene was preposterous and yet somehow appropriate to a museum: the weird struggle was not unlike Laocoon and his sons gripped by the knot of suffocating serpents. Norma Jean, like an unsuspecting forest creature, was about to be swallowed by the iron jaws of a snake. A very professional snake.

"Miss Lincoln! Miss Lincoln . . ." the familiar voice came caroling down the corridor. "Mr. Shelfmore and I—" Astonished at the scuffle taking place in the dignified marble halls of culture, Mrs. Shelfmore stopped speaking, then turned to her husband. "Let's go," she said, and hurried toward Norma Jean's attacker.

Seeing Bertha Shelfmore's approach, and the ex-Boy Scout a foot behind her, Norma Jean managed to regain her balance. She shoved, she wriggled and flailed her arms, at the same time beginning to scream.

Removing a metal comb from her purse, Bertha attacked the attacker, scraping some face skin. "The idea," she called out. "Take your hands off her this instant—"

Horace Shelfmore, less excitable than his wife, merely

pushed, but his efficient pressure freed Norma Jean from the arms of the assailant. The woman in the blue suit scrambled up from the floor and took off in the opposite direction, leaving her handbag behind.

The ruckus, whose echoes rang down the hallways and through neighboring galleries, had finally brought two museum guards. "I've never seen such a thing in my life," Mrs. Shelfmore said to the guards. "She attacked poor Miss Lincoln while our backs were turned."

"Yes, and she went that way," added Horace.

One guard went after her, the other asked Norma Jean if she was okay.

"Yes, I think so. I was right, she *has* been following me."

"Following you?" said Bertha. "Dear me."

"I'll call the police," the guard said.

"Oh, no, please don't," Norma Jean said quickly. "If it's all the same to you I'd rather forget about it. She's some weirdo who's been after me since I got here. I just want to get out of town—the sooner the better. If you call the police I could be stuck here for days."

"Well, if you're sure you're not hurt . . ."

"No, I'm fine and dandy," she said. "But I wouldn't be if these wonderful people hadn't rescued me." She embraced Mrs. Shelfmore and kissed her on both cheeks. Then she hugged Mr. Shelfmore, who said, "Think nothing of it."

Examining the handbag dropped by the assailant, the guard found nothing but a piece of crumpled yellow paper with a cryptic message: "Poison Ivy. Chicago. Extreme prejudice." He scrutinized the pencilled words, then passed the note to Norma Jean. "Any idea what it means?" the guard asked.

Norma Jean had heard the phrase before. Not "Poison Ivy," though. As far as she knew, it just meant something that itched. But Jack had mentioned "extreme prejudice" at a secret rendezvous in Los Angeles . . . he had tried to explain to her why Fidel Castro's very existence represented a threat. "Why can't you just ignore Castro as long as he doesn't make trouble?" she asked. "Come on," Jack had said, "he's like a time bomb on our doorstep. If we don't eliminate him, he'll explode. No, the only solution is extreme prejudice." She was shocked. "But what about civil rights, and Freedom Riders, and sit-ins?" "No," he laughed, "*extreme prejudice* is a code word. It means, in the vernacular, to bump somebody off."

Norma Jean signaled Mrs. Shelfmore by tilting her head slightly in a gesture that meant "Let's get out of here." Outside, she explained the ominous meaning of the message.

"Why would anyone want to harm you, Miss Lincoln?" asked Mrs. Shelfmore, incredulous.

"It's a long story," Norma Jean said. "If I make it to New York I'll be safe. I mean, I can wear disguises, change everything about myself. Throw these people off the track. They'll never find me again."

"Can we help?" asked Mr. Shelfmore.

Before Norma Jean could answer, Bertha Shelfmore demonstrated her presence of mind once more. "We're like sitting ducks here on the sidewalk. That . . . that *person* may still be around."

Mr. Shelfmore hailed a cab and instructed the driver to take them in circles for a quarter hour, ostensibly so that the three tourists could have a look at Chicago. It was his wife's idea. From reading mysteries and watching them on television, she knew the importance of giving the slip when you're being followed.

After a long powwow at their hotel, they decided on a course of action.

CHAPTER

19

"Train Flying Round the Bend"

Winter covered the Midwest like a white feather comforter. With Thanksgiving out of the way, shopkeepers in the little town beside the Missouri River rushed to display Christmas spirit. Fancy wreaths hung on every shop door. Inside were evergreen trees freighted with colored lights and gold and silver ornaments, with stacks of beribboned boxes piled underneath.

Prices had been marked up for the season of joy. But not in Horace Shelfmore's hardware store. Prices there were the same as in July. Honest Horace, he might have touted himself in advertisements if he had been less modest. The Shelfmores, however, did not have to advertise. They were well known for the quality of their goods and for the good will of their business. Customers came from all over the small town, and from distant farms, to trade at the H&B Hardware and Dry Goods Store.

Early in December Bertha Shelfmore had taped last year's Christmas cards across the large window at the front of the store, spelling out "Merry Christmas" in Hallmark art. That done, she had spent the rest of the afternoon tying red ribbons on the handles of shovels, rakes and hoes. She had not, however, decorated a tree. She and Horace felt it somehow gaudy to put up a Christmas tree in the store. For many years they had trimmed one tree, and only one, and that was in their living room.

Although Christmas Eve was still several weeks away, the Shelfmores glowed with happiness. They believed, perhaps more sincerely than any of their neighbors, that it was more blessed to give than to receive. And, indeed, they had given.

Norma Jean had five hundred dollars in cash and a train ticket, compliments of Aunt Bertha and Uncle Horace. She had asked for nothing. They had done too much for her already. But an hour after she announced that she must move on, the bills and the one-way ticket from Kansas City to Washington were in her hand.

"Thank you ever so," she said, embracing them both. "I'd like nothing better than to stay here forever." But she had already explained about searching for her destiny, for who she was. Aunt Bertha and Uncle Horace understood.

"Dear Martha"—she remained Martha Lincoln to the Shelfmores—"you can stay here forever anytime you want." Mrs. Shelfmore, unconsciously, had picked up some of Norma Jean's way of talking. Mr. Shelfmore, echoing his wife, said, "When you get fed up with the big city come back out here. Spend two weeks or forever, whichever you like."

"You're both living dolls," Norma Jean said. "If you hadn't saved my life, who knows where I'd be right now. Why, I might have sprouted wings right there in the museum."

On that Indian summer day in late October, the Shelfmores had convinced her that the only safe thing was to come home with them. Norma Jean had resisted, telling them she was in a rush to get to New York. "And I really couldn't impose. Besides, you'd soon get tired of me. I'm a slob, I can't seem to pick up one thing off the floor without dropping half a dozen others."

"Nonsense," Mrs. Shelfmore had answered. "Our daughter's room is just waiting for you. She's married and lives in Hawaii, and you're invited to stay as long as you want. Absolutely no imposition at all, Miss Lincoln. But you can't stay in Chicago. Not with that madwoman chasing you."

"An armed madwoman," Mr. Shelfmore amended.

And so it had been settled.

Since moving in with the Shelfmores, Norma Jean had learned about tranquility and composure. For the first time in years she felt safe. She had outsmarted her tormentors again, and apparently this time they had lost the scent.

The rhythm of life in a small Missouri town had changed little in a hundred years. If Mark Twain had returned he would have felt right at home. The long unhurried days gave Norma Jean time to relax—without drugs, something she had never before accomplished in her adult life. Sleep, too, came easily and unbidden. Sometimes she slept seamlessly for fourteen hours.

But her greatest pleasure came from the presence of other human beings around her—undemanding, uncritical friends whose kindness concealed no ulterior motives. She had never realized how a pleasant morning could direct the course of the day. Most of her life she had awakened in a drug haze, faced a husband or a housekeeper, then a set full of frantic studio employees whose every word, every move jangled her nerves and increased her paranoia.

The contrast here was astonishing. When she awoke around nine-thirty, Uncle Horace had left for the hardware store but Aunt Bertha was usually reading the newspaper or knitting by a warm fire in the parlor. "Good morning, Martha," she greeted Norma Jean without fail. "How about . . ." And each day the breakfast menu changed. Eggs, bacon, toast with steaming coffee or hot chocolate was the perennial favorite, Norma Jean's as well as the Shelfmores'. But on other days Aunt Bertha brought out country ham with grits, or a basket of warm bran muffins loaded with raisins. She made tea in a big white porcelain teapot, which reminded Norma Jean of delicious tea in England when she was filming "The Prince and the Showgirl." Somehow it tasted even better in Missouri.

These breakfasts stayed a while; Norma Jean could have skipped lunch most days but Aunt Bertha wouldn't hear of it. "You don't eat enough to keep a kitten alive," she chided, even though Norma Jean's waist demonstrated otherwise. Her appetite had rebelled against years of dieting; now it demanded large portions at breakfast, again at lunch and once more at dinner. As best she could calculate she had gained ten pounds in the past month and a half, with the result that she looked more womanly than ever before. Curvaceous, buxom, voluptuous—these were the words gossip columnists and fan magazine writers would have used if they had seen her. And yet Norma Jean's ripeness differed from the overripe Marilyn of "The Misfits." In that last sad movie, Marilyn's skin, hair and eyes seemed in decline. Her bones were pushing through.

Now Norma Jean's skin glowed, her eyes were lustrous, and her hair—was auburn!

Aunt Bertha suggested it. "Before you go back out in the world, Martha, I want you to look as different as possible. Just in case. Mind you, I'm not trying to frighten you. But better safe than sorry." Meaning the woman in Chicago.

Norma Jean picked out a dark auburn shade. The best beautician in town applied it, and when Norma Jean looked at herself in the mirror she laughed. "Now I'm Arlene Dahl," she exclaimed. "But if the tip of my nose stuck up a little higher I'd look like Susan Hayward."

"The main thing," said Aunt Bertha, "is that any roughneck looking for a blonde won't give you a second look."

A few days later Aunt Bertha and Uncle Horace drove her to Kansas City to take the train. "Don't forget to write," they said on the cold station platform. Aunt Bertha wiped her eyes with a lacy white handkerchief, and Uncle Horace reminded Norma Jean that she could come back—"back *home*," he said—anytime she wanted.

"Merry Christmas, Happy New Year," called the Shelfmores as the huge black train puffed steam, then chugged out of the station.

"Thanks again for everything," Norma Jean called through the closed train window. Uncle Horace put a hand over his ear, signaling her that he hadn't understood.

"Thank you ever so," she enunciated, putting her mouth against the glass and exaggerating the movement of her lips. Aunt Bertha nodded vigorously, then turned to repeat Martha's last words to her husband. The whistle blew, long and shrill, and the train accelerated. "Maybe I should stay," Norma Jean thought as the station slid out of sight and the brightly lighted train pushed into the darkness of late afternoon. "I may never find such a happy home again."

* * *

Early the following morning she changed trains in St. Louis. At the newsstand she saw a familiar face on the cover of Motion Picture. The same face appeared on Photoplay, Silver Screen and half a dozen others. On every magazine, beside the face or under it, bold, black cover lines announced mournful tributes inside: "Hollywood Tragedy: Marilyn's Dying Wish," read one. On another, "The Sad, Lonely Death of Marilyn Monroe." She looked through several of the fan publications. Reading about herself—her *former* self—made her shiver. These reports at least proved that Marilyn had been loved and that she wasn't forgotten.

Even Hedda Hopper had a good word to say; now that she could no longer mistreat Marilyn, her entire column this month was a memorial. "In a way we are all guilty," she wrote. "We built her to the skies. We loved her, but left her lonely and afraid when she needed us most."

Reading these pious words, Norma Jean imagined watching a movie with the wrong soundtrack playing. What if "Moulin Rouge" were projected on the screen with Zsa Zsa Gabor singing her heart out in great earnestness while the music you heard was Debbie Reynolds and Carleton Carpenter racing through "Aba Daba Honeymoon."

Her smiled twitched, she couldn't stop it. She pursed her lips but couldn't control the merriment. Even when she clapped her hand over her mouth like a geisha it didn't help; the giggle spilled out. A second later she was helpless with laughter while the salesgirl and three or four customers looked at her curiously.

The distinguished gentleman nearest her at the magazine rack looked her way. He smiled, too, vicariously enjoying her amusement. "I can't help it," she said, dissolving again into laughter.

"A funny joke, eh?"

"The old bat hated me while I was alive. Now she can't say enough nice things." Wiping her eyes, Norma Jean realized that the gentleman seemed perplexed and then suddenly uneasy. He took a step back. "Oh, I didn't mean it that way," she said, not wanting to draw attention. "What I mean is, there's a woman in

Hollywood who was after me. That is, she wormed all my secrets out of me, then told them."

"I see," said the man, walking briskly to the cashier to pay for his purchase.

"So, they think I'm a freak," thought Norma Jean. During her years in Hollywood she had tried to be as normal as possible but it never worked. Her attempts to conform, to blend into the Hollywood crowd only made her stand out. For instance, when she told interviewers what she thought they wanted to hear, everyone reacted as though she were the funniest woman alive. A reporter, asking about the famous nude calendar pose, said, "Didn't you have anything on?" and she replied truthfully, "Oh yes, I had the radio on." For years, literally years, writers quoted her remark as though it were equal to "Frankly, my dear, I don't give a damn," or "I'd like to kiss you but I just washed my hair."

But she wasn't funny, she thought. Not really. Carole Lombard was funny, Lucille Ball was funny, she was not like them. Another time, on the set of "The Seven-Year Itch," she ad libbed a line that caused uproarious laughter at the premiere and reportedly everywhere the movie was shown. "My fan is caught in the door," was all she said. She said it because her fan really was caught in the door, but the director, the producer and everyone else loved it so it stayed in.

Well, Marilyn had tried to act normal and it didn't work. So now she, Norma Jean, wanted to be herself for a change. "Let people think I'm weird if they want to. The things I've been through lately, I'm lucky I don't have the screaming meemies," she thought.

All day she read and wrote as the train crossed the flat belly of America. Illinois, Indiana and finally, late in the day, Ohio. The new play she had bought in Denver, *Who's Afraid of Virginia Woolf*, was sensational. She had intentionally saved it, even though she could have read it a hundred times at the Shelfmores. But it somehow seemed fitting to read a play on the last leg of her journey. Or the next-to-last leg, since she was making a detour through Washington on her way to New York. She read the play for the first time in the morning, then again in the afternoon. She hoped it was still playing on Broadway. If only she could have played Martha—sad, funny, a walking wound full of salt. "And I could play her, too," Norma Jean wrote in her notebook. "I know I could."

She had chosen a new name. Between performances of the play—for she had more than read it, she had acted it out in her head the way she had re-enacted movies as a child—she had taken as her alias the name Georgia Philco from the Shelfmore's Philco television set. It reminded her of one of the characters she had played in the movies. She also knew the importance of a memorable moniker. How many times had she heard Hollywood agents, directors, publicists and actors haggle over a name—the number of letters in it and whether they would fit onto a marquee; the letter beginning the last name, in case a contract stipulated alphabetical billing; the sound, the rhythm, the sex appeal of a name. It was an art, and some names stood out as masterpieces: Rock Hudson, John Wayne, Theda Bara, Rita Hayworth . . . Marilyn Monroe.

Of course, Broadway names were never as flashy as Hollywood handles. Jessica Tandy, Alfred Lunt, Lynn Fontanne—these names shone like polished oak, while Hollywood names glittered like sequins. She had noticed years before in New York that supporting actors' names always sounded made up even when they weren't. She recalled Hortense McGinnis, Lil Vanderpool, Evans Shapiro—all of them actors who worked steadily in New York theater, at least when she lived there in the fifties.

So maybe Georgia Philco could get work too. As long as nobody ever found out about that other name, the one that used to glitter like sequins until it was smashed and then buried in a crypt in Westwood.

"What are you doing?" the little girl asked. She stood calmly in the aisle as the train lurched over an especially rough piece of track. Her large, penetrating eyes took in Norma Jean and the books, pens and notebooks spread carelessly on the seat beside her.

"Hello there." ("I wish you were my little girl," she thought.) "My, you're pretty. I'm reading a play and I'm writing things in my notebook."

"What are you writing?"

"I'm writing my name."

"That's funny." The little girl giggled. "Why're you writing your name?"

"So I won't forget it," Norma Jean said, and they both covered their mouths and giggled together.

"I hope she's not bothering you," the girl's mother said, reaching out a hand to her daughter. "She just woke up from a long nap and now I'm afraid she wants to socialize."

"She's adorable," Norma Jean said. "And we're having a nice talk, aren't we, honey?"

"Yes," replied the child with a grownup nod. Then, "What's your name?"

"Why, my name's Georgia," said Norma Jean. "What's yours?"

"Marilyn," said the little girl.

Norma Jean looked stunned, as though the child had uttered a profanity. Finally she managed a weak "Oh, how nice."

"We named her for Marilyn Monroe," the mother explained. "My husband and I saw 'The Prince and the Showgirl' a few days before she was born. He wanted to name her Elsie, after the character Marilyn played but I told him that name didn't stand out. Lots of girls are named Elsie. But Marilyn—if we named her that it would always remind people of Marilyn Monroe."

Norma Jean nodded, and looked out the window, trying to regain her composure.

"Poor Marilyn," the young woman said. "I still can't believe she's dead. I've seen all her movies."

Her husband strolled up, holding onto seatbacks as the speeding train rolled and twisted across Ohio. A few lighted houses beside the railroad tracks, a blur as the depot disappeared, and on they went.

"Marilyn, are you ready to eat?" he said, and Norma Jean said, "Yes, I'm quite hungry—" Then realizing, she said hurriedly, "Well, I don't know about Marilyn, but I'm really famished. Shall we go to the dining car?"

The husband and wife were in their late twenties. He was

Dennis and she was Amy; they would spend the holidays with his parents in Delaware, then take the train back to their suburban home in Indiana.

"It's so interesting," commented Norma Jean. "I mean, that you named her for an actress. And such a famous one, too."

"My mother-in-law didn't like the idea too much," Amy said with a smile. "She's a devout Catholic and she said Marilyn Monroe was a sinful woman."

"I'm glad we didn't listen to Mom," Dennis said. "Marilyn's a prettier name than Elsie, which is the one I chose as a compromise."

"I don't know the details of . . . of Marilyn Monroe," Norma Jean said. "You see, I've been away. On a ranch. There wasn't even a television."

"Say, you really *have* been away," Dennis said.

"The end of the world." A moment later, trying to appear nonchalant, she asked, "What do you think she died of?"

Amy and Dennis told her as much as they knew—the newspaper accounts, the television reports, the special network programs about Marilyn Monroe's life and career—and her death. "I finished ironing early that Monday, made Dennis's dinner and turned on Huntley and Brinkley," Amy said. "I was going to watch a few minutes of the news until Dennis came home. And there it was. I'll never forget it. A picture of Marilyn the first thing. David Brinkley looked a lot more solemn than usual. He said something like, 'Marilyn Monroe, one of Hollywood's legendary stars, was found dead early yesterday in her Los Angeles home, an apparent suicide.'"

She paused, letting sadness sweep over her again. No death, it seemed, was sweeter than the death of a movie star.

"I couldn't stop crying. I cried all through dinner," she said. "I hugged Marilyn. She started crying too."

Norma Jean, feeling uncomfortable before such undraped emotions, asked about the funeral. "Did the President make a statement?" she asked suddenly.

Dennis, puzzled, looked at Amy. "Did we hear anything about that on the news?" his wife asked him. Then, answering her own question, "No, I don't think so. But Joe DiMaggio cried at her funeral—we saw it on TV. His son, Joe DiMaggio, Jr., walked beside him." Recalling more and more, Amy went on, "Her lawyer and her friends—they wanted the funeral private. You know, to keep out curiosity seekers and the like. So only a dozen or so got in. Invitation only. Let's see, now, on television they interviewed all kinds of stars. Jane Russell gave a statement, Betty Grable, Frank Sinatra, Jack Benny, Dean Martin—you know, he was making a picture with Marilyn when the studio fired her last summer."

"A lot of directors and producers and big shots were interviewed," Dennis said. "It went on for days. And you know, another sad thing was, nobody claimed the body for the longest time. About a week went by before it was claimed."

"Oh," came out of Norma Jean's mouth, although she seemed not to have spoken. She looked very troubled. Finally she asked, "Who claimed it—her, I mean?"

Neither Dennis nor Amy could say. "Was it Joe DiMaggio?" Dennis asked. "No, it was somebody else connected with her, but I can't remember who," Amy said. "A woman, maybe."

"Paula Strasberg?" Norma Jean asked. "Not Mrs. Bridwell! Oh no! Not her." Realizing she was now fishing in troubled waters, she asked no further questions. *Me and my big mouth*, she thought. *I'd better not know too much if I know what's good for me.*

She had eaten mechanically, scarcely tasting the food she put in her mouth. Little Marilyn was sleepily munching a cookie, her mouth lined with brown crumbs.

Norma Jean looked at her, finding solace in the child's innocence from the grotesque details of that recent death in Hollywood. Little Marilyn, pleased with this sign of adult attention after so much uninteresting grownup talk, said "You're pretty."

"Why, thanks. So are you."

"Up, little girl," her father said. "Time for a goodnight story."

They heard a long, shrill whistle from the engine four or five cars ahead. They were walking away from it. It was just as Dennis turned to comment about the loud, prolonged whistle that a tree plunged through the heavy glass window at the end of the brightly lit dining car. Glass rained on them like sleet, except that it wasn't falling from above. It flew furiously in from the darkness outside the train. Norma Jean hurtled through space toward the wall at the opposite end of the dining car. She flailed her arms, struggling to regain her balance. It was like dropping an object and trying to snatch it before it crashed to the ground. This time, the object was herself.

Her grasping fingers caught nothing stronger than a starched tablecloth as the impact of the crash hurled her body across tables and chairs. She had time to wonder why the bright lights flickered once and then went out. And however did those tough, massive pieces of steel scrunch up like a beer can?

Plates and cups seemed released from gravity as they hit her like baseballs thrown in a carnival game. Where was the child? Where was Marilyn? Unable to find the little girl who had been holding her hand just a second ago, Norma Jean covered her head with her arms.

Then she was dropping down, down a great empty hole like Alice tumbling into Wonderland.

When help arrived half an hour later the police and ambulance attendants heard groans and screams from the engine to the observation car. The quiet Ohio night had changed into a cacophony of sirens and whizzing motors and machinery chopping up the train in search of the dead and wounded. A reporter from the local newspaper wrote on his pad: "The nine passenger cars folded into each other like an accordion."

Heavy casualties and odd maimings transformed the nearby wheat fields and apple orchards into a hellish Hieronymous Bosch landscape. Bodies—dead and alive—were laid side by side under the bare apple branches on one side of the track. On the other side, in the wheat stubble, more bodies. Some of these crawled, even walked upright. Eventually the walking wounded fell to the ground and lay silent.

Pulling an elderly gentleman from a sleeping car, a policeman discovered a hairbrush sticking out of his forehead. The gentleman's last activity was frozen in time, embedded in his flesh like a horn. A stout middle-aged lady screamed, "Put on the brakes, Henry, put on the brakes." No one stopped to comfort her. At least she wasn't bleeding, although the horror of it had driven her out of her mind.

In the dining car rescuers discovered the waiter, a black man of fifty with graying temples. His arm was severed at the elbow. His hand, discovered later, still held a menu between two bloody fingers.

A young man who looked to be in his twenties, and a woman about the same age, were unconscious but still breathing. As the woman was loaded into an ambulance with several others, she moaned. Trying to speak, she said something that sounded like "Mar Line, Mar Line." No one had time to question her. She was unable to say more, unable to ask if Marilyn, her little girl, was all right.

Using axes, saws and blowtorches rescuers eventually opened a corridor in the Pullman behind the dining car. There, under mangled steel beams and frayed cables, they found a child wedged under a seat. The delicate body was pitched into its corner by the force of a railroad train skidding on and off the tracks. As one car buckled into another, making the train warp like plastic over a flame, only the laws of physics remained constant. All else was chaos. But the primeval laws of motion, force and resistance held true, mindless and pitiless, mixing steel, glass and flesh into a hideous concoction. Little Marilyn was not breathing.

CHAPTER

20

"Between Disasters"

In the white hospital room the woman lay very still, as though in a deep sleep. Her arms were stretched beside her, undamaged. Her legs, too, though covered by a sheet, appeared whole. Auburn hair framed her face, which looked the same as yesterday except for a large bandage on her left cheek and a smaller one covering her chin.

When the doctor entered she slept on. He touched her shoulder, then clasped her hand. She opened her eyes. "Hello," he said. "How do you feel today?"

"I can't go on. I forgot my lines," she groaned. Then, dimly recalling the scene before the lights went out, she asked, "Where's Marilyn?"

"Who is Marilyn?" asked the doctor. A nurse had now joined him at the bedside.

"A little girl," the patient answered.

"Is she your daughter?" asked the nurse, holding the hand which the doctor had released in order to write notes in the patient's chart.

"No, I don't have a daughter. I don't have anything left."

"Can you tell us your name?" the doctor asked. He looked at her closely, interested in this woman who had survived with only superficial injuries.

"What's in a name?" she said, closing her eyes and smiling as though someone had told her a funny joke at bedtime that she hoped to remember in her dreams.

Stay awake just a few seconds longer if you can," said the nurse. "Can you help us a bit? We need to find out who you are, where you're from."

". . . Georgia Philco," came the faint reply. But she was too sleepy to hold her eyes open. She wanted to ask these people if they'd excuse her because it was time to go back into that hole where she had slept for a long long time.

"Where do you live, Miss Philco? Can you remember?"

"I'm from out of town."

The doctor smiled. "Yes, we know that. Can you tell us *where* out of town you're from?"

"Aunt Bertha and Uncle Horace—" She stopped, waited, then resumed—"put me on the train in Kansas City." A heavy sigh, followed by, "That was before Christmas. I've had some bad luck. Is it after Christmas now?"

"No, don't worry about that. Today is December fourteenth, nineteen sixty-two. Can you remember Aunt Bertha's phone number?"

No, that was unfair. She had questions of her own. "What about Marilyn? And Norma Jean?" Not waiting for an answer she quickly told the doctor, "I'm not taking any medications. No drugs at all. But I did have my appendix removed some years ago." Someone had told her, or maybe she had read it, that in case of emergency you should always tell the doctor your medical history. Boy, it'll take a while to tell him mine, she said to herself.

"I believe you're improving," said the doctor. "Let's take one thing at a time. Who is Marilyn?"

"The little girl."

"On the train?"

"Yes. How did you know?"

"Do you remember what happened to you?"

"Not exactly. Did they try to bury me again?"

The doctor stopped writing in the patient's chart. "Who?" he asked.

"Oh, nobody. Please tell me what happened. But if it's too, too terrible, make up a story. You know, a girl likes to have a little relief between disasters."

"Miss . . . Philco, you are definitely improving. And your attitude is good. Yes, you could call it a disaster but you survived. And you're going to be all right."

He took her hand again; warmth radiated from his skin to hers. "Now, I know you don't feel like talking, but there's one thing you must try to remember. We need to telephone your aunt and uncle. For two reasons. You'll recover faster if you have family members nearby. Also, we need to consult them about doing a bit of cosmetic surgery on your face. If we don't take care of it soon, you might not be as pretty as you . . . are now."

Norma Jean wondered if this was a dentist. Dentists always woke her up just as she drifted off to sleep under the influence of their drugs and her own. "Open wide" or "Close down" or "Bite": dentists never failed to issue one of these commands the minute she relaxed. Now this one wanted phone numbers.

She told him the name of their town. "You'll have to look it up," she said groggily. "They are the . . . Shelfmores."

"Yes, this is Mrs. Shelfmore. Bertha Shelfmore speaking." A long pause as the doctor filled her in. "You don't say. Yes, I heard about the accident on the news. But I don't know a soul by that name."

The doctor described his patient. "Why, I can't *believe* it. It sounds exactly like Martha."

"My patient said her Aunt Bertha and Uncle Horace took her to the train in Kansas City," the doctor said.

"That *must* be her. It's got to be Martha. I'll be there as soon as possible." Even as she said it, she was looking around for belongings to pack. "Tell me, doctor," she said. "Do you think airplanes are safe? I've never been in one, but it seems to me this is a matter of life and death."

The doctor assured her that she couldn't find safer transportation. He also said that it wasn't such a dire emergency that she must come by air.

"Tell Martha I'll be at her bedside before dark."

Mrs. Shelfmore sat bolt upright in row twelve, seat D. She wore a new hat trimmed with dark silk begonias and a wisp of veil. Her matching blue suit, handbag, gloves and pumps were suitable for a funeral, or the next worst thing, a train wreck. Bertha Shelfmore's mother had brought her up to wear dark clothing during a crisis. Somber colors might somehow mitigate the upheavals in life's smooth flow. If not, they were at least appropriate for grief, should mourning become necessary.

She might have been in the front row at church, under the preacher's direct gaze. She paid attention to every word, every sound, every rustle and click. As the plane gathered speed she opened her handbag and took out the small black book that she kept on her night stand. Opening it at random, she tried to concentrate on the words: "And I saw an angel come down from heaven, having the key of the bottomless pit and a great chain in his hand. And he laid hold on the dragon, that old serpent, which is the Devil, and Satan, and bound him a thousand years." She closed her Bible and put it back in her bag. The Book of Revelation was too stimulating; it increased her heart rate alarmingly. She was now in the air, high above the world where she had spent her life. How could she be sure of coming down?

"Ladies and gentlemen, in a short while we'll be landing in Columbus, Ohio. At this time the captain has requested . . ."

Bertha Shelfmore hit the ground running. The travel agency at home had arranged not only her flight but transportation to the hospital and a hotel room to receive her afterward.

"Martha, what a terrible thing," said Mrs. Shelfmore at the bedside. She grasped Norma Jean's hands, then leaned down to kiss her. "You're lucky to be alive. You don't have any broken bones, I hope."

"Aunt Bertha! How did you get here so fast?"

Mrs. Shelfmore explained it all. She assured Norma Jean

that she planned to stay until every hurt was healed, every bandage removed. "The doctor mentioned plastic surgery," she said. "I don't know a thing in the world about it. Is that what you want? Won't it ruin your looks?"

Norma Jean repeated what the doctor had told her. The cuts must be taken care of; otherwise large ugly scars would zigzag across her cheek and down to her chin. Her face would look like somebody had carved his initials in it.

She motioned for Aunt Bertha to lean down. Norma Jean whispered, "Tell then I want a couple of other changes, too. In case you-know-who is still after me."

"I couldn't agree more," replied Mrs. Shelfmore. "A very wise precaution." An hour later it was all arranged with the doctor. Early the next morning, a surgeon smoothed Norma Jean's wounds like wiping smudges from a mirror. In addition, he snipped off the black beauty mole. While sculpting the injured face he tightened some of the skin that had begun to creep down her jawbone. A nip and tuck to the chin widened it a few centimeters at its narrow point. A turn of the scalpel narrowed it ever so slightly where nature made it wide. When the job was done, all that remained was the healing.

"Not much more than a haircut," the surgeon assured her when she woke up.

"What?" asked Mrs. Shelfmore, hovering at the bedside.

"You know how a little bit of hair removed from the front or the sides makes you look different for a few days," he explained. "Well, it's the same with a little bit of skin. Cut a little here, sew it back on there, and voila! a new look for spring." Mrs. Shelfmore wondered if all plastic surgeons were so lighthearted.

Norma Jean, remembering how a nose bob had improved Marilyn's looks long ago, was eager to see her new face. The surgeon warned her, however, that complete healing would not come for weeks. "But," he added, "you'll be out of here in a week. Your face will retain some black and blue—a shade I call 'heart disease purple.'" He winked conspiratorially at her. "If anybody asks what happened, just say you were in a cat fight." With that, he was out of the room, leaving Norma Jean and Mrs. Shelfmore with a new impression of a bedside manner.

Mrs. Shelfmore sat beside the bed, accompanied Norma Jean on walks up and down the hospital corridors, brushed her hair, read to her, brought in fresh flowers. In a week, as the surgeon had promised, she was out of the hospital.

The offer tempted her—Aunt Bertha's invitation to spend Christmas, even the rest of the winter, in Missouri. But Norma Jean, after all, was only twenty years old; or so she had convinced herself since that day back in Denver when she realized that Marilyn had departed, taking with her the sixteen-year occupancy of Norma Jean's body. Like every girl of twenty, Norma Jean couldn't wait to go into the world. Her destiny beckoned—if she squinted, she could almost see it bending its finger, gesturing "come here."

Like millions of other girls, Marilyn had been bitten by the show-biz bug. Now it was Norma Jean's turn. She tried to explain this to Aunt Bertha, but it was no easy thing to do, especially since she couldn't mention Marilyn and those sixteen years. But finally Aunt Bertha said, "Well, my dear, if you need us, all you have to do is call."

Norma Jean's belongings had been found in the wreckage of the train and brought to her hospital room. Mrs. Shelfmore helped her pack, and they parted again. "But not for long, I hope," said the fairy godmother from Missouri. "Remember, my dear, if you wish hard enough I'll appear." She smiled. "And don't you dare lose the telephone number. I'm as close as your phone."

CHAPTER

21

"The Ghost of Christmas Yet to Come"

The Washington Monument loomed like a giant icicle. Stark and cold, it dared anyone to approach. No one did. Who would think of visiting it on Christmas Day, anyway?

Norma Jean regarded it from a distance. She had spent an hour, from noon to one o'clock, in the Lincoln Memorial. During that hour she had talked with President Lincoln. She wanted to let him know how much she admired him. She recited the Gettysburg Address without once looking at the text carved into one wall of the memorial. She had memorized it long ago because she loved the ringing cadences of Mr. Lincoln's language.

She remembered snatches of his speeches, letters and addresses from her reading. "With malice toward none, with charity for all, let us strive on to finish the work we are in," she said, looking up into the enormous marble face of her hero. These words reminded her of Brentwood long ago, and home. They conjured up a more ominous association, too—the day she told Bobby Kennedy off. Yes, she told him off, then went to her bedroom, where she sought comfort looking at President Lincoln's picture. That summer day she had said these very words aloud: "With malice toward none . . ."

"With malice toward Marilyn," she muttered now. "Please excuse me," she said quickly, again looking up at his gigantic face.

"But it's the truth. I'm just being honest. Like you, Mr. President."

Her infatuation with President Lincoln had lasted much longer than the one with President Kennedy. She'd never bothered to memorize one of Jack's speeches, but she knew by heart passages from Lincoln and used them depending on the occasion. Like the opening lines from his Farewell Address: "No one, not in my situation, can appreciate my feeling of sadness at this parting."

That's how I feel, too, she thought, waving a reluctant goodbye to Honest Abe. She descended the staircase and walked onto the dry brown grass beside the Reflecting Pool. For the first time in years she recalled what a journalist had written when she married Arthur: "La Monroe thinks Abraham Lincoln is the sexiest man in the history of the U. S. of A. Could it be that's why she is attracted to Arthur Miller? After all, the famous playwright is long and lanky, just like Abe, and if he had a long black beard the resemblance would be striking."

She walked around the Tidal Basin to the Jefferson Memorial without seeing a soul. By the time she returned to the Mall, the afternoon was waning and she still hadn't made it to the White House. Half a dozen people now strolled on the Mall, trying to walk off their holiday meals of turkey and fruitcake. "Merry Christmas," said a tweedy gentleman smoking a pipe. His wife, a few paces behind with their golden retriever, smiled at Norma Jean. "Happy Holidays," she called.

"Thank you," Norma Jean answered uncertainly. "And a pleasant Noel to you."

The bare branches of trees on the Mall were full of twittering birds, hungry in Washington's dreary winter. Gray had crept over the city like fog, making museums and government buildings look as lifeless as turnips.

Norma Jean sat on a bench. Her heart told her to look for Jack, her head warned her not to. She had come to Washington in the vain, absurd hope of seeing him. He, of course, would never see her.

But even knowing that the President must be at least partially responsible for her troubles, she still wanted him. Surely he had loved her—otherwise why would he have even considered making her First Lady? Even mentioned it? "And he'd have kept his promise, too, if Bobby hadn't butted in." She wrote that in her notebook. Two squirrels scampered up to her, looking for a handout. Rummaging in her bag, she found half a packet of raisins, which became the squirrels' Christmas pudding.

Nightfall was approaching as she crossed the Ellipse and walked slowly up East Executive Avenue, the road beside the White House. Behind the heavy iron White House fence magnolia trees spread glossy black leaves over the dead lawn. Further on, the gnarled branches of naked hardwoods threatened to seize her like King Kong picking up Fay Wray.

Approaching the guard booth, she detoured to give it a wide berth. For all she knew, the Secret Service might have bloodhounds trained to lunge at her. She pulled her scarf over her face. Nowadays she used this plaid scarf from Aunt Bertha as Spanish ladies used fans—to conceal her features. It would have to be a prop until all evidence of her surgery had disappeared.

She stared at the White House. Upstairs, where he lived, all was dark. Would he be working on Christmas Day? "No, silly, they're all downstairs in the ballroom, where—"

"Can I help you, Miss?" the voice was low, threatening. A guard emerged from the booth, which resembled a white stone cottage with bars on the windows.

"Oh no." She gulped, ready to take off. Then she thought better of it. What if he shot her in the back?

"Is anything the matter?" he asked.

"No speaka English," she muttered, rolling her eyes like Blanche Yurka in "Hitler's Madman." "No speaka, no speaka," she repeated, stiffening a leg to make herself look old and lame as she shuffled away. She pulled her scarf further over her head until she looked like a tartan mummy.

She felt his gaze following her. Half turning, she sniffed indignantly over her shoulders, another gesture borrowed from Miss Yurka.

Rounding the corner onto Pennsylvania Avenue, she glanced back. No one was around her. She walked on until she had an excellent view of the entire North Front of the White House. Water gushed from the fountain. Chandeliers, lamps and floodlights made the President's home as bright as the Pantages Theatre on Oscar night.

The second-story windows, however, were all dark, like blind eyes in a beautiful face. She grasped the iron fence, stepping up to gaze at the house. Where she might have lived?

The chandelier at the far end blazed even brighter. "Jack's probably having Christmas dinner in there right now. With her. I wonder if they've unwrapped the presents." Suddenly the main door opened. "Oh my God, it's the Prez."

She froze. Not able to unclench her hands from the iron railings, she wiggled her feet, attempting to step back down onto Pennsylvania Avenue.

John F. Kennedy glanced absentmindedly across the darkness toward her as she gripped the cold iron bars. Then he smiled at the woman beside him, who wore a sequined crimson gown that lit up the night. Still grasping the fence, Norma Jean squinted; she had never seen Jacqueline Kennedy in person. Like everyone else in the world, she was curious about the First Lady.

She would have liked to wave but couldn't move her hands. "Hey, Prez," she said weakly, "over here." Not a chance he heard her. "Even if he did hear me it wouldn't matter," she told herself. "I'm not the glamor girl he fell for. I'm plain Norma Jean now. I mean, plain Georgia Philco."

She squinted again. "Wait a minute! Jackie Kennedy doesn't have blonde hair . . ." Indeed not, nor was it Jackie Kennedy on the President's arm. The beautiful woman in the dazzling red dress with a diamond tiara on her platinum hair, this woman lighting up Washington with sequins and lipstick was none other than—Marilyn Monroe! Norma Jean watched as the President's eyes crinkled in merriment when he said something to her, and throwing her head back, Marilyn laughed, eyelids lowered, teeth white as the majestic Doric columns rising beside her and her husband the President. Flashbulbs popped all around them, warming the chilly gray air. Marilyn let the white fur stole slip off her shoulder. Leaning forward, she blew a kiss to the photographers. They went wild for her decolletage. She blew another kiss, this one to the whole world. Somewhere out of Norma Jean's sight a band struck up "Hail to the Chief." After a few bars of the rousing march the music changed. As the President helped Marilyn, his one and only First Lady, into the sleek limousine the band was playing "Diamonds Are a Girl's Best Friend." Now Norma Jean saw them in close-up. Their limousine was driving right by the spot where she clung to the fence. Suddenly she seemed to be looking up at a silver screen, with Marilyn and the President projected in Technicolor and she could hear every word they said . . .

"I can be smart. When it's important," Marilyn told him. Norma Jean thought she sounded a lot like Lorelei . . . "You, ah, certainly said the right thing to, ah, Mr. Khrushchev," the President said, beaming at his gorgeous blonde wife. She fluttered her long lashes, her lips trembled seductively . . . "Well," she said in a whispery voice, "he's a man, isn't he?" . . . "Miss Monroe—I mean, darling—I'm sure he feels more a man than ever, now that he's met you." . . . "Oh, Jack, was he enraptured, do you think?" . . . "I *believe*, sweetheart. The whole evening. When he invited you to Moscow and you said, 'I'd adore it to death', I could almost imagine the end of the Cold War and I, ah, have never imagined such an event before."

The music swelled. In the last scene in Norma Jean's movie Marilyn and the President laughed, talked and cuddled in the gleaming black limousine as it rolled out onto Pennsylvania Avenue, crossed the Potomac and drove all the way across America. Finally, in long shot, Marilyn turned and looked out the back window. She waved goodbye to the thousands of fans lining the route. She blew them a kiss. As she waved, Prez leaned over and kissed her cheek. Marilyn smiled and winked at Norma Jean, and the enormous silver screen faded to dark . . .

Out of the corner of her eye Norma Jean saw the man who had growled at her a few moments ago. The one wearing a gun and holster and a shiny badge on his shirt. He hurried toward her, waving his arms and yelling something. *What a rude awakening*, she thought.

The guard was running toward her. More floodlights flashed on; a siren wailed nearby.

"Hey, you," the guard yelled. "Get off that fence."

As he grabbed the tail of her coat she managed to loosen her hands from the iron bars that had magnetized her. "No speaka, no speaka," she said from under the plaid scarf as she bolted into the middle of Pennsylvania Avenue, where because it was Christmas Day no cars whizzed by to knock her down. She ran across Lafayette Square and down a narrow alley beside St. John's Church, not daring to look back until she was sure the bloodhounds were no longer after her.

The holiday dinner seemed more elaborate than usual. Twelve people sat down to a long rectangular oak table. Twenty-three others took their seats at three smaller tables in corners of the large dining room. As the family grew and grew, seating everyone together had become increasingly difficult. Perhaps dining rooms with tables of sufficient size could be found at the Waldorf. Or the White House. No one in the family, however, desired such formality. No, the decision was unanimous: everyone would spend Christmas Day in the informality of home at Hyannis Port.

The unwrapping of gifts would go on for hours and if the weather was mild a game of touch football would spring up on the lawn. Everyone in the family loved the rambling old house on Cape Cod, with its porches and sea breezes, its cozy rooms that seemed to retain political debates and rollicking laughter long after the actual sounds died away.

A car had picked up Cardinal Cushing and whisked him down to the Cape at the end of High Mass in Boston. Rather than kissing his ring, the Kennedys kissed the Cardinal's cheek. No one could remember when he hadn't been one of them. "Jack," the Cardinal said when the President embraced him, "you look splendid. These crises seem a tonic for you, my boy." Cardinal Cushing hadn't seen him since August. He had thought then that Washington was aging Jack rather fast.

"Don't let the, ah, Russians hear you say that. I wouldn't want them preparing another dose of it for the new year."

In Massachusetts winter days fade fast by four o'clock. It was already three-thirty and the Kennedy clan had not yet sat down to Christmas dinner. Noisy children and their noisy parents ignored the dinner bell that Rose Kennedy rang. The clear bell tones had no effect on the hubbub. "Boys," Rose Kennedy announced to her grandchildren. She included granddaughters as well as grandsons in the category of "boys."

She walked through the rooms like a town crier, ringing her bell and repeating with a quavery note of vexation, "Boys! Boys!" Eventually she stopped the loud merriment and made a speech.

Aromas drifted through the room from the distant kitchen. After Rose's speech the Cardinal said grace, and then the first course was served: consommé brunoise, dipped with a silver ladle from a heavy antique tureen.

Rose Kennedy's favorite china, which she had bought at Harrod's when her husband was Ambassador to the Court of St. James's, added a festive touch to a house already bursting with festivity. The pattern, called "Nightingale," had wide vermillion borders and fanciful blue-and-yellow birds that swooped across plates, cups and saucers. Waterford crystal and eighteenth-century English silver anchored the celebration in the past while everyone present discussed the future.

"You can't do it without Texas," one of the President's sisters said across the main table. "And you won't carry Texas without Lyndon Johnson." The First and Second Estates occupied a majority of the twelve most important places at this long oak table. At one end sat the resplendent Rose Kennedy, at the other her ailing husband, the former Ambassador. From her right to her husband's left stretched the illustrious: the Cardinal, the President, Patricia Kennedy Lawford, Sargent Shriver and Ethel Kennedy. Opposite them, from the left hand of Rose to her husband's right, sat the Attorney General, Eunice Kennedy Shriver, Senator Edward Kennedy, Jean Kennedy Smith and Peter Lawford.

To be sure, the Third Estate was represented at this baronial board. Its majority, however, was dispersed to the satellite tables. There, among the grandchildren, sat Stephen Smith, a son-in-law. Joan Kennedy, Ted's wife, looking young enough to be a grandchild, had Rose's grandchildren as her only dinner companions.

Jacqueline Bouvier Kennedy sat with her children and their nanny. She disliked loud conversation at mealtime. The nanny enforced the First Lady's rules of decorum, such as that beverages be tasted only with an empty mouth and that bread be broken so as to avoid a volley of crumbs over the tablecloth.

The next course was oysters Rockefeller, jokingly known here as oysters Kennedy. At the main table, the clatter of forks on plates blended with long-range planning for the election of 1964.

"It'll take a million dollars at least for the television ads."

"I never said it would be easy to dump Lyndon. But if he's Vice-President for another term, he'll be very strong in '68."

"Why not Adlai?"

Oversized platters of goose stuffed with sweet potatoes and apples appeared next. Not everyone liked goose, so turkey was also served. A third entree elicited applause when it was put on the table: a ham glazed with cloves and cherries, surrounded by chunks of pineapple, sections of orange, and herbs designed to form the Presidential seal.

In the middle of dinner a servant brought the President a note on a salver. Handwritten by a member of the Secret Service at the Kennedy compound, it said: "A woman created a minor disturbance outside the White House this afternoon. Clutching the fence on Pennsylvania Ave., she was calling out 'Jack.' A guard attempted to apprehend her but she escaped. Message rec'd 6:05 P-EDT, SS Lancer Detail, Hyannis."

Reading it, the President grinned. "What's up?" said Bobby.

"These fellas really take me literally. I told the Secret Service that I, ah, want to be kept abreast of anything that's likely to appear in the newspapers. Whether I'm in Washington or elsewhere." Taking a mouthful of hazelnut souffle, he swallowed, then leaned forward to tell Bobby across the table, "Some business about a woman trying to scale the fence and gain access to the White House. From too much Christmas cheer, I guess."

After dinner, the gathering broke into small groups. Seated on a sofa between Patricia Lawford and the Cardinal, Rose Kennedy was discussing theology with His Eminence when two Kennedy moppets raced by, shrieking as they played cowboys and outlaws. A chubby hand banged into the Cardinal's brandy snifter, knocking it to the floor and taking Rose's with it as well.

"Now, cut that out!" scolded one of Rose's daughters, leaving her caucus on the other side of the room to pursue the miscreants.

"You will both leave the party for the rest of the evening."

Rose smiled at her disgraced grandchildren. "It's spirit like that that makes Preidents."

The celebration went on until past midnight. Late in the evening, after children were asleep and the open fire had burned to embers, conversation quieted and the various groups drew together in a circle around the sofa. Current topics having been exhausted, the Kennedys now reminisced. The Ambassador had retired to his room but Rose remained, telling stories of long ago that she and everyone else knew by heart. The Cardinal, too, recognized every story from afar, like old friends seen down a long corridor. The punchlines were as familiar as the beads on his rosary.

When the Cardinal excused himself a little later to retire for the night, he kissed Rose's cheek. "Rose, another Christmas; and another Christmas blessing it is to spend it with you and your family. Let's all agree, right now, never to change this custom. It's perfectly all right to add a few youngsters," he laughed, "but let's pledge that this family will never diminish."

The happiness of the day seemed fleeting and fragile and so, for an obscure reason that the Cardinal himself did not quite understand, he did something he ordinarily wouldn't do in the presence of such intimate friends. He raised his hand and made the Sign of the Cross as a general blessing upon the house and the family. Then, thinking he must appear sentimental, like Bing Crosby playing a priest on-screen, he quickly left the room.

CHAPTER

22

"Start Spreading the News"

It was her first time in the Port Authority Bus Terminal. On previous visits to New York she had been a movie star, and movie stars arrive by plane. What an odd feeling for Norma Jean: she had come home, and not a living soul new it. Or knew her.

En route from Washington she had asked her seatmate on the bus—an English girl who worked as a secretary for BOAC—the location of the bus station. "Why, it's where we'll be getting off the bus. It's called the Port Authority, isn't it?" was the girl's puzzling reply. It echoed Norma Jean's question without giving her an answer.

"But where's the bus station—you know, the terminal—in Manhattan?"

"Why that's it, duck. Just what I said. Port Authority." The way she said it—"Putta Thuddity"—sounded like hooves clopping down the racetrack.

Inside the station she asked a policeman where she was. He told her Forty-second and Eighth. On the sidewalks she put down her bag and looked around. She couldn't recall this part of town. Her elusive sense of geography kept her from realizing that Madison Square Garden, where she sang "Happy Birthday" to the President less than a year before, was so close by.

For a day in early January the weather was mild. The sun

felt warm on her cheeks in spite of a brisk breeze coming off the Hudson and whipping down the avenues.

Like everyone who has been away from New York for a while, she immediately looked up. Midtown resembled an Art Deco forest: the green McGraw-Hill Building, the silvery, birchlike Empire State, brown skyscraper tips climbing toward the sun. Lunch-hour crowds surged toward food and shopping, filling up every space on the sidewalk.

Winifred Welles, her seatmate, had proved more helpful on the question of lodging than on the clarification of Port Authority. "Now look here, duck," she counseled Norma Jean en route, "as soon as we arrive you must ring up the Hester Dolan Residence for Women." As a former resident, Winifred recommended it highly as a place for "any young woman of slender means," as she put it.

"I wish my hips were as slender as my means," Norma Jean said with a straight face. Winifred, finding this hilarious, rummaged in her bag until she located a telephone number for the Hester Dolan.

"It's a smashing location," she said. "Just round the corner from the Riverside Park. I had a wee bedsit overlooking the water. And when you're peckish, love, you can nip round to this little delicatessen called Zabar's. It's most extraordinary. D'you know, it smells like Babylon or Jerusalem, or some such."

Now, alone on the street and trying to spot an unoccupied taxi, she wished Winifred were still with her. Unable to hail a cab, she wondered how long before she could make tracks from Forty-second and Eighth.

"Is this the way to Mama Leone's?" an odd young man in a seersucker suit asked her. Even if he hadn't been dressed in a summer suit he would have looked peculiar. But his June-in-January outfit made Norma Jean shiver.

"What's the matter, you cold?" he said, standing closer to her. His slick brown hair looked as if he had put Vaseline in it, and his mustache looked like Captain Hook's. "Hey, c'mon, baby, lemme take you to lunch at Mama's. Bring your suitcase along."

"I'll thank you to shove off," she said, surprising herself with the command and also with the frown that she felt wrinkling her forehead.

"No offense, babe, I just thought you might be a little lost chick in a big bad town."

"Take a hike," she said. "If you're not out of here by the time I count three I'll scream *bloody* murder. One, two . . ."

Shrugging, he wandered off into the crowds of Times Square.

Taxis roared past, ignoring her dainty hand held up in supplication. She had been trying to get one to stop for a quarter of an hour. Between anger and despair, she wondered if she'd done something wrong.

Then she remembered that New York cab drivers loved to snub prospective riders. "They won't get away with it," she said aloud. "The big lunkheads—who do they think they're kidding?"

Stepping to the curb, she put two fingers to her mouth, drew in a deep breath and whistled like the Staten Island Ferry. Tires screeched; a big yellow taxi lumbered to a stop inches from her.

"So how long you been outta town?" the driver asked, making conversation as he sped up Eighth Avenue.

"Oh, I'm a stranger here," she said seriously. "Of course I've visited New York before. But this time I've come from far away." She said it as though she were telling a favorite bedtime story to a sleepy child. Saying rude things to that masher on the street, then making an undignified noise to get a taxi had made her feel coarse and a little cheap. She resolved to speak in feminine tones from now on and to be a lady.

"You tryin' to tell me you ain't a New Yorker? You coulda fooled me. Where'd you learn to whistle like that?"

"Oh no," she giggled, "that wasn't me. What I mean is . . . you see, I'm an actress. Well, I still have to find work, of course, but suppose I had to play a girl who's good at whistling? I could do it okay, huh?"

He thought he had seen every kind but this one was different. Innocent, real friendly and yet somehow very exciting. He wanted to ask her for a date. The only thing was, he also felt like he wanted to protect her . . . like his sister or something. "You take care, now," he said as she climbed out at the Hester Dolan Residence on Riverside in the low Eighties. "You need anything, just whistle."

"Thank you ever so." As the taxi drove away she felt pleased to have been mistaken for a seasoned New Yorker. "But I've got to stop talking like . . . Lorelei, and like *her*. If I don't, somebody will guess. After all, New Yorkers are smart. They ask a lot of questions, too."

The Hester Dolan Residence was tucked between a wide apartment building and a much older, stubby brownstone. Its sedate brick facade reminded Norma Jean of houses she had seen in London. A green awning stretched from the entrance to the street, like a real hotel. But there was no doorman in livery to escort her in.

"Your room is ready," said the matron at the reception desk in the lobby when Norma Jean identified herself as Georgia Philco, who had phoned an hour earlier. This woman filled up the tiny enclosed space, a literal hole in the wall. Even so, it had a switchboard, a miniature writing desk and one chair crammed into it. To enter or leave this niche the receptionist on duty had to follow a ritual—lift the chair out into the very small lobby, squeeze herself in, stand flat against the switchboard without becoming entangled in any of the various wires, then gingerly lift the chair back in; leaving, one performed the ritual in reverse.

The lobby could accommodate four persons, provided all were trim and standing straight. Otherwise it seemed more like a crowded elevator. Inside the actual elevator, two were a crowd. A hand-lettered sign posted in the lobby warned of the consequences of overloading: MAXIMUM WEIGHT 275 POUNDS. DANGER IF EXCEEDED. Someone had scrawled across the bottom of the sign, "Please empty bladder before boarding."

"I'll take you up," said the matron, lifting her chair into the lobby in order to leave her hole. "I hope no calls come in. There's no one to mind the switchboard. We're terribly understaffed, you see."

They got off at seven, the top floor. The matron, Mrs. Wockner, unlocked a door, revealing a room slightly smaller than the lobby. The walls were painted bird's-egg blue. The room contained a very narrow single bed, a chest with four drawers and a chair upholstered in imitation brocade. Sunlight streamed through the pair of small windows.

"Well, it's . . . charming, I'm sure," said Norma Jean. "It reminds me of the orphanage."

Mrs. Wockner was startled. "I hope you won't say that to any of the other girls. We hear quite enough noise from them already."

"Oh, sorry, I don't mean to sound like an ingrate. You see, what I meant was, it's not like a hotel room. It's more"—she glanced down, as though the right word might be written on the floor—"more homely."

Not sure that was an improvement, Mrs. Wockner smiled stiffly and said, "You share a bath with the girl next door." She opened the door to the bathroom that connected the suite. "Your neighbor, Miss Costello, has been here five years. She's in show business."

"I'll be in show business, too," said Norma Jean. "As soon as I find a job."

"Yes, they all say that." Mrs. Wockner sighed.

"But the first thing I need is a public library card. Is there a public library in the vicinity?"

"That's a new one," Mrs. Wockner said. "Most of the girls here wouldn't know a library from a lavatory."

"Well, I do. I go there to get books."

After giving directions to a branch library on Amsterdam Avenue, Mrs. Wockner said goodbye and returned to her cramped niche.

Norma Jean unpacked her suitcase. Her clothes filled up three of the drawers in the chest. Unsure how to dress for job-hunting in New York, she changed into a bulky brown sweater and a plain, narrow beige skirt. Checking her makeup in the bathroom mirror, she wondered if she would ever again be blonde. Her dark auburn hair gave her a mellow look. She might almost have been a university student—a pair of glasses would have done it. And her hair was longer now than she had worn it in years. She imagined letting it grow as long as Rita Hayworth's.

A few scars remained slightly red, as though she had stayed out in the winter wind too long. The shape of her face, changed only slightly, worked the way she had hoped. As long as she stayed away from *her*, no one would guess. But if she ever shifted personalities, lapsed into Marilyn, the hair and the facial modifications wouldn't hide enough. "Now that's something I'd better not forget," she thought. "There's one big secret I can't *ever* joke about."

After scrutinizing her face, she left her new home and walked the two blocks to Broadway. "I'm a new girl in town"—she imagined singing the line as the opening to a musical number. An orchestra cue would play, then suddenly dozens of singers and dancers would materialize for a big production number. And Marilyn would be the star—"No, no, no," Norma Jean lectured herself. "*She's* dead."

She wanted to get to know her new neighborhood. This was a part of New York she hadn't seen before. It reminded her of Brooklyn.

She—or rather Marilyn—had once told a reporter, "I want to retire to Brooklyn." Strolling on Broadway in the Eighties, and on into the Nineties, she perceived the same earthiness, the same smells of bread baking and onions frying that had drawn her to Atlantic Avenue and Flatbush. Today the seediness of the Upper West Side, the untidy mix of culture and grime, welcomed her home, even though she had never been there before. "What a swell New York this is. I love it to pieces."

Here she felt no constraints, no expectations. If she wanted to hop down the street like a rabbit, who would care? In fact, a woman wearing a hat with floppy white ears sewn on it was doing exactly that, and no one paid her the least attention as she hopped around the corner onto Eighty-sixth Street, her hands folded in front of her like Peter Cottontail.

Used furniture stores, kosher butcher shops, ballet studios, dingy pharmacies with flyblown advertisements propped in grimy windows, secondhand bookstores, macrobiotic restaurants and the headquarters of all those organizations that made J. Edgar Hoover see red—these streets were like a carnival. And nearly every face she met was a sideshow.

The carny crowd was intentionally, even arrogantly, unfashionable. These intense, bespectacled inhabitants wore coats and jackets from army surplus. They carried heavy canvas bags, knapsacks, plastic and paper shopping bags, oversized pocketbooks, briefcases—all seemingly filled with manifestos, books and bagels.

Long black beards covered many a handsome face. As for the girls, Norma Jean divided them into two categories: those who had put on a year's worth of makeup that morning, and those who should have but hadn't. Walking here was like crossing the back lot at Fox: she saw models, professors, cowboys, dwarfs, Black Muslims, a juggler performing on the sidewalk, dogs wearing sweaters, and children who seemed to be discussing all manner of serious topics with their parents. But unlike such a crowd in Hollywood, every one of these looked like the genuine article.

"I didn't come here to gawk," she reminded herself. "I've got to find a job. Now, what's the first thing you do?" She had always heard that half the waiters and waitresses in New York were really out-of-work actors. "If they can do it, why not me?"

On the other side of Broadway she saw a sign full of black squiggly lines. Beside the squiggles, in big red letters, was the name of the restaurant: Plum Orchard Chinese Restaurant and Cocktail Garden. She crossed the street and entered. A smiling maitre d' greeted her.

Lowering her eyelids slightly (it seemed a pity not to use that foolproof technique) she smiled warmly, hesitated a moment, then said languidly, "I'd like nothing better than to speak to the manager. Could you direct me to him?"

Accustomed to outlandish requests from the foreign devils who ate at the Plum Orchard, the maitre d' smiled, bowed slightly and replied, "Manager eating. Not like be disturbed."

"Is that him over there?" she asked, indicating a short, chubby man at an obscure table half-hidden behind a red-and-black dragon screen. She took a step in his direction.

The maitre d' smiled. "Not like be disturbed."

Mr. Wa, the manager, was dining at four o'clock because he had to supervise a banquet scheduled to begin in an hour. His plate of squid, bean curd and bamboo shoots reminded Norma Jean of a color reproduction in her art book. She recalled the caption under the picture, which described Jackson Pollock's procedures for slinging and dripping paint onto his canvases.

"I saw your sign outside," she said brightly through a big smile. "I'd like to apply for a job. As a waitress, of course."

"Must speak Chinese," he said, slurping a bean sprout into his mouth.

"Oh my, I hadn't thought of that."

"Cook not speak English. Waiter must speak Chinese."

"I could learn. At least enough to get by," she added, realizing that the cards were stacked against her.

Grinning as he lifted the teapot, Mr. Wa said, "You drink tea? You eat fortune cookie?"

"Why thanks! I'd adore some," she said, glad for something sweet to lift her spirits.

He invited her to join him as he removed a cup from a nearby table and signaled a waiter to bring a dish of cookies. Norma Jean cracked one open and pulled out the white slip of paper. "Bend and you need not break" was the fortune printed on it.

"How charming," she said to her host.

"Ahh, that very famous Chinese saying of Lao Tzu. Long, long time ago. It mean, You not resist too much. If bad luck come, you go 'long with it till it pass. Not fight too hard. Then bad luck leave, you be okay."

"I've done *that* forever. Did that old fellow mention how long it takes for the bad luck to play out?"

"You sad 'cause you not find a job?"

"Yes, you might say that."

"You try in next block. Broadway and Eighty-seven. Place call Jaffa. You ask for Mo."

The Jaffa Dairy Restaurant welcomed her with lovely smells. A steamy odor of dumplings, cabbage and potatoes pervaded the place, mixing with warm soup smells and an irresistible sub-odor that Norma Jean recognized as cloves and apples stewing in the same skillet.

The waitress led her through the kitchen and down a long passageway to Mo's office, an immaculate little room with Israeli museum posters on the walls and shelves of books in Hebrew above his desk. Expecting an elderly Mo, she was surprised to encounter a tall handsome young man who spoke in a deep voice with a slight

French accent. His yarmulke was as black as his hair. Without the letters embroidered in gold thread on the black fabric, she wondered if she would have noticed his skullcap.

"How do you do?" he said. "I am Moise Shamanesh-Halevi."

"Delighted," she said. "More than delighted, really. My name is Georgia Philco. I'm new in New York—brand new, you might say. Just a new girl in town." She stopped chattering and smiled shyly at him. He was making her nervous in a nice sort of way.

"Well, the thing is," she rattled on, "it's like this." She rushed as though talking for dear life. "You see, I need a job real bad. I'm here to act—you know, an actress—and my dough is running out."

"Of course I understand," he said. "New York is an expensive town. Tell me, Miss Philco, what is your experience? As a waitress, I mean."

"I've done lots of modeling," she said irrelevantly, using a line that had often helped when she was first making the rounds in Hollywood. She didn't point out that her last modeling job was in the late forties. "And then I've—" Crestfallen, she interrupted her resume. "Oh dear, I was afraid you'd ask. Well, I cannot tell a lie, as President Lincoln said. I haven't had lots of experience."

"I see," he said with a twinkle in his dark, liquid eyes and a fleeting smile at the corners of his mouth. "This reminds me of a story my grandfather used to tell. An old story passed down by Jews in Russia—that's where my *zaida* grew up. Anyway, a beaver was working on his new home, busily damming up the river to construct it. A turtle floated by. 'Why are you working so hard on your house?' he asked the beaver. 'You know the peasants will only destroy it for sport.'

" 'It's easy for you to be insouciant,' replied the beaver. 'You were born with a roof over your head and clothes on your back. But for me, the good Lord only grew a forest. On my own I learned architecture and engineering.' "

Norma Jean looked faintly puzzled. "Oh yes, I love animals, too."

"Perhaps the story suffers in translation," Mo conceded with a laugh. "But like the beaver, you must apply your skills to a new job. Since you have no experience as a waitress. Anyway, the point is that we can use you. One of our girls, Bella, is going back to her kibbutz in Israel. She leaves in three days."

When Norma Jean returned to her room she heard a voice in the shared bath. "I vant to drrrink your blood," it said. "Gif me a bloody Mary. Und hold the Mary." To Norma Jean, it sounded like a parrot. The moment it paused, she called out, "Hello, are you Miss Costello?"

"Yeah, baby, who wants to know?" answered a whiskey voice. Finally, the bathroom door opened. Miss Costello's black hair hung to her waist. She smoked a cigarette through a long ebony holder. Her makeup covered the spectrum of blue: deep blue eye shadow, a Della Robbia blue as rouge, and lipstick Norma Jean learned was called "Deep Purple," and blended by Miss Costello's own hand.

Her first name was Magda, she informed Norma Jean, and she was "an underground star." Unclear on the qualifications for such a job, Norma Jean said, "What do you think of my name? Georgia Philco."

"It's memorable, I'll say that. Provided anyone can remember it." Miss Costello guffawed at her own wit, coughed heavily and said, "So what do you do? Singer, actress, dancer, all of the above?"

After Norma Jean had explained her ambitions, Miss Costello said, "You know, kid, you remind me of somebody. Have you done any commercials? Toothpaste—that's it. Ipana—you did that Ipana commercial about the girl who's kissy fresh."

"Oh no, that wasn't I. Me. You couldn't have seen me on the networks. But someday you will. That's a promise, I hope."

Miss Costello was the kind of New Yorker who told her life story often, and in detail. For her—and others given to unabridged autobiography—it was as natural as a handshake. An Irish childhood in Queens, followed by several boyfriends, an early marriage, a divorce. Dramatic lessons from unspecified sources, a fling with a producer, then "Bingo, I got a part in the chorus of 'The King and I.' Followed by commercials, and I also spent five months playing Lucille Prescott on 'The Guiding Light.' Oh, I forgot to tell you, I was Miss Subways of nineteen—well, it helped my career." She guffawed at her own shtick. Norma Jean giggled politely.

Then, Miss Costello narrated, it had been her good luck to land a local TV job as hostess of a late-night show called "Graveyard Shift." A weekly horror movie. She played Transylvania, who opened the show with deep-voiced patter about vampires, werewolves and assorted monsters. From time to time Transylvania would interrupt the movie with more horror-chat, some of it rather suggestive. These interruptions, of course, were commercial breaks, and the sponsors were pleased with sales of cleansers and special-offer phonograph records. During the year the show had been on the air, Transylvania had developed a following. She appeared regularly at certain small nightclubs in the Village and below, often in the audience as a stipendiary guest but sometimes on stage with specially written patter that let her go much further than she could ever hope to on TV.

Tonight she was performing, hence the blue makeup, which meant her face looked somewhat like a varicose vein. Her slinky black dress and mournful accessories added to the effect. Miss Costello referred to her outfits as "funeral fashions."

"You wanna come along, Georgia? It won't cost you a cent. The club even pays my carfare downtown."

"Simply elegant," was the answer. Although it came from Norma Jean the redhead, it sounded a lot like the blonde girl upstairs in 'The Seven-Year Itch.' And no wonder; surrounded by show business, even small time, she became terribly excited. How could she suppress that show-biz love of performance that had driven you-know-whom to stardom and beyond? Norma Jean's stimulation was not only mental but physical as well. Miss Costello noticed it. "Hey, you're quivering, Georgia. Well, no wonder, it's cold in here. I'll have a word with Wockner next time I see her."

Here she was, her first day in New York and already she not only had a job, she had also been asked out. Maybe that fortune cookie was right; maybe she had bent so far that she wouldn't break, after all. "No, I'm okay, thank you," she told Miss Costello, who had put an arm around her trembling shoulder. "I'm still nervous from the train wreck, I guess."

The spotlight made Transylvania look even bluer than before. You could say she matched her material, Norma Jean thought.

"Did you hear the one about the undertaker?" Before Transylvania could tell the joke, the room was rolling with laughter because of the droll, suggestive faces she made. They loved her, even though in Norma Jean's opinion the routine seemed a bit stale. She had heard variations on most of these risqué jokes years ago. All the same, seated at a front-row table, she laughed appreciatively.

". . . and so the mortician says, 'Quick! Wrap a shroud around that stiff!' " The corners of her mouth were turned down in disdain, while her eyes roved around the room. Hilarity and applause went on and on. Transylvania stayed in character, bowing only slightly; earlier she had explained to the audience that she had something stuck through her heart.

After the show Norma Jean went to Transylvania's dressing room. Or dressing booth, actually, since it was no more than a piece of dark muslin suspended from a rope in a corner of a storage room full of beer kegs and wine bottles. Several fans—teenagers, as well as some who would never see fifty again—had come for autographs. After they left, Miss Costello said to the only remaining visitor, "Here she is now." The man was helping Magda put on her coat. "Georgia Philco, meet Mike Bonnadella. I was just telling him you've done some acting and commercials. Mike, tell her what's cooking."

"Why don't we do it over drinks?" he said, surveying Norma Jean as she excused herself and walked toward the powder room. When she was out of earshot he returned his attention to Transylvania. "So she wants a job, huh? Have you seen her do anything?"

"No, but that's the funny part. You take one look at her, what's the first thing you think? Star material. You know what I mean? She's got that quality I'd give a million bucks to have."

"Hmmm, I kinda see what you're talking about. But it's star quality trying to get out. She's got it covered up."

"That red hair's not hers," Transylvania allowed. "She's no more a natural redhead than I'm a natural blue. But her complexion—it's delicate, it attracts even when she's not wearing makeup. Of course she's had a lift of some kind. I know a lift when I see one. But why? She's not old enough to need it. I'd say she's thirteen going on thirty-nine. Agree or disagree?"

"*Mezzo, mezzo.*" He shrugged. "She could stand to lose fifteen or twenty pounds. But then she might wrinkle around the edges."

"What I said earlier about that quality she's got—have you ever known a mature woman who was kittenish without seeming fake? No, I haven't either," Transylvania declared. "But with her, it's somehow natural. Nothing fake about her. Mysterious, yes. But dishonest? Uh uh. She's like a big grownup tabby cat that still wants to play with string."

Looking in the mirror in the dilapidated powder room, Norma Jean worried that she didn't look her best. It had been a long, long day, and she was tired. This habit of self-criticism was a hard one to break; she had spent her life looking in mirrors and tormenting herself with what she saw. Marilyn, of course, had receded far into the depths of her eyes. They still held a trace of the old sadness, but at least the desperation was gone—that desperation that used to creep in the moment she stopped her posing for the camera.

Much of Marilyn remained—relics of the pre-blonde Marilyn. The recent surgery had returned her face to a square, undoing the oval shape established by a previous Hollywood operation. Norma Jean's auburn hair worn straight down the shoulders accentuated the perfect widow's peak of her hairline more distinctly than studio hairdressers had ever permitted. Even Alice Mulligan had insisted on covering it with a blonde sweep brought forward across the forehead.

Norma Jean was unaware of any remaining star quality. Always somewhat gullible, she had tricked herself into believing that heat and light, the glow of glamor that had created Marilyn, could be willed away, covered up with a new hairdo and meager makeup. Now, unknown to her, the same light burned, if at a lower wattage. Had she chosen to revert to Marilyn, she would have commanded the same attention.

The Double or Nothing Club on a cobbled Village street was loud and rambunctious when the trio entered. Several patrons paused to look at Transylvania, who was still in costume. Their glances lingered but briefly on her getup; after all, half the people in New York were in costume at any given time. But they did stare at Norma Jean; somehow so familiar yet so nondescript. She had to be a new girl in town, not yet hardened and worn down by the mean, dirty city. She was . . . luminescent.

"This is the deal," Mike said after ordering a Fuzzy Navel for himself, a rum-and-Coke for Transylvania and orange juice for Norma Jean. "I've collaborated with two guys on a musical that we hope will make it to Broadway eventually. But of course we have to start off-Broadway. I mean, way off. So my partners and I are putting on a backer's audition next Thursday in a church basement in the East Nineties."

"What's it about?" asked Norma Jean.

"The title is 'Maggie and Jiggs.' Based on the old comic strip. Did you ever read it?"

"Oh sure. Maggie is a tough broad"—Norma Jean had to laugh, thinking about the big-boned woman in the funny paper—"who's always trying to improve her husband. She seems not to like him the way he is, although I think she really loves him a lot. Jiggs is her husband. But all he wants to do is hang out with the boys at Dinty Moore's saloon."

"You *got* it," Mike said. "Jiggs is a kind of a slob. And wants to stay that way. But Maggie has social pretensions. Big ideas. You know, she wants to be a lady of fashion but doesn't quite know how to go about it."

"I'm too young to remember them," Transylvania said drily.

"Now," continued Mike, "we've cast Jiggs—a terrific comedian with bug-eyes, name of Marty Broshears. Perfect for Jiggs. But my partners and I have been round and round trying to get the right Maggie. I'll spare you the gory details but basically one of them wanted to put his girlfriend in the show and the other two of us said, no way, José. She's thin and serious—goes around reading Ayn Rand all the time."

"What's wrong with Ayn Rand?" Transylvania demanded.

Mike waved his hands at her in a shooing motion. He continued telling Norma Jean about his problems with "Maggie and Jiggs." "I mean, his girlfriend couldn't open up and really sing if her life depended on it. You know? Her idea of a showstopper is probably Blossom Dearie." With a change of tone from impatient to interested, he asked Norma Jean, "Would you read Maggie? I mean, read a few of her lines for me sometime soon? I can imagine you being very funny pretending to be a grande dame. Could you do her with a Brooklyn accent?"

"Me read Maggie?"

"Like I said, it's only a backers' audition," said Mike. "Even if you get the part. But if you're not interested I'll look for—"

"Not interested? I'd adore it to death!" She clapped her hands. "I'll do more than read, I'll memorize the whole play!"

Mike laughed. "That's above and beyond. Tell you what. If you're up to it, let's go by my place. You can read a little for me, then if Trans will be good enough to play the piano I can also hear you sing. By the way, how good a singer are you?"

"Well, I'm not Patti Page, mind you, but I have vocalized from time to time."

"You won't have to sing that much. At a backers' audition, the actors only sing about half the numbers. The composer and lyricist do the rest. That's because they know best how they want their songs interpreted. So my partners, Eliot Silverman and Wayne Weeks, will be the stars of this audition, as far as music's concerned."

On the way to his apartment on West Tenth Street Mike explained that the book, written by him, was conceived as blackout skits, with musical numbers between episodes. For variety, the script called for the actors to burst into song a few times in the middle of a skit.

* * *

Norma Jean stood by the big window looking down into the quiet, tree-lined street from Mike's apartment on the fourth floor. The old brick row houses reminded her of Hollywood movies where the characters were Old Money. Like Bette Davis's family in "Mr. Skeffington," or in "Now, Voyager," and especially in—

"Wake up, Georgia," Transylvania said. "You're about to nod out on us. This won't take long. I promise I won't let Mike take out his etchings."

Mike read from the opening notes: "The play takes place in New York in the nouveau-riche upper Fifth Avenue apartment of Maggie and Jiggs. The action goes from the mid-nineteen-thirties to the early forties. The play opens with Maggie and Jiggs in their living room. Maggie is disgruntled."

He handed Norma Jean the script. Reading the lines cold, she felt adrift with nothing to hold to. Until she remembered Michael Chekhov's words: "Everything depends on the text." Then she began speaking Maggie's stilted English, which barely concealed the loud Brooklyn accent just beneath it.

MAGGIE: The goils are coming to play bridge. Afterward we shall have tea. I've invited Mrs. Vanderbilt—she's such a delight. Now, you, scram.

Mike went on reading:

JIGGS: But Maggie . . .

MAGGIE: I ain't foolin'. This is a tete-à-tete for goils. You've gotta be crazy, trying to butt in on my afternoon of culchuh and refoinement.

JIGGS: (*aside*) Maggie is right. I'll just clear out till her hen party's over.

MAGGIE: Why don't you just go down to Dinty Moore's bar—that's where you'd rather be anyway. (*He exits*) Now, what shall I serve for tea? The fancy hostess in that movie I saw last week served petite finger foods and something called trifle. I know—I've got just the thing: graham crackers with peanut butter. I'm sure that's what that finger food was. And that trifle just had to be Jell-o with maraschino cherries. This is going to be some elegant tea party! Why, I bet Mrs. Vanderbilt will be asking me to join her bridge club in no time.

"That was great, Georgia," Mike said. "Your accent's perfect. Now let's do the number that comes right after the party. I'll sing Jiggs."

Transylvania played the intro to the song.

JIGGS: (*in a tenor voice*) Sit down, sit down.
MAGGIE: (*running around the stage, hysterically*) Shut up! Shut up! It wasn't your party. They didn't laugh at you. I'll never play bridge with Mrs. Van-derbilt.

Mike interrupted. "Hold it even longer. Hold *Vanderbilt* as long as you can. Make it funny and pathetic at the same time."

JIGGS: (*his tenor becomes caressing*) Sit down, my dear, sit down. You're exciting yourself.
MAGGIE: (*belting, near hysteria*) I won't sit down, I can't sit down. My liiiiiife—is ruined. I can never show my face. Will I ever be in the soc-iiety colyum?

"Georgia, you've got the part," Mike said. "You're a *natural*. In a way, yes, she thought. For a change.

CHAPTER

23

"Some Candle Clear Burns"

Dear Aunt Bertha and Uncle Horace,

Spring is a little early this year. I mean, in my life not on the streets of New York. I'm afraid the slush is still yellow and black and dirty, and March has come in like a lion with sharp teeth. Wow, however—I'm almost doing what I came here to do.

Believe it or not, my first day in New York I got a part in a play. Well, not a big Broadway splash but a reading. This one is called "Maggie and Jiggs"—just like in the funny papers. Guess who I was. I'll give you a hint, I wasn't Jiggs.

After the reading, this rich old gent put up money for the play. He told the authors he adored my acting. Imagine that! So "Maggie and Jiggs" opened in February at a small theater called The Open Window Playhouse. We perform on Friday and Saturday nights.

That's the good news. I also got a job as a waitress, but it didn't work out so well. My first day on the job, I brought out a tray of hot food to this guy. I set his soup on the table and also a basket of bread. Then I turned around for the coffeepot so I could pour him a cup. You know what he did? Well, I wouldn't want to write it, but it felt like a pinch. On my tush, as New Yorkers call the part you sit on. I turned back around to say something. You see, by then I had the coffeepot in my hand. "You're fresh," I said, "and besides, you've probably bruised my epidermis."

He said, "Oh, I know what you are, girlie." And he made this very uncivilized face. Taking liberties, you know.

Before I could stop her—I mean, before I could stop myself I said, "Here's your hat what's your hurry," and I handed him his hat. Honest Injun, I did. That was bad enough, I guess, but the manager said later that's not why he had to fire me. The manager's name is Mo, and he's quite swell. From France originally although that's beside the point. Well, anyway, I was furious with that blankety-blank man who pinched me. So I said out loud, "You want to be a masher, go mash somebody else, but keep your lousy hands off me." And I poured his coffee on his lap. "There," I said, "see if that cools you off."

Well, forks hit plates—that's how my friend Miss Costello describes it, and she wasn't even there. She's such a card. But as I was saying, or writing, you could have heard a pin drop on velvet. It turns out this guy that can't keep his hands to himself is famous, at least in New York. He's built all kinds of parks and playgrounds and freeways. Ditto buildings, and might run for governor or police chief or something. At least, that's what Mo told me when he gave me my pink slip.

The Hester Dolan Residence for Women, look at the address above, has lots of interesting tenants. My favorite is Miss Costello, my next door neighbor. She helped me get the role of Maggie. And she is a dictionary of knowledge, like how to ride the subways and how to defend yourself against a New York wolf.

I have to close for today. That's because I start a new job tomorrow, one where I don't have to pour hot coffee in anybody's cup or lap. The job pays enough to get by, and the best thing is it's in a *bookstore*. I mean, a huge real one on Fifth Avenue. Somebody said it's the bookstore of the stars. Whether that's true or not I don't know, but as an employee I get a fifty percent discount on almost any book in the place. What better way to get an education at last?

I hope you're both peachy. Keep your fingers crossed for me.

By the way, I have a new name. Please address letters to Georgia Philco. You've heard this name before. I was trying it out when the train wrecked.

Love and kisses,
Georgia

P.S. Miss Costello says she is a star of TV, nightclubs and mortuaries. Isn't that so delicious?

* * *

It might have been called a book emporium without sounding pretentiously misleading. Instead, it bore the fine old name of the publishing firm and bookseller—Doubleday. And while there was not one but two bookstores on Fifth Avenue with this name, it was to the larger one, the one that appeared to contain every book in print and then some, that Norma Jean reported for work one fine March day. The very location, Fifth Avenue and Fifty-seventh Street, bespoke elegance and good taste.

A few steps in either direction led to some of New York's most splendid sites: the Plaza Hotel, Central Park, Tiffany's, St. Patrick's Cathedral, Rockefeller Center, the Museum of Modern Art. Who wouldn't be enchanted among such legendary, even mythic, institutions?

Georgia Philco, née Norma Jean Baker, was no exception. Although the store opened at ten and she was to report at nine-thirty, she woke up at six. Unable to go back to sleep, she got up, dressed and ate a hearty breakfast in a coffee shop not far from the Hester Dolan Residence. But it was still only seven-thirty. She strolled to Central Park, where daffodils had already jumped up in anticipation of spring. Now they stood stiffly in the snow, determined to prevail.

The sun, rising over the thousands of buildings in the city, seemed to promise riches and splendor, even to those without a cent in their pockets. Norma Jean whistled as she walked briskly over a knoll near the Sheep Meadow.

She was far too sensible and intelligent to ask herself, "Who am I?" and then attempt to answer the question. Such simple-minded probing, she knew instinctively, belonged to the unimaginative and the boring; the kind who not only answered the question for themselves but repeated their tedious answers to anyone who couldn't run fast.

And yet during the upheavals of recent months, and especially now that she had apparently survived, she had often considered the question of her identity. Her literal identity, of course, was multifaceted: she was by turns Norma Jean, Georgia, MM, Lorelei and half a dozen others. But the teasing thought that tripped through her mind was . . . Put them all together and what do you get? And which one do you want to be?

A blueprint of her mind, with the chambers of her emotions clearly labelled, might have resembled one of those houses in London damaged in the war. Repeated shelling by big bombs and small ones had very nearly shattered the walls. The blueprint showed several rooms in ruins with an entire floor gutted, unsalvageable. But the other stories, despite their buffeting, remained intact. The dining room, for example, with china and glassware on the table, had come through unscathed. A dinner party could take place anytime. In the parlor only a broken vase and a cracked windowpane betrayed the repeated attacks. Other rooms showed greater or lesser destruction, but the walls still stood. The house would again hold life, maybe even laughter.

Doubleday seemed as big as an airline terminal, soaring three floors and containing purchase counters, an elevator, soft gray carpet and modern decor. Books punctuated the store with color. Glossy, laminated jackets of art books gleamed like lacquerware. The reds, blues, yellow, mauves and greens of Cézanne, Goya, Michelangelo and a hundred others blazed on shelves to the right of the revolving door.

Norma Jean waved to the solitary clerk inside to let her in. He pointed to the sign in the window: Hours Ten A.M.–Midnight. Continuing the pantomime, she pointed to herself, then acted out the process of removing money from her pocket, punching keys on an imaginary cash register, wrapping purchases. Finally the salesman got the point and unlocked the door. "I'm the new girl," she said, introducing herself.

"Just look around a few minutes," her colleague instructed. "Mr. Hatalom is in his office. He'll be down in a jiffy."

Across from the art volumes stretched row after row of fiction. Trendy novels with jackets in kaleidoscopic patterns; bestsellers emblazoned with romance and action; classics in hardcover and paperback showing pastoral scenes of the English countryside, or Paris or Spanish windmills.

Poetry, biography and science followed. Norma Jean wandered downstairs. The basement bulged with history, political science and dictionaries. Upstairs she saw cookbooks of every cuisine, volumes on weddings and manners and gardens, and a hundred baby books. Religion, philosophy, cults; and a demure lower shelf on marriage techniques and deviant sex, the latter roundly condemned by leading American psychiatrists.

It was paradise. "Miss Philco," a voice called. "Ready when you are." Mr. Hatalom was tall and thin, so thin that his clothes seemed not to touch him anywhere for lack of anything to touch. He looked about fifty-five. He had sandy hair and whitish eyelashes. "Delighted you could come," he said.

He spoke in overstatements. Whatever he said sounded momentous as he invested every sentence with implications.

He taught her how to use the register. "Utterly crucial," he said, "never to miscount a cent. Upon pain of banishment."

"I certainly wouldn't want that," she said. "I'll do a super-duper good job." His overemphasis was already rubbing off on the new employee.

"A welcome note in your voice is sure to please customers," he instructed. "And without our customers, where would we be? And smile always, Miss Philco," he said sadly. "A smile lights up the world." He blinked his frosty eyelashes as though peering through a blizzard. "Not a false smile, of course. People see too much of that on television."

She smiled at him, as though to convince him she knew how. He saw auburn hair turning dark brown close to her head. He saw opalescent skin, dancing eyes, teeth white on white. He saw a voluptuous woman. He heard pure enunciation and quirky speech rhythms, as though she had carefully rehearsed from a script.

Mr. Hatalom was a poet. Unable to support himself on poetry, he had been assistant manager of the Doubleday bookstore for twenty-five years. He had trained many salesclerks, whom he selected for their resemblance to lines in his beloved poems. His superior, of course, had no inkling of his criteria for the Doubleday work force.

Nor were the salesgirls and salesmen aware that Mr. Hatalom had invested them with art. They came in the revolving door, and departed hence, never guessing that they were mere verses in the album of Mr. Arpad Hatalom. Born beside a melancholy *puszta*, a prairie, on the great Hungarian plain and brought to New York as a baby, Mr. Hatalom spoke English and Hungarian with equal fluency and wrote in both tongues. He found it a simple matter to learn languages, and had acquired a reading knowledge of thirty-one others, but speaking them was of no interest to him since he never traveled and never intended to.

The young man who opened the door for Norma Jean was Hector Palma to everyone who knew him—except for Mr. Hatalom. In his eyes, Hector Palma was "Bare Ruined Choirs," so named because Mr. Hatalom was thinking of Shakespeare the day Hector applied for work. Rochelle Himmelfarb, a middle-aged saleslady upstairs, was hired because Mr. Hatalom knew instantly that she was none other than "Ah Sunflower, Weary of Time."

Over the years Doubleday had employed the Dantesque young Italian "Nel Mezzo del Cammin di Nostra Vita"; a German emigré pastor dubbed "The Lord is My Shepherd"; and a flighty would-be critic who reminded Mr. Hatalom of Emily Dickinson's "Because I Could Not Stop for Death."

"Learn to love these books as though they were intimate friends," Mr. Hatalom continued, training Miss Philco, whom he now thought of as "Some Candle Clear Burns" from an obscure poem by Gerard Manley Hopkins.

"Oh, I love them already."

"Most people do not. Especially the mortals who toil in bookstores."

"Gee, you must know a lot about books. I hope you'll recommend some to me."

And so their friendship began.

On her first day as a bookseller Norma Jean worked with Hector Palma, who despite his Italian name looked like a northern European. He had blue eyes and hair the color of maple syrup. At the black, circular, polished central desk in the middle of the main floor, he manned the east register, she the west.

"Standing inside this round desk is like working at a bar," she said.

"You'll meet some of the same kinds of characters," he said. "Oh, by the way, did Hatty tell you how to fill telephone orders?"

"Hatty?"

"Hatalom."

"As a matter of fact, he said I should ask you how to do it."

Hector explained that books were delivered in midtown until one hour before closing. He showed her the slips to fill out, the information to collect from customers and pointed out the pneumatic pipe where order forms were sent flying to the stock room. "A lot of famous people call in orders," he said. "They expect you to swoon when they say their names. But don't, even if you'd like to. Otherwise they'll expect every kind of favor. Joan Crawford ordered a fifty-cent paperback last week, then had the nerve to ask if the delivery boy could also bring up a bottle of vodka on the way to her apartment."

"Oh my," Norma Jean sympathized. "She's like that. I mean, according to Louella. Louella Parsons." She quickly added, "Do you read her column?"

"The *Times* doesn't run it. Anyway, who cares?"

"What do you read?"

"Dickens, Trollope, Flaubert. Jane Austen, I try to read all of her novels at least once a year. And Proust. T. S. Eliot, Auden, Garcia Lorca. Virginia Woolf. How about you?"

"Please make me a list," she said, impressed by Hector's familiarity with such stars of literature. She still ventured to answer his question. "I've read Whitman, and Thoreau, and Abraham Lincoln. Oh, yes, and Oliver Wendell Holmes. Shakespeare. Edgar Allan Poe. He's too scary, though. I'll never read his stuff again." Producing a sheet of paper from under the desk, she said, "Please, before you forget. Write down the books I have to read to become a smart blo—uh, redhead."

At the end of the day she had a list of some thirty books, a few of Hector's favorites. Using her employee's discount, she bought *Pride and Prejudice* and an anthology of twentieth-century poetry.

At six o'clock her day ended. She wasn't tired but exhilarated, unlike the weary, frazzled days in Hollywood when Marilyn needed amphetamines to walk from her dressing room to the limo after a day on the set.

Rounding the corner from Fifth Avenue onto Central Park South she remembered Rumpelmayer's, a sweet shop full of stuffed animals and dolls. A treat for children, and a treat for MM many times when she lived in New York before. She went in.

Drinking rich hot chocolate with a head of fluffy whipped cream, Norma Jean suddenly knew the answer. It came to her like the solution to a problem that has teased the mind for days. When the mind relaxed, the elusive answer often appeared unbidden. The resolution to her long conundrum went like this: I've really accomplished something. I'm free from booze and pills and depression. Of course I'm flat broke or close to it, but so what? I was always underpaid in Hollywood. Liz Taylor was getting a million a picture when I was getting a hundred thousand, fifty after taxes . . . And now I can walk around without being mobbed by a gang of idiots with cameras and microphones. But I sure wish I could see Alice, and Terry, Lee and Paula and Jane. And Prez. The son of a bitch, I'd like to kiss him again, then slap his face for the trouble he's caused me. But all the other men? I don't miss them, not really. I mean, after a while they're depressing. All they want is an hour of your time, then you could be a pound of chicken salad for all they care . . . Marilyn, honey, it's too bad you can't be here. You always loved the hot chocolate at Rumpelmayer's. *Hold a good thought for me*, that's what Marilyn used to tell her friends. So, Marilyn, wherever you are, I'm holding a real scrumptious thought for you.

"Cheers," Norma Jean whispered, swallowing the last drop of chocolate.

"Thank you ever so," said a voice far away, an echo no louder than a butterfly's wing skimming the air.

CHAPTER

24

"The Envelope, Please"

"Do you want to go to Fire Island for Labor Day?"

Vernon Bridge, like half a dozen Doubleday employees, had grown quite fond of Georgia Philco, the pixilated mystery girl who devoted herself to books and reading like a nun to crucifixes. Since her arrival five months earlier the store had become familylike. She had, in fact, drawn them all together. Everyone looked out for Georgia. Not that she was defenseless, far from it. But as Vernon asked Hector, "How can she be this really intelligent chick yet seem so naive?" Hector shrugged, turning his palms outward.

She called Vernon "London Bridge." Hector was no longer Hector, but "Hector Proctor," a name she recalled from an old Jimmy Durante routine about "Hector Proctor, Chiropractor."

Even Rochelle Himmelfarb, the shrinking violet of the stock department, had bloomed a bit. She would now occasionally join in the coffee-break repartee whereas formerly she had skittered about like a scared rabbit, sniffing and nervously blowing her nose.

Norma Jean's colleagues were fond of her, yet they never felt they knew exactly who she was or where she came from. She was mercurial, teasing, mischievous, and fiercely dedicated to improving her mind. Beneath the fun and frivolity, however, it seemed she and her soul inhabited a cave where no one, not even good friends, was permitted to visit.

Norma Jean, Hector and London Bridge had a race in July to see who could read *David Copperfield* the fastest. It was her first time reading the book; they had read it in high school ten or twelve years before. She won the contest; her reward was a banana split at Rumpelmayer's. "Which I need like a run in my stocking," she sighed. Still, she ate it with pleasure and resigned herself to buying her next dress a size larger. Could the dreaded middle-age spread really be pointing to her and saying "next"?

All summer, at her instigation, they talked Dickens. For example, when customers approached a cash register, the signal was, "Janet, donkeys," in homage to David Copperfield's Aunt Betsey Trotwood.

"You're so very 'umble," Hector told Norma Jean one day when she looked delicious in a new sleeveless summer dress. He writhed lubriciously like Uriah Heep.

"Just waiting for something to turn up," she replied, à la Mr. Micawber. And indeed, something did. Before the day ended she was asked out, quietly and discreetly, by one of the store's regular customers.

Rex Winchester had seen her before. Several times, which was why he read so many books that June. But he hadn't found the right moment to talk to her. She seemed friendly but quite businesslike with customers, although he noticed a good deal of camaraderie among the staff manning the circular desk in the center of the store.

Late one afternoon he found her alone at the desk and approached. She smiled pleasantly while ringing up his purchase. "I've always wanted to ask you something," he said.

"Oh my. What is it?"

"Will you have dinner with me sometime?"

"You're very kind. I'm not sure I can, though. You see, it's frowned upon. I mean, for us to mix pleasure with business."

"I promise to spend a hundred dollars in the store if you will."

"Gee, you make it terrifically difficult for a girl. Who could blame me for drumming up business? I'll ask Hatty if he has any objections."

And so, two nights later they went to Caravans, an Indian restaurant near Gramercy Park. At her request they met at Rockefeller Center. The night was balmy but not hot, so they walked downtown.

"I haven't meant to stare at you when I've been in the store," Rex said, "it's just that I can't seem to stop myself. There are two reasons. The first one, quite frankly, is that I find you very attractive. And the second one—well, it's hard to explain, but I'm sure I've seen you somewhere. No, don't laugh—it's not a line I've ever used before. But tell me—could I have seen you on the stage or TV?"

"I don't know if you travel a lot," she said. "If you do, it's possible you could have seen me in 'Maggie and Jiggs.' But it played so far off-Broadway that you'd need several roundtrip tickets just to get there in the first place."

"Do you always speak in such interesting nonsequiturs?" he asked, taking her hand.

"Well, I always try to enunciate," she said firmly. "Being an actress it's required. But enough about me," she added warily. "Tell me about yourself—do you have any oil wells?"

He laughed. "Now what makes you ask a thing like that? As it happens, I do handle other people's oil wells, also their diamond mines and dude ranches and yachts. I'm a money manager—for people with lots of money to manage."

"Do any of your clients produce plays, by chance?"

"I believe some of my clients have theatrical connections. But let's save that for our next date."

At the end of a hot spicy dinner of curry, biriyani, chutney and cooling, rose-scented lassi, she agreed to see him again soon. She liked his distinguished salt-and-pepper hair, his smooth tanned skin and deep voice, which was both relaxed and relaxing. And his smarts; he could talk about everything, but only when she asked. "I'd almost call him modest," she told Transylvania. "Not at all like the usual."

She couldn't see him again until after Labor Day, but she looked forward to the ocean at Fire Island. Hector Proctor and London Bridge had friends who owned a beach house covered in clematis vines and surrounded by tall cedars. Hector and Norma Jean made the eight o'clock ferry. London Bridge, who was scheduled to work late, arrived after midnight.

The hosts, Julian Schaeffer and Paul Spring, had planned a costume party for Saturday night. Guests were to improvise costumes from whatever they could find on the island. The theme was "Oscar Night," and the only rule was that everyone had to dress up as Academy Award winners or candidates.

Norma Jean had to laugh. Maybe as Georgia Philco she'd finally get her Oscar.

Around nine o'clock Saturday evening the "nominees" started arriving. Those party guests who were also house guests wouldn't come down until later, to make a grand entrance via the circular staircase.

"Greetings, Miss Colbert," Julian said, kissing the cheek of his friend Annabella da Fonseca, the interior decorator. She was the first to arrive. Wearing men's pajamas, men's slippers, but looking amazingly feminine with short brown hair, super-thin eyebrows and a cupid's-bow mouth, she was very much the image of Claudette Colbert in "It Happened One Night." A few minutes later two other "nominees" stepped into Julian and Paul's sunken living room. The first uttered not a sound, sign language being the basis for her Oscar-winning performance. Leonora Smith was Jane Wyman, the deaf mute in "Johnny Belinda." With her was a tall man in a white robe and white burnoose who carried a pail of sand. "How d'you do?" he said in an Oxbridge accent. It was Lawrence of Arabia impersonated by Leonora's husband, the novelist Al Steinhardt.

Soon the house was full of stars: Scarlett O'Hara, wearing a dress made from somebody's curtains; a very bald young man—the restaurateur Erwin Ammen—in billowy Oriental pants, barefoot, and convincing as Yul Brynner in "The King and I"; half a dozen Jets from "West Side Story."

A gaunt young man then entered wearing black pants and a black turtleneck, with two oversized shoulder pads perched on either side of his neck like a therapeutic device for the treatment of whiplash. No one could figure it out until Johnny Belinda scribbled the guest's identity on a memo pad: "Mildred Pierce."

Suddenly, at the top of the stairs three figures appeared. London Bridge, tall and muscular, wore a gold body stocking. Arms folded across his chest, he might have been mistaken for Mr.

Clean except that the "nominees" yelled, "Oscar, Oscar." For indeed, he had come as the famed statuette. And Julian announced that Oscar had agreed to be taken home by the star lucky enough to win him at the end of the evening.

Flanking Oscar were two beautiful women of the movies. Hector wore a blonde wig, a red dress covered in sequins with matching red gloves, and coats of glossy lipstick. Guess who, thought Norma Jean. Oscar stood aside to let the girls precede him down the stairs. But suddenly the other beautiful woman ran back for a final makeup check in the large bedroom mirror.

Uncrossing his arms, Oscar motioned her to come on, they couldn't make their entrance without her.

Striving for perfection, she smoothed an eyebrow, patted her dark wig, licked her glossy lips made glossier with coats of Vaseline and beeswax, straightened a red sequin that she imagined was slightly out of place on her gown, and sucked in her cheeks to make herself look thinner. Not daring to keep Oscar waiting, she ran out of the bathroom, waltzed gracefully to Hector's side and, while they waited for the applause to die down, posed for the photographer. Paul had brought out a camera and was flashing one picture after another of the two girls and Oscar.

"We're just two little girls . . . from Little Rock," Hector sang in a breathy voice, lowering his eyelids.

At the bottom of the staircase Leonora Smith whispered to Julian, "He's terrific as Marilyn."

"Poor Marilyn," Julian said.

The girls preceded Oscar slowly down the curving staircase. Oscar's face was impassive, while the two girls smiled vivaciously as they kicked their legs, preened and wiggled.

"We lived on the wrong side of the track." It was Georgia singing. She looked very much like Jane Russell, even though Jane was tall and statuesque while Georgia was on the *zaftig* side.

The noisy party had become still and quiet as all eyes were now on Dorothy and Lorelei, who glittered and blazed down the stair singing the song from "Gentlemen Prefer Blondes." Four steps from the bottom they changed their tune. Norma Jean began it, singing in Jane Russell's clear voice, "A kiss on the hand may be quite continental . . ."

"But diamonds are a girl's best friend," chimed in Lorelei played by Hector. The song then became a duet, and when it ended the party applauded wildly.

"I didn't know he had it in him," Paul said to Julian. "I didn't know Hector could do Marilyn."

"He told me this afternoon he had no idea how to do her but Georgia promised to coach him."

Everyone wanted to congratulate the girls from Little Rock. "You all win the prize," Scarlett O'Hara said in her tart southern accent. Johnny Belinda moved her fingers. Even Lawrence of Arabia's stiff upper lip gave way to a "jolly good, jolly good."

Scarlett was right. When it was time to vote on the winners of the Academy Award, Hector and Georgia tied for "Best Actress." The door prize, Oscar, was able to sleep in his own bed after all.

And Georgia-Norma Jean-Marilyn felt together for the first time in years.

CHAPTER

25

"November 22, 1963"

New York, out of step with the rest of the world, claims autumn, not spring, as its time of awakening. In spring New Yorkers plan their escape from the city; after Labor Day they find pleasures in town. New plays fill theaters of every size, from twenty-five seats to a thousand. Museums assemble exhibitions of old masters, neglected masters and young masters demanding admiration. New books flood the market, new movies, new fashions, new music. No one wants to leave Manhattan in the fall. New Yorkers endure New York the rest of the year just for the autumn renaissance.

Anyone phoning Georgia Philco in the fall of 1963 had to call back repeatedly. Reaching Mrs. Wockner at the switchboard, or one of her underlings, callers heard the familiar line: "Sorry, she isn't in. Do you wish to leave a message?"

"Where do you suppose she could be, Horace?" Aunt Bertha asked her husband after making three long-distance calls to New York City in as many days. After the third one Georgia phoned her to say hello and to tell her she was all right and sorry to have missed her.

"Guess what, Aunt Bertha, I've got a part in another play. That's why you couldn't reach me. I'm at the theater every night. When the house is dark, when there's no performance, we rehearse or make changes in the play. So I'm only here to sleep for a few hours, then it's back to work at Doubleday and off to the playhouse."

The new play was "an absurdist farce" called "A man, a plan, a canal, Panama." Norma Jean thought it sounded sort of weird, but who cared? The entire play, like the title, was conceived as a palindrome, she learned—it read the same backward and forward. Not every line was as ambidextrous as the title, but the author had constructed it so that the actors could start with the final curtain and play it backwards, which they did on alternate evenings. Played in reverse—the title was the same—the play unwound backward as it moved forward.

Whew. Strange. But for the first time ever Norma Jean had to depend on her use of language instead of her body.

Her new friends came to see her. Mike Bonnadella, Transylvania, and Marty Broshears, her co-star in "Maggie and Jiggs," were all there opening night. A few nights later the Doubleday tribe filled the house. Julian Schaeffer and Paul Spring sent her two dozen roses. Not to be outdone, Leonora Smith and Al Steinhardt gave her a Tiffany lamp—not a full-size one but a miniature lamp made in the studio of Louis Comfort Tiffany around 1900 and intended for the drawing room of a little girl's dollhouse. It was four inches tall with a base of swirling metal and a lampshade of brilliant glass, purple and gold to represent violets and daffodils. Al and Leonora had enclosed a card: "Congratulations to a brilliant shade."

Rex Winchester saw a small advertisement for the play in Cue and buzzed his secretary. But then he realized he didn't want to see the play, it would be too painful. "Never mind, Gloria."

He wasn't ready to see her again, even on stage where there was no possibility of another rejection. Not rejection, actually, because she never had said no. She had said, "Not now, Rex. It's too early." But she had hurt him. He had been married once for a short while in 1938 after he graduated from Williams but he could hardly recall what his wife looked like, or even her name. He had had plenty of chances since then; women often went out of their way to make him notice them, and it wasn't unusual for them to get serious on a first date.

But he didn't like gold diggers. And even though Georgia had asked him on their first date, "Do you own any oil wells?" he knew it was her funny way of getting to know him. When he proposed six weeks later as they walked along East End Avenue she turned him down. "Not now, Rex. It's too early, I'm afraid."

"Too early? Too early for some real happiness? Because that's what I promise—"

"Gee, you're awfully sweet, sweeter than you'll ever know, I guess." She beamed at him, as though she were saying "I do." But she was saying "I don't."

"You see," she went on, "there was someone else. Before I met you, before I came to New York. You could almost say it was in a different lifetime." She put her hand over her mouth as though embarrassed by her figure of speech.

"I can help you forget him."

"Well, I've already forgotten him. The thing I'm thinking about now is whether to see him one more time. You see, there's something I need to find out."

"But if you've forgotten him, what difference does it make?"

"You wouldn't believe me if I told you." She sighed. "Well, it's like this. He probably thinks I'm dead. But if not, then chances are he'd try to have me bumped off."

"What! That's crazy! Do you mean to say some jerk tried to hurt you?"

"I'd rather say he didn't but his brother did. And then, well, before I knew what was happening I was in a coffin. Only it turned out to be a ranch house near Boise—"

"Georgia, I know you don't drink. I know you say you don't touch the stuff but I have to ask you—have you started drinking in secret?"

They were walking across town now, taking a long stroll from East End Avenue toward Central Park across Eighty-sixth Street. It was a crisp autumn night, full of promise and festivity. Crowds filled the East Side as though it were Times Square.

"Rex, please . . . you see, that's why I don't want to talk about the past. That's why I can't explain it to you. It's just too weird to explain. Pretend I never said a word about it—"

"No, I'm in love with you. No secrets, *please*."

"But I can't help it. I could get in a lot of trouble." Snuggling closer to him as they reached the Metropolitan Museum, she whispered, "Why, a girl could get killed, knowing some of the stuff I know."

Autumn was dying. The bright blue skies of September and October were gone, invaded by rough gray November clouds etched in black. The sun's warmth had spilled out of the sky like liquid from a bowl. Bitter winds stripped the trees in Central Park, turning dead leaves into projectiles.

New York had moved indoors. Norma Jean wondered once or twice how she ever had time, in warmer days, to take long walks in Central Park, sometimes crossing Columbus, Amsterdam, Broadway, West End, continuing her walk another hour or so in Riverside Park until her body felt numb and her heart beat in exhilaration. "If people walked more in L.A.," she thought, "maybe they wouldn't be so cuckoo."

Now she scarcely had time to look out her window at the blazing sunsets across the Hudson. For the first time in her life Norma Jean had learned to write down appointments, and the pages of her engagement book were full. "I wish I had thought of this years ago," she said to Transylvania one day. "I used to be late all the time. That's because I tried to remember everything in my head. But you know what? Since I have a calendar I'm always on time. Just like those swallows at Capistrano."

Transylvania, off to another club appearance, answered, "I'm glad you're such a busy girl. That means you don't tie up the bathroom when I need to put on my makeup."

Norma Jean's spiral-bound engagement calendar had fifty-two photographs of silent movie stars, one at the beginning of each week. A picture of Rudolph Valentino preceded the page that was lined off for the week of November 17–23, 1963. In the slot for Sunday the seventeenth she had written, "Lord of the Flies"—meet L. Bridge at 34th St. East for 7:00 movie."

For some reason she insisted on writing "Work" five times a week on her calendar; from Monday the eighteenth to Friday the twenty-second a neat column of that one word traveled down the page. Also in Monday's slot she had noted: "Paul & Julian—dinner

Le Chat Noir. Meet there." Tuesday she planned "Fab.—Met," which meant that on her lunch hour she would go to the Metropolitan Museum to see an exhibition called "The Art of Fabergé"—according to the newspaper a show of Fabergé eggs, miniature pieces of furniture and other objects by the Russian master. Wednesday, also during lunch hour, she would see the paintings of Francis Bacon at the Guggenheim ("Gug—F. Bac."). Knowing her desire to learn more and more about art, Hector had told her not to miss this one. He promised to go with her. The word "Play" formed a short column from Thursday to Sunday, indicating the performances of "A man, a plan, a canal, Panama."

The week before, she had seen paintings and drawings by e. e. cummings at the Downtown Gallery just a few steps from Doubleday. She had seen three plays, "The Ballad of the Sad Cafe" and an off-Broadway double-bill. The first was "Opening Night" with Peggy Wood; the second was "A Matter of Like Life and Death"; Mike Bonnadella, who had taken her and Transylvania, had called this second play "as silly as its name." Norma Jean tended to agree. Now she didn't mind saying so but she had had to learn how. In Hollywood she had been terrified to express contrary opinions.

Leonora Smith and Al Steinhardt had invited her to see "The Blacks," which everybody was talking about, but she couldn't fit it into her schedule. Finding herself so busy, she made a list of events she mustn't miss, including "Spoon River" and "Barefoot in the Park" on Broadway, half a dozen plays Off and Off-Off, concerts, art exhibitions and a new movie, "The List of Adrian Messenger," opening the twentieth. She had always been a fan of John Huston's, even after working with him on that exhausting and scary production of "The Misfits." "I'll write to John after I see his movie," she planned. "I'll sign the letter—Roslyn Tabor! No, I wouldn't dare. He's so smart he might really get wise."

The week started badly. On Monday she woke up with a sick headache and missed work for the first time. She had to cancel dinner with Paul and Julian at Le Chat Noir, a place they had raved about over the Labor Day weekend.

On Tuesday she felt better, even though her head was still stuffy. Unable to breathe through her nose, she was afraid her sinuses were infected. She took a taxi to work, even though she couldn't afford it. But the wind was raw; she couldn't face walking and her head was too sore for a bumpy Manhattan bus ride. Besides, she was weak and if she turned her head too quickly she felt dizzy.

At work everything went wrong. An old lady in a mink coat approached her as she was arranging a display of *Ship of Fools*, which had just come out in paperback. Each copy had to be placed just so in order to form a mountain of books that would tempt customers to lift off the top without toppling the pile beneath it. "Young woman," said the dowager, "where might I find *Amaryllis*, by Giess?"

Norma Jean, whose ears were blocked by the infection in her head, stood up too fast. Bookshelves tilted madly, like the library on a ship tossed by rough weather. The woman seemed to be unmoored from the floor.

"*Excuse* me," Norma Jean said, clutching a nearby display table. "What did you say?"

"*Amaryllis* by *Giess* come come where is it?" The dowager's words and syllables all ran together, making her question sound, to Norma Jean's afflicted ears, something like, "I'm renting some geese."

"Uh, well, you see . . . " Norma Jean began, still woozy. The only word she could be sure of was "geese." She smiled weakly at the glaring dowager, who said sternly and impatiently, "Well? Don't you *know*?"

"Oh, that's got to be upstairs with the animal books, I guess," she finally said, hoping to remove the threat that breathed fire and alcohol so close to her.

"I've never heard such *insolence* in my life! That's a famous composition for the pianoforte, and *you're* attempting to joke about it. Animal books, *indeed*! I'll have you fired for this, you insolent jade." And she stormed off, accosting Hector at his post and demanding to speak to the manager.

Hector stepped into Mr. Hatalom's office and explained that an irate customer demanded to speak with him.

"Good day to you, madame," said Mr. Hatalom, thinking how much the furry old prune reminded him of Milton's phrase, "obdurate pride and steadfast hate." Bowing almost imperceptibly, he continued, "I trust you've sustained no injury?"

"That, that *person* out there insulted me. I demand that you fire her immediately."

Mr. Hatalom asked for an account of the incident. After hearing, he assured her that no harm had been intended. Of that he was certain, he added. Having smoothed the ruffled feathers, he personally escorted the old witch to the music department, where she pawed and scratched through a number of books without finding anything satisfactory. And at last she remounted her broomstick and was gone.

On Wednesday Norma Jean felt no better. Oddly, her sick headache, along with her sore throat and sniffles, had disappeared. And yet her balance remained off. She ached, and her hands shook.

It was the kind of rainy day that puts all of New York in a bad mood. Rain and wind ripped umbrellas; taxis sped through puddles, drenching everyone on the sidewalk; piercing street-noises set nerves on edge.

No sooner had she scurried inside Doubleday then she saw a new book display that hadn't been there the day before. On a good day it wouldn't have disturbed her, but this wasn't a good day. She felt so lousy, so depressed and jittery that she considered going to a bar. Or buying a bottle of champagne and hiding it in the cloakroom.

Arthur Miller was looking at her with a thousand eyes. One of the night clerks had filled a huge table with copies of his books—hardcover, paper, anthologies, theater collections. A big poster gazed at her like that eye atop the pyramid on the back of a dollar bill. He didn't look unfriendly but he definitely seemed to be watching her. "What if he recognizes me and tells?" she couldn't help thinking, even though she knew such thoughts were foolish. Still . . .

An hour later Mr. Hatalom asked her to arrange several copies of a new Ibsen collection in the drama section. As usual, she looked through the book. This edition of Ibsen's plays contained new translations, which, according to the introduction, were more accurate than any previously published in English. Norma Jean picked up five of the new books. Finding them heavier than she expected, she laid down one copy and made her way to the shelf with the four remaining books.

The Arthur Miller display was unavoidable. She tried not to look, but as she passed it she cut her eyes furtively toward the large poster. And saw it looking back at her . . . the eyes moved like the eyes of a statue when they appear to follow the viewer first this way, then another. An optical illusion? She was too startled and upset and sick to reason with herself.

She squealed, and as she did it, the topmost Ibsen slid out of her arms and crashed to the floor. Attempting to grab it, she lost control of her other books, which flew out of her arms and collided with the works of Arthur Miller. Plays and anthologies wobbled, then tumbled, mixing up Miller and Ibsen in a mess all over the table and on the carpeted floor.

Frowning customers turned to stare as Norma Jean burst into tears and ran into Mr. Hatalom's office.

"Miss Philco, *what* is the matter?"

"Arthur Miller . . ." and she said something else between sniffles that Mr. Hatalom couldn't understand.

"Yes, I know," he comforted, thinking a bit of drollery might lighten the situation. "I too sometimes wonder about him."

It didn't help. She was still crying.

"Has anything happened? Here, at home?"

"Everything is *awful*," she gasped. "I'm sick, I'm depressed . . ." Again she dissolved into tears and couldn't go on.

"Why not use a sick day?" he asked. "You've accrued several." And so they decided she would take the afternoon off.

The following day, Thursday, she was not much improved, so she stayed home. Not daring to miss a performance, however, she forced herself to the theater. By Friday she was really worried. Although symptoms of infection were gone, her gloom remained. She hadn't felt this bad since the old days . . .

Friday she overslept. When she eventually struggled out of the murkiness of sleep, she couldn't clear her head. Familiar sensations—ominous, threatening—lingered in her brain. Had she dreamed again about MM and the old life that was no more? The echo of such a dream played around the edge of her consciousness. She phoned Mr. Hatalom to tell him she would be late. Several hours late.

Although Altman's was out of the way, she went there for lunch. To Charleston Garden, which resembled the set of an old melodrama. Palm trees and antebellum southern mansions covered the walls, painted in a style obviously influenced by "Gone With the Wind." Nice ladies sat eating pale sandwiches and drinking tea, followed by desserts they referred to as "sinful." The entire department store seemed concentrated in this one room. Other ladies waited in line for a table. Laughter and gossip filled the restaurant. It belonged to women; the three or four men having lunch seemed uncomfortable, as though they had somehow strayed into a fitting room.

Transylvania had introduced her to Charleston Garden. They went there for tea one afternoon because Transylvania found it "camp." Pointing out overdressed or otherwise ludicrous ladies, Transylvania made up stories about them. Whispering, "Look at her over there," she told salacious tales about the unsuspecting matrons. Norma Jean thought that a bit cruel. She herself found Charleston Garden relaxing. It reminded her of outmoded department stores in Los Angeles where she had gone as a girl with Aunt Grace Goddard. Before the orphanage.

Waiting for her lunch to arrive, she started a letter to Curly and Tunafish, the two cowboys she had met on the bus. She had occasionally dropped them a line on a postcard but without a return address. Curly was so infatuated he just might set out for New York to marry her. Now, a year later, she felt that she owed him and Tunafish a long letter, bringing them up to date about herself. After all, she had promised to stay in touch.

". . . more books than you've ever seen in your life," she wrote. "The only thing I don't like is trying to decide which one to read next. I couldn't read all the good ones if I worked there a hundred years. Right now I'm reading this long novel called *Vanity Fair*. Plenty of famous celebrities come into Doubleday. Just last week Jackie Kennedy bought a new book about herself. Fortunately I was at lunch when she came in. Otherwise, who knows what I might have said."

Hearing a sound like someone weeping across the restaurant, she looked up. All around her, ladies were talking, eating, laughing, drinking, everything normal. Waitresses hurried about, squeezing between tables to serve soup and replenish water glasses. "And this play I'm in has a funny title," she wrote. "But try reading it backwards and see what it says."

There it was again, someone was crying. She was certain that's what she heard. Then a gasp and a scream, and far away on the other side of the noisy restaurant she heard staccato sentences that sounded like "oh no" or "no no." At the next table a young woman in a brown hat asked her friend, "What's going on?"

A hush rapidly spread over the room, erasing the chatter and merriment. Silence swept from table to table like a wave, bringing in its wake the sounds of shock and mourning. Norma Jean frowned, staring intently at the wave rushing toward her. The line of women waiting for tables had suddenly disappeared, replaced by another line waiting to pay at the cash register. They were all ashen-faced. No one took their money; the girl at the register had disappeared.

The waitresses had stopped serving. They dabbed their eyes with the white aprons they wore over black uniforms.

Distress had now reached the next table. The girl in the brown hat said, "Oh my God!" and her friend opened her mouth and didn't close it. Norma Jean, baffled, leaned over. "Excuse me," she whispered, "could you tell me what's happening?"

The open-mouthed woman merely shook her head. The girl in the brown hat turned slowly, staring at Norma Jean without seeing her, and said, "The President . . . has been murdered."

The words didn't sink in. Norma Jean couldn't understand it—the president of what? At first she thought incongruously, the president of Altman's—I wonder if it happened in the store. Still her mind would not, or could not, fill in the blank. President. *The* President?

The girl in the brown hat said, "They've shot the President. In Texas. Jackie was with him. They got the Vice-President, too."

The Charleston Garden had become a funeral parlor.

Norma Jean said, "Thank you" to the girl in the brown hat. And returned to the letter she was writing. *I ought to tell Curly and Tunafish the news. And then I'll write Aunt Bertha and Uncle* . . . Her fingers guided the fountain pen but no words leaked out through the sharp point. A few moments later she realized that the letter was ruined. The paper was wet and wrinkled, the words had dissolved into soggy drops.

The restaurant emptied. Following groups of women downstairs, Norma Jean wondered if they were evacuating the building. She had overheard a panicky voice in the restaurant saying, "They might drop the bomb any second." Soon she realized where everyone was headed; to Appliances, where a dozen television sets spoke at once.

Walter Cronkite, his voice breaking, said, "In Dallas, Texas, President Kennedy lies gravely wounded. According to the latest report from Parkland Hospital . . ."

More shock. More weeping. Norma Jean, feeling faint, sat on the floor in front of the bank of televisions, as others had done already. *These people didn't know him. For them he was only the President. But for me, he was the man I loved. The man who promised . . . But something went wrong. Bobby, that's what went wrong. And now it will never be right . . . again . . . oh my God . . .*

And then Walter Cronkite was saying, "We have just received word from Parkland Hospital in Dallas . . ."

She sat there from early afternoon until the store closed at six. Many others remained also. Around four o'clock two employees of Altman's appeared with coffee, tea, soft drinks and plates of cookies. Very little merchandise was sold in the store during the afternoon. A thief could have walked out with everything, the salesclerks were so distraught. But not even thieves felt like stealing that day.

November 22, 23, 24, 25—an extraordinary weekend, followed by an extraordinary first day of the blank new week. The days trudged by, as though Norma Jean and the rest of the world were acting out their lives underwater. After leaving the department store she remembered that Mr. Hatalom had expected her at work. She walked up Fifth Avenue toward Doubleday. The city seemed wrapped in black newspaper headlines. Occasionally, in a shop that was still open, she saw the gray glare of a television. Always repeating the same scenes: the motorcade, the shots, the new President arriving in Washington.

Doubleday was closed and all her friends gone home.

On Saturday she stayed in bed. *I'm a widow, too, but no one knows.*

On Sunday another shock: the President's killer killed. On Monday, Jack's funeral. On television, his widow lighted the Eternal Flame. *Jack, do you remember me? I mean her, Miss Monroe.*

CHAPTER

26

"Little Girl Blue"

"I'm so blue," the torch singer sighed in a breathy voice full of pain.

"I'm so blue." This time she held the word "blue" until it died on her lips. The audience in the smoky cabaret knew what she meant. She was blue.

The Cellar, a down-the-steps place that could hold forty-five, was known for singers like this one. They weren't always torchy, but often enough their repertoire was full of sad songs about a sad life. The Cellar was so far west in the Village that some of its regular clientele joked you had to go there by stagecoach.

Out-of-towners never came to the Cellar. Wouldn't like it even if they found it. Even many New Yorkers—those who lived above Fourteenth Street—had trouble getting there. The Cellar was not on a picturesque little street between a patisserie and an antique shop. No, it was beyond the meat packers, past the trucks, in sight of the piers. Down a dark smelly little side street paved in greasy stones. River dampness made the Cellar's brick walls sweat.

The singer had a question in her song. "I'm so blue, will I always be this blue?" She sang it with style. She had real tears in her eyes. When the song ended, the audience waited before bursting into applause. The singer had revealed intimate secrets and no one wanted to break the spell. It seemed almost irreverent to clap.

She did not smile, she had no patter, she did not say "thank you, ladies and gentlemen." She stood, eyes to the floor, as though she were all alone in the room. When the audience stopped its loud cheers and applause she looked them over as she had done at the beginning of the set, as though she were searching for someone who wasn't there.

She began her next song. The words of "Cottage for Sale" dropped over the audience like cold drops of rain. No one moved; no one lifted a glass or struck a match. Why wasn't this singer making records, singing at the Rainbow Room, appearing at Carnegie Hall?

One night a fan waited for her outside and told her she should record her songs. "Gee, you're sweet," she said, smiling, "but you see, I'm no singer. I'm just an actress who can't find work." Touching his hand briefly, she whispered, "Goodnight," and walked away over the oily cobblestones.

The previous November her voice had drastically changed. She had heard of hair turning white after a harrowing experience. But a voice? She asked Transylvania, who said it sounded richer. "However, that's probably because of air pollution," she added, expecting a giggle from her friend. But Norma Jean had not laughed in weeks.

After Dallas, America's hair had turned white.

Those dark days and weeks changed into months, yet Norma Jean couldn't shake off the depression. Jack was gone forever and she was left with the big question: did he kill Marilyn when he died? She used all her sick leave from Doubleday, then took off a week without pay. Later she overslept a couple of times. When she managed to wake up, she couldn't make her face look right. One day her lipstick looked all wrong and she decided to remove it and put on a different shade. By the time she was ready to leave her room the sun had set. Mrs. Wockner was angry. As Norma

Jean passed the reception desk, the matron said, "What's wrong with you? Your boss has been calling since this morning. I can't write messages for you all day long."

By the time she reached Fifth and Fifty-seventh Mr. Hatalom had left for the day. Hector said, "Georgia, sweetheart, tell me what's wrong. How can I help you?" She had no answer.

It happened again the next day. The day after that she made it to work but she couldn't function, so she had to return home and sleep. Finally Mr. Hatalom was called on the carpet by his own boss. An hour later her final check had been cut, a note prepared for her personnel file, and everyone in the store had heard. They missed her already, knowing the special fun had stopped.

Bad luck bred more bad luck. The play closed; no one wanted to see absurd farces in cramped theaters off-off-Broadway. Suddenly the whole world had become more absurd than any playwright could ever imagine. Even Samuel Beckett hadn't written anything as desolate as the winter of 1963–64 in the United States.

She walked around. Sometimes she forgot to report for unemployment compensation. The long lines scared her, the bureaucratic process was an ordeal she couldn't face. When she did remember to sign up she spent most of the money on sweets. Suddenly her body couldn't get enough chocolates, cookies, puddings, ice cream. She thought about champagne, vodka, gin, but they didn't have enough sugar. The years of dieting had caught up with her, or so she believed. The mere thought of cottage cheese and toast made her want to retch; she unwrapped another Baby Ruth and ate it quickly to settle her stomach.

Wandering in the Village on a blustery day in March, eating her third cannoli, she had turned into Gansevoort Street and stumbled all the way to the river. She considered jumping in, but since it smelled so bad—a vile soup of oil, salt and sewage—she decided to eat another dessert instead. She was ravenous; if the pavingstones on the dirty little street had been edible she would have ripped out one and devoured it.

She saw a small sign: The Cellar. A red arrow pointed down a flight of gritty stairs. "Maybe they serve ice cream," she said to the empty street.

Cora Jones, the club owner, unlocked the door. "Sorry, Miss," she said. "We're not open."

"Please, *please*," Norma Jean said. Cora Jones wondered if she had robbed a bank, or if she planned to rob her to get money for a fix.

"What's your trouble?" Cora Jones asked in a no-nonsense tone. Before slamming the door she wanted to make sure this wasn't a girl she had dated.

"I'm so sorry," Norma Jean said. She started to cry. "Holy smoke, I feel like a dummy. You see, I've been eating sugar so I wouldn't drink, then all of a sudden I got the shakes. So I came down here for ice cream. If you'll sell me some."

"A lot of folks come here for a lot of reasons, but ice cream . . . that's a new one." She looked at Norma Jean. "Say, don't I know you from somewhere?"

"I doubt it. I'm nobody." Then, trying not to seem rude, she said, "About the ice—"

"Tell you what. I'll give you a piece of carrot cake. I brought it for myself, but, honey, you need it worse than I do." She opened the door, ushered Norma Jean into the Cellar, where only one small light burned, and pulled a black chair from under a table covered with a red-and-white-checked cloth.

In the darkened room, redolent of stale cigarette smoke and clammy from the river nearby, Norma Jean pulled her jacket tighter. Cora returned with a slab of bronze cake on a paper plate and smiled for the first time. "The coffee is brewing," she said.

Cora's face was copper brown, her hair was shiny black with wisps of steel gray on the sides. Tall and slender, she looked strong enough to pull a barge. She pronounced every word slowly and carefully, as though she might lose control if she spoke faster.

"Not that it's any of my business," Cora said, implying she'd like to know anyway, "but who are you? And how did you happen to descend my staircase in the middle of the day?"

"I'm just a little girl from Little Rock," was the answer.

Cora didn't catch the allusion. When "Gentlemen Prefer Blondes" came out eleven years earlier in 1953 she was struggling to save enough money to leave the black ghetto in Cleveland and come to New York, where her prospects seemed better. Playing piano in a bar called Miss Behavin, and working days as a short-order cook, she had no time for movies.

"You don't have a southern accent," Cora said.

"I'm not really from Little Rock, it's just something I say when I'm nervous. You want to know who I am? I'm Little Girl Blue. Lost in the crowd, down on my luck. Sister, can you spare a dime?" She laughed for the first time in months. The laugh tasted bitter but it forced her mouth to smile.

"It's that bad, huh?" Cora said. "You know, honey, I've been there. I've been all those things, and more. I'll get your coffee."

An hour later they were still commiserating. "My momma begged me not to leave Cleveland," Cora said. "She wanted me to stay there and be polite all week. Say 'yes'm' and 'no'm' to white ladies and sing in the choir every Sunday. I tried to explain but she never understood. When she passed, I hated myself. I wished, oh God I wished, I'd stayed there and worked full-time in the diner and done just what Momma wanted."

"We can't go back, can we?" Norma Jean said vaguely. "Well, I'm not sure I'd want to even if I had the chance. It's true I had more money when I lived in California, but you know what? Other people spent it for me. I was too busy. Or too depressed."

"What did you say you did out there?"

"I worked in the motion picture field. Behind the scenes, of course. But I've done some singing, too."

"Really? What do you sing?"

"Ballads. Show tunes. Did you ever hear 'My Heart Belongs to Daddy'"?

"How good are you?"

"Well, I've made a few records. Under another name. But they're not very good, at least I don't like them anymore. I could sing a lot better now."

And so, one thing leading to another as often happened in New York, Cora Jones gave Norma Jean an impromptu audition in the murky little room at four o'clock in the afternoon. And liked what she heard.

MM being dead, or at least out of the picture, Norma Jean had no reason to effect the breathy voice that was one of her trademarks. Of course, it sometimes returned like the memory of a dream. But the singing voice had deepened and matured. It was darker; champagne had turned to rum. And once it warmed up, the voice dropped even more, becoming cello-rich.

Cora had heard Nat "King" Cole's recording of "Lost April." His voice was so silky that the song never made her sad. But this girl with the unlikely name of Georgia Philco who had walked in off the street trying to buy ice cream—the way she sang it underscored the true hopelessness of a dead love.

Lost April, where did you go?
Like winter snow, I saw you vanish . . .

Cora was amazed. This girl made the whole year, not just April, sound as lost as first love. The Cellar's regulars might go for her—if the sadness in her voice didn't make half of them commit suicide.

At the end of "Lost April" Cora exclaimed, "My God, girl, you're damn near up there with Lady Day. Where'd you learn to do stuff like that?" Cora had stopped enunciating and started talking. "You sure you not black? I mean way down underneath your pale complexion?" Cora laughed at her own joke, and Norma Jean laughed too.

"I'm not black," she said, "but you know what? If I keep eating sweets I'll look like Aunt Jemima."

As part of her effort to nurture talent, Cora sent regular mailings to the Cellar's clientele. Two weeks later, when her next one went out, it listed "Georgia Philco—Friday 20/Saturday 21 March 1964." A flyer, added to the calendar, called the new singer "an undiscovered sensation" and urged the Cellar's patrons to hear her now before fame took her away.

On Friday, May 9, the *Herald-Tribune* carried this item in its "Out on the Town" section:

If you can find your way to the deepest, darkest part of Greenwich Village, consider a low-priced, high-caliber evening at the Cellar. You can't get there by subway or bus; if you take a taxi, be prepared to produce your own map for the driver. But it's worth the trouble of finding this hole-in-the-wall *boite* to hear a new singer on the New York club scene, a young lady with the unforgettable name of Georgia Philco. What she does with a song is unforgettable too. Accompanied by Cora Jones at the piano, she signs her name to every number in the set.

On a recent evening she told a sad story with three well-known numbers—"Something Cool," "Lush Life" and "Love for Sale"—tracing the path of a fallen woman. At the outset, Miss Philco sang in a frou-frou, dumb blonde style (even though she is a redhead), making her audience believe that the most important thing in the world was that much-needed highball. By the time she reached the second song, her tone was dark and serious. No longer a giddy barfly, she was in the throes of depression and ruin. Finally, she brought to Cole Porter's bold song about a prostitute the heartbroken warbling of an American Edith Piaf.

To lighten the mood she followed these torchy vocal showpieces with a medley of songs about spring, including "April in Portugal" (sung in French as "Avril au Portugal"), "It Might As Well Be Spring" and "When the Red, Red Robin Comes Bob-Bob-Bobbin' Along." Her interpretations, however, made the audience more melancholy than buoyant. She must be one of the few vocalists who can sing about spring as if it were the dead of winter. After hearing her slowed-down versions of these peppy numbers you might understand why the poet said that "April is the cruelest month."

By the first day of summer the *Times*, the *Post* and the *Daily News* had printed short reviews of Georgia Philco's unique style and interpretations.

Cora wasn't stingy, and so Norma Jean was once again solvent. Sometimes she thought of looking for an apartment downtown but immediately wondered if she wouldn't be terribly lonely without Transylvania in the next room. They found time to visit for at least a few minutes every day, if only for a "hiya" and a "*ciao*" called out as the doors of their shared bath rapidly opened and closed.

Norma Jean's former colleagues at Doubleday's hadn't forgotten her. Hector, London Bridge, even Mr. Hatalom came to the Cellar. Mike Bonnadella told her he had mentioned her name to a Broadway producer. She was invited to parties, clubs, movie screenings, gallery openings. Cue and The New Yorker ran items about her, called her "talented" and "scintillating."

Norma Jean ignored most invitations unless Transylvania or another friend convinced her to attend—with a guest. She appeared often at the Cellar, and when she wasn't singing she was scouting new material. She relished nights off as a time to read one of the books in her expanding collection. She plunged into *War and Peace*, which she had started in New York in 1956 and hadn't finished because of her return to Hollywood to film "Bus Stop."

One night in early July Rex Winchester turned up at the Cellar. Not wanting to distract her, he sat near the back. After the show he waited for her in the street. Usually Cora or one of the waiters scanned the sidewalk to make sure everyone had left. Only then did Norma Jean exit. She found it draining to talk to admirers and stage-door Johnnies, especially since they frequently asked questions about her background that could not, must not, be answered. The best way to discourage was to stay inaccessible.

"Georgia," Rex said as she emerged from below street level. "I wanted to tell you how much I enjoyed your singing."

"It's good to see you, Rex. You're looking terrific. Where'd you get that tan?"

They spent the next hour weaving through Village streets, finally arriving at Washington Square. Rex hinted that he was ready to try again if she'd give him the slightest encouragement.

"Things have changed," she said. "The man I told you about last year—well, you see, he died. A terrible death. I'm still affected by it. By him. Maybe I always will be. Rex . . . can't we be friends, do I have to say yes or no?"

"I'm not getting any younger," he said quietly. "You are, though, or at least it seems like it. You look better now than you did the first time I saw you."

"Can you imagine me getting younger?" she exclaimed. "Why, I'm not that far from forty. I won't tell you how far."

"And I won't ask," he said.

"Please try to understand," she told him. "Half my life could be over and I'm just now getting started at what I've always wanted to do. Even if I had nine lives, and sometimes I think I do, it's not as though I've got any time to spare." Snuggling closer, she continued, "It doesn't matter a lot whether I'm acting or singing. I just need the reassurance of an audience." She paused for a moment. Now that she was explaining her needs, they seemed clearer to her.

"Gee, it's like a test," she went on. "You see, I have to know that I'm good, and that people like me, or I go into a slump. The problem was . . . that is, earlier in my life, well, the problem was that people really disapproved. The harder I tried to please them the meaner they became. But now, you know, I'm almost . . . adored? That's not too extravagant a word, is it?"

Rex shook his head. She intrigued him more than ever.

"By people who matter," she said. "People who come all the way down here to the jumping-off place just to hear me sing. Wow, what's more exciting in life than that? It's what I've always wanted."

Convinced, if reluctantly, Rex agreed to be her friend even if she never allowed him to become her lover. He realized that what she desired was much more than success. As she sang he had watched her communicating her deepest feelings—love, sadness, fear, yearning—and he understood that she was expressing life for those unable to interpret it for themselves. They sought her out, as they sought out all artists, to learn the truth about life. That truth, or truths, might be sad, but an artist transformed sadness into beauty. Indeed, that was precisely why they came to hear her in this smoky dive with its sticky, gritty floors—because she had something to say to them, and about them, even though every note she sang was about herself.

A few nights later Cora invited her home for a drink after the show. Norma Jean had been to Cora's spacious loft a couple of times before but always with two or three others. This time they were alone.

Cora said, "I want to tell you, honey, I'm glad you've stayed on at the Cellar. Thanks to you, the club's making a little money for a change." She laughed at the unintended pun. "I know you could do better, and when the time comes I won't try to hold you back."

"Jeepers, Cora, could I find a better accompanist? Or a better friend? I wouldn't bet on it."

"Oh, g'won."

"No, no, it's true. I mean, first you saved my life with a piece of carrot cake."

Cora threw back her head and roared at the memory of their peculiar meeting.

"No, really," Norma Jean said. "Then you gave me my big break. You think I'm so ungrateful I'd use those Cellar stairs to climb up? No, I'm staying right down here in the dumps with you!"

As late night became early morning, Cora said finally what she had sometimes thought. "Georgia, have you ever considered settling down? Not that it's possible to settle down in Manhattan, of course, but I mean the closest thing to it. Which is to find a companion."

"Oh, I've had offers," Norma Jean giggled. "Like you wouldn't believe."

"Would you listen to another one?"

"Why, do you know something I don't?"

"Would you?"

"Say what's on your mind, Cora."

Cora took a deep breath, then quickly came to the point. "I could comfort you. All that pain, honey, I hear it even though you're always smiling outside. Always polite and kind. But Cora hears. Uh-huh, Cora hears it."

"Thank you, I'm sure," Norma Jean said quietly, meeting Cora's gaze. "You see, I'm flattered—don't think I'm not. But it's like this. After what I've been through . . . now isn't that just like a New Yorker to say 'what I've been through'?" They both giggled. "*After what I've been through*," she declaimed, but soon became serious again, "it will be a long time before I give this lil ol' heart away again. Maybe years, maybe never."

"You know, honey, you could tell Cora what you been through. But you never have."

"You know what? I'd like to." She brushed a strand of hair

off her forehead. "I really would. But it's such a long story. And I'd have to begin all the way at the beginning, I guess, but really, I'm not at all sure where that is."

"There you go again, talking in riddles. Sometimes I think you're a Russian spy, or maybe a spy from Mars."

"You remember what I told you that first day? I'm just a little girl from Little Rock? Say, maybe that's really true after all. By the way, I've got a new song. The name is 'Surabaya Johnny.' And when I sing it I'm going to smoke a cigar."

As the sun rose over the thousands of buildings, bringing a hot steamy day to the overheated city, Norma Jean and Cora were working on the new song.

The cigar made Norma Jean gag the first time she tried it. Transylvania said, "No, silly, don't inhale. It'll kill you. Not only that, you'll puke on the bathroom floor." A wisp of the strong smoke drifted into her chest and she dashed to the bathroom while Transylvania made exaggerated howling noises.

She persisted, and by the time she was ready to sing "Surabaya Johnny" she could have smoked half a dozen cigars and still have been on her feet. There was a hint of Marlene Dietrich in her interpretation and phrasing, a whiff of Tallulah Bankhead, even a hint of Patti Page. But the edges of her creamy voice were all her own, inspired by no one.

Her followers loved it, they loved everything she sang. And they were her followers, devoted and faithful. If she had wanted a cult she could have herded them together and charged them for the privilege of worshiping her. It was harder and harder for "outsiders" to get into the Cellar because every table was occupied by her devotees. When they were not gathered in front of their diva, they talked about her, thought about her voice and waited impatiently for her next performance.

Every night fans stood around outside the Cellar, but she waited them out in her dressing room, reading. One night a boy and girl, relative newcomers to the flock, endured longer than all the rest, and when Norma Jean emerged at the top of the stairs the young man called out, "Hey, Georgia, why don't you ever talk to your fans? Without us, you wouldn't have anyone to sing to."

"I agree," she said, nonplussed by the note of accusation underlying his tone. Perhaps he was showing off for his girlfriend. "But without me, you'd be at home watching Ed Sullivan." As she walked away, she called back, "Good night, boy. Good night, girl." On stage she seemed so vulnerable, but in her street voice there was now a note of iron.

The first week of August was an anxious time for Norma Jean in 1964, as it had been the previous year. In memory she relived the nightmare of August 1962, the year she lost Marilyn, the year she herself was taken captive.

One hot night in July she had had dinner with Rex, who sensed her anxiety and restlessness. "Is anything bothering you?" he asked.

"What makes you ask a question like that?" she snapped. "Forgive me, please, Rex," she said in the next breath. "Yes, I'm so jumpy I can't stand it. Maybe five nights a week is too much to sing. What I need is a vacation." She brightened at the thought of leaving the city for a week. "How much does it cost to fly to Italy?"

Rex explained that Italy in summer wouldn't necessarily be the best place to relax. "However," he said, "if that's where you'd like to go, I'll send you a ticket tomorrow. A birthday present for next year, since you wouldn't let me buy you anything expensive in June."

"You're such a dear," she whispered, "may I tell you a secret?"

"You've decided to marry me?"

"No, silly. Now listen, this is serious. Last night while I was singing . . . well, it's hard to explain, but I had the darnedest feeling that someone in the room had come to—no, it sounds too dumb, forget it."

"I won't forget it. Out with it, someone in the room—go ahead."

"Okay, someone was watching me. I don't mean watching in the normal way, you know, but, well, *staring*. Not even hearing my songs but studying me." She sighed impatiently. "There, now

I feel silly. It must have been my imagination. Let's forget it, okay?"

"Look, you say the word and I'll hire a bodyguard to sit at a table—"

"No, no. Then I'd get nervous being reminded about him."

Embarrassed because her suspicions sounded hokey, she changed the subject to a book she was reading. "One of the boys from Doubleday gave it to me. He said I was the only person in New York who hadn't read *1984*. He said I'd better hurry up, too, because that's only twenty years from now. And then Mr. Hatalom—he's the one who fired me but I still drop by to see him—well, he recommended this novel about Hollywood called *The Deer Park*. The author's name is Norman Mailer—he's a new one to me. It's quite a book."

"How many books do you read at the same time?" Rex asked, surprised at her ambitious reading schedule.

"Well, only three right now. Since I'm so busy, you know. The other one is by Wilkie Collins. It's called *The Woman in White*." She shivered. "Talk about thrills and chills. It's so exciting, maybe that's the reason I've had the jitters."

As usual, she felt relaxed after spending time with Rex. The next night she sang with more confidence, all but certain that her fears were unfounded.

As a surprise for her audience she included two comic numbers in her second set. "Experiment," by Cole Porter, which sounded so innocent until she started to think about the lyric. She sang it like a wide-eyed virgin, then at the end she tilted her head and winked the way Marilyn used to. The audience gave her a standing ovation, knocking over several beer bottles as they sprang to their feet.

"Ladies and gentlemen," she said, "I wonder how many of you remember this song. It's an oldie, but oh-my." They were amazed; she almost never talked. To hear an entire sentence from Georgia Philco was like getting a toothpaste smile from Greta Garbo.

". . . but please don't dance, there isn't room enough." Probably no one in the audience had thought of the song in years, but when she began a steamy arrangement of "Papa Loves Mambo" they laughed and cheered. Between verses she did a hip-swinging mambo patterned on Jack Lemmon's gyrations in "Some Like It Hot," with an added spritz of Carmen Miranda.

That man in the dark glasses, she thought abruptly. He's new . . .

The third set was made up of such trademark songs as "I'll Be Seeing You," "My Ship," "Smoke Gets In Your Eyes." Singing her last number, "What'll I Do," she thought how much the audience resembled children at bedtime, engrossed in a story as they drifted to sleep.

She sang slowly. Her voice filled the room the way honeysuckle fills a summer night.

And she saw that another man in dark glasses had joined the one at the table.

"What'll I do . . ." Suddenly she gasped sharply and stuttered, "W-What'll I do . . ." Cora looked up sharply from the piano. How could she forget this lyric? It was the most familiar one in the set.

One of the men in dark glasses stood up and walked out the door. No one in the audience paid attention, but at that moment Norma Jean realized who the men were, and why they had come.

CHAPTER 27

"Assassino!"

Finishing her piano accompaniment with a subdued flourish, Cora decided to lecture Georgia on the importance of never, under any circumstances, forgetting the words of a song.

The enthusiastic applause lasted as long as usual, but Cora sensed that something was wrong. Georgia, who seldom deviated from her performance patterns, had stayed on stage instead of disappearing as usual. Her fans clapped on and on while she gazed toward the back of the room, almost as though she were in a trance. Cora had never before seen this expression on Georgia's face.

Slowly, she raised both hands as though ready to plunge off a diving board. Her expression was tight; no softness in her eyes or on her lips. Her face was as pale as her white dress. Instantly she commanded the silence she wanted. The audience seemed poised at the top of a collective breath, uncertain whether to exhale or freeze.

"Ladies and gentlemen," she panted. "Ladies and gentlemen, please stand up."

Every lady and gentleman in the room immediately stood.

"Please join me in singing 'The Star-Spangled Banner.'"

Cora shook her head. What the hell did she think this was, Yankee Stadium? But she dutifully played an intro to the national anthem.

"Oh, say can you see, by the dawn's early light," sang Norma Jean as though her voice were suddenly amplified. She beat her arms up and down as though conducting a symphony.

This is like Pearl Harbor, or the *Titanic*, Cora thought sourly as she tried not to miss any unfamiliar notes.

"And the hoome of the braaaave!" Cheers, yells, screams, and the stamping of feet.

"I want to go home with all of you," the singer said matter-of-factly when the noise died down and everyone sat, wondering if more surprises were coming.

A chorus of "Let's go," "Whadda we waitin' for?" "Hear, hear," sprang up.

She attempted a smile as she walked over to the piano and whispered to Cora, who looked even more perplexed. Then, smiling radiantly as though playing the most important scene in her life, Norma Jean walked into the middle of the room and stopped at a table of two young men and two young women who looked like beatniks. They wore dark colors, the men had beards and the girls wore no makeup. Norma Jean had noticed them many times before. "Ready?" she said. Obviously surprised, but game, the group said "sure" and "okay," thereby becoming her instant entourage. The remaining stranger in dark glasses watched, like everyone else in the Cellar.

Outside she told them, "You see, it's an emergency. Some nut case in there was threatening me. Two nut cases, as a matter of fact. One of them left but the other one's still in there. Would it be too much trouble for you to take me to Seventh Avenue? From there I'll either take the train or grab a taxi."

"That's cool," said one of the guys. "But like, who'd threaten *you*?"

"You're the grooviest," added his girl. "You really shake my cage. Why don't we all, like, stop in this joint for some vino?"

Everyone agreed, and the five of then piled into a tavern on Hudson Street. Before they did they were careful to look around for anyone wearing dark glasses and looking suspicious. The coast was clear.

An hour later her beatnik fans left, promising Norma Jean to see her at the Cellar the following night. She stayed on at the bar, sipping a glass of champagne. Badly scared, frozen in place, she debated whether any spot in New York was safe now. What if there were more than two? What if she was surrounded? She ordered another glass of champagne. "I'm so nervous that even chocolate won't help," she confided to the bartender, who gave her a puzzled look. "If you say so, lady."

Around three in the morning she ventured out of the tavern. Hudson Street looked quiet. A few cars, a few people walking alone or in pairs. A wino asleep in the doorway.

The night was balmy, the oppressive humidity of the August day had dissipated. A narrow wedge of moon gleamed in the sky. A breeze skittered through the streets and around the corners of buildings; soon it would lift the warm night and push it into the harbor. In a couple of hours the sun would blaze up out of the ocean, igniting the city.

Norma Jean had finally relaxed some. At least she could now draw a deep breath, talk without panting, stand on her legs, which earlier seemed flimsy and ready to wilt. Should she take a taxi home? Should she wake up Cora and tell her . . . tell her what? "I'm Marilyn Monroe, or I was, and the men who kidnapped me when I was Marilyn were sitting in the club tonight"? Fat chance.

She detoured a couple of times, looked around, then headed toward the river. Remembering what she had learned at the Actors Studio, she told herself, "I'm a shadow. I'll play a shadow so well no one will notice me. I'll be just one more transparent shadow among all the other shadows of the night."

The night population of the Village was still on duty. Men and a few women roamed the tangled streets, coming out of bars, looking at each other, making furtive signals, continuing their search or finally forsaking it until the next night. A lone taxi wheeled around the corner. Someone got in. The taxi lurched off, leaving the street dead quiet.

Wooden piers jutted into the river like giant fingers pointing at the Jersey shore. Traffic on the West Side Highway was sparse as on a desert road. Waterfront warehouses loomed in darkness as though closed not for one night but forever. This quiet, still little sliver of Manhattan might have been severed and set adrift in the sea for all the human activity visible on it between three and four in the morning.

Until a woman came in sight. She wore a white sleeveless dress with a full skirt that billowed in the river breeze. Someone seeing her might have guessed that she had left a party to stroll beside the water. In a sense she had left a party, a happy party that began when she arrived in New York a year and a half before. Now, however, the party had ended. The past had come back to claim her.

Walking on the waterfront, occasionally stopping to gaze at the deep river that flowed rapidly a few feet away, Norma Jean felt resigned. It was too good to last, she told herself. *Who do I think I am? Of course they won't leave me alone. No matter where I go they'll find me. But this is the last time. After this, who cares? I won't.*

The champagne had raced to her brain like poison on the end of a dart. Three or four glasses, maybe more, had ripped the veils. Norma Jean now saw it all clearly. Soon the old days would return, the old days of depression, exploitation, rage. *Methought I heard a voice cry, "Sleep no more! Macbeth doth murder sleep!"* If sleep was dead, then so was she. She wouldn't go through it all again, not for anything. Better to go quickly, tonight.

Walking fast, weaving as she went, Norma Jean saw another woman at the end of the pier, motioning to her. Who could it be? What a coincidence—she too was wearing a white dress. She was blonde, her moist red lips burned the night, her eyes were half closed, her head was thrown back in silent laughter.

Norma Jean left New York behind and walked onto the wooden pier. Far out in the river, against a backdrop of twinkling lights on the opposite shore, Marilyn motioned for her to come. Something whizzed by, maybe a speedboat, and suddenly Marilyn's skirt blew up, blew above her waist as though she were over a wind tunnel. She turned her head this way and that, savoring the cool night air. "It's so refreshing!" she cooed in a sweet, breathy voice. Her white skirt billowed out like a parachute and wouldn't go down. She smiled seductively at Norma Jean. "Come join me," Marilyn invited.

Norma Jean swayed as she walked quickly toward her old friend. Friend? "Hello," she called out to MM. "It's been a long time. An eternity." Soon they would be together again, just like sisters. Maybe that billowy skirt would lift the two of them up and take them far away, high over New York, beyond the world.

Back on the shore a figure moved swiftly and silently along the edge of a massive freight warehouse. Approaching the water, the figure headed for the pier, where he had just spotted a woman. Now he was running to get to the pier. He reached it without making a sound, like a hunter in the middle of a forest closing in on his prey.

The figure crept along the pier. At the end of it stood the woman he had stalked all these months. Seeing her arms moving wildly, he wondered what she was up to. He couldn't make out her words. Then the breeze blew them toward him . . . she was singing a cockamamie song about diamonds. This songbird's gotta be put out of its misery, he thought.

Bledsoe reached into his windbreaker and pulled out the Luger with a silencer already in place. He took aim at the redhead in a white dress who swayed tipsily on the end of the pier. Any second now she would be on the edge, so when the bullet hit it would knock her into the water. Neat. The body wouldn't even need a shove from his feet. The songbird was gonna sing to the fishes, down deep. Goodbye, Poison Ivy.

The moon had dropped to the edge of the black sky. Over the water the wind rose, pushing the moist night air. A shot rang out, a muffled pop no louder than a rude belch.

Norma Jean turned around. The first thing she saw was the Empire State Building. Her eyes darted from that bright beacon just in time to see a man falling off the pier into the Hudson. He had been only a few yards away from her.

Terrified, she started to run. The heavy wooden boards were rough and uneven and she was afraid she might catch her foot in a crevice. She sped down the center of the pier in a desperate rush to escape from Marilyn, from the river, from the murderers in dark glasses who had come to kill her. Where was the other one?

She neared the end of the pier. In a split second she would be back on land, back in New York where she could get help. She decided to go to the police, to tell them everything. Let them lock her up, it couldn't be worse than this.

A figure crouched behind a high storm fence at the water's edge. He could see her although she couldn't see him. Not until she ran past. At that instant, from the corner of her eye, she spotted the tall dark man. She screamed as he stepped in front of her. Running too fast to stop, she collided with him and he grabbed her arms.

"Leggo," she screamed, and kicked hard, hitting him in the shin. Wriggling to free herself, she flailed her dark captor with elbows and knees and butted him with her head.

"Norma Jean, cut it *out*. Cut it out, I said!"

The voice. The voice was not the one she expected. It wasn't the man who killed Grushenka.

"You're okay, I won't hurt you," he panted. "For God's sake, stop kicking me."

Wheezing, gulping for air, she dropped her arms to her sides, planted her feet on the ground and raised her head, which a second earlier she had used as a battering ram.

"Tom!"

"Hey! Hey, calm down," he gasped. "Just wait a minute while I catch my breath."

Norma Jean stood looking at Cathcart, whom she knew only as "Tom" from their months together in the Colorado wilderness. "I recognized you in the club," she said. "Even under your new beard. And your dark glasses didn't fool me, either."

"I'm real sorry it came to this," he said. "Believe me, there was no way around it." He dusted himself off. "Look, we need to get the hell away from here. Somebody might've seen and called the cops. The thing we don't need right now is to be implicated in a killing. Neither one of us."

Putting his hand on her arm, he guided her away from the murky no-man's land. As they crossed the West Side Highway, the morning sky was turning gold.

Norma Jean was too dumbfounded to ask a coherent question, so Cathcart explained as concisely as he could what had led him, and the late George Bledsoe, to New York, to the Cellar and to the fateful pier in the Hudson River in pursuit of her.

As they ate breakfast he told her how Bledsoe was obsessed with tracking her down and killing her after her escape. "He swore he'd kill you for drugging the food that night," Cathcart said, "and making him look so bad."

"But who was behind it?" was Norma Jean's first question. "I mean, who had me kidnapped? Was it Bobby?"

"Norma Jean, don't ask me. There are certain things I can't tell, certain things you'll never know. I will tell you this much, though. Nobody wins against the CIA. Okay, is that clear? Don't try for details. I've given you enough, don't push any further. If you do I can't guarantee your safety."

"Oh, Tom—by the way, is that your real name?"

"It's close enough."

"Tom, I have to know one thing. Just one. You see, I loved him . . . the President, and I believe he loved me. I can't believe he was involved in this. I mean, I was kidnapped, held captive—Bobby threatened me, and I think it was all his idea. But not Jack . . ."

Cathcart paused. "No, that I can say for sure. He never knew. End of discussion." He looked quickly away.

"Well, the other question I have is—why did you," she lowered her voice, which was already *sotto voce*, so that Cathcart was forced to read her lips, "why did you shoot *him* last night instead of me?"

"What you never knew in Colorado was that I liked you. He didn't. Nope, he didn't like you at all, even though you tried being nice to him. And you were smart to escape when you did. After he shot the cat . . . you'd have been next. Anyway, to answer your question, you reminded me of somebody—somebody I never had, like a daughter, maybe, or even a wife. And of course, I'd seen all of your movies."

"Why didn't you tell me that back there?"

"I brought you books, didn't I?"

"Yes, and I really was in no shape to talk about . . . her. I mean, me. The old me that everyone saw in the movies."

"I love this country," Cathcart said quietly. "I've spent my life working for it. But hell, Marilyn Monroe . . . Anything happened to her, it'd be like sticking dynamite under Mount Rushmore."

"Anything else, sir," asked the waitress.

"A bagel with a shmear, please," Norma Jean answered.

"Cup of coffee, for me, ma'am," said Cathcart. To Norma Jean: "You look about ten times better than you did on the ranch. I don't know if I oughta say this, but looks like you've gained some weight, too."

She raised her eyebrows.

"Oh, hey, it looks good on you. Makes you look sorta like you did in 'River of No Return.' That tight pair of blue jeans, and all." She stared at him, making him squirm.

"Maybe I've gained a pound or two," she said, "and maybe I haven't. Playing chase all night gives a girl an appetite. I mean, how would I know about running from killers? Last night was the first time I've done it. If you want my opinion, that kind of thing is okay for the guys in 'On the Waterfront.' But just include me out."

She was making him laugh with her wide-eyed patter. It was awfully familiar. If the voice weren't so much lower, Cathcart was sure she'd sound like she used to when he saw her in pictures.

Her mind was still on last night. "Gee, that night air could make a girl hoarse. Then what? I couldn't very well stand up in the club and sing 'Old Girl River', could I?"

He laughed so loud that people in nearby booths turned around.

"No, I guess not. But let me give you one piece of advice. Stay the way you are. What I mean is, keep the red hair. Don't change into a blonde. You know why? Because it's not healthy. You read me?"

"Like a book," she said. "Does that mean others have got wise? I'd sure hate to look out over that sea of faces one night and see J. Edgar Hoover. And you know something else? Bobby Kennedy is running for Senator! Right here in New York. Maybe I should leave the country—could you get me a passport?"

"Norma Jean, I don't think you have to worry. I could probably arrange a passport. But just stay put. I'll leave you a phone number and a code. If there's ever a reason to get in touch, you can. Otherwise, just keep on singing. Let me tell you one thing, then I've gotta leave. That person you just mentioned—he thinks you're six feet underground somewhere in the woods in Colorado."

"Are you kidding? Where'd he get an idea like that?"

"You figure it out. Better yet, don't try to. Just go on with your life. I hope it'll be long and happy. I mean it."

Outside the coffee shop she kissed him on both cheeks. "I'm awfully sorry I kicked you last night," she said. "And I'm sorry I put Valium in your soup, too. Next time I go strolling along the river I'll take a hatpin. A long, sharp hatpin. So no more surprises, Tom, okay?"

As his taxi zoomed off and disappeared in the congestion of Sixth Avenue, she realized that she hadn't remembered to get his phone number. Would he get in touch?

CHAPTER

28

"Do You Look Like Her?"

Not long after Norma Jean's close call on the waterfront, the cult of Marilyn Monroe began. It was impossible to pinpoint the onset; nobody noticed it until it was full blown, like an immense cloud that sprang up from a puff of moist air.

Perhaps the fan magazine Photoplay was the incubator that nourished the cult. An odd story appeared in the issue of August 1963 bearing the provocative title, "One Year Later, Marilyn Monroe's Killer Still at Large." The article was daring for the time, because no one—in print, at least—questioned the official conclusion of death by suicide. And yet that fanzine began its story like this: "You can see him in a crowd. You can reach out and touch him, because he is a great man, famous, known all over the world . . . But what you will never know is that this man is a killer. He is the man who killed Marilyn Monroe."

No name was revealed, and few readers gave the story a second thought. After all, magazines of that sort regularly ran such teasers as, "Fabian Breaks His Mother's Heart," disclosing somewhere in the innocuous prose that the teenage star did so "By Missing His High School Graduation!"

Fueling the cult was the appearance of books with such titles as *The Strange Death of Marilyn Monroe* and *Who Killed Marilyn Monroe?* Serious writers, among them several professors, wrote appreciations of the star and her heretofore undervalued acting talents. Elegiac fan clubs sprang up with names worthy of epitaphs: "The Marilyn Forever Fan Club," "Marilyn Remembered Fan Club." Her image refused to fade; matchbooks, decals, cups and plates, sofa pillows and magazine covers perpetuated the lipstick smile, the white platinum hair, the heavy lids, the look of innocence and heat. Her movies became increasingly popular in revival houses and on TV.

And in the summer of 1965, The Great Marilyn Monroe Look-Alike Contest was announced. Although it lacked the wide appeal of the Miss America pageant, it was perhaps the first public declaration that MM's light was not extinguished.

Norma Jean had popped into the Eighth Street Bookshop to buy a volume of Wallace Stevens' poetry. The day before, she had attended a poetry reading uptown. Hearing the rich music and the strange images of Stevens' poems, she decided to delve into his work the way she had into Rilke years earlier. (The Hollywood press, having no idea who Rilke was, had refrained from the usual mockery of her intellectual interests.)

On her way out of the store she glanced at the bulletin board. Among the notices for teach-ins, peace marches, folksong concerts and lectures on Buddhism she noticed an announcement on pink paper. Suddenly her anticipation of an afternoon spent reading poetry was forgotten. She felt as though she had looked into a mirror that reflected both future and past.

THE FIRST ANNUAL
GREAT MARILYN MONROE LOOK-ALIKE CONTEST
DO YOU LOOK LIKE HER?
$500 PRIZE TO THE MOST CONVINCING DOUBLE
ALL SEXES WELCOME
SUNDAY, AUGUST 1
HOTEL RICHMOND, WEST 48TH STREET

She had heard of lawsuits for trademark infringement. For a moment, in anger, she wondered if she could sue. Then she had a better idea.

That night she had dinner with Transylvania and Mike Bonnadella. "Maggie and Jiggs" was, it seemed, headed for Broadway next year and Mike wanted to talk to Norma Jean about playing Maggie. He and Transylvania hadn't seen each other in months, although they talked on the phone. And now that Norma Jean had left the Hester Dolan Residence for an apartment in the Village, she and Transylvania had a standing appointment for dinner on Monday nights.

"Fifteen pounds!" gasped Transylvania. "Where's the rest of you? You're the shadow of the girl I know."

"Do I look wonderful, or what?" asked Norma Jean.

"Your neck is most appetizing," said Transylvania in a Hungaro-Romanian accent. Even though she wasn't wearing her usual blue and purple, she had played a vampire for so long that she drifted in and out of character.

"You're gorgeous," Mike said. Norma Jean decided he meant it by his look of appraisal when she came in.

"What did you do to that sweet tooth—pull it?" asked Transylvania, who had suggested in the past that losing weight might lead to career advancement.

"Running. I've been running in Central Park, around the Reservoir. I used to run years ago, but in California people stared at me like I was off the funny farm."

She told them about her set of weights and her new membership in a swim club. They wanted to see her apartment on Sullivan Street so she promised to invite them for dinner.

"The way your career has taken off," Mike said, "we may have to wait a while."

"It's true I'm working all the time," Norma Jean said. "But gee, if I'm ever too busy to see my friends I'll retire and apply for anti-Social Security."

She had played the mother in "Our Town," and recently had opened off-Broadway in "The Bald Soprano." Several reviewers singled her out for praise. One wrote that she was "a new actress who plays the Englishwoman Mrs. Smith as though the character were a combination of Ethel Barrymore and Gracie Allen."

Her name had slowly moved from the bottom of cast lists to the top, becoming familiar to regular theatregoers. Meanwhile, her fans, missing her at the Cellar, flocked to see her on stage. They wrote letters begging her to take a break from acting and make a record. Or at least sing weekends at the Cellar, "where you *belong*," as one devotee wrote.

"Oh, I almost forgot," Norma Jean said at the end of dinner. "I've decided to enter a contest. Transylvania, I need your help."

When she told them the name of the contest, Transylvania jumped. "That's who it is! That's who you've always reminded me of. Since the first day I saw you! Well, I'll be damned . . . Marilyn Monroe."

"I can see you as Marilyn," Mike said, scrutinizing her. "The right makeup, a blonde wig—you've already got the right figure . . ."

Holding a fork as though it were a microphone, Transylvania said in a voice like a Congressional investigator, "Are you now, or have you ever been, Marilyn Monroe?"

Making her voice higher and breathier, Norma Jean said through tremulous lips, "I was in the Miss North Dakota contest once." She batted her lashes, then lowered her lids. Her friends had never seen this kittenish femme fatale. They were nonplussed, as though a stranger had sat down at the table.

Marilyn, seeing their surprise, wiggled her shoulders and demurely turned her head. When she stopped giggling she was Norma Jean again; the visitor who had occupied her for an instant had fled.

"So you do imitations?" Transylvania said. "Why haven't I seen them before?"

"I'm not at all certain I can do *her* —MM, I mean," said Norma Jean.

Mike and Transylvania pooh-poohed. "Even without costume and makeup," Mike said, "you'll be ahead if you stick to the mannerisms, the trimmings. You've really got them down pretty good."

* * *

It was a role like any other, and she had to prepare. She wondered if she could still do it. After all, she hadn't played Marilyn, hadn't *been* Marilyn, for three years. She persuaded Transylvania to accompany her to a drag bar where she could observe in advance some of the competition. Mike and Transylvania had reminded her she would be competing mostly with transvestites.

The clientele at the Pink Ribbon at first mistook Transylvania for one of themselves. Decked out in a range of blue-and-purple hues, she could have passed for a deadly nightshade. At first no one believed it was Transylvania, the horror-star of local TV. They thought she was just a good imitation.

The crowd at the Pink Ribbon spilled onto the sidewalk. The transvestites and their admirers paraded in and out of the bar like exotic fish circling in an aquarium. Norma Jean wondered how long these large, handsome "girls" had spent on makeup, hairstyles and clothes. She decided they must have sat in front of their mirrors as long as she used to.

Transylvania blended easily into the pageantry even though she was merely herself and not a glazed imitation of a movie queen. Several versions of Bette Davis swept through the crowd, smoking cigarettes and pausing to deliver the inevitable line, "Fasten your seatbelts. It's going to be a bumpy night."

The word "dahling" filled the air like heavy birds. Only two Tallulahs were in evidence so far, although their exaggerated mannerisms and raucous baritones suggested a battalion.

"The calla lilies are in bloom again, relly they are," declaimed Katharine Hepburn. Anna Magnani answered in a torrent of arm-flinging Italian.

Norma Jean was fascinated. "New York's answer to Disneyland," she said to Transylvania.

"Or Madame Tussaud's," said Transylvania. The drag queens did have a waxworks quality as well as the same spooky unreality. Magnifying the screen personalities of their favorites, the transvestites seemed to have stolen the soul of certain actresses for use as a playtoy.

Garbo arrived. So did Judy Garland, Jayne Mansfield, Jean Harlow. And Hedda Hopper in a ridiculous hat. Norma Jean, seeing her, shrank back. She knew this was New York in 1965, yet she believed a chunk of the past—Hollywood fifteen years earlier–had broken off and crashed like a meteorite in front of her. Mae West, Jacqueline Kennedy, Jane Russell, Marilyn Monroe—

"Transylvania, I have to leave. I don't feel too well."

"But it's getting good. Look at that Marilyn over there. You can do better than that."

"Oh, yes," Norma Jean whispered weakly. "He's too tall and his face is skinny. And the way he moves his upper lip is all wrong. It looks like something's caught between his teeth. No, you see, Marilyn smiled with her upper lip drawn down. Like this. It was because Emmeline Snively at the Blue Book Modeling Agency told her there wasn't enough upper lip between the end of her nose and her mouth. That's what made her mouth tremble so."

"How do you know all that?" Transylvania asked.

"How do I know? I must have read it somewhere, I guess." No more slip-ups like that, she sternly reminded herself.

"You must have been quite a fan of Marilyn Monroe," Transylvania continued. "I liked her, too. I was upset when she died. Weren't you?"

"Now there's one who really looks like a woman," Norma Jean said. Her heart raced and she felt removed from her surroundings, disoriented by anxiety and a strange déjà vu brought on by these false figures of Hollywood. She whispered to Transylvania, "Look at Elizabeth Taylor over there. That little chubby guy has her eyes, no kidding. I want to hear him talk. You know, no one can imitate her squeaky voice. She told me once—"

"You *know* Taylor?" asked Transylvania.

"Oh no. I mean, not really. Well, we had the same gynecologist and once we were in the waiting room together."

"Is she beautiful in person?"

"I don't remember. I think I'd better concentrate on these stars, though, if you don't mind. What I mean is, I want to learn from their mistakes. And they're making so many, I could get a college degree."

A week before the Great Marilyn Monroe Look-Alike Contest, Norma Jean's agent called to ask if she was interested in auditioning for a television soap opera.

"I've never even *thought* about that. As a matter of fact, I've never really watched one, although I used to hear them on the radio."

"This one's your basic alcohol-and-agony soap," her agent said. "And it's got the fluffiest title on any network—'This Above All.'"

"That's from 'Hamlet,'" Norma Jean said.

"Hamlet, shmamlet, here's the deal. There's a story change coming up and they need an actress to play the minister's new wife. He's been a widower for a year or two, his first wife died of the big C—"

"Cancer? Why, that's terrible."

"Don't worry too much about her, babe. The producer bought out the actress' contract just to get her out of his hair. But that's irrelevant. Now tell me—do you want to read?"

After the audition Norma Jean hurried into St. Patrick's to pray that she'd get the part. The role of Ruth Goodman, wife of the Reverend David Goodman, required an actress of a certain age who was all smiles and platitudes on the outside with a mean edge under her sweetness. The character was to make her debut the first week of September. Thereafter she would only appear a couple of times a week, which meant the actress who played Ruth Goodman would have time to pursue more serious roles.

"Can you believe it?" Norma Jean said to Transylvania that night on the phone. "Three hundred fifty a week. Ruth Goodman turns up for weddings, funerals and christenings. She wears tailored suits and pearls and white gloves. Oh yes, and she spreads cheer at sickbeds, especially in hospital scenes. It's all so delirious." Her giggle was light and rippling.

"So Georgia Philco moves from honky-tonk singer to the First

Generic Church of Pleasant Valley. Do they know you're Jewish?"

"Oh, they must. After all, Ruth is a Jewish name, isn't it?"

"So's Goodman, if you want to get technical," Transylvania said. "The Reverend David Goodman—hmm, why do I think that church is a front for rabbis?"

That year, Norma Jean was too busy for apprehension as August approached. On Thursday, July 29, her agent called to tell her she had gotten the part of Ruth Goodman. On Friday she went to the TV studio for wardrobe fittings and picked up the script for her first episode, which was set for the next week.

And the weekend was devoted to the look-alike contest, the time when Norma Jean would grapple with Marilyn. For the first time in her life she felt capable of facing MM—and pinning her to the ground, if necessary.

CHAPTER

29

"The Return of Marilyn Monroe"

Transylvania had searched Manhattan without finding it. She had poked through department stores, she had scoured the Lower East Side and pawed through racks of hideous dresses, she had even considered buying the material and having a seamstress make it from scratch. Finally, just a few days before the Great Marilyn Monroe Look-Alike Contest, she found the right dress in a thrift shop in Yorkville. The red satin evening gown must have belonged to a very *zaftig* dowager, because Transylvania knew instantly that it was several sizes too large for Georgia. The waist was about forty inches around. But the gown had possibilities, and when it was altered and dry cleaned it glistened. "Now that's you," Transylvania said when she presented it.

"Yes, it's exactly what I had in mind," Norma Jean said, running her hand over the cool satin. "It's a lot like the dress Marilyn wore in 'Gentlemen Prefer Blondes.' Now, let's see, I have long white gloves, a blonde wig, high heels and earrings. I guess I'm all set." She looked at Transylvania. "Should I arrive late at the contest? I mean, she was always late. At least that's what I've read."

"No, every contestant will have the same idea. If you're all late, then there won't be a contest. What time does it begin—eight o'clock? We'll start on you at noon."

On Sunday, the day of the contest, Transylvania, true to her word, struggled out of bed at ten o'clock and arrived at Sullivan Street at noon. Norma Jean's second-floor apartment had three rooms. The living room, which faced the narrow street in the heart of Greenwich Village, had a high ceiling, a fireplace that didn't work and a varnished pine floor. Norma Jean had added two large green plants and three nondescript chairs. A tall wooden bookcase sagged, double-lined with her library. On the floor beside it, and stacked all around the room, were books, books and books.

Her small bedroom overlooked an air shaft, so she kept the blue shade pulled. A loft bed filled half the room. Instead of sleeping on top of it, and using the space underneath for storage, Norma Jean had put her mattress under the sheltering loft and hung bright Indian bedspreads and African fabrics all around, creating a colorful tentlike sleeping nest. When her friend Hector paid a visit he suggested that she wear golden earrings and tell fortunes in this room. The kitchen was barely large enough for two people. A table was out of the question, so she ate her meals from a TV tray. A few pots and pans were stacked on top of the refrigerator, along with more books. In the bathroom a wigstand occupied the tub. Resting on the stand was a carefully coiffed, silver-blonde wig. The rest of the room was full of makeup, moisturizers, conditioners and perfume. A clothesline strung from corner to corner sagged under the weight of bras, slips and panties.

Norma Jean, up early and fretting, polished her nails. Since she kept them short, and since her fingers were slender and graceful, the bright crimson didn't seem vulgar. She applied the same shade to her toenails.

Transylvania, rummaging in the kitchen, called out, "Is there any coffee in this library?"

From the bathroom Norma Jean answered, "Look beside the ice cubes, it's freeze-dried."

Transylvania, doing a double take, muttered, "Now she's

turned into a dumb blonde. That's from taking this contest too seriously. If I believed in ghosts . . ."

Norma Jean, glued to the bathroom mirror, evaluated and critiqued for an hour. Eventually she tweezed a few stray hairs from her eyebrows. Holding her splayed hands beside her face, she framed it, then changed the angle like a photographer setting up the perfect shot.

Hormones, she thought as she looked at the delicate down that crept from her hairline and dusted temples, cheeks and upper lip. She had applied peroxide to the tiny hairs yesterday; now they were practically invisible, like a light frost disappearing in midday sun.

At four o'clock Transylvania went out for croissants. Norma Jean, too nervous to eat, drank coffee, adding tepid tap water to dilute it.

Using techniques remembered from studio days, as well as her own secret inventions, Norma Jean recast her face so that it resembled the Marilyn Monroe of unposed pictures. After her manipulations, it was pale, smooth and round, open and trusting.

She regarded herself in the mirror, examining this face poised on the frontier of the past, then added dark color and volume to her eyes. The metamorphosis from child to woman was in progress. The first phase took half an hour and enough brush strokes to complete a portrait . . . which in a real sense was what was happening here.

Transylvania was now barred from the bathroom. Norma Jean required absolute concentration. Besides, she was trembling. But under her artful brushstrokes the lips deepened from natural pale lilac to light red, then redder red, finally to flashing scarlet.

A little later, with Transylvania's help, Norma Jean squeezed into the red dress that matched her lipstick. "What a dish!" Transylvania said, giving a wolf whistle. Next they maneuvered the shimmering blonde wig onto Norma Jean's taped-down auburn hair.

Transylvania wondered if the ancient Egyptians who earned their living as mummy-wrappers had the same weird feeling she had now . . . the astonishment of watching a mortal transformed into an eternal object. Georgia Philco, her friend, had disappeared under the layers of fabric and paint. The figure standing before her in this unremarkable apartment on an ordinary street in the Village was a wondrous fabrication, a form to stimulate the imagination and the senses.

For once Transylvania didn't know what to say. She said nothing and phoned for a cab.

The Richmond Hotel, a great cavern of faded elegance on West Forty-eighth Street, was past its prime but still highly respectable. When approached about the Great Marilyn Monroe Look-Alike Contest, the management blanched. The Richmond's ballroom had often been the site of debutante parties, the place where stars of theatre and radio held their wedding receptions. But, on second thought, there hadn't been such an event in fifteen years at the Richmond, so the management sorrowfully agreed to this contest that was sure to bring out every freak in New York.

As it turned out, however, the management got more publicity than it could have bought through every press agent in the city.

The small, discreet sign in front of the hotel was like a magnet; passersby couldn't resist it. They stopped, read it two or three times, pondered, then went into the lobby to buy tickets. The sign said:

Tonight, Marilyn Monroe and Company
The Look-Alike Contest

By six-thirty a crowd had gathered, forcing hotel employees to put up police barricades as though a parade or a premiere were taking place. By seven o'clock papparazzi outnumbered spectators; by seven-thirty, when the first Marilyn tottered up the pavement, a hundred people thronged the entrance, with a couple of hundred more inside. Reporters and newspaper photographers, happy for a splash of color in the dog days of late summer, came up to get their human-interest shots and three-graph features.

Between seven-thirty and eight o'clock twenty Marilyns converged on the scene. Twelve were women, five were men, and the rest might have been either, or both. Tall Marilyns, short Marilyns, thin ones and fat ones, black, white, yellow and brown Marilyns—it was like a big noisy party where every guest was the same person. These Marilyn mutations fascinated the crowd of New Yorkers, who gaped like tourists. Whispers and comments ran through the crowd.

Inside, amplified music filled the ballroom. Even with the volume turned loud, however, Marilyn's voice on the recordings sounded intimate. "There's a river, called the river of no return," she sang in a melancholy kitsch.

At ten past eight the music stopped. The audience quieted, expecting the emcee to appear. Instead, they heard more recordings of Marilyn singing "One Silver Dollar," "Bye Bye Baby," "When Love Goes Wrong," and "I Wanna Be Loved By You."

Outside, the crowd was beginning to disperse. Those who had watched the contestants felt a little sad that it was all imitation, sad that the real Marilyn Monroe could no longer light up New York with her smile.

Suddenly a taxi horn warned them to stand aside, to clear the street. The driver pulled to the curb, stopping exactly in front of the hotel entrance. He got out, walked around the cab and opened the back door on the curb side.

A tall blue woman with long black hair slithered out. Her eyes were circled in blue, her cheeks were mauve shadows and she smiled through fuchsia lips. She wore a blue-black dress and held an ebony cigarette holder. Several people on the sidewalk called out, "Hey, Transylvania, what're *you* doin' here?"

She held up a long, thin hand as though to say, "Keep silent, peasants." Then, like a footman, she carefully held the door open so that her companion could emerge. Nothing happened. To the spectators on the pavement it looked like a pantomime. Would Transylvania pretend to escort an imaginary person into the hotel? She did things like that on television.

Finally, the crowd glimpsed a platinum head, graceful arms gloved in white, then a lot of red: red dress, red lips, red high heels. A roar started up, spreading until the entire block of West Forty-eighth Street was cheering, applauding, screaming for "Marilyn! Marilyn! Marilyn!"

She looked startled for a moment. Frightened, like a doe caught in the headlights of a speeding truck. Then the roar of the crowd reached her and she waved. First her right arm, held aloft like a banner, then her left. Her smile stunned them; none of the other contestants had it. Flashbulbs popped like lightning.

Transylvania stood aside, as unobtrusive as a tall blue vampire could be.

"You're all terribly sweet," said this new Marilyn. It was a whisper, but at that instant a hush fell over the crowd. "You're all terribly, terribly sweet," she repeated. "I love you all . . ."

The crowd pressed forward, holding out scraps of paper, newspaper sections, dollar bills for her to sign. A boy thrust his Selective Service card at her.

She seemed out of breath when she spoke, as though she had run several blocks. Or just left the arms of a lover.

In the lobby, hotel employees gawked. The desk clerk ignored a guest asking for his room key. "None of the others looked this convincing," he told a bellhop. "She's even a little older, the way Marilyn would be."

"Thank you. Thank you ever so," said the blonde signing autographs. "Why, thanks, dear," she said. "I love you, too. My next picture? I'm afraid you'll have to ask Fox about that. They fired me, you know. What do I sleep in? You really want to know? Why, Chanel Number Five, of course. The same as always."

Word had reached contest officials backstage that a zinger of a look-alike was out front and they mustn't start before she came in.

Meanwhile, she was autographing the cast of a teenager with a broken leg. "Get well soon," she wrote with a red Magic Marker someone handed her. "Love and kisses, Marilyn Monroe." She leaned over and kissed his cheek. Flashbulbs popped. She kissed his other cheek. More applause, more flashbulbs. The reporters asked who she really was. "Why, fellas, can't you tell? I'm just a little girl from Little Rock." She threw back her head in a dazzling pose.

It was nearer nine o'clock than eight when the crowd released her. Or she released them. Parched for love and adulation, she signed autographs, answered questions, posed for pictures. Fans, starved for beauty and glamor and dissatisfied with Hollywood's current offerings—Carroll Baker, Ann-Margret, Stella Stevens—grasped her like a sensuous dream that would vanish on awakening. The unexpected pleasure of this apparition thrilled the crowd, adding a poignant note to its obsession.

Finally contest officials sent a messenger to inform the latecomer that no further delay would be tolerated. And so she swept into the hotel, with Transylvania beside her and an entourage of photographers and reporters behind, begging for one more.

The audience had grown restless waiting; as the final contestant rushed into the ballroom she heard catcalls, the stamping of feet and more than one Bronx cheer. She quivered; any sign of hostility still terrified her.

When they caught sight of the gossamer blonde hesitating in the entrance, their jeering stopped. For a moment the room was silent. All eyes were on her, and she was scared to death. She put her hand to her face and looked distraught. Tears filled her eyes. She wanted to apologize for making them unhappy. *They came to see Marilyn but I've upset them.* She turned to Transylvania, intending to say, "I can't go through with it, let's leave."

"I can't go through—" was all that Transylvania heard. Before Norma Jean could finish her sentence the noise of approval burst forth. "Marilyn! Marilyn! Marilyn!" The chant spread through the ballroom and turned into a demonstration. They rose. "We want Marilyn!" People left their seats, rushed to her and joined the entourage that was moving toward the stage.

"Thank you, I love you, thank you," she said as she moved slowly across the enormous ballroom toward the stage. "I'm so very happy," she said, smiling and brushing away tears at the same time. She loved them. She really did.

The emcee met her at the steps, led her to the stage and helped her up. Transylvania whispered something in her ear, then took a seat in the front row. The emcee adjusted the microphone.

"Ladies and gentlemen," he said, "welcome to the Great Marilyn Monroe Look-Alike Contest. It's appropriate that we're late getting started." He looked at Norma Jean, who was standing beside him and now covered her face with her hands in mock-embarrassment. Someone called out, "It was worth the wait."

"We have a lot of beauty and a lot of talent tonight," the emcee continued. "There will be three winners. The best Marilyn Monroe imitation, the best talent, and the best costume. He introduced the judges, then said, "and so, without further ado, let's go on with the show." He paused, then added, "I wonder if we could have a chair brought onstage for, ah, Miss Monroe here." The audience approved loudly. Someone appeared with a fauteuil and Norma Jean sat like a queen on her throne.

If the other contestants had been jealous of the attention showered on the glamorous late arrival it would have been understandable. But mostly they seemed awed. They were immediately curious, and as they came on stage one by one they could barely resist gazing at MM seated a few feet away. At the end of each of their performances she applauded enthusiastically, the expression on her face one of intense interest and enjoyment.

A willowy young blonde who looked no more than sixteen sang "That Old Black Magic"à la Marilyn in "Bus Stop." Her saloon-singer's costume was identical to the one in the movie, down to the fringe and the black net stockings.

Several look-alikes reenacted scenes from Marilyn's movies. An inventive contestant performed the scene from "Anna Christie" that Marilyn had done at the Actors Studio years before. Others sang "Diamonds Are a Girl's Best Friend," "You'd Be Surprised," "Running Wild" and "Heat Wave."

And then the mood changed. A young man who looked very much like Peter Lawford came onstage. He grasped the microphone, then said in a clipped British accent: "Ladies and gentlemen, the late Marilyn Monroe."

A smattering of applause came from the audience. It was obvious, however, that this reminder of Marilyn's last performance was not a crowd pleaser.

A would-be voluptuous but haggard Marilyn Monroe tottered

out. Obviously a man, although with edges softened to create the illusion of vulnerability, he wore a see-through dress into which he, like the real MM at Madison Square Garden that night in May of 1962, had been sewn. Sequins glittered, he smiled wanly at the audience, then looked distractedly into the wings as though someone had called out. He made an effort to collect himself. When he finally did so the familiar music started; he sang a phony, breathy "Happy Birthday, Mr. President" to an imaginary JFK. When he finished the spotlight wheeled into the audience, where a Kennedy look-alike stood and repeated the late President's words: "I can now retire from politics after having had, ah, 'Happy Birthday' sung to me in such a sweet, wholesome way."

The audience remained silent. It seemed to be waiting for the response of the woman seated in the armchair onstage.

Something twitched inside Norma Jean's head. Perhaps it was a blood vessel in her brain, overtaxed by the stress of seeing her life pass in review. Or maybe it was just the wayward Marilyn reentering Norma Jean's personality, clicking into place like a new lens on a camera.

Seated there in front of adoring fans, Norma Jean smiled and accepted the addition of that other girl, the famous movie star MM she had thought was dead but who constantly came back like a butterfly, only to sail out into the world again, and then flit home. *I guess there's room for her in my head*, Norma Jean thought. *Maybe that's why I was mistaken for a dumb blonde—so many people staying in my head that there wasn't any room for brains.* She smiled at the notion.

And then it was time for her to perform. The emcee said, "Ladies and gentlemen, it gives me great pleasure to introduce the final contestant in the Great Marilyn Monroe Look-Alike Contest. Marilyn, take it away."

Her eyes lit up, her smile beamed to the far corners of the ballroom as she moved to the microphone.

"My friends," she said in her breathiest MM voice, "I was scared to death to come here tonight. You see, I was afraid you might say, 'Who does that girl think she is, trying to be Marilyn Monroe?' But as soon as I felt all the *love* in your hearts, well, I wasn't frightened anymore. Not the least teeny-weeny bit." She paused while her audience responded. "You've made my day. In fact, you've made my life. And now, if you'll let me, I'd like to sing for you."

Her song, of course, was "Diamonds Are a Girl's Best Friend." At the end of it, however, instead of singing the line "Diamonds are a girl's best friend," she sang, "You all are a girl's best friend."

After her number she went backstage rather than sitting down in the armchair again. She heard the emcee say, "Ladies and gentlemen, the judges have recommended that the last contestant be awarded all three prizes—for best Marilyn imitation, best costume, and best talent." A wave of approval roared through the house.

She accepted the prize money, kissed the emcee, blew kisses to the audience, then ran off stage and retired to a dressing room, where she sank into a chair as though she had completed a marathon.

In a way, of course, she had, because fame had overtaken her. Just as young Norma Jean in the late forties had entered the public domain as Marilyn Monroe, so the middle-aged Norma Jean, in 1965, was once more playing that demanding, exhausting role. The goddess, it seemed, refused to stay dead. And she preferred the body of Norma Jean.

CHAPTER

30

"Hold a Good Thought for Me"

The following day, August 2, 1965, New York newspapers ran stories and pictures of the contest: "MARILYN RETURNS!" proclaimed the *Post* headline beside a photo of Norma Jean. The *Times* relegated its feature to page 27, calling it "Miss Monroe Is Remembered." Despite the cool prose of the *Times*, however, readers paid more attention to the Look-Alike Contest that day than the progress of the Cold War. The *Daily News* ran a large close-up of Norma Jean with the headline: "MM II."

The wire services picked it up, and for the rest of that week pictures and features appeared around the country. The following week Time, Newsweek and dozens of other magazines ran the story. No one, however, had information on the woman who bore such an amazing resemblance to the late movie star. Like Cinderella, she had vanished from the ballroom in the company of a local TV personality known as Transylvania. Television producers were interested, as well as a couple of Hollywood studios toying with the idea of filming the Marilyn Monroe story.

Senator Robert Kennedy saw the newspapers, looked at the magazine pictures, and found it all too painful to dwell on. Marilyn was dead, and so was his brother. Meanwhile, he had plans to change the world for the better by becoming President himself, an agenda that left no time for such memories.

Clippings of the contest also made their way into a file at the FBI. J. Edgar Hoover pored over them, eventually going so far as to have agents in New York watch "the degenerate known as Transylvania" and report on her activities.

Deep within the CIA the pictures were, understandably, studied with great interest.

In Los Angeles those who had loved Marilyn, and those who hadn't, were mesmerized by pictures of the audacious imitator. Sarah Bridwell looked at the grainy newspaper photo again and again. "I tell you," she said to herself, "this girl's the near-spittin' image of poor Marilyn." No one heard her declaration. She now lived alone, her son and daughter-in-law having been killed two years before in a smash-up of the 1962 Valiant she had bought them.

Before discarding the newspaper, she clipped the picture, folded it and stuck it between the pages of the family Bible. The memento safely put away, she shuffled into the kitchen. "I just don't have the appetite I once did," she muttered to no one. "When I think how good the food tasted at Marilyn's in the old days I could just cry."

Hedda Hopper's hands shook so she couldn't read the caption under the photograph in the *Hollywood Reporter*. She now spent most of her time in bed attended by a nurse. Her fantastic hats, each one garish as a carnival sideshow, were all packed away. Hedda's hair was snowy white, her face had collapsed under an avalanche of wrinkles, and her teeth tended to slide off her gums when she tried to talk.

In the rest home where she had been for almost a year, Louella Parsons knew nothing of Marilyn's "return." Often she would say to other ladies, "Have you heard the news? Marilyn, that dear girl, is going to tie the knot with President Hoover. Oh, oh, not Hoover, I mean . . . Eisenhower. And *that's* my latest exclusive."

Alice Mulligan, seeing pictures of the girl who looked like Marilyn, knew immediately she was wearing a wig. "Marilyn's hair was prettier than that," she told her sister. "But this is how Marilyn would look if she was still alive . . . I still miss her."

The photograph in the Los Angeles *Times* made Dr. Gruber think about the psychopathology of cross-dressing. He was seeing more and more of it in his practice. The wealthy transvestites who consulted him invariably mentioned Marilyn Monroe as the woman they most wanted to resemble. They sought psychiatric help, he learned, not because they wanted to stop wearing women's clothes but to have a medical alibi in case of arrest.

Seeing pictures of this new Marilyn, Joe DiMaggio no doubt ached for the original one.

Jacqueline Kennedy, remembering her statement to the press at the time of Marilyn Monroe's death, wondered if she had perhaps anticipated this growing cult when she said that Marilyn would go on eternally. Paris Match photographs of the contest held her interest for a few moments and she read several lines of the article titled "Le Retour de Marilyn."

"I'm calling to cancel our appointment," Terry Pavka told a regular client. "I'm very sorry but I've been called out of town on an emergency." In three hours his plane would depart Los Angeles for New York. Never one to read newspapers, he belatedly learned about the Marilyn Monroe contest from photographs in Newsweek. Then he knew that he had to fly east and do some psychic detective work.

The letter from Aunt Bertha and Uncle Horace was full of praise for her portrayal of Ruth Goodman in "This Above All." Norma Jean often sent them postcards and Aunt Bertha usually wrote detailed letters full of the minutiae of life in their small town. This missive, however, was full of real news. Uncle Horace, who would soon be seventy, had decided to sell the business and retire. They had always looked forward to traveling—their trip to Chicago had brought them such good luck in the shape of their new friend Martha Lincoln, or Georgia Philco as she was now known to television viewers all over the country—and so they had decided to sail to Europe on the *Queen Mary*. Their travel agent called their itinerary a "Deluxe Grand Tour." After docking in Southampton they would continue on to London, then Paris, Geneva, Milan, Rome, Venice and Vienna.

They had decided to fly to New York first, and hoped their "dear friend and niece" would be able to show them around. "P.S.," wrote Aunt Bertha, "we would love to visit the Metropolitan Museum. However, we do hope to avoid any dangerous females like that one in Chicago. Ha, ha."

Norma Jean was thrilled about their visit, although she wondered how she would have time to show them the interesting spots in New York. Playing Ruth Goodman took more time than she had expected. One reason was that the character appeared in four weekly episodes so that viewers would accept her as a regular. In addition, the show was live and required rehearsals from early morning until it went on the air at 3:30 in the afternoon.

Norma Jean was still petrified in front of television cameras, just as when Edward R. Murrow interviewed her, as Marilyn, on "Person to Person." Nevertheless, she refused to let fear conquer her. Every day she got up around dawn, ran four times around Washington Square as the sun rose over the city and ate a large breakfast. Physical activity helped take the edge off her anxiety. Then she reviewed her lines, which she had memorized so well the night before that they echoed in her sleep. She took the subway to the studio in midtown and worked without a lunch break. A few minutes before air time she ate a Cadbury chocolate bar, which calmed her jitters as efficiently as champagne.

Now, almost two weeks after the contest, Transylvania was still besieged with questions about her friend who had won the prize and then vanished. And suddenly her own fame had doubled because of her association with the mysterious blonde. She was interviewed in newspapers and on television, but no one could get a word out of her on the subject of MM II, as the unknown but tantalizing woman was now regularly referred to in the press.

Norma Jean threw the Cadbury wrapper in a wastebasket and waited for the countdown. Her initial appearances on "This Above All" had drawn such favorable mail that the writers had enlarged her role. Today Ruth Goodman had to inform her new husband, the Reverend David Goodman, that his secretary Beth had been seriously injured in an automobile accident. They would rush to the hospital, only to discover that Beth had died.

". . . seven, six, five, four, three, two, one," and the director's signal that they were on the air.

The electric organ surged. The theme music was a combination of Stephen Foster and Richard Wagner. The announcer declaimed, "Welcome to 'This Above All', brought to you by Foam dishwashing liquid. Remember, Foam is the liquid that makes your dishes ocean-fresh."

After a word from the sponsor the show opened with Ruth Goodman answering an urgently ringing telephone in her family room. "Hello," Norma Jean said brightly as the camera showed her in medium shot wearing a demure tailored suit and a wavy brown wig. As she listened to the message her face became troubled. "Why, I can hardly believe it," she said. "This is a tragedy. Beth is one of the finest young women in our town." A pause. "Yes, of course, my husband and I will come immediately . . ."

In the next scene the Reverend Goodman and his wife talked about his faithful secretary Beth and the horrible thing that had befallen her. The minister was particularly upset. "Without Beth," he said distractedly, "I don't know how I could go on. I mean, I don't know how I could do my work in the parish."

"We should try to look on the bright side, David," said his wife. "The Almighty gives us strength to bear our trials. I know how close you are to Beth." A pregnant pause. "Yes, I knew even before I married you." Organ music surged again as the scene faded to ocean waves pounding a load of dishes, and a box of Foam rising from the sea.

Viewers who wrote in about the new character Ruth Goodman said they especially liked her because the actress was so *sincere*. The producer, not sure exactly what that meant, instructed the writers to make Ruth even more artificial. Then he told the director he wanted her played like Jane Wyatt in "Father Knows Best." The director was impressed by the ability of this new actress to make love to the camera without, apparently, even trying. He had never worked with anyone so photogenic. She loved the camera, the camera loved her.

As soon as today's segment ended, Norma Jean hurriedly removed her makeup and changed into street clothes. She was meeting Aunt Bertha and Uncle Horace at LaGuardia Airport at six o'clock. She would accompany them to their hotel, then they would have their reunion dinner at the Blue Mill Tavern.

Because of thunderstorms in the New York area Terry Pavka's plane could not land at JFK International. After circling for half an hour, the pilot was instructed to divert to Philadelphia. After an hour on the ground in Philly the plane took off again for New York. The storm was over but JFK was congested, a nightmare. With apologies for the inconvenience, the co-pilot of United flight 240 from Los Angeles announced that they would land in ten minutes at LaGuardia.

Aunt Bertha and Uncle Horace, arriving from Kansas City, were also delayed by weather. Unaccustomed to flying, they didn't realize that their plane was traveling in wide circles for the last hour of the flight. "I wish I could see something through that window," Aunt Bertha complained, shaking her head so that the plumes on her new hat bobbed up and down. "Nothing but fog, fog, fog, and Georgia said to be sure to look for the Empire State Building."

Finally, though, the plane cut through the cloud cover and they were on the ground—and there she was. "Aunt Bertha, over here! Uncle Horace!" The reunion, punctuated with tears and laughter, went on for several minutes. "My, my, you look better than the last time we saw you," said Aunt Bertha, remembering the aftermath of the train wreck. "In fact, you're a *very* pretty girl. I can tell you're eating right, too. You've filled out. Lost that gaunt look you had."

Horace was unable to speak because his wife and Norma Jean were chattering so, like long-lost friends brought together on "This Is Your Life."

At the baggage counter they were still at it. "I looked and I looked and never saw a blessed thing but fog," lamented Aunt Bertha.

"Clouds," put in her husband.

"Well, I could see clouds in Missouri," she said. "I want to see New York. I want to paint the town red. By the way," she asked Norma Jean, "do folks who live here call it Gotham? Walter

Winchell calls it that on the radio but I'm not sure he's typical."

Norma Jean said, "I've got a delicious surprise for you. The producer gave special permission to bring you on the set tomorrow. Would you like to watch 'This Above All' in the studio?" The Shelfmores were delighted.

As they crawled into a taxi a gust of wind blew Aunt Bertha's grand new hat onto the pavement in front of the terminal. Norma Jean hopped out to retrieve it. "Thanks loads," she said to the man who picked it up and handed it to her.

"You're welcome, Marilyn," said Terry Pavka in a quiet voice. "It's good to see you again."

"*What?*" How could it be him? Where did he come from? *How did he recognize her?* "Oh dear, I beg your pardon," she said, lowering her voice and affecting a New England accent. "I'm afraid you've confused me with someone else."

He took off his dark glasses and stared at her. He based his certainty not just on her face, her voice, or her figure but on her Marilyn aura, which *no* amount of surgery or wigs or disguises could change for her. He had recognized it all the way across the terminal, and had followed her. The hat he'd retrieved was just a convenient accident, a prop.

Norma Jean, flustered, turned back toward the taxi.

"*Please,*" he said quietly, softly, "it's taken three years. I always knew you weren't dead, even though I couldn't prove it."

She was overcome. But, she instructed herself, a disciplined actress knows how to contain, or at least postpone, even the strongest personal feelings. Bertha and Horace must not see her lose control . . . "I'm sorry, I'm Georgia Philco . . . but if you're convinced that I'm . . . somebody else, well, I know these things can be upsetting, I'll be happy to talk with you about it. Only not now, okay, sir?"

Instantly she felt remorse for being curt with him. "I didn't mean to be rude," she apologized, "what can I say? The truth is, I'm not who you think I am."

"All right," Terry said slowly. "If that's how it is, I can understand."

"My number is Circle 2–8094," she said very quietly, reluctantly. "I'll be in late tonight." Biting her lower lip, she crawled back into the taxi with the Shelfmores. But they noticed that she seemed suddenly distracted.

They rode a carriage through Central Park, they zipped to the top of the Empire State Building, then strolled through the Village. Norma Jean showed her apartment to Aunt Bertha and Uncle Horace, giggling as she apologized for the disorder. "There's not a thing wrong with it," Aunt Bertha said firmly. "If I lived in New York I wouldn't waste my time cleaning house, either."

After dinner Norma Jean put them in a cab and rushed home to wait for the call. It was close to midnight. She decided that if Terry hadn't phoned by one o'clock she would take the receiver off the hook and go to sleep.

At twelve-thirty Terry called again. He had tried numerous times before without reaching her. "I don't really know what to say," he told her. "I'm afraid you're not very happy to see me."

"No, no, please don't say that . . . You see, this is a *shock*. At first I thought you might have been sent by . . .But after a moment I realized you had come as a friend. But if you knew how *hard* it's been to escape . . ."

"I wouldn't be a very good psychic if I didn't perceive your pain."

"Yes, yes, I realized that."

"After . . . after the reports of your death back in nineteen sixty-two," Pavka said, "I knew that the real story hadn't been told. I still felt your presence. Your living presence. I don't know if I ever explained it to you, but a psychic can feel the difference between life and death. If he's keenly attuned. As you might expect, life is warm and colorful, death is a little like smog in Los Angeles. Gray and soiled."

"No, I haven't heard that before," Norma Jean said. "Los Angeles was always full of smog. At least when I lived there. But go on, tell me more about life and death." Norma Jean's and Marilyn's, she added to herself.

"Real psychics, of course, can't contact the dead. That's only done on television. I was determined to contact the living, though, namely Marilyn Monroe. But where to start? Three years later I was looking through a magazine and there she was. I knew. The picture was uncanny, of course. But the aura around the face was warm and bathed in color. I also recognized it because, after all, it belonged to an old friend."

"Terry . . ." she said. It was the first time she had called his name since the last time they had spoken, years before. "It's like this. *You must not tell.* Most people wouldn't believe you, but . . . I'm not ready yet to have my secret told, and there *are* people who could hurt me. People with a lot of money and power. They tried before but I got away. Next time, though, I won't be so lucky . . ."

He paused. "I understand. I understand that Marilyn is dead," he said quietly. "And I'm flying back to L.A. in the morning."

"Yes," Norma Jean said like an echo, "Marilyn is dead. But you know what? Something of her is still alive."

"I agree," Terry said. "She's everywhere. Magazine covers, TV, you name it."

"It seems to me," Norma Jean went on, "that Marilyn's . . . attraction is still alive, too. So in a way, sure, I'm Marilyn—just like nearly every woman back in the fifties wanted to be."

"What about all the publicity that Marilyn got recently?" he asked. "Isn't that risky? You know, since Marilyn is still in danger."

"Yes, a little, I guess. But that was Marilyn II. It's a red herring, like those mystery writers use to draw attention away from something. Well, yours truly did the same thing. I shouldn't tell, of course, but after all—you could probably find all this out from your crystal ball anyway." She giggled like the playful, teasing Marilyn he remembered.

"Besides," she went on, "who knows what can happen? After the reception I got at the Marilyn look-alike contest I just might—I mean, she just might—be on more magazine covers than ever. If I wanted to, which I don't. Who could stand it? It would drive a girl bananas. Wouldn't it . . . ?"

"I'll be waiting to see what happens if she ever decides to

make a *real* comeback," Pavka said. "In the meantime I'll keep putting flowers on the grave of that poor girl in the Westwood Cemetery."

"Oh yes," she said. "You realize, of course, that Marilyn couldn't really be alive today." She sounded eager to convince him of something, to make him see her point. "It's true, Marilyn and I have a lot in common. And we're a lot different. Thank God."

The woman on the phone—whether she was Norma Jean, Georgia, Lorelei, or even Marilyn Monroe—had the last word on the subject. "But Terry, just one thing, sweetheart. Don't forget. Marilyn is best left just where she is. Okay?"